THE DREAM RUNNERS

ALSO BY SHVETA THAKRAR

Star Daughter

∞ THE ∞
DREAM
RUNNERS

SHVETA THAKRAR

HARPER TEEN
An Imprint of HarperCollinsPublishers

For my dearest Lindsey pie: my heart sister in Devi,
tea dragon to my nagini, and staunch believer in my magic.
All the rose hot chocolate, desi feasts, and dreamstone vials forever.

HarperTeen is an imprint of HarperCollins Publishers.

The Dream Runners
Copyright © 2022 by Shveta Thakrar

For information address HarperCollins Children's Books, a division of HarperCollins
Publishers, 195 Broadway, New York, NY 10007.
www.epicreads.com

Library of Congress Cataloging-in-Publication Data
Names: Thakrar, Shveta, author.
Title: The dream runners / Shveta Thakrar.
Description: First edition. | New York : HarperTeen, [2022] | Audience: Ages 13 up.
   | Audience: Grades 10–12. | Summary: Spirited away to the subterranean realm of
   Nagalok as children, seventeen-year-olds Tanvi and Venkat are charged with harvesting
   human dreams for the entertainment of the naga court—until one of them begins to
   remember the mortal life she left behind.
Identifiers: LCCN 2021041937 | ISBN 978-0-06-289466-3 (hardcover)
Subjects: CYAC: Dreams—Fiction. | Memory—Fiction. | Fantasy. | LCGFT: Fantasy
   fiction.
Classification: LCC PZ7.1.T4472 Dr 2022 | DDC [Fic]—dc23
LC record available at https://lccn.loc.gov/2021041937

Typography by Corina Lupp
22 23 24 25 26   PC/LSCH   10 9 8 7 6 5 4 3 2 1

❖

First Edition

Come away, O human child!
To the waters and the wild
With a faery, hand in hand,
For the world's more full of weeping than you can understand.

—FROM "THE STOLEN CHILD,"
BY W. B. YEATS

THE DREAM RUNNERS

PART ONE

*E*ons ago, when time first spun out of nothing like the whorled shell of a nautilus, there lived a boy who loved to swim. The blood of all nagas runs brackish, of course, yet this boy's affinity for the aquatic surpassed that of even the rest of his kind: at the moment of his hatching, he wiggled free of his gold-speckled egg, his tiny tail uncoiling behind him, and slithered unerringly toward the nearest of Bhogavati's many beaches. His astonished parents, who had been reaching out to embrace their infant son, were instead forced to pursue him into the layers of lacework foam cast off by the waves that crashed on the lavender shore.

"I want to swim everywhere!" he cried, squirming in his mother's grasp. No matter how keenly his parents attempted to dissuade him, he would not yield.

When it was clear their pleas would bear no fruit, his mother sighed and relinquished his arm. "As you will, my hatchling. If it is that important to you, then swim."

"But," his father said, less willing to surrender his fresh-born child so

1

easily, "only until you have run out of new waters to try. After that, you must return home and make a life among us."

With all the worlds yet to wander through, the boy gamely agreed, then disappeared into the sea.

As millennia passed and the small boy grew into a young man, he spent his days undulating among a multitude of ever-changing companions. From sunrise to sunset, through storm and shine, he frolicked with sand dollars and starfish, crooned lullabies to guppies and goblin sharks, and idled with tortoises and tube sponges. In between, he collected conch shells and multicolored pearls, which he left on land for treasure hunters to find. Their iridescent sheen matched the meghdhanush he occasionally glimpsed in the sky, Lord Indra's mighty seven-hued bow.

From stream to swamp to lake to ocean the young man splashed, from realm to realm, wading through the bluest of hot springs and the brownest of mudflats. From pond to river to lagoon he slipped, through salt water and through sweet. He swam, and he swam, and he swam, the current sometimes calm, other times enraged, but always swaddling him as soundly as his absent mother's arms.

Yet all things must come to their natural end, and in due course, the young man found he had exhausted the cosmic supply of water in which to play. But despite his promise, he was not yet ready to return home.

He desired one last great plunge, but that would require finding a new medium in which to move.

First he tried sand. Then he tried soil. He readily dismissed both, for they offered neither water's buoyancy nor its flow.

If the earth was of no use, then he would try elsewhere. Above him swelled the sky, its fleecy clouds so like the froth of his beloved white-capped sea.

The young man's questing heart kindled with joy. For what else was the firmament but a boundless ocean of air?

He would, he determined, swim through the sky.

Lacking the wings of the glorious Mansa Devi, he searched for ways to ascend. He tried to scale the sky, to catch hold of a cloud, to barter for passage with a bat in flight. For centuries, he only fell back down.

At last, weary and feeling the pull of his age-old promise, the young man nearly gave up. Thunderheads blustered above him, darkening the heavens from brightest day to a semblance of deepest night. Their needles of rain stabbed down as Lord Indra seethed upon his throne in the clouds.

Then a single ray of Lord Surya's golden light burst through the gloom. Where it grazed the walls of rain, Lord Indra's meghdhanush appeared. In its arc of seven bold colors, the young man found his answer.

But Lord Indra never brought out his bow for long. The young man scampered up its vast curve.

He climbed and climbed, often backsliding, for the meghdhanush was far more slippery than it looked, until finally he arrived at its peak. Aglow with triumph, he prepared to dive into the ether.

Suddenly Lord Indra shook the massive bow, and bolts of thunder shot through the air. "Who dares lay a hand on my meghdhanush?" he bellowed.

In his fury, he slammed the bow down, down, down until it smashed into the kingdom of Nagalok far below. Down, down, down, too, tumbled the young man.

3

And so, he swam through the sky.

Where the bow struck the soil, it shattered, all seven colors fragmenting into crystals: rubies, carnelians, topazes, emeralds, sapphires, lapis lazuli, and amethysts, and many others besides. Lord Indra retrieved his bow and resumed his business, heedless of the jewels sparkling behind him. They in turn sank deep within the crust of our world, where they multiplied into the limitless riches that bless us today.

Some claim the boy sprouted cloud-wings and swam on into eternity, for he was never seen again, but his gift of the gems will scarce be forgotten.

—FROM *THE NAGA PURANA: A FLORILEGIUM OF FOLKTALES*, PROPERTY OF THE OFFICIAL ROYAL LIBRARY AT BHOGAVATI

1

Wind whooshed past the rolled-down windows and sprayed Tanvi's bangs back into wings as she floored the gas pedal. The old Honda Civic's engine growled in response, underscoring the music blasting from her phone, and the tires gobbled up the curving highway mile by mile. On her left, the mountain glinted in the afternoon light like someone had painted it with honey. *"Never gonna stop, never gonna stop, never, never, never gonna stop,"* Tanvi belted out, her voice high and breathy, and zoomed around a bend in the road.

Suddenly she stood on a bridge spanning a green-brown lake, the relentless sun glaring down over everything. So hot. Too hot. Tanvi was going to melt.

Wait, where was the car?

She turned to find it idling next to her at the edge of the bridge. No, not idling so much as smashed into a guardrail, the front half folded into a perfect accordion. The pleats in the metal twinkled at her like a taunt.

Acidic horror ate through Tanvi, from the pit of her stomach right down to the tips of her toes. It wasn't her mom's Civic—but her stepdad's precious Maserati GranTurismo. Cherry red and flashy, the car he'd dubbed his baby, the one whose black leather interior he spent hours buffing to prevent cracks. He'd never let Tanvi sit in it, let alone drive it.

He was going to *kill* her.

Her phone rang from the mangled passenger seat, and Tanvi wrenched it free. Somehow, unlike the car, it was fine. She tilted the screen to see who was calling—

And woke to find herself gasping for air in a stranger's shadowy bedroom. A phone chirped inches away, half tangled in the actual dreamer's sheets.

Tanvi yanked back her empty hand from where it hovered above the sleeping girl's forehead, coaxing out the nightmare's substance one translucent wisp at a time, and muted the phone. She scowled down at the girl. Who slept with their ringer on?

The scowl turned to a shudder. Though her dream had been interrupted, the girl's distress still pulsed, slimy and wet, in Tanvi's chest. It made her small. Terrified. Weak.

She hated this part of harvesting—having to inhabit the dream and become the dreamer. Knowing their innermost thoughts. Wanting what they did. Feeling what they felt, even when it was as banal as this.

Desperate to shove the dream residue away, Tanvi pulled the cork from the waiting amethyst dreamstone vial a little too hard. It came loose with an audible *pop*.

6

She swore under her breath, bracing herself to be caught, but the girl only shifted and mumbled.

In the meantime, led by Tanvi's will, the smokelike wisps she'd reaped floated over to the vial. Now she physically motioned them inside. As if the girl knew her dream had been lured elsewhere, she twisted again, craning her neck at an awkward angle. But as long as she didn't wake up, Tanvi couldn't care less if the girl sleep-somersaulted onto the floor.

The instant the final wisp entered the vial, Tanvi jammed the cork back in. Just like that, the glut of emotion dissolved. Tanvi was herself and only herself. Her head clear, she examined the vial. She'd definitely captured the nightmare—the purple dreamstone flickered with a faint inner fire—but it had cut off right as things had gotten interesting.

"Come *on*," she muttered into the gloom. She'd made the trek to this upscale apartment complex, staking her night's take on the people who lived here. She'd let her inner sense tell her, with its bright and dark spots, who dreamed and how deeply. And all she'd gained for her efforts was the sludge at the bottom of the barrel?

At least this one had some meat to it; the scraps she'd harvested from the girl's neighbors weren't worth the vials Tanvi had stored them in—running out of toilet bowl cleaner and studying for an exam that got canceled. Junk-drawer dreams.

A last bit of residual fear quivered through her. *What if Venkat doesn't want them?*

Dreams were Tanvi's bread and butter, or in naga terms, her roti and ghee. Without engaging ones, she had no boon. No boon meant no bracelet. She'd have to keep hunting if she wanted to bulk up her skimpy harvest.

Shaking off the fear, she stowed the vial next to the other dreamstones in the pouch at her waist and pulled the drawstring shut.

The bedroom and the hallway past it were silent. Sometimes pets detected her presence and would meow or bark until their owners woke up. Nobody was home to check on this girl, it seemed. Good.

Not bothering to glance back, Tanvi tiptoed to the window, sucked on a lozenge that made her as boneless as liquid, and stole out into the night.

A haze of exhaust shrouded the early autumn sky over Philadelphia. It seared Tanvi's lungs as she prowled through the city streets, determined to fill her two unused dreamstones.

In the distance, the Ben Franklin Bridge arced over the river, glittering like the sea goddess's giant tiara it had been in a vision she'd harvested a few months ago.

Now *that* had been a boon-worthy dream.

Even though it was late, a buffet of potential dreamers drifted around her, from the wealthy people in Rittenhouse Square leaving swanky restaurants to the buskers and tourists on South Street to the office workers heading home from bar crawls in Center City. If only she could follow them all and reap every one of their dreams.

Glass crunched under her shoes, a pair of ballet flats Asha had given her to help her blend in on Prithvi. Tanvi vaguely registered that she'd stepped in the shards from a smashed bottle. She kicked them into a nearby drain.

The smart thing would be to call it a night. She had three dreams, even if two of them were boring.

But Venkat might not want them, and Tanvi knew she could do better than the meager wares she'd pulled in so far. Besides, it wasn't like she'd be back in Philadelphia anytime soon.

Dream runners circulated around the mortal world, never staying in any one place. That meant they could harvest from the full spectrum of dream flavors without the risk of being recognized. Recently Tanvi had gone to Beijing, Aix-en-Provence, Rio de Janeiro, and a tiny hilltop town in Mongolia where the sheep outnumbered the people—and often starred in their nocturnal rambles. Even there, she'd found the best wares, so how could she accept anything less tonight?

All she had to do was hurry.

Her mouth growing dry with excitement, she quickened her pace. What sorts of dreamers would get her closest to her bracelet?

Something collided with her, all muscle and hard bone. "Watch it!" a voice ordered, as near as a breath—way too near.

Tanvi's stomach clenched. Dream runners weren't supposed to let themselves be noticed, never mind getting so wrapped up in possibilities that they bumped into people. She might as well have been daydreaming.

"Sorry," she muttered, avoiding the boy's eyes, and brushed past him. The faster she got away, the faster he would forget her.

She marched toward a crosswalk, her breath coiled, snakelike, in her lungs. Fifteen seconds passed, then thirty. But the boy wasn't in pursuit, and Tanvi could exhale again.

That had been careless of her. Foolish.

Her whole body still tensed for discovery, Tanvi peeked over her shoulder. No sign of the boy. The traffic light changed. Using the crowd around her as her shield, she stepped into the crosswalk.

"Wait up!" someone else shouted.

Tanvi kept walking. What potential dreamers said to one another outside their dreams wasn't any of her business.

"Hey! Didn't you hear me, Nitya?" the voice asked from beside her. "I saw that guy plow right into you. He didn't even apologize."

Another step, and Tanvi made it to the other side of the street. So did the speaker, a Hmong girl with a shiny bob. No one Tanvi had ever seen before. But the girl was clearly talking to her.

Her insides swirled. *Two* people had noticed her? She had to get out of here—now.

"You look kind of out of it. Are you sure he didn't hurt you?"

Tanvi stared past the girl, gauging the best direction to run.

"Um." The girl gave a nervous laugh and changed the subject. "God, Mr. Collins is a *sadist*. Two pop quizzes in a row, like chem's the only class we have?"

"You're confused," Tanvi informed her. "I'm not whoever you think I am."

"But—" the girl began. Tanvi took off before she could hear the rest.

It's okay, she told herself, even as her stomach churned harder. So she'd been spotted. The boy would never remember, and the girl

10

had mistaken Tanvi for someone else. She'd just have to be much more careful from here on out.

But the tight feeling wouldn't leave her chest. She kept checking behind her as if someone might be there.

Tanvi had never been afraid before, had never worried about anything but earning the boon that would get her bracelet. She didn't like it.

Stupid dream residue. It made you feel, and that was the last thing any dream runner would want. Stupid dreamer and her stupid phone.

Tanvi clutched her pouch close. Soon she would be home, and soon she could buy her bracelet. Nothing else counted.

The thought of the bracelet soothed her, with its dangling charms and alluring gold. *Soon.*

But first, she had a job to do.

Tanvi ducked into a side street in Queen Village to finish her harvest. She inhaled deeply and felt around for dreamers.

Her mind lit up like a radar screen. Almost everyone on the street was dreaming, and like a bonus, two of the row houses blazed with especially promising options. If she hustled, maybe she could nab both.

She slipped inside the first house and followed the beacon to the couch. The man she was after lay before his blaring TV, drunk enough to have blacked out. Perfect. Without much effort, Tanvi harvested his vision about a ship that sailed through sweet meringue oceans to a land of salted caramel almond bark trees. Sweet and quirky, with the flavor and texture of candy.

One down, one to go, and the boon was hers.

The second house had a pineapple knocker. Annoyed, Tanvi filtered it out. Details were only relevant if they had to do with her harvest. Every runner knew that. She homed in on the source of the dream instead, a teen boy located on the third floor.

Tanvi crept inside and up the stairs, her awareness pinned on the dream above her. As she reached the second floor, a woman shuffled out of a bathroom, yawning. Tanvi pressed herself back against the wall, a lozenge at her lips, while she waited for the woman to pass.

Then, fueled by adrenaline, she streaked up the last flight of stairs and toward the boy's bed. After swapping the lozenge for a dreamstone, she swooped right into his dream—the boy and his friend had broken into an abandoned mansion at twilight to film their documentary. It was scary and silly both, with giant spiders that attacked from the ceiling before turning into plush toys.

The boy didn't move while she was harvesting except to grunt when she corked the vial.

There. Tanvi had done it—and had two awesome dreams to show for it, dreams Venkat would be begging to buy. She coasted back down to street level.

No one burst out of the night to misidentify her as she raced toward the river. No one talked to her at all.

That, Tanvi thought, was more like it.

At Penn's Landing, Tanvi leaned out over the railing and studied the murky water. The Delaware River wasn't something she wanted to dive into at any time, but it was almost dawn. She'd stayed out too long as it was.

Tanvi fingered her pendant, a writhing black-and-gold serpent, and tapped it between its round emerald eyes. The river below immediately rose up, forming a sapphire doorway with shimmering arches. She leaped through it and landed on a sloping liquid platform that funneled her downward. The wavering walls surrounding her merged back into the water as she descended.

When she reached the bottom, no other runner was reporting to the guards flanking the cramped side entrance to the palace. Tanvi shivered. She'd never been this late before.

A younger naga beckoned her forward. Keeping her head lowered, she gripped her necklace.

"Name?" the guard barked, his voice oddly loud and grating.

Any other night, he would have faded into the background. Now, though, she could feel his smirk boring into her. He didn't expect a reaction, and she didn't give him one. Still, her hand trembled as she flashed her pendant at him.

"Tanvi," she said, without inflection.

"Cutting it close, are we, Tanvi? I doubt Lord Nayan would like that."

The mention of Nayan made her lapse sting all over again: If she'd been paying attention, that boy wouldn't have run into her. That girl with the bob wouldn't have seen her. Tanvi had already forgotten the girl's face. Too bad she couldn't erase their conversation so easily.

She'd been reckless. There was no denying it.

Her muscles stiffened with something new and awful. It took her a few seconds to name the feeling.

Panic.

Never again, she vowed, praying the guard couldn't tell.

The guard waved her through without another word, unlike some of his colleagues, who inevitably demanded to see the wares. They couldn't afford what Nayan and Venkat charged for a dream, so they tried to steal brief glimpses of what lay within the jewels the runners brought back with them.

Tanvi stalked through the hidden passage to the dream runners' quarters and then her own door. A jerk of the knob, and she rushed into the room. She wouldn't be able to sleep until she'd reassured herself that *it* was still there, exactly as she'd left it.

With the same fluttering in her belly she always got, Tanvi went straight to the closet.

The wooden shelves sat empty except for a lone gold-lidded enamel box. Her panic ebbing, she undid the lid. The lush pink velvet setting greeted her, ready for the bracelet she would soon earn with her boon.

Tanvi drew in a relieved breath. An image of her bracelet appeared in her thoughts, its golden links and charms untarnished and glossy like naga scales. She would never wear it, of course, never risk losing or scratching her treasure. It would be enough to spend endless hours here in this closet, gazing at the bracelet's perfect beauty.

The ghost of Tanvi's extinguished heart twinged with contentment. She didn't get why humans wanted anything else. The promise of her bracelet was all *she* needed.

For the chance to win it, she would gladly harvest dreams. Even if that meant going into the humans' world and dealing with their messy, irrational behavior.

Like that girl. Anger flared in Tanvi again, galling but remote. She would never endanger her bracelet like that again. Not ever.

Next time, Tanvi promised her bracelet as much as herself. *Next time I'll get it right.*

Alone in Nayan's appraisal vault, Venkat prodded the lack-luster dream fragment again, as if that would somehow make the panel in the wall across from him slide to the right to reveal Jai. But the runner who'd sold him the fragment a week ago was nowhere to be seen.

A mix of irritation and concern spread through him. This was the third time Jai had been late in a fortnight. Venkat's stable of runners all knew how important keeping these dawn appointments was. Every third morning, in the privacy of the vault, they brought him the dreams they'd harvested, the best of which were packed with drama and emotion, and Venkat paid them accordingly. He'd often thought it would be easier if his runners could walk around in public, but then their identities would be known, and anyone could try to poach them.

Still no Jai. Venkat's concern grew. Could he be—?

No. Venkat peered through the lone window, which was as translucent as a topaz lover's tear on this side but opaque golden wall on the other. In contrast to the cramped vault, the vast palace archives beyond buzzed with people: messengers sent by King Vasuki and Queen Naga Yakshi, wealthy patrons impatient to purchase dreams, merchants looking to horn in on the dream trade, would-be suitors and admirers, and scholars combing the stacks for novel ways to strengthen the nagas' defenses against their ancient enemy, the garudas.

Lord Nayan, a notorious firebrand in his youth, now presided over the archives as their curator and court historian. Nephew to the ferocious, exceedingly poisonous Nagaraja Takshaka, he also held a seat on the royal war council. And he was the only dream broker in all Nagalok.

So of course everyone wanted to get close to him.

That was where Venkat came in. As Nayan's apprentice, he served as gatekeeper, redirecting and deterring, leaving Nayan free to address his larger duties.

It was a job, Venkat thought, he couldn't do while waiting here. He didn't want to give up on Jai, but the archives beckoned.

"So?" a familiar voice demanded, making him jump. "How much?"

He wheeled around to find Jai slouched against the panel in the wall, his impassive, shadow-ringed stare fixed on the fragment in Venkat's hand. He looked like he hadn't slept or eaten since his last visit, and his crumpled kurta wore him instead of the other way around.

Relieved that he'd shown up at all, Venkat said gently, "I paid you for this last time."

Jai scoffed. "Not that one." He thrust an orange dreamstone vial at Venkat. "This one."

A new harvest? Curious, Venkat accepted the carnelian vial. Maybe things weren't as bad as he'd suspected.

He slid the cork out with ease, and the escaping wisps formed a scene in the air, the prelude to a feature film only he could see. Unlike his customers, who fell into them, Venkat observed harvested dreams from the outside.

The dreamer had illustrated her soul mate on a canvas, expertly rendered in oil pastels. But once she set it on her altar, a spell to summon him to her, the pigment peeled off in ribbons until it lay on the floor.

When at last she found him in real life, he didn't recognize her. Tears dripped down her cheeks, and she threw herself at his feet, intent on convincing him they belonged together. Her raw, naked anguish made Venkat cringe in sympathy, even as he estimated its value. Dreams like this, ripe with naked pining and need, were a naga favorite. Jai had chosen well.

The sequence hiccuped a few times before going dark, a decaying reel with bits eaten away. Sorrow bloomed in Venkat's chest. So things *were* that bad. Jai had plainly lost control of the wisps mid-harvest, and some of them had evaporated into the ether.

When the choppy nightmare resumed, the dreamer huddled, devastated, in a patch of unripe strawberries while her soul mate tucked a blue flax flower behind the ear of a laughing woman in a pretty sundress. Venkat assumed the man must have rebuffed the dreamer for this woman, but he'd never know for certain, not with the middle section missing.

Dodging Jai's dull gaze, Venkat steered the remnants of the dream into the dreamstone and set it down. "Show me what else you have."

Jai's frown lent some feeling to his face. "That's it."

Fighting to hide his dread, Venkat crossed his arms. "You only harvested one dream?"

What survived of the dream was good quality, its level of immersion deep and its quotient of heartbreak high. Yet in two nights of harvesting, all Jai had managed was a single half-reaped dream. Venkat wasn't sure Jai had even perceived the holes, and that only made him sadder.

He considered quietly buying it anyway, but the damage was too extensive.

Venkat knew better than to care about his runners this much. But while his kin were gone, at least he had Nayan. His runners had no one. He'd promised himself that no matter how long it took, no matter how many times his experiments failed, he'd come up with something to help them.

Jai pushed the carnelian vial at Venkat again and held out his empty palm. "One boon."

Venkat knew he was itching to get his hands on his particular obsession, a tricycle. Jai was way too old to ride one, not that he cared. It didn't matter that the boons could invoke anything at all; the dream runners wanted what they wanted.

Venkat imagined telling Jai that getting the tricycle wouldn't grant him any lasting happiness. "I'm sorry," he said instead. "Bring me something else, all right?"

If only Jai would argue. If only he'd do something to prove Venkat wrong.

There was no reason to expect that, not after the initiation had done its work, but Venkat couldn't help scrutinizing him. *Something. Anything. Please.*

Jai closed his fist around the rejected vial, snuffing out that wish along with the soft light from the ruined dream. "One boon," he said flatly. He darted back through the panel, presumably toward his room in the runners' quarters.

Swallowing a sigh, Venkat opened his logbook to the day's acquisitions and drew a blank line after Jai's name. At any rate, he consoled himself, running his finger down the page, Indu and Srinivas had both delivered excellent wares earlier.

All dream runners burned out eventually. Venkat knew that, he'd always known that, and yet his heart still hurt. He was failing them, like he'd failed his family back on Prithvi.

He pressed his forehead down on the page. If only he could disappear into the workshop and focus on his trials.

But the line by the desk wasn't going to get any shorter. Venkat groaned, picturing ants swarming over him like he was a juicy ball of rose syrup–drenched rasgulla dropped on a sidewalk. There'd be nothing left of him if he wasn't careful.

Donning a noncommittal smile like well-oiled armor, Venkat left the vault through his own panel. The dream runners weren't the only ones with clandestine routes through the palace.

Once he emerged at the scallop-arched entrance to the archives, he strode past the queue of gem-stippled and silk-swathed patrons, all touched by the river sky's glow spilling in from the skylights like liquid aquamarine. Madhu, her white plait swinging behind her, dismissed her latest client with a curt flick of her wrist.

Princess Asha of the clan of Vasuki promptly sashayed forward, as imperious as the nagarani and three times as showy in a zari-embroidered scarlet choli. "You cccccertainly dallied this morning!" she scolded, jhumka earrings tinkling as she tossed her waist-length black locks over her shoulder. Rhinestone flower clips sparkled like a rainbow of dreamstones against its waves, in striking contrast to the green-black scales of her powerful cobra tail. "Ssssome among us have absolutely *arduous* days ahead."

Venkat had learned early on not to react to Asha's theatrics—after all, they both worked for Nayan—but the nagas closest to her began stage-whispering, precisely like she'd intended.

"Surprises are what keep life interesting. Thank you for your patience," he called, nodding at Madhu as he deposited the vial on one of the many shelves warded to repel anyone but him or Nayan.

Her expression might have withered a field of crops as she moved to let Venkat reclaim the immense ivory desk. He could already hear her irate voice in his head: *I serve as Lord Nayan's eyes and ears, not his secretary. Do not keep me waiting again.*

Two nagas, who might have been the equivalent of Venkat's age of eighteen, followed in her wake. The bigger of the pair, Prince Chintan, offered a shallow bow. "Venkat, is it? I am Chintu."

21

"Oh?" Venkat asked with extra politeness. He'd seen the prince and his friends clowning around the palace like the spoiled nobles they were, and he was fairly certain Nayan didn't need whatever it was they thought they could provide.

"I have heard a great deal about you," Chintu continued. "All superb things, needless to say." His friend leaned back on his chevron-patterned orange-and-white coils and shot Chintu a *hurry up* look.

Venkat pointedly eyed the line of people behind them. "I'm sorry, but I can't really chat right now."

"Of course, of course," Chintu said, the epitome of arrogance. "I merely thought perhaps we might help each other out. I am searching for dreams, and you—"

Venkat gestured to an elegant registry beside the giant ledger on the desk. "You know the rules; all barter must be sanctioned by Lord Nayan. However, if you register to become a new patron . . ."

Chintu's slit pupils widened and contracted. When he spoke, his fangs flashed, as tapered as freshly whetted daggers. "Do you realize who it is you are denying?"

Venkat had known cocky boys like this his whole life. Whether back on Prithvi or here in Nagalok, they thought all they had to do was demand what they wanted, and it would be theirs. Unlike Venkat, they had no concept of the sacrifices others made so they could enjoy the luxuries they took for granted.

Chintu had no clue that with a maximum of thirty dream runners in their stable, even with the citywide lotteries held every week, Nayan and Venkat could never hope to meet more than a fraction of the demand. Selling dreams to those with clout was a stopgap measure at best—they'd been turning away more and more buyers—and Venkat had no time for the whims of petulant princes.

"I do know," he said blandly. "Prince Chintan of the clan of Anant Shesha. An old and respectable line, and one we would be pleased to do *official* commerce with."

Chintu was still glaring, but at that, he reached for the peacock feather pen in the inkwell by the registry.

"Why trouble yourself?" asked his friend, who'd sprawled back against a bookshelf, hands in his kurta pockets. "There are other means to obtain what you want." Grinning, he jabbed his chin toward Asha, who, by some miracle, said nothing.

Chintu paused, the quill dripping viscous gold ink the color of his irises, then dropped the pen back into the inkwell. If he noticed the shining splotch he'd made on the immaculate desktop, he ignored it. "Tell Lord Nayan I came by, would you?" he bade Venkat, looking down at him with the detachment of a stranger.

Everyone has an agenda, Nayan had told Venkat at the outset of his apprenticeship. *In many ways, the obvious ones are preferable. With them, you always know where you stand.*

Chintu and his friend slithered away. They were probably headed to the marketplace, in search of the seedy pop-up shops that claimed to peddle dreams sourced directly from the palace's stock. Nayan always laughed them off. No one except for Venkat and Nayan had access to their inventory, and anyone who believed otherwise got what they paid for.

Asha hissed, her forked tongue tasting the air. "He attached himself to me for the better part of this week, even insisting I should take him along to Prithvi. Hatchling royalty can be so ridiculously *tiresome*!"

Venkat started to point out that she was a hatchling princess, so maybe not one to talk, but the doors to the hall had opened again, and a reverent hush cascaded out in waves until the archives almost rang with it.

Nayan swept in, the council emblem of eight snakes entwined in an ouroboros glimmering from the cobalt-and-gold dupatta draped over his broad shoulders. Though he was no taller or larger than the other nagas, Nayan's proud bearing somehow felt grander, more substantial, enough that the shadows themselves seemed to sway like snakes in thrall as he passed.

He smiled slightly before announcing, "I bear news from the council. Our scouts have learned of another attempt to breach the gates to the realm."

The garuda army. Venkat couldn't imagine what Garuda thought he stood to gain from attacking Nagalok. Wasn't it enough that the nagas had been forced to retreat here from Earth two centuries ago, when his forces had resumed their ancient onslaught? Now even Nagalok wasn't safe?

A susurration of alarm flooded the archives, and Nayan, night-black eyebrows drawing together, waved it off. "Calm yourselves. This is the reason we shelter underground. I know many of you miss traversing the mortal realm, and the nagaraja and I both intend for our people to one day be able to return to Prithvi. But for the time being, it is imperative we remain under the sky of our own world."

Though no one dared openly question King Vasuki's trusted advisor, Venkat didn't miss the disquiet glistening in the many gold-brown eyes around him. The nagas of the court had heard this speech often during the past two hundred years, and cabin fever had long since set in.

That was why Nayan had first suggested brokering dreams. It gave those who wanted one a substitute for interacting with humans while the council and its scholars searched for a solution to the garuda threat.

"The nagaraja and nagarani," he continued, "along with the council, will hold an audience this afternoon, which I encourage you to attend and where you might voice any lingering concerns you have."

The disgruntled mutters grew louder, matched by dark looks. "The council!" someone mocked. "Always so eager to talk. What are they actually *doing* to stop the breaches?" When Nayan faced him, the man sputtered. "I— Naturally I did not mean *you*, my lord."

"I understand," Nayan said, unperturbed. "You did not ask for our predicament, and yet you languish because of it. It is unjust. Nevertheless, if you cannot trust me that we will endure, then trust your liege. King Vasuki and Queen Naga Yakshi desire nothing more than security for their entire kingdom and its revered inhabitants."

The room fell quiet again, grimaces turning on the man who had spoken up.

Nayan took advantage of the silence to glide through the crowd, which parted before him. "Now vacate this chamber. My apprentice and I have much to discuss before the audience."

"But what of my—" someone else protested.

"Whatever business you have with my office can wait until tomorrow, I assure you," Nayan said, halting beside Venkat's desk. He smiled fully now, a dangerous upturn of his lips like the blade of a sickle.

The chamber emptied abruptly, making the pearlescent walls loom as high and wide as a cavern's. Venkat sat up straighter and looked at Nayan, who laid a hand on his shoulder. "Well done, holding down the fort while I was in council." He turned to Madhu. "I will expect your report this afternoon."

Venkat's heart lifted at the praise. Back when he'd lost his family, he'd never imagined he'd end up raised by a naga. And yet here they were.

After he'd failed the dream runner initiation, Nayan had saved him from being exiled back to Prithvi, taking him in as a son and an apprentice. He'd let Venkat cry out his grief and rage for the earthquake that had left him to watch, helpless, while it murdered the rest of his family. It was Nayan who'd then nurtured Venkat's love of stories and shown him his true potential for working with dreams.

What was the hassle of dealing with entitled customers compared to that?

Madhu put her palms together before her face. "As you wish." She undulated away, her scales gleaming in the jewel-toned light.

With far less grace, Asha huffed and hastened after her.

Once the double doors had closed behind them, Nayan spoke one word: "Upstairs."

Warming with anticipation, Venkat hurried to the statue of Mansa Devi, sister to King Vasuki, at the rear of the hall. There were four such statues in the archives, each standing guard over one stack of shelves, but only this one contained a hidden lever. The rooftop sanctuary it uncovered had originally been created for the visiting queen as a refuge from court politics, but in her absence, Nayan had found a different use for the space.

Venkat located the fifth feather on the statue's right wing and pressed down. A pulley-driven lift materialized, undetectable to anyone who hadn't been granted admittance to the sanctuary. Then he and Nayan boarded the lift, which carried them to their workshop overlooking the distant marketplace.

Here, within these walls of cobalt and gold with their cobra-scale motif and embedded gemstone murals, Nayan had introduced Venkat to the most important aspect of his job.

For Venkat was a dreamsmith. He didn't simply catalog and sell the scraps of dreams brought in by the runners; he also mined those scraps and soldered the extracted elements together into tangible objects as strange and fanciful as the visions they came from. His was an ability rarely seen and even more rarely developed.

And Nayan was the one who'd helped him develop it.

Up here, in their secure retreat, he'd guided Venkat until about three years ago, teaching him between their other tasks. Then, once Nayan was pleased with his skill, they had begun their project. Section by section, Venkat was forging a landscape of dreams, one

Nayan promised would end the war with the garudas and change everything for the nagas.

"How are the runners?" Nayan asked.

Venkat had to tell him about Jai. Their system relied on monitoring and replacing the dream runners as necessary. If it was time to recruit another candidate, Nayan needed to know.

But Venkat's trials to help them were so close to success. He could feel it.

"Look!" he said, producing a pair of stone-blade scissors he'd designed to cut right through the most elaborate of lies. "This one's still holding its shape. I think we might be onto something."

He would tell Nayan. Just not yet.

"Indeed!" Nayan surveyed the bustling terrain far below them, the nagas only small dots of color against the green. Then he took the scissors and held them up to the boundless sky. "My son," he said, his words steeped in satisfaction, "I believe you are ready for the next step of our project."

3

Tanvi jerked awake to the sound of rattling. Golden charms glittered all around her—a carousel horse, a quarter note, a toadstool, a rearing unicorn's head, an open book, two hearts intertwined, and a daisy—then winked out. Her neck ached. She'd fallen asleep in the closet while imagining the bracelet again, her pouch full of fresh wares from Dubai.

Dream runners didn't dream, but sometimes they held on to memories of their harvests. One swam up in Tanvi's mind.

Her fourth time venturing out on her own, she'd lucked into a dream about a man winning the lottery and completely transforming his life. He'd traded in his basement studio apartment for a grand villa in Paris, quit substitute teaching, and bought his aunt the motorcycle she'd always wanted. It had been an enchanted vision, packed with beauty and luxury and pleasure—up until the moment when Tanvi had accidentally woken the dreamer while guiding the wisps into her vial. Not only had the story cut off halfway through, but the man's horror as reality sank back in had been a total waste. Why couldn't that have happened *inside* the dream, so she could have bottled it?

Her limbs felt as clumsy now as they had all those years ago. She might not dream, but she did need to sleep if she wanted to stay alert, and passing out on a hard floor for the second night straight wasn't going to cut it.

The rattle came again, hurtling up her spine. Someone was shaking the doorknob. Still groggy, Tanvi pressed her palms over her face.

"Ssssilly creature," crooned an incredibly aggravating voice through the door, right on cue, "would you sssssleep away the entire morning?"

It wasn't even dawn yet. "Go away!" Tanvi called, jumping up one second too late.

The knob turned, and Princess Asha glided in, the shine of her chevron-patterned scales an assault on Tanvi's sleep-raw eyes. "Why is it always so *dismal* in here?" she demanded, waving at the ceiling until the overhead lanterns flared to life. "One might almost believe you runners prefer to dwell in drabness."

Tanvi headed her off by the foot of the untouched bed, then stabbed a finger at the doorway.

Asha, of course, ignored the hint and flounced past her. "Do you like my new barrettes? Sameer gifted them to me."

"Why are you here?" Tanvi mumbled, her thoughts slowly defogging. "My appointment with Venkat's not until tomorrow."

"How perfectly *sssstultifying*! Do you not want barrettes of your

30

own? A necklace? A pair of jhumka earrings? Or . . ." Asha edged toward the closet. "I realize we are dipping our tails into unknown territory here, but perhaps even a dress or a sari? Some flowers to freshen up the space—jasmine to start with?"

The ambush made Tanvi's teeth hurt. Asha didn't usually badger her like this. And she definitely knew better than to poke around the closet.

Asha suddenly slithered over the threshold. "You and this fixation," she called, shaking her head. "What exactly do you think this charm bracelet will bring you?"

Tanvi barely heard her. "Get away from there," she growled.

With a single ripple of her coils, Asha reappeared in the room proper. She huffed. "You dream runners are all so predictable. I shall tell you about my day, then." In less time than it took Tanvi to blink, Asha morphed into her human form and reclined on the bed, hugging a cushion to her chest before diving into her story.

Tanvi itched with impatience. Until recently, Asha had been busy scouting potential candidates for Nayan's stable, leaving Tanvi to her own job of harvesting. She'd been the one to spirit Tanvi away to Nagalok in the first place.

But now that they were both physically—if not chronologically—seventeen, Asha had decided she was bored with her cushy life as a princess and invented a human boyfriend.

Except everyone knew that nagas were forbidden to consort with mortals; it put them at risk of being captured by the garudas. Not even Asha could get away with *that*.

So instead of burdening her actual friends with her daydreams, she constantly barged in and prattled at Tanvi.

Tanvi scowled. If Asha had pointless fantasies, that was her problem. But why did she insist on making them Tanvi's?

". . . 'Did I not just say that?'" Asha mimed sulking at someone. "And then I told him, 'Surely you know better than to fear sssssnakes.'" She turned the sulk on Tanvi. "You are not even listening, are you?"

Tanvi only pointed to the door again.

Asha let out a huge, dramatic sigh and changed back into her nagini form. "Why do I trouble myself so? You are no better than Jai."

Tanvi and Jai had been in the same group of dream runner recruits. They'd gone through the initiation together. Tanvi didn't recall much about that time, which was fine with her, and she hadn't talked to Jai since then.

She figured Asha must be annoying him regularly, too.

Asha undulated over to the table and rapped twice on it. A tiffin, a goblet, and a plate appeared there. "Eat, at least." When Tanvi didn't move, Asha added, "Without proper nourishment, you will have no strength for harvesting dreams this night."

That was all Tanvi had to hear. She didn't care about food any more than she cared about clothes, never mind flowers, but Asha was right. She did need the fuel to succeed.

A tiny blossom sat next to the food. Tanvi rested her goblet on top of it, ignoring the perfume it released. The tiffin opened with a *click*, revealing vegetable biryani instead of the normal simpler roti and sabzi.

Asha launched into more nonsense about her latest exploits on

Prithvi, none of which Tanvi bothered to acknowledge. She could feel Asha probing. Waiting for her to respond.

But Tanvi only chewed mechanically, chasing each bite of biryani with a huge gulp of mango nectar. They might as well have been chalk dust, for all she tasted them.

Within a dream, treats like this would have meant everything. From Venkat's reports, his customers—who had no way to access any ingredients found on Prithvi—practically drooled at the chance to experience mortal foods, both gourmet and comfort. Dumplings especially fascinated them: even scraps featuring anything from cheese-stuffed pierogi and creamy malai kofta to savory xiao long bao and fluffy Knödel in vanilla sauce went for high prices. Whenever Tanvi could, she tried to find dreamers who'd just eaten.

Outside of dreams, though, why bother?

Two more bites, and she got up. "There, finished. Now will you go?"

"Did you hear what I said?" Asha challenged. "Navratri is upon us, and this year, I wish to dance at mortal garba with Sameer."

Tanvi rinsed her hands at the sink and opened her storage cabinet. Three rows of unused sapphires, rubies, emeralds, topazes, tourmalines, and amethysts flashed in welcome, vibrant with the promise of the dreams she would fill them with.

That, and her bracelet, was all she wanted. That was all any dream runner wanted, and Asha knew it. "I don't get why you think I need to hear this."

Because Asha was Asha, instead of backing off, she slid up beside Tanvi. "I have been planning, and I believe you should accompany me." She wiggled on her coils, beaming. "Would it not be fun to come to Philadelphia? We could dress you up like me!"

Philadelphia. Tanvi's hands closed around the nearest dreamstones, and their polished facets cut into her skin. It took everything she had to hold her face still.

"What do you mean?" she asked as vapidly as she could, even though the breath lodged in her lungs felt like it would strangle her. Was Asha trying to trap her? Get Tanvi to admit she'd screwed up the other night?

Did Asha know?

"Truly, Tanvi, you are the most unobservant person I have ever had the misfortune of meeting," Asha complained. "Sometimes I wonder if the only way you would even realize I am here is if I gave you one of the jewels from my hair for your harvest."

Were the dream runners under some kind of surveillance to track their progress? The idea jarred Tanvi to her core.

The girl in the street, the girl who had called her a name, loomed in her mind. Had that been a test?

Sweat pooled under Tanvi's arms. What secrets had she given away? Would Nayan kick her out?

Was she going to lose her bracelet?

"Of course I know you're here," she snapped, her fear acute enough to sound like anger. "You never stop talking!"

"That settles it," said Asha. "Since you are too foolish to comprehend when someone is trying to help you, I shall decide in your stead. You are coming with me."

"Why?" Tanvi burst out, knuckles scraping the dreamstones. Too bad it wasn't already night, so she could take off with them.

If Asha was going to turn her in, cost her the chance to earn her bracelet, why wouldn't she just say so?

Asha flipped her long hair. "Because fresh air would likely do you many worlds of good."

"But my—"

"Yes, yes," Asha interrupted, waving a hand. "Your appointment with Venkat is not until tomorrow. I heard you the first time. Unlike *some* people, I actually listen when others speak."

The disaster from two nights ago replayed itself in Tanvi's head all over again. Why hadn't she looked where she was going? Why hadn't she run as soon as the girl had started talking?

What was it the girl had called her? *Nitya.* Was that supposed to mean something?

The questions caromed off one another, but Tanvi couldn't connect any of them with an answer.

Asha watched her with sly eyes. "Is something the matter?"

"I thought you wanted to tell me more about Sameer?" Tanvi suggested, the words sitting oddly in her mouth. But if that was what it took to distract Asha from her blunder, she'd do it. Anything to keep her bracelet safe.

"Interesting." Asha tilted her head. "Sssssuddenly I have your attention?"

Tanvi let her expression go slack. "Well, this way, maybe you'll finally leave."

35

"*We* will leave, yes," Asha said. "Now, in fact, after I see Nayan Uncle. You will stay out of sight while I obtain authorization for my scouting mission. Come."

"You want to go *now*?" What was Asha thinking? Tanvi hadn't seen proper daylight on Prithvi since she'd become a dream runner. And did it have to be Philly? "I was sleeping!"

But if she didn't go, Asha might get even more suspicious. Then Tanvi might never get her bracelet.

The idea almost broke her in half. She could survive without the harvest if she had to, but not without the bracelet. Its gold links, its dangling charms, the way it would fit around her wrist and make that tinkling noise . . . what else was there?

She wouldn't let that happen. If Asha was testing her, she refused to fail.

"That is when I scout, yesssss," Asha replied, even her hiss amused.

"Fine." Tanvi stomped to the door without waiting for Asha. "Let's get this over with."

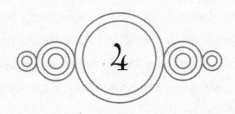

4

Every so often, even though he didn't need it, Venkat liked to wear a jeweler's loupe while alone in the workshop. He remembered sneaking into Mummy's and Papa's closets as a kid and cobbling together costumes—Mummy's Indian and Western jewelry and bindis, Papa's ties and hats. He'd told anyone who would listen that he'd be a treasure hunter when he grew up.

That was all gone now, of course, just like his family, but Venkat had never quite outgrown the urge to pretend. According to Asha, role-playing was popular in the mortal world these days, and while he had no plans to leave Nayan, Venkat did wonder what it would be like to attend a convention dressed up in an elaborate outfit, even donning someone else's identity. But the character he had in mind wasn't one anybody would recognize. No, he would zip himself into the Venkat who might have been and discover the path his life could have taken.

Was that any different than the nagas' desire to experience mortal dreams?

He had maybe a quarter hour before his first appointment of the morning, but Venkat drew out the loupe from its silken case in a drawer anyway. Then he spun the dial on the burnished brass device and stared through the diamond lens at the shelves upon shelves of dreamstone vials lining the gold-and-cobalt-and-grass-green walls. His own well-stocked wizard's laboratory, courtesy of the nagas, keepers of precious metals and jewels.

Like liquefied gold, the extracts of melted-down dreams could be combined and fashioned into something new, overwriting the past. Creation stemming from destruction. Human imagination distilled into story.

And Venkat loved a good story.

These brief snatches over the past year, when he worked on his own experiments, felt like he'd stepped into one. His favorite creations so far included a replica of his grandmother's golden elephant necklace, which he'd animated so the elephant actually flapped its ears and trumpeted; a living rose with petals of brine and a perfume of ocean air; and, of course, the pair of scissors he'd shown Nayan. Unfortunately, except for the scissors, none of them had lasted more than a week or two before separating into their dream components.

Venkat just had to identify what made the scissors different. Once he did, not only would he be able to complete his project with Nayan, but he'd also craft a way to save his runners. He glanced at the shelf reserved for the sections of the project he'd already forged, each preserved as an individual dream fragment in its own vial, and all awaiting the day when he would solder them into a whole.

The pain in his heart, which had been poised to spring, relaxed.

Today, he'd put the finishing touches on his most recent design, a hand-sized couch that soared among the stars. He'd been turning it over and over in his mind, exactly as Nayan had taught him, conceptualizing the carved frame, the indigo upholstery, the halo of silver stardust, and considering the particular arrangement of elements he'd need to bring it to life.

If this one held like the scissors, next he would try a tincture, one that would extend the life of a plant. Then that of an animal. And finally, one to heal burnout.

He raised his arms, inviting the vials on the shelves to speak to him. To help him help Jai.

A jar he hadn't really noticed in years twinkled at him, the lucent green-yellow of marrow-deep desire.

On his ninth birthday, to mark the beginning of his apprenticeship, Nayan had taken him to a place called the Night Market, which lay in its own pocket dimension between the worlds. The entire Market might have been a dream, from its golden peacock-beak entrance to the kinnara and vetala vendors to the eerie singing that serenaded the patrons from all directions at once.

Do you see how these wares are like dream elements? Nayan had asked, leading Venkat past the stalls. *Dreams are stories, Venkat, and what is a story if not reordering the familiar in a novel form?* He motioned to a nest of spectral eggs, then to a bleeding-tooth mushroom collar. *Mix this element with that, and you come up with something wholly yours. You spin a new tale.*

As they continued the tour, Venkat had marveled at the eyeballs that offered glimpses through time and space—but only if they were eaten raw—and the dagger that cut the thread binding the wielder to their destiny, at the risk of also cutting the thread binding them to their life.

Then he'd spotted the jar of fireflies like luminous soaring peridots. He'd lifted the jar, transfixed by the flickering jewels within. *Dreamstones with wings!*

No, corrected Nayan. *Not dreamstones. Hearts that sought but never found, hearts that even now seek. Let these inspire you as you forge.*

He'd purchased the jar for the price of a single scale and gifted it to Venkat.

The memory faded, replaced by the tangible vials of dream elements Venkat had selected for the next section of their project. They winked at him from the gilt-edged marble counter, brilliant-cut reds, greens, purples, and blues all brimming with potential.

Potential for what, though? Venkat frowned. While Nayan had encouraged Venkat's experiments from the beginning, he still hadn't shared the full scope of his own vision.

It is hard to spot a single leaf if you are ogling the entire forest, he'd noted a few months into the project. *Let us glean wisdom from the sages of old and progress section by section, devoting ourselves fully to each one.*

And he'd held to that, insisting if Venkat had expectations, they would stifle the story he was forging and force it into preconceived notions. When Venkat had argued that he could handle knowing, and Nayan should just let him in on the plan, Nayan had run him through a series of tests proving otherwise.

That didn't make waiting to find out any easier, though. Or

wondering what moving to the next stage actually meant.

The garland of small golden bells above the workshop's back door jingled, startling Venkat. His first runner was downstairs. Somehow Lord Surya's flaming chariot had already crested the horizon, and the pink striations of Ushas Mata's dawn were feathering through the sky.

Though the shelves of elements hummed to him, each a tale in miniature, Venkat reluctantly put down his loupe. No matter how much time he spent here, it was never enough. He hadn't even gotten to finish his floating couch.

But he was the closest thing to kin his dream runners had, so he pressed the button for the lift.

"And what did you get?" Venkat asked politely, studying the motley collection of dreamstones laid out before him on the rough-hewn table, wares he'd purchased from the four runners who'd stopped by earlier. They were the only spots of color in the stark cell of an evaluation room, so unlike the rest of the palace.

"Cats." The runner, an athletic boy named Bharat, held up a topaz vial. "Worth a boon all by itself."

Venkat hid his amusement as he uncorked the vial. Bharat said the same thing about every dream he harvested, and at this point, his overconfidence had worn as soft and reassuring as an old letter unfolded and reread over the years. It proved he was still functioning, still nowhere near burnout. "We'll see about that."

A gaudy color palette and fuzzy texture brushed past Venkat as the reel began to play, revealing human-sized cats dancing in a musical number punctuated by a chorus of mews and yowls. The whole thing was very strange and off-putting, even what he would qualify as a nightmare, but the joyful haze surrounding it indicated the dreamer had felt very differently.

Then the dream stage went up in flames. Through their cater-wauls of dismay, the cats donned top hats and mourned the black lump of a theater. In the next scene, they'd gathered a pile of sticks and, still singing, prepared to rebuild.

Venkat mulled over the vision. He wouldn't have conceived of a use for warbling felines anywhere in Nayan's scheme, but the second half was a nice surprise—it had exactly the feeling he'd been look-ing for. "I'll give you a fifth of a boon for this," he said.

"A half," countered Bharat, his passion sparking. He sounded like Asha and her friends when they talked about their current crushes. But his eagerness only made him seem even younger than almost fifteen.

Guilt smoldered like cobra venom in Venkat's veins. Bharat and the other runners might not make it to his age, and that was his fault as much as anyone's.

The initiation all dream runners underwent—the one Venkat himself had failed—silenced their traumatized hearts and eased their suffering. He'd seen it for himself: whenever a recruit arrived, they'd been heartbroken or terrified or both, with no one to turn to. Asha deliberately limited her invitation to candidates trapped in miserable situations, and only if they were under the age of twelve and still able to adapt to their new role. But once Nayan had guided the poor kid through, rooting out the memories that had tormented them, their face inevitably relaxed. Their back grew straighter, and their chin lifted. Harvesting dreams filled the hole where their past had been, giving them a purpose, something stable they could count on.

Venkat's heart rallied every time, too. While he'd never have the option not to remember losing his family, at least he could see how much lighter the candidates were after being initiated. Bharat's previous home life had been horrifying, just like all the runners', and forgetting it was a gift. But knowing they'd been spared more pain didn't mean Venkat could accept them burning out.

Especially considering he'd almost been one of them. How was he *not* supposed to care?

"One-third," he declared, "and that's my final offer." He dropped the fraction of boon into Bharat's hand.

It fused with the two-thirds Bharat had previously accumulated, a soft white orb shining over his skin until he, too, glowed. "My console," he said breathlessly, invoking the boon.

The boon wavered, then dissolved into a handheld video game console.

Bharat immediately began punching buttons. When the panel he had stepped through minutes ago slammed aside hard enough to shake the bare wall, Venkat jumped, but Bharat didn't even react.

Princess Asha burst into the appraisal room, her night-dark hair streaming out behind her in bejeweled waves, and her green-gold eyes with their slit pupils blazing as intensely as the gold-and-pearl belly chain that marked the point where her brown midriff merged into her undulating serpentine tail. She might have been a dreamstone herself, the mauve of her gold-trimmed choli shifting in the light of the overhead lanterns, one second a shimmering ruby, the next a vivid amethyst.

Three people already put the room at capacity, but just beyond the panel, Venkat caught a glimpse of Tanvi—her own loose hair unadorned, her simple salwar kameez a muted yellow, and her dark eyes cast down—before she slipped out of sight again.

Odd—she wasn't on today's appointment roster. For her to show up like this, she must have run low on dreamstones. Venkat made a mental note to check that the other runners were still well stocked.

"I must speak with Nayan Uncle," Asha announced. "Where is he?"

Venkat pointed Bharat and his new console toward the exit. His fingers still tapping away, Bharat left.

"I'm busy, Asha," Venkat said. He adopted his best fake fawning tone. "But never mind *my* work; it loses all meaning before your fulgurating presence. Pray tell, Princess, how may I best serve your every arbitrary whim?"

Asha hissed, long and loud, her serpentine gaze glinting and her fangs flashing, as if any of that would intimidate him. "Do not test me. Where is he?"

"On his morning stroll," Venkat said lightly, trying not to laugh. "You know, the one where you're not supposed to disturb him? That one."

"Yet I am in need of him." Asha gestured to the dreamstones left by the other runners, positioned in a row like a necklace waiting to be strung. "I am overdue to return to Prithvi, and I must remedy that straightaway."

A scouting mission. The laughter turned to spikes of dread in Venkat's throat. Asha couldn't have noticed Jai's condition. She hadn't even been around much lately.

But if she had . . .

Everything was happening too fast. Venkat should have updated Nayan already, but he had made excuses, had let himself keep hoping, as if things would somehow fix themselves.

Calm down, he told himself, swallowing the dread before it could climb any higher. *She doesn't know.*

To buy some time, he held up a hand. "Let me take care of this first," he said, his voice as soothing as he could make it. "Come in, Tanvi."

When she did, he offered her his friendliest smile. "What can I do for you? Do you need more dreamstones?"

Tanvi stepped closer, but her movements were jerky, like she was fighting herself. She glanced at Asha, then back down at the floor. Venkat studied her more carefully. She looked off somehow, one hand curling in a fist at her side and her gaze not quite catching his.

Alarms blared inside him. She wasn't burning out, too, was she?

In the next instant, however, her hand relaxed, and she raised her head. "Yes, more dreamstones," she said, her tone as distant as her eyes.

Venkat sank back on his heels. He should have realized; the

initiation had left his runners so dependent on routine that even something as simple as forgetting to order more dreamstones could throw them off. Unlike burnout, he could work with that.

Asha, of course, was listening to the conversation with no shame. "Fassssscinating," she drawled, each syllable soaked in condescension. "I am *utterly* riveted. Shall I help you two select more vials? It will, without a doubt, be *precisely* the thrilling diversion I had envisioned for my day."

Venkat shot her a sidelong glance. "I can handle my job, thanks."

"Splendid! Then let us return to my request."

"You're incorrigible," he muttered, but he felt better. She didn't know about Jai. He'd had time to pick out her tells, ever since she first brought him here on the promise of a chance to start over. "What do you want me to do, conjure Nayan out of thin air?"

He'd half expected her to say yes, but in one of her mercurial changes of mood, Asha motioned to Tanvi. "Navratri is upon us. Do you not see how bored the runners are becoming?"

Bored? Venkat glanced skeptically at Tanvi. The dream runners couldn't get bored.

Tanvi didn't react to the exaggeration. He honestly couldn't blame her if she'd stopped listening. "Why the rush in going to Prithvi, Your Royal Highness?" he asked, turning his attention back to Asha. "Got a craving for artisanal lavender-blackberry éclairs?"

Asha, as she well knew, had no business shopping or attending the theater or taking any of her myriad other detours while on scouting trips to the mortal realm, but she'd never let what she called pointless rules hem her in. Life, she insisted, was meant to be lived.

"Perhaps," she allowed, angling her head in a move she probably intended to come off as mysterious. "I do not suppose you wish me to find you more novels?"

She had Venkat there. "Fine," he said. "I'll put in a good word for you with Nayan when he gets back. But no promises." Asha preened. "Now can you please let me do my job? I still have to get out there and deal with the customers!"

Her lovely features screwed up in annoyance. "I suppose so. But only if you agree to leave this stuffy prison and celebrate with us tonight. You never have any *fun*."

Venkat sighed. Every year, Asha tried to drag him out during Navratri. Like a spoiled older sister, she'd harass him with her constant need for the limelight, but then, right when he was ready to toss her out the window, she'd charm him with a little gesture like this. Even though he never brought it up, she hadn't forgotten what that date meant to him.

"Oh, do come!" wheedled Asha. "You never go anywhere. Even Nayan Uncle says so." Her scowl had turned as bright and cloying as the jalebi pops she'd once brought back from the Night Market, oozing enough sweetness to send him into a sugar coma.

But Venkat had had years to build up a tolerance. Channeling his best evasive Nayan, he shrugged. "We'll see."

As though she'd gotten the answer she wanted, Asha beamed and slithered out, leaving him alone with Tanvi. "Thank you for waiting," he told her, and pulled a pouch of dreamstones from the cabinet beneath the table.

47

She held out her hand for it. The hollow way she stared at nothing, her pretty face blank until her fingers dipped into the pouch and found the loosely packed vials, snagged on something inside him.

He'd seen that detached look thousands of times before, but as if Asha's invitation had pried open the floodgates of memory, he suddenly recalled Tanvi the day she'd arrived—she'd been ten, curious, and feisty. As she took the pouch from him now, an echo of that girl radiated around her like an aura before dispersing.

The dreamsmith in him had to wonder: Who might she be if things were different?

That question was its own kind of forbidden fruit, and he shook it off. "Happy harvesting. I'll see you tomorrow, then." But when she didn't leave, he frowned. "Yes?"

She'd lost herself to the pouch, her fingers digging into the fabric and letting go, digging in and letting go. He resisted the urge to wave his hand in her face.

"Tanvi?" he tried. "Is there something else?"

The silence between them hung as dense and dark as smog. *Was she burning out, then?*

"No," Tanvi said after what felt like an hour. She turned and scuttled through the panel.

Venkat stared at the place she'd been. If only he could believe that.

5

Back in her room, door shut, Tanvi chanted one word over and over and over: *bracelet.*

Her skin flushed with fear, and she broke into a sweat. Her bracelet. She'd nearly blown everything.

So Asha *didn't* know what she'd done, after all, but Venkat had almost caught her. She was slipping.

She was going to lose the only thing she cared about.

So many thoughts. Too many thoughts. Tanvi wanted to squeeze her head until every one of them shut up. All she should be thinking about was her bracelet with its delicate gold charms and how great they would feel on her wrist.

There was one good thing, she told herself, trying to cut through the panic. At least Asha had given up on that half-baked day trip to Prithvi.

Legs trembling, Tanvi sank to the floor in the middle of the closet and stared up at the velvet case waiting to be filled. It screamed for the bracelet.

Her skin hurt. Her head hurt. She needed the bracelet, needed to count off the charms on their slender links. She itched to disappear into its metallic shine, to get hypnotized by the play of the light on the polished gold.

Not having her bracelet made Tanvi's fingers prickle. It left her empty. Craving.

She *needed* it.

Normally she could spend hours like this, entranced, everything else obliterated. But the fatigue tackled her again, and Tanvi couldn't sit up straight anymore. Her knees ached, her eyes burned from staring, and pins and needles pierced her thighs.

Normally she would have gotten plenty of sleep, leaving her fresh for her afternoon routine: calisthenics for maintaining agility and speed, bathing, eating for energy, sorting her latest wares, and settling on her destination for the next harvest.

She blinked rapidly, her eyelids too heavy to fight off, and trudged to bed, where she buried herself under the covers. The oblivion she'd missed earlier rushed in, shutting down her mind.

Dream runners didn't dream. They went away until it was time to wake up, refreshed and ready to harvest. If Tanvi ever had dreamed before she came to Nagalok, she couldn't remember it.

Just like she always did, she let go into the nothing. Just like it always did, it enfolded her, taking her room, her bed, the darkness with it. Taking her.

And it was all there was. Sweet, restful silence.

Except then the void vanished.

An elderly woman with deep frown lines brandished a bouquet of withered blue and yellow pansies at Tanvi. Their stench slashed through time and space like an olfactory sword. "Are you happy now, with all your awards and TV shows?"

Tanvi glanced down at herself and realized she was in the body of an old man.

Terror stabbed through her. *No!*

She slapped at the air. She scratched at her crepey skin. She screamed to be let out.

But as hard as she pushed, she couldn't break free, and the words she shouted only emerged as static.

Every muscle in her borrowed body cramped up. She was in one of the dreams she'd harvested last night, the baker's!

"Ngh—" she tried, reaching toward the woman. *Help me!*

The woman shook her head, spraying desiccated petals like poison darts around them. "I trusted you, Hrithik. You stole my recipe. All that money, all that fame—that should have been *mine*!"

"Ngh, ngh!" Tanvi pleaded. *I'm not who you think I am!*

"I could never stop thinking of you. Never move on. You hijacked my world, and you didn't even care." Teeth bared, the woman advanced on her. The rotted flowers gave a sickening crunch and burst, spewing bloodred beetles with silver razor blades for wings. "And now I'm going to make you hurt the way you hurt me."

She launched the bouquet at Tanvi.

Tanvi struggled and bucked, and right as the first set of wings sliced into her shoulder, the dream tossed her out.

Panting, her mouth even drier than the bouquet had been, she

51

fell back into her sweaty pillow. Her body quivered with adrenaline, and if her heart hadn't been silenced, it would be thrashing hard enough to break her ribs.

That couldn't have just happened. Tanvi focused on the lantern hanging from the dim ceiling. It couldn't have. Dream runners didn't dream. Everybody knew that.

Her body was overheating. She was going to short-circuit.

A whimper escaped her, and she jammed her face in the pillow. *But how?*

Dream residue. Of course. Harvesting dreams meant experiencing them, and the residue took a while to wear off. Maybe this time, some of it had gotten stuck to her.

Yes. Tanvi exhaled hard, the tension easing from her muscles. She'd never had residue last so long before, but anything was possible.

She breathed long and slow, waiting out the residue's effects, and slowly her surroundings came into view. Tangled, limp sheets and a pillow punched flat underneath her. Bare walls all around her. Across from her, a cabinet. She knew that cabinet—it was where she stored her dreamstones. The table where she sat to eat her meals and admire the bracelet she'd soon have.

And the door, as red as a ruby dreamstone.

Someone knocked on the other side.

Her breath caught. Was she late for *harvesting*? Apologies already leaping to her tongue, Tanvi raced to answer.

The door swung wide at her touch, and the girl from Philadelphia beamed at Tanvi. "I was just looking for you!"

Tanvi stumbled backward, but she couldn't escape that too-broad grin.

The girl shoved a folder full of loose pages at her. "Don't forget to study for the quiz, Nitya! Mr. Collins won't like it."

"Go away!" Tanvi shouted before slamming the door in the girl's face. Somehow the folder still landed at her bare feet, scattering paper everywhere.

Tanvi's eyes wrenched open. The first thing she saw was the door to her room—unfinished brown wood. No fallen folder lay on the floor.

Suddenly the sheet was balled up in her fists, her knuckles paling with the force of crushing the cloth.

No. No, no, no.

Say it, she ordered herself. *Say it!*

She'd been dreaming. And this one couldn't be blamed on residue.

Tanvi choked down the scream that wanted to rip loose from her throat. *Nobody needs to know. Nobody needs to know. Nobody needs to know.*

She repeated the sentence until it quit meaning anything. As long as nobody knew, she was safe. It would be okay. She would be okay.

No matter how hard she tried to convince herself that was true, though, she couldn't deny the most fundamental rule of all: dream runners collected other people's visions, yes—but they were vessels, and empty vessels never, ever dreamed. That was the point.

Tanvi's breath shuddered out of her, ragged and frantic. Her eyes felt gritty, as if she hadn't rested them in weeks.

Why was this happening? She'd passed the initiation. She'd successfully harvested dreams all this time. She was a natural dream runner; even Asha said so.

It was her own fault, she decided, flinging the sheets away. She'd been too careless with her last harvest, too cocky, and the dream residue had clung to her. It was the only explanation. She could fix it, though. She could slow down and make sure every last bit of the dream ended up inside the vial.

Except, a cold voice insisted, residue didn't create *new* dreams. It couldn't.

If anyone found out, she was done for. No more dream running meant no more boons—and no more bracelet. Her hand encircled her wrist, feeling the bare skin.

No. The dream had to have been a fluke. She wouldn't let it be anything else.

This time, when Tanvi slept, she didn't dream.

6

Well, mused Venkat as Asha hauled him toward the palace's grand audience balcony, where the nagaraja and nagarani would soon be speaking, *the nagas do like their holidays.*

The Hindu lunar calendar was packed with festivals from different regions and traditions to the point that someone could practically find something to celebrate every day of the year. And in the capital city of Bhogavati, they did.

Sharad Navratri, the post-monsoon autumn jubilee, was really just an excuse to break out the treats and the fanciest of already impossibly fancy clothes. Monsoons might be common on Prithvi, but here they were nothing more than the stuff of myth and legend, and most people's spiritual sentiment lagged behind in a distant second place to the shopping and feasting.

Lovers wearing the yellows and oranges of fire meandered hand in hand, their lithe tails sinuously tangling together and untangling, their adoring stares locked on each other. Parents chased after children clutching sparklers and sticky sweets. Musicians played rousing folk songs, energized by the enthusiastic clapping of their listeners. And like confetti sprinkled by an unseen hand, clouds of pastel champak blossoms showered down over everyone.

Asha led Venkat past two naginis crouched on a marble pathway, constructing rangoli in alluring colors that might have come straight from a candy factory. The intricate rice powder patterns depicted the usual images of mandalas and Durga Devi's knowing gaze, but as Venkat stopped to admire them, one divine kajal-ringed eye winked up at him.

A snatch of the women's conversation reached his ears, a competition to determine who had paid more for their bangles of gold and silver: "It certainly seemed like more than I could afford, but Mahadevi deserves to have Her devoted servant represent Her in nothing less than the best!"

"Oh, yes!" The second woman waved her wrist so that her surfeit of bangles clinked together. "What would it look like if I did not trouble myself to commission a fine new design from Jitendra? The cost of custom work may pinch, yet how would She otherwise ever know I would sacrifice all things for Her?"

Venkat repressed a laugh. *Right. Durga Mata is the one who gets the credit when you show off how rich you are. Of course.*

Deepavali didn't actually fall until a couple of weeks after Navratri, but vividly painted clay diyas had already appeared across the palace grounds, along with mirror-studded cloth lanterns strung on slender cords and the constant pop and fizzle of firecrackers like tiny starbursts. And the best confectioners in the land had set up stalls festooned with beaded torans to take advantage of every minute.

One had currently roped in Asha, who handed over a coin and then bit into a piece of sunlight leaf–topped kaju katli. "In your hands, the humble ivory cashew has transcended into a supernal delight," she declared, eliciting a beam from the vendor.

The gods must have been on Venkat's side in that moment, because he managed to keep a straight face.

As Asha made her way back to him, he let himself remember. That first year in Nayan's house, Venkat had loathed Deepavali here. Sure, it had resembled Deepavali on Earth, even if the people celebrating had scales and bifid tongues, but he'd been alone. No parents telling him he'd eaten too many laddoos. No brother complaining that Venkat's sparklers always stayed lit longer than his. No grandfather recounting the story of Lord Rama's triumphant return to Ayodhya after having defeated Ravana, no grandmother folding a rupee note into his hand for offering during Lakshmi pooja at the mandir. No friends from school to race him through the streets. For their part, Asha's friends had only seemed interested in siphoning free dreams out of him.

Not to mention that Navratri was the last time he'd seen his family alive. With that memory emanating like an apparition from the flame in every diya, he'd vowed then never to celebrate it again.

And yet here he was in the thick of the revels, decked out in a sherwani woven from green-and-yellow plumage and embroidered with tiny gold parrots while toting a bag of the dream scraps Nayan had sent with him. Venkat had to admit this wasn't so bad. He didn't even mind the curious glances or speculating murmurs. Meeting a particularly attentive—and cute—nagini's gaze, he flashed her a playful smile.

Asha bared her fangs, startling him so he almost tripped over the rangoli's winking eye. The women on the ground glowered, their slit-pupil stares heating up from brown to blazing gold. "Ceasssse your shameless flirting with everyone!" she hissed in his ear.

He backed up as fast he could. "What? I'm not—"

"Do you not see how they look at you?" She swept her arm to take in the landscape as they resumed their trek.

Arguing with Asha was a fool's game, so he changed the subject. "Where's *my* barfi?"

"You did not say you wanted any," she retorted with a smirk, happily munching.

They passed a series of stages arranged to mimic a wave, all blues and greens, as if the ocean itself were taking part. Children crowded around each one, where troupes performed scenes from the various epics: Queen Kunti telling the Pandava brothers to share whatever they'd brought home, which that afternoon happened to be Princess Draupadi, who then married all five of them; Princess Sukanya recognizing her husband, Rishi Chyavana, though he'd been enchanted to wear the same youthful, dashing face as the Ashvini twins, who'd hoped to win her for themselves; the nagas fleeing their cousins and mortal enemies, the garudas. The nagas, of course, were sleek and graceful, while the garudas were monstrous, their eagle heads overripe red melons with cruel hooked beaks, their feathers and talons dirty yellow knives.

Venkat listened, amused, as an unseen narrator recited, "Due to an accident of birth, our blessed first ones had the grave misfortune to be kin to the first of the unscrupulous beasts known as the garudas."

Two human women appeared on the stage, their similar features making it clear they were sisters. They perched on either side of a bearded man in a dhoti, watching him with identical smitten expressions.

"Sage Kashyapa's two wives had everything—everything except children to complete their happiness. To right this grievous wrong, Vinata and Kadru both performed great devotions, and at last Kashyapa granted them this boon."

Blue-white sparkles showered the stage, and then Vinata stood between two children, human Arun and nightmarish avian Garuda. Beside her, a thousand gilt-flecked eggs hatched into nagas in a ring about Kadru.

"They were fulfilled for a time. But ambition and rivalry poison all peace." A seven-headed horse the exact white of drifting snow appeared, wings aloft. "When mighty Uchchaihshravas, King of Horses, surfaced from the Ocean of Milk, Kadru and Vinata entered into a wager, the loser of which would become enslaved to the winner. Kadru bet that his tail would be black, while Vinata guessed white."

People in the old days sure got bored easily, Venkat thought. *Who did* that?

He tried to envision his mother and any of his aunties betting their freedom away just for something to do. The bittersweet image

59

of their faces made his eyes well up, but the idea was so ridiculous he had to laugh, too. His quiet mother would have picked up her sewing or tended to her garden or gone for a walk, while his far more outspoken aunties would have given anyone who suggested a bet like that the tongue-lashing of the decade.

"Determined to win," intoned the narrator, "Kadru commanded her naga children to cover the equine's majestic tail so that it appeared black. Though initially reluctant, they in due course understood the need to respect one's elders, and they obeyed."

Venkat groaned. Why did so many adults feel compelled to ruin a good story by preaching?

The nagas onstage streamed over the horse's voluminous tail. Kadru grinned in triumph, while Vinata hung her head. The sisters' expressions contorted in hatred as they turned to each other, and Garuda glared out at the audience. "This would not stand," the narrator added, and the audience drew in an audible collective breath.

Asha, though, huffed. "Today is hardly the occasion for a dismal history lesson." She linked arms with Venkat. "Everyone is awaiting us for the opening ceremonies. No more of your dawdling!"

"I was watching!" Venkat protested, but he already knew how this saga went. All of Nagalok did. Garuda had proposed a bargain: he would bring the nagas the amrit of immortality in exchange for an end to Vinata's bondage. It was a con, however; once his mother was safe, Garuda had absconded with the amrit, in his haste spilling a handful of drops on the kusa grass, and the nagas, ravenous for a taste of what they'd lost, licked it off the spiky blades, causing them to have forked tongues ever after.

Yet not even getting Vinata back had quenched Garuda's blood-lust. He'd recklessly hunted his cousins as food and encouraged his brethren to do the same, until Lord Vishnu had interceded and officially prohibited the eating of one's relatives. Though the nagas had fought back with fang and venom, their casualties had grown too great, driving King Vasuki and Queen Naga Yakshi to order a retreat to Nagalok while they regrouped.

Nayan and the council were certain they'd find a solution, and Venkat believed they would, too, one that meant the nagas wouldn't need dream runners anymore. In the meantime, he'd keep at his own experiments.

Beside him, Asha made a revolted face. Venkat opened his mouth to tease her, but then he spotted the reason for her grimace.

In the wake of the council's morning dispatch, sentries now patrolled the perimeter. He'd heard this was coming, but actually seeing the scabbarded swords, the bows and quivers packed full of arrows, and the maces hefty enough to smash through walls had him edging closer to Asha. The sentries' expressions were just as much of a weapon as anything they carried, keen with a barely leashed ferocity.

Asha nodded at Venkat. "I believe it is time," she said.

He returned the nod. The people needed reassurance, and so as Asha glided and he strode along, he began to hand out the bounty in his bag, Nayan's promise of the future.

Asha slithered over to a man Venkat recognized as belonging to the lesser nobility. He moved to follow. It made sense to give the dream fragments to those in positions of power, because they had the most influence, but something his grandmother had once said stayed with him: it wasn't how rich or connected anyone was that made them special, but rather the potential waiting to be uncovered in their heart.

He knew what he should do, but he couldn't do it. Asha's minor lord didn't need the fragment. He could afford to buy one anytime.

Instead, Venkat headed back the way he and Asha had come until he found a solitary old man. "Here you go, ji," he said, offering the fragment to the stunned man and then joining his palms before his face. "Shubh Deepavali."

The man took a moment to catch his breath. "For me? Truly? But they are so rare!"

"Yes," Venkat said, his heart warming. "For you."

The man smiled, his joy as brilliant as the heliodor vial he now held. "Many thanks to you, apprentice to Lord Nayan. May the gods bless your generosity."

After that, Venkat dispensed the rest of the dreamstones as randomly as he could—a toddler, a woman amidst a large group of friends, a girl swaying along with her father.

Their wide eyes and elated exclamations told him everything: his grandmother had been right.

The whole palace, from servants all the way to the highest ranks of the monarchy's advisors and kin, stood in attendance in the manicured gardens, which boasted a wealth of plants and flowers guaranteed to dazzle any mortal horticulturist. Venkat's mother would have exploded from pure happiness at the incredible spectrum of colors, the alternately frilly and jagged shapes of the blue and green leaves, the vines that hung like streamers with blossoms of glowing suns and moons and ringing bells. The ever-present intoxicating perfume of champak and jasmine wafted over the gathering like an olfactory dream.

But if anyone else noticed, Venkat couldn't tell. He was an island in a shimmering sea of scales. All around him, gorgeous yet grim faces tilted up toward the royal balcony, where two massive green-and-black thrones, each with a seven-headed cobra corona, awaited their occupants. Rumors about the attempted invasions floated above him, an ominous cloud, and no one, not even Asha's gleefully gossiping friends, could ignore the somber presence of the guards.

A court messenger wove his way through the onlookers to Asha's side. "Princess, you must come with me now. Your parents require your assistance."

"*More* diplomatic duties?" Asha released one of her trademark sighs. "I suppose it cannot be helped." She strutted away, leaving the messenger to scurry after her and Venkat to make small talk with her friends.

They moved closer, their brown-gold eyes kindling with interest. Venkat recognized Chintu's friend Karan among them and swore he would get back at Asha later. "What is this?" Karan asked, gloating. "Or did she not tell you, her dear friend?"

Bansuris sounded, their haunting tones saving Venkat from having to do anything but smile politely. He hadn't known Asha had been doing any diplomatic work, aside from entertaining Chintu. Not that he'd let on to Karan, of course.

Clad in fabrics so fine they rivaled Lord Surya himself for incandescence, King Vasuki and Queen Naga Yakshi settled onto their thrones. In fact, the raja of the nagas looked to have been gifted a full day's worth of the sun's rays made cloth, while his rani wore a winter's measure of moonlight in the form of a silver sari. Ornate, gem-studded gold crowns sat heavy on both their heads, a perfect match for the lavish jewelry glittering on their necks and fingers and wrists. The plainest of their rings put the bangles Venkat had seen earlier to shame.

"Shubh Navratri, beloved citizens of Bhogavati," King Vasuki began, his cobra-hood corona framing him like a halo. "Here we find ourselves again, giving thanks for another fruitful turn of the cosmic wheel."

The speech continued, and Venkat knew he should be listening, but Karan's insinuation had gotten to him. Why would Asha be called away now? Had something happened?

Only when the nagas around him traded surprised stares did Venkat snap back to the present. "I do not need to tell you," King Vasuki said, "that our beleaguered realm has long been in need of glad tidings, and on this first night of sacred celebrations, it is my distinct privilege to deliver them to you."

Glad tidings? Worry sparked in Venkat again. He could feel Karan studying him, so he smiled as if this pronouncement were exactly what he'd been waiting for.

Nayan appeared behind the balustrade, his head bowed, and knelt before the nagarani's throne.

What was he doing there? Venkat couldn't help feeling doubly betrayed. Nayan hadn't mentioned any announcement, and it wasn't as if he hadn't had the opportunity.

"If the garudas seek to sow division among us with their assaults, then it is up to us to find ways to reunite," Queen Naga Yakshi said, her soft voice as mysterious as the words it spoke. She signaled to Nayan. "Rise, Lord Nayan, and tell them of your triumph."

What triumph? Venkat felt like the parrots on his clothes, repeating the words of others without understanding them.

Nayan stood, his palms pressed together before his face. A breeze blew back his black hair, and his smile was remote as his eyes raked the crowd below. He looked every inch the member of the royal family he was.

"Indeed," he said, his gaze stopping briefly on Venkat's, "it is my pleasure to have brought about the circumstances of those glad tidings." Then he waved someone forward from the wings. Chintu and an older naga Venkat thought might be his uncle came to stand on King Vasuki's right. "Many of you know that Prince Chintan of the clan of Anant Shesha has stayed among us as ambassador these last two years. It seems he has agreed to extend his tenure, for . . ."

Asha sauntered into view from the left, dressed in a sapphire-and-emerald silk choli worked through with gold. Her hair had been gathered in a loose bun studded with gemstone lotuses. Her parents followed her, all exultant smiles.

"Ah, Princess Asha," said Nayan with another bow, "right on time."

Venkat's mouth grew dry with dread. Good news that included

both Chintu *and* Asha? Asha, who couldn't wait to be rid of the annoying prince just the other morning?

She shone bright, altogether the enchanting princess, but Venkat knew her, and to him, that sheen was brittle—a patina of iron pyrite for those who expected to see true gold and wouldn't bother to look any deeper. If his hunch about the announcement was right, it wasn't anything she wanted.

Even so, she could have given him a heads-up it was happening.

Sandwiched between her parents, Asha mirrored Nayan's greeting. "Your Majesties," she said, smooth and practiced.

The nagarani granted her a benevolent nod before turning to Nayan. "As you were."

Nayan opened his arms in invitation. Asha's parents led her forward from the right, while Chintu's uncle escorted him from the left, until they both stood before the king and queen. Then Asha's parents placed her hand in Chintu's, offered up by his uncle.

"The clans of Anant Shesha and of Vasuki join hands today in betrothal: Prince Chintan and Princess Asha are to be wed in a month!" Nayan announced. "The ceremony will be held here on the palace grounds."

Their parents and uncle scarcely waited for him to finish before flinging handfuls of marigold and rose petals over the happy couple.

While Chintu grinned out at the spectators, Asha demurely cast her eyes down.

Though Venkat had already presumed she was faking, that single gesture only drove it home. If demure was one end of the emotional spectrum, Asha was the other.

Her duty was to put the clan's welfare first. Venkat couldn't fault her for that.

But why hadn't she *told* him? Why hadn't Nayan?

And then it was hard to think, because waves of people surrounded him, cheering and dancing, and the gardens themselves had blossomed into extra greens and blues, as if their foliage were living gemstones, with flowers growing larger and lusher and even more fragrant—the palace grounds' reaction to their rulers' proud state of mind.

He'd known any event that centered on Asha would mean drama; he just hadn't predicted this.

Suddenly Venkat was eight again, lonely and despondently circling the borders of naga society. All he wanted was to be in his workshop among his dreamstone vials, or in his room, reading one of his favorite books. At least there, he knew what to expect.

Fireworks boomed against the nocturnal sky, forming pink lotuses and intertwining serpents in gold and green, and lively music streamed from the shadows. People called out questions and congratulations and chattered in excited knots. Up on the balcony, Nayan and the rest of the royals waved. Asha, her bejeweled head held high, even blew kisses.

She knew her duty. Probably she always had.

Disgruntled as he was, Venkat knew his duty, too. As he pasted on his smile and readied himself to dole out the rest of his dream scraps, he reminded himself that Asha wasn't the only one who knew how to pretend.

This was the end. Tanvi knew it.

Her harvest last night in Belfast had been excellent, rewarding her with top-tier dreams. She'd focused fully on each one, conducting the wisps of the vision into the dreamstone she'd selected for it and patiently waiting out the effects of the residue before moving on to the next. In a handful of hours, she'd been a grandparent racing their team of flying pigs in the Indianapolis 500, a comic-book alien from the rings of Saturn, a werebook switching genres from romance to thriller to cozy mystery, and a kid winning an international burping championship with an all-time record of ten minutes.

The bracelet was hers.

Daybreak had found Tanvi snug in her bed and her dream-filled vials safely stored in the cabinet, ready for her appointment with Venkat in the morning. She'd pictured how her bracelet's delicate charms would swing on her wrist. Settling into her pillow, she'd closed her eyes and given herself up to the void.

Everything had been the way it should be.

Until she *dreamed*.

This time, she was five, and she stood in line at a museum with a woman and a man in their thirties, their skin glowing brown under the pink lights. Off to the side, a girl Tanvi's height peeked out from behind a shiny purple-and-green book sculpture so big that only the tops of her striped butterfly-frame sunglasses showed. Tanvi couldn't tell what the book cover said, and she didn't care. They were finally going to see the exhibit on virtual reality from other dimensions! She'd been waiting months for this.

The woman bought their tickets, along with a steaming pretzel as tall as a giraffe and flecked with salt crystals that were actual cut crystals. It smelled so good and yeasty that Tanvi wanted to devour the entire thing. She tried to break off a foot, but the woman laughed. "You can't eat a friend," she said. "Now give him your ticket."

A ghost-white teen boy with a shaggy mess of sandy hair and an employee uniform had appeared before them, his hand out. The woman offered him her tickets—one for herself and one for the pretzel—and the boy waved her through, along with the man and the other girl, who'd hopped back in line when Tanvi wasn't looking.

So excited she could burst, Tanvi bounced toward him with her ticket. The boy tore it in half. "Sorry, not valid."

Tanvi stomped her foot. "This is so unfair. We just bought it!"

The boy only shrugged. "You're not allowed."

She watched helplessly as the other four vanished down the color-changing hall. "Wait!" she called after them. "I'm coming!"

If they heard, they didn't stop.

"Please," she begged the boy. "There has to be some mistake. You let them go. You have to let me go, too!"

But he just blocked her path. "You're not allowed," he said again. "Only Nitya is."

The neon lights flashed a violent purple veined with venom yellow, and klaxons blared, forcing Tanvi to clap her hands over her ears. All the exhibit posters became distorted mirrors that turned the cheery yellow museum into a fun-house nightmare. She dodged around the boy and started running, but before she got to the hall-way, a red door with a half-moon window and a deadbolt slammed down. And beyond that, another. And another, into infinity.

Not allowed. Not you.

The marrow in her bones melted in anguish. Whoever those people had been, she'd lost them forever.

Tanvi woke with a start. Snapshots zipped through her mind: The poster of the exhibit. The woman walking away with her giraffe pretzel. The girl and her sunglasses.

And there had been a name . . .

Something about the setting had felt so familiar. Almost like Tanvi was remembering it. But she'd never been anywhere like that.

The false sense of recognition gripped her, dream residue she couldn't scrub off.

Horror clogged her chest. If she couldn't even separate dreams and reality anymore, she might as well hand in her remaining dreamstones now.

The sunlight pouring through the strip of window had grown stronger, a reminder that she was due to meet with Venkat in half an hour.

Her body and the bracelet screamed at her to get up. Tanvi had a routine to follow. A boon to claim. But no way could she face Venkat with the ugly dream—*her* ugly dream—spinning around inside her skull like this.

Resisting lit her nerve endings on fire, and she bit down on her lip to keep from screaming.

She rolled herself up in the covers and fought the urge until it finally died away.

When the door banged open, Tanvi had no idea if she'd been huddled in her bed for five minutes or five hours. "Why are you sitting like that?" Asha demanded. "Are you ill?"

"Get out," Tanvi croaked, reluctantly lifting her head to glare at Asha.

Just because Asha was a princess, did she always have to wear such flashy clothes? The bold red of her choli hurt to look at.

Behind Tanvi's nearly screwed-shut eyelids, the dream replayed itself, and the horror grabbed hold of her all over again, biting through her skin and into her mind. A mewl rose in her throat. She was going to crack into a million pieces.

Tanvi pinched the skin between her index finger and thumb hard. *Stop.*

Asha started pacing, like this was her room and not Tanvi's. "It was never meant to be this soon. Sameer is still expecting me to help with his documentary!"

Spots smudged Tanvi's vision as she hauled herself up, and her stomach gurgled. She was going to be sick, she knew it.

"Oh, fine," Asha babbled. "I did not promise *him*. But I promised myself."

Still dizzy, Tanvi fumbled over to the tiny ablutions area. There, she brushed her teeth with turmeric paste. The yellow-orange color stabbed at her eyes, like she'd never really noticed it before now, but at least she didn't have to see it once it was past her lips. Then the flavor exploded on her tongue, so intense that she gagged. "Why are you here?" she spluttered.

"I wanted to check on you," Asha said. Even her voice—had it always been so high?—made Tanvi's nerves screech in protest. "You missed your appointment."

A clash of aromas suddenly stung Tanvi's nostrils: sweet, sour, savory and all strong enough to knock her over. Shocked, she turned to find breakfast on the table. Asha had even stuck a bouquet on the windowsill.

Tanvi couldn't stand to look at the flowers, but she dared a glance at the spread. Rose-gold apples, jewel-mangoes, jewel-figs, spiced ivory almonds, piping hot payasam—all things normally wasted on her. Food was fuel. It should have no scent, no taste. It just needed to fill her stomach.

But now, when she could almost smell the various spices on the almonds and the tang of the toothpaste still sat in her mouth, she couldn't bear the thought of eating. The second Asha placed a loaded plate in front of her, Tanvi pushed it aside. "Why are you *really* here?"

"Navratri is upon us," Asha said, "and night has fallen, when you may roam free. Perhaps we could select our outfits and venture to Prithvi for one of the mortal celebrations? Sameer assures me the dancing is something to be seen, and the sweets, oh, the sweets!"

Tanvi squinted in her direction. Asha was the one who had helped train her, the one who had brought her to Bhogavati in the first place. No one understood more than she did how little Tanvi or any of the other runners would be tempted by a scheme like that. "No."

"Venkat suggested you—"

"No!" Even the thought of Venkat brought the panic back. If he found out about her dreams . . .

Asha frowned. "I see."

The air between them grew as cold as the blizzard Tanvi had endured last winter in order to fill her quota, and remembering that left her even madder. Her memory of that night was smooth and glassy, a time when she didn't make out things like colors and scents and textures—or feelings.

All she wanted was for everything to go back to the way it had been.

"I am betrothed," Asha said, her eyes sparking gold. Tanvi immediately dropped her own stare to the floor. "My friends, my family, are of course overjoyed."

If she was expecting an answer, Tanvi didn't have one. It seemed weird for Asha to get engaged when she was still so hung up on this imaginary boyfriend of hers, but that was her problem.

With a loud sigh, Tanvi got up and headed to the cabinet. "I have dreams to harvest," she said bluntly. "Do you not want me to do my work?"

"Certainly not. Indeed, I will come with you."

"What?" Panic apparently came in different flavors. Who knew? Tanvi made her face as indifferent as she could. "Dream runners work alone. It's the third—"

"Rule. Yes, yes, I realize that." Asha brushed that aside with a flick of her wrist, making her bangles tinkle. That small sound grated on Tanvi's eardrums. "Surely you have heard the mortal adage that sometimes rules are meant to be broken?"

She sniffed and helped herself to Tanvi's rejected plate. "If you do not plan to eat these delicacies I strove to bring you, I suppose I will have to. So sssssstubborn."

Tanvi hadn't been ready to look at the plate again, and the glimpse of the rich food sent her reeling. She was going to pass out right here in front of Asha, who would go straight to Venkat and Nayan. And then the game would be over.

Asha daintily nibbled on an apple. "Sameer thinks Binh would not approve if I joined them on their urban explorations. How silly boys can be!"

It was all too much. Tanvi couldn't stop thinking about the moment she'd been seen, when the strange girl had talked to her. It sent goose bumps over her arms.

That girl. My dreams.

My bracelet, my bracelet, my bracelet.

The mad racing of her thoughts broke off, and Asha's chatter dimmed into static. Tanvi mentally traced the familiar charms of her bracelet, counting until she'd reached the end of the circle, and then starting over.

When she finally left the safety of the imagined bracelet, everything around her had returned to normal, smokelike shadows with the vaguest of proportions. She breathed out in relief and grabbed her Prithvi wardrobe of jeans and a T-shirt.

Only the dreamstones were real. Their range of shades called for dreams to fill their vacant depths. For Tanvi to find those dreams.

After she'd finished getting dressed, she packed her pouch with vials from the cabinet. "I'm leaving," she announced. "You should, too."

"Nayan Uncle has not yet approved my request." Asha's mouth tightened. "Then again, nor did he leave me time to make said request, what with the influx of sudden betrothals demanding his attention."

Tanvi had no clue what she was talking about and couldn't care less. "You can't come. I told you, I have work to do."

Asha grinned. "Suit yourself. I am certain you will enjoy being thoroughly interrogated by the guards. *I*, however, possess methods of travel that permit me to bypass the gates."

Tanvi hesitated. She hated the thought of rewarding Asha's boasts about how she could use water to go anywhere nagas had set foot or tail. Apparently she only had to choose a location, and the water would transport her there.

But lying low after the other night was a good idea, especially if the guard who'd questioned Tanvi was on duty again. "Fine. But we have to leave right now."

"What Nayan Uncle has not known all this time has not hurt him." Asha transformed into her human aspect. Her fangs receded, and her forked tongue rounded out and turned pink. "Let us have some fun!"

"But how do we—?"

"Watch." In one flowing motion, Asha tipped water from the pitcher onto the table, linked arms with Tanvi before she could protest, and swept her into the puddle.

They plunged into another dimension, teal and aquamarine and jade and cobalt—the conjunction of all the bodies of water in all the worlds. The colors were muffled, like Tanvi saw them from a remove. There was the Ganga River, which led to the domain of Princess Uloopi and her father, King Kauravya. There was the Kalyani River bordering King Maniakkhika's realm. There was even the galactic Ocean of Milk, where the first nagaraja, Anant Shesha, served as Lord Vishnu's floating couch while he dreamed.

Asha must have chosen the location, because then the two of them stood on a familiar street on Prithvi.

Philadelphia in soon-to-be twilight. Tanvi recognized the ritzy neighborhood—Society Hill. She'd just been here, hurrying by these same stores and homes. Her failure mocked her from every building, every sign. The sooner she could get out of here, the better.

Asha tapped the screen of a cell phone. "I have not yet glamoured you." She pulled a small jar of vermilion from her bag. "You could be recognized in this neighborhood."

Tanvi eyed her doubtfully. Was she trying to say that she *did*

76

know about the other night?

If so, Asha didn't let on. She dipped a fingertip into the vermilion, then dabbed it right between Tanvi's eyebrows. A flush ran over her body as the illusion took hold. "Flawless. Now come; we are running late."

"For what? I need to harvest!" Tanvi was already regretting letting Asha come along.

"I have a stop to make first." Asha clamped her hand around Tanvi's elbow. "It will not take long."

Then Asha propelled her through a series of turns and alleys, finally stopping in front of a brick row house with a bronze pineapple knocker. *Weird*, Tanvi thought.

Asha pouted at herself in a compact mirror and blew her reflection a kiss before rapping the knocker against the door.

A human boy answered. At the sight of Asha, he broke into a huge grin.

So, Tanvi allowed, *he really is real.*

She tried hard not to notice anything about him, but the details pushed themselves on her, anyway. His skin was the same medium brown as hers, and he seriously needed to comb his messy black hair.

Asha, though, giggled and flipped her hair behind her. "If I were not already a princess, I would make a wonderful president, I agree."

Sameer's smile faded. "I wasn't sure you'd come back."

"Have I let you down yet?" *Tsking*, Asha nudged Tanvi forward. "This is Tanvi. She lives in Nagalok and finds herself in desperate need of a holiday. Perhaps to the infamous Cheesesteak Corner?"

"Nice to meet you," Sameer said. "I'm Sameer." But his gaze went right back to Asha. "Come in. Both of you."

Asha glided past Tanvi, up the step, and into the house. Not knowing what else to do, Tanvi trailed after her.

The crystal chandelier in the foyer rocked slightly, reminding Tanvi of something. She snatched at it, but it slipped out of reach like stray dream wisps.

Being inside the house made her skin feel funny in a way she couldn't put a name to. The compact layout and the family portraits on the walls . . .

"My parents won't be home until ten, and my sister's got rehearsal," Sameer said.

"Alas, I can only stay long enough for you to feed me." Asha mimed wiping away tears. "I will be expected back for the festivities." She tweaked his nose before darting into the kitchen. Sameer joined her, leaving Tanvi in the foyer with only her disorientation for company.

His voice drifted out to her. "I think my mom made blueberry lemonade. Want some?" Liquid splashed into a glass, once, twice. "What about you, Tanvi?" he called.

"No," she replied, still trying to pin down all the weird sensations. She peeked into the kitchen. Asha and Sameer stood close together, their heads touching, and watched something on his phone. They both laughed, and Asha kissed his cheek.

Tanvi was putting off harvesting for this?

"I told Binh about you," Sameer said. "But he says pictures, or it didn't happen, and you won't let me take any." He held up his phone to her, and she instantly switched into snake form, dropping to the floor. The glass she'd been holding vanished with her. "Okay, okay! I won't take any, I promise."

Asha changed back into her human shape. "Some things are better an enigma, do you not agree? This way, you need not share the wonder of my company!" Sipping her lemonade, she leaned against his side. "Have you made any progress on the film? Found any new sites?"

"I wish," said Sameer, and even Tanvi could tell how irked he was. "I had these great ideas—I know I did—but when I woke up the other morning, there was this gap. I can't remember."

The suspicion that had buzzed just beneath the surface of her thoughts burst free.

I've been here before.

Suddenly she knew why this place and its pineapple knocker were so familiar. Why Sameer was.

Her whole body quavered, and it hurt to breathe.

She'd harvested his dream. The one about breaking into a house with his buddy. She'd harvested a dream from Asha's secret human boyfriend.

His house pressed in around her. The chandelier's crystals turned into serrated prisms designed to carve Tanvi into ribbons.

"What about Nitya?" Asha asked, cupping Sameer's face in her hands. "What about her ideas?"

Nitya.

Sameer bent forward. "Ask her yourself at garba."

Tanvi couldn't stay here any longer. Not even the thought of the bracelet, with all its golden charms, could soothe her. That terrified her more than anything, more even than her own—she hesitated to think the word—dreams.

Nitya, Nitya, Nitya.

Tanvi backed out of the kitchen and fled.

A lambent mist bathed the workshop balcony, varnishing the blues and greens of the walls in salmon and violet as Venkat finished setting out the dream elements for Nayan's inspection: a tree of ebony apples growing in a barren sandscape; a first date despite a sultry, suffocating lust for someone else eternally beyond reach; a fully ripened wrought-iron lantern fallen from its lamppost-tree, rich with custardlike glowing pulp and seed; and of course, the restaurant fire.

"Rebirth and renewal," Nayan said, appraising the table. "What have you come up with?"

Impress me. Venkat heard the challenge in the question, and he selected the isolated element from Bharat's harvest.

"I think the restaurant fire works best here. It's both"—he opened his awareness to the emotions in the vial—"poignant and hopeful. A broken heart, but paired with the promise of healing."

Dreamsmithing was, at its core, an art of revelation. Venkat listened to each element in turn, the way a composer selected a note or a chef sprinkled in the perfect spice, until he found the one that fit, letting it lead him through a winding labyrinth of imagination. The rightness of it always sang in his chest, a logic beyond words.

Nayan nodded, then held up the agate dreamstone containing the custard lantern. "And why not this one?"

How Venkat answered was the real test. He thought hard. "It could've worked, too. Except something was missing. That sense of loss to be overcome."

"But you felt it with the fire?"

"Yes."

"Well chosen." Nayan smiled, and the pressure was off. "Your sense of nuance has grown by leaps and bounds these past few months. Shall we begin, then?"

Pride swelled in Venkat, only to be stained by the confusion and hurt he'd felt during yesterday's royal audience. Why hadn't Nayan told him about the betrothal? Wasn't he Nayan's foster son? But he didn't know how to say that.

"Sure," he agreed instead.

With Nayan guiding him, Venkat began to forge the newest section of their project, welding the mood of the dream element into each movement. A single branch of what must be an ancient and massive tree bloomed into being, bursting with small pink-and-white buds. With life.

Whatever story the two of them were piecing together would be breathtaking, crafted from the blended ore of invention and vision.

But that was exactly the problem: Nayan still hadn't told him what that vision was. Venkat's exuberance eroded like sand beneath a crashing wave. Not to mention, *he* still hadn't told Nayan about Jai, Tanvi had never shown up for her appointment, and—

The branch withered, gnarling into a blackened wraith tree straight out of a horror movie. What remained of the dream element slipped from Venkat's now-shaky mental grasp and disintegrated. He swore.

"My son, is there something you wish to ask me?"

Busted. Venkat glanced up to see Nayan's arched eyebrows. "I guess I don't understand why . . ." He couldn't force the words out.

Nayan waggled his head. "Ah. You wish to know why I did not inform you of the betrothal beforehand."

The nagas had a term for this level of feeling exposed: *scale-stripped*. As Venkat stared at his ruined handiwork, he felt as small as the day he'd arrived here.

Nayan moved to the parapet, where the currant-and-papaya flames of sunset had long since given way to the saturated blue of the gloaming. "Asha herself did not know; the negotiations were only completed yesterday." The first pearly bands of starlight lingered on his imposing features, softening them until they were something close to approachable. "I should say, she suspected such a union in her future. Just not quite so soon."

But why? Venkat nearly asked. He knew why, though. The garudas' attempted breaches of Nagalok had brought the war to the nagas' doorstep, and nerves were fraying like worn thread. The people needed a symbol of clan solidarity to bolster their faith, something they could root for and see themselves in.

"She must have been livid," he said, trying to laugh it off, like he was Nayan's apprentice and not the wobbly, desolate kid Nayan had taken in all those years ago. Like he didn't need any validation.

Nayan's own chuckle was grim as he turned back to the table. "Oh, I would not have called her happy, no. But some things are greater than the individual."

"So she *doesn't* want to do this?" Venkat pressed, sitting down on the marble bench. Poor Asha, marrying someone she didn't love but would have to spend a long, long lifetime with.

"Grasping the need to perform one's duty does not always make the actual undertaking of it any more pleasant," Nayan said, joining him. "Asha's companions do not know how to support her in this; they see only the opportunity they all desire, a rise in station and attendant power. You, however, do."

He laid a firm hand on Venkat's shoulder. "I have known since I first brought you into my employ that you are special. That you possess a talent to create beauty far surpassing any artist I have encountered in my many years. But as my representative, you must become more practiced in other arts as well—the politics of our court."

Venkat didn't quite know how to interpret that last sentence. He'd already been shadowing Nayan at official functions, quietly noting any unusual conversations and interactions and reporting them later.

Again, Nayan read him as easily as his favorite volume of folktales. "I have kept you on the sidelines for too long, my son, and it is time you learn to hold your own among our people. Starting tonight."

Please, no. Hadn't last night been enough? Did Venkat really have to show up at the impromptu betrothal party, too? A whole stack of books waited by his bed, urging him to refuse.

But Asha could probably use his encouragement. "I'll be there," he said, injecting his voice with all the fake enthusiasm he could muster.

"Will you?" Nayan's slit-pupiled gaze sliced through him. "How can I believe that when my own dreamsmith is being less than truthful with me?"

"What? I don't—"

"Everyone and everything has its day, including our dream runners," Nayan stated, and in the fathoms of that gaze, Venkat saw only compassion. "Even Jai."

Jai. Venkat's breath calcified into that single syllable.

The dam in his chest toppled, and the serpent of grief coiled behind it sank its fangs into his heart. Nayan knew. Of course he did. Nayan was the one person Venkat had never been able to hide from.

"That he has endured as long as he has is a testament to the depth of your care and devotion." Nayan's voice grew brusque. "Nevertheless, you must not attempt to shoulder such burdens yourself. You know this."

Venkat's eyes swam, his pulse seesawing between regret and guilt-streaked relief at finally having the truth out in the open. He asked thickly, "I— Shouldn't this get easier?" Flames of rage at his own failure licked at him. "*Why* doesn't it?"

"The only way it would get 'easier' is if your heart were to harden, and I will not permit that." Nayan released Venkat's shoulder. "All this grieves you, and with good reason. Nevertheless, you must always be forthright with me. Without trust, our objective has no foundation."

Venkat nodded. "I wanted to save him," he mumbled, because otherwise he would shout it until even the hills on the outskirts of the city boomed with how much this hurt. "I was hoping . . ."

"Indeed, and that is what we are striving toward here. To change the story so we no longer need mortal dreams."

"But what's the *point*?" Venkat tried and failed to moderate his tone. "What are we really doing for him? For any of them?"

The gleam in Nayan's eyes pinned him in place. "We give them dreams. A reason to keep going."

"Dreams," he echoed, numb.

"Their dreams," Nayan agreed, "over and over, in the hope of one day satisfying them. Dreams, like stories, distract people. They give them something to hold on to. To work toward. It is no different than our own customers."

He rose and moved toward the door. "In any case, *you* must not fall for the dream and so forget to cultivate distance in this work. It will only become more demanding."

Venkat reluctantly stood, too. Nayan wasn't saying anything he didn't already know, but he still couldn't shake the feeling he'd let Jai down. There was so much he wanted to say, to do. "Shouldn't someone stay with him?"

"No need. I will handle the situation," Nayan said. "You must only prepare yourself for the party. Madhu has arranged for your attire to be waiting in your rooms. I will meet you there in two hours."

Nayan had always insisted on escorting the burned-out runners to Prithvi himself. A small mercy, but Venkat's heart still contracted. He would never see Jai again, let alone say good-bye.

Not that Jai would notice.

"It will be all right," Nayan promised. He handed Venkat a small parcel. "Remember our goal."

At last, with another nod, Venkat left to get dressed.

J ai. Tanvi had to find Jai.

She didn't bother to shut Sameer's door behind her, just ran toward the alley.

A floodlight dazed her, so garish the night might as well have been noon. It left her seeing spots. Raucous laughter and shouts from South Street bombarded her. Whiffs of stale coffee and cooking grease made her stomach rebel.

More details she didn't want to see or hear or smell. They should be bouncing right off, not tugging at her hard enough that she almost bashed her head against the nearest mailbox.

Until now, there had never been a time when Tanvi had gone to Prithvi and *not* harvested dreams to sell in Nagalok. The wrongness of it made her bones hurt. She was a dream runner. She was supposed to be harvesting dreams in exchange for boons. Everyone knew that.

"Tanvi, ssssstop," Asha hissed, so close Tanvi could feel the *s*'s on her neck. It wasn't fair; no matter how hard Tanvi trained, nagas could outpace her without breaking a sweat.

"Leave me alone!" she growled. But before she'd even reached the next row house, Asha had circled around to block her path.

"I will not." Asha grabbed her arm. Her eyes flared green-gold against the dimly lit narrow street. "Why did you vanish so abruptly? What happened?"

Tanvi stared at her shoes. Her breath ripped out of her, steaming in the chilly air. She thought of the bracelet so she wouldn't have to think about what she'd just learned.

What she'd heard Asha say. That *name*. So many things that had no right to be there stuffed Tanvi's head, getting crammed tighter and tighter until she knew she'd lose it.

"I left Sameer for you!" Asha cried. She shook Tanvi's arm. "Would you at least do me the courtesy of looking at me?"

The pressure in Tanvi boiled over, and she wrenched away. "I didn't make you do anything! *I* came for dreams. *You* ruined that."

Asha sighed. "Tanvi, I have no time for this. I am expected back at the palace for my own betrothal party."

Tanvi almost screamed. Asha, always pushing. Always wanting her way. But she couldn't make Tanvi think about that name.

She stuck her face in Asha's. The words tore free, on fire like her breath. "If you want to be stupid enough to chase after some mortal boy when you just got engaged to a prince, that's your choice. Do what you want. But don't expect me to blow *my* chances."

Then she stalked past Asha, who let her go.

89

Right now, Tanvi needed to be around another dream runner. To remember what normal was.

Right now, all she wanted to do was forget.

When Tanvi burst onto the stairs in Bhogavati, the gold of the palace walls, dramatic even in the dark, gleamed with an aura of blue-green light. So much light tonight. Too much, showing her all the things she didn't want to see.

She could've slapped herself. She'd lost control and yelled at Asha. But who cared what Asha did? Asha didn't matter. Nothing but the bracelet did.

Still berating herself, Tanvi skulked toward the dream runners' private entrance. The guard on duty, the same one from the other night, flashed her a strange look. "Back so soon? It must have been a particularly fruitful mission."

Tanvi waited for him to wave her through. She just had to get to Jai's room.

The guard inspected her lowered face. "Show me what you brought."

Her head jerked slightly. She didn't have any wares to show him.

"Well?" he asked.

Every bit of her wanted to bolt. She'd let her panic show, a total rookie mistake. All these stupid feelings she wasn't supposed to have—they were wrecking her life. And now she had to give this guy something before he got too suspicious.

His eyes narrowed. "I told you to show me."

A sudden spark of defiance replaced Tanvi's terror. She didn't answer to this guard—or any guard.

He's just an obstacle. An obstacle keeping her from Jai, and she thought she knew how to get past him.

It was worth a try.

Smoothing out her expression, Tanvi thrust an empty vial from her pouch at him. Let him call her bluff. Let him scoff and say he couldn't see any glowing wisps. *I dare you.*

For once in this nightmare of the past few days, the gods blessed her. The vial was jasper, red-brown and opaque, and when the guard raised his lantern, the stone trapped its beam, appearing lit up from the inside.

"Fascinating," the guard said. "Perhaps one day, I also might try one."

She almost nodded but curbed the impulse in time. Instead, she slowly walked toward the entrance.

Once she was sure he couldn't see her, Tanvi launched herself into the back passages of the palace, the ones only the dream runners used. Her hair, which she'd left loose, floated behind her like a second shadow.

Quit it, she scolded. *No more pointless details.*

Still, even as she ran, Tanvi couldn't keep from registering the gloom of the tunnels. They were so stark, like no one thought the dream runners needed beautiful things. Or even plain old sconces to keep them from crashing into the wall.

And then she wanted to claw *that* observation out of her head.

She reached Jai's door, one down from hers, and pounded on it. No one answered.

Her breath coming fast and harsh, she tried again. Had he already left to harvest?

Still no answer.

Tanvi turned the knob. The door opened, and she rushed inside.

The room had basic furnishings—a bed and a table and a cabinet. The cabinet was probably stocked with dreamstones, too. All that was missing was Jai.

Tanvi glanced around again, confused. *Her* room was the same, wasn't it?

Her eyes blurred, refocusing to take in specifics. No, Jai wasn't the only thing missing. The bed had been stripped.

Dread bitter on her tongue, Tanvi opened the bureau. The clothes had disappeared, too.

Already knowing what she'd find, she checked the closet. Nothing.

She was too late. Jai was gone. Gone for good.

Was it because he'd started to dream, too?

Her flagging energy gave out, and Tanvi dropped to the middle of what had once been Jai's floor.

As she lay there, her face pressed against the cool marble, a long-hidden memory crept to the surface, dusty and faded but still in one piece.

That first day, when they'd been initiated into dream running, Asha had gathered the nervous candidates together in Nayan's study to hear him speak. *This is an honor,* she'd explained. *Each of you was specially selected for an essential job.*

Nayan had emerged from behind the desk and nodded at the

group. He'd been so tall and stately, like a king in a movie. Mommy would probably call him brooding and handsome. Like Asha, he had pretty clothes.

Dream runners, he had said then, *have a purpose. Nagas do not dream, so your purpose is to harvest human dreams for them. It is a grand and necessary service. Without you, there are no dreams.*

The candidates, including Tanvi, had all nudged one another and puffed up like peacocks.

Nayan's fierce glare had landed on her, as if what he had to say next was meant for her ears alone. *We have brought you here because you each longed for something more. And something more you will have—on the condition that you are able to perform your duty.*

The candidates had listened with their full attention, eager for the rewards he'd promised.

His mouth had hardened into a line before he spoke again. *But only on that condition.*

"No," moaned Tanvi now. She didn't want to remember. Had she done something to bring all this on? Had Jai?

She tried to push it back down, but the memory resisted. The other kids in it—Archana, Hemant, Kavya, and the rest—when had she last seen them?

It had been a long time. So long that maybe they were all gone.

Now that she was thinking about it, Tanvi couldn't even say how long it had been since the initiation. Her mind iced over when she tried.

Good. She closed her eyes and imagined her bracelet.

But, whispered the doubt in her chest, if she and Jai were the

only ones left from their cohort, did . . . did running dreams somehow *break* the runners?

Jai wasn't here to tell her. And if she didn't do something to help
herself, it would be curtains for her, too.

Tanvi needed a boon, and she needed it now. It was the only way
she could fix things before anyone realized she'd been dreaming.

And *then* she could finally buy her bracelet.

Wincing, she struggled to her feet and opened Jai's cabinet.

10

Venkat had wanted to skip Asha's betrothal party, but now, standing in Jasmine Hall, he privately admitted that the palace staff had outdone themselves. And on such short notice, too. Even the ever-present sentries couldn't spoil the sight.

The majestic chamber sparkled like the inside of a dreamstone, its baroque inlay walls gleaming beneath the banners featuring the devices of both clans: red-and-yellow intertwining vipers for the clan of Vasuki and a cobalt-and-silver cobra springing at a crescent moon for the clan of Anant Shesha. Clusters of silvery flowers tucked into the jade mosaic ceiling sent their perfume dancing down like playful paris. The carved gold-and-green pillars lining the perimeter had been tied with bands of mirror-worked silk, their tiny reflections pinhole portals to other worlds. Gold filigree lamps studded with an array of jewels furnished the hall with multicolored light, their beams braiding together into a bedazzling fresco that formed and re-formed over the marble floor. On a dais near the entrance, the royal musicians played veena and nagasvaram at a volume low enough to encourage conversation.

A buffet station lined the far wall, watched over by a relief of prancing naginis. Long tables groaned under the weight of a lavish steaming banquet featuring Asha's and Chintu's favorite dishes, their wonderful smells taunting Venkat's empty stomach. He could have devoured the chafing dish of jewel-rice biryani all by himself, and once the guests of honor made their grand entrance, he would do his best to bring that about.

They weren't the only ones late, however. Nayan had also been delayed, marooning Venkat by a statue of the nagarani in repose. At first, he'd distracted himself from thoughts of Jai by mentally tracing the beadwork of the banners and going over all the naga lore he knew, all the tales of the various clans and their escapades.

But when he ran out of stories and Nayan still hadn't arrived, Venkat sighed and approached the guests closest to him, a refined older naga couple practically dripping kundan jewelry. They put him in mind of high-society people in movies, as at home in their extravagant pear-and-gold embroidered sherwani and richly worked dusty rose choli and dupatta set as if they'd never even conceived of having to settle for anything less.

Venkat put his palms together in greeting. "It's a fine evening for a party."

The couple beamed in unison. "Lord Nayan's apprentice!" said the woman. "Where *is* dear Lord Nayan?"

"He'll be here soon," Venkat said. Feeling awkward, he repeated, "It really is a nice party."

"Such a lovely kurta!" the woman exclaimed. "The colors suit you."

"Oh, it's nothing compared to yours," Venkat said politely, but the compliment warmed him. He knew he looked good. Madhu had chosen peacock colors this time: rich blue, vivid green, and deep violet, all embroidered with gold dots. The stylish kurta fit him like silken armor, and his freshly combed hair shone.

The man's tail wound in sinuous patterns behind him as he moved closer. "Such a position of prestige, to work with Lord Nayan in the dream trade."

Venkat stiffened, then smiled even wider to hide it. He could already tell where this was going. Worse, more guests were gathering around them, boxing him in. He should have just waited for Nayan.

"You must be quite knowledgeable," the man continued. "Given great responsibility. Tell us of the trade; is your supply truly so limited as they say?"

Venkat had seen Nayan easily deflect people who thought they could wring favors out of him. Asha, too, in her flamboyant way. She'd have the man laughing about something else completely by now. Too bad Venkat didn't know how to do that when he wasn't sitting behind the big desk in the archives.

"It's fine?" he hazarded. "Busy."

"I have been waiting months. Surely it would not be much— such a *small* gesture—if you were to make an exception for me?"

A server in an impeccable ivory kurta passed by with a tray of golden goblets, and Venkat almost ambushed him in his haste to grab one. "I'm thirsty. How about a drink? To the glory of the betrotheds, Princess Asha and Prince Chintan!"

"A drink"— the man laughed and clinked his goblet against Venkat's—"and perhaps a dream as well."

Venkat's smile felt nailed on. Where was Nayan?

Even more guests had joined them, eyeing Venkat like a shark that had found fresh chum, and he had to resist the urge to back away. "Apprentice," another nagini purred, sipping her amrit, "is it true the council fears another breach?"

The first woman offered him a suggestive grin. "You can certainly confide in us. Lord Nayan would not mind."

Yeah, right. Time to go. Venkat stared over her shoulder and made an apologetic face. "Speaking of Lord Nayan, I think I see him over there. Excuse me." He loped off, only stopping when half the hall separated him from his covetous audience.

On this side of the grand chamber, the palace architects had erected a pond designed to mirror the holiday celebrations outside. Golden plates coasted on the pond's surface, each covered with enameled diyas, a little pot of oil, and a dark blue lotus with a flame at its heart. Venkat knelt next to the pond and focused on the flame.

They were only people, he reminded himself. He could do this. He dealt with people every day, even if it was from behind his desk.

"That was not so terrible," Madhu said, gliding up in an indigo choli and matching ornaments. It was strange to see her in her nagini aspect for once. "A tad clumsy, perhaps, but finesse can be learned."

His neck flushing, Venkat ducked his head. He hadn't known she'd been observing him. "Thanks?"

"Shall we circulate?" she asked.

Venkat held up a finger, then selected an unlit diya painted with a pink-and-green paisley motif. He dipped one end of the cotton wick into the pot of oil and touched it to the flame. Once it had ignited, he said a silent prayer for Jai's successful return to Prithvi and set the diya back onto the floating plate. It glowed like a carnelian dreamstone against the dark water.

A pair of giggling children ran by, chasing the fiery damselflies fluttering out of the diyas' flames. "Come back here!" one cried, grasping at a damselfly that zigzagged around her, its wings trailing smoke. If she caught it before its spark went out, her dearest desire would come to pass. Or so the nagas believed.

Venkat rose and gazed through the skylights, wondering if his family was up there in Svargalok, or if they'd already begun new lives with new identities. What was it his grandfather had said? That nothing ever ended, only changed shape?

The thought was sad, but hopeful, too, and as the age-old stars twinkled and flashed above him in their secret language, Venkat felt comforted. He folded the memories into their box at the bottom of his heart and nodded at Madhu.

And just in time; flanked by their families, the guests of honor paraded toward him. The vivid plum and peridot of Asha's diamond-bedecked choli and gauzy dupatta, shot through with gold and silver zari, subtly complemented the goldenrod of Chintu's brocade sherwani. Venkat couldn't begin to count the various ornate pieces of jewelry glittering from the crowns of their heads to the tips of their tails. Together, at least superficially, they were the ultimate royal match.

"Well, well." Mischief brewed in Asha's large, heavily lined eyes. "Look at you, here all on your own."

Venkat treated her to the shallowest possible bow. "I wouldn't have missed it for anything, Princess."

Shooting him a lazy grin, Chintu slung an arm around Asha's shoulders. "I am glad you could join us."

Was Venkat the only one to catch her tiny flinch? But then she laughed and leaned into Chintu's embrace, so maybe Venkat had imagined it, after all.

Someone nudged him in the side. He glanced over to see Madhu, who tipped her head toward the pair. Oh, right. Nayan had given him a complete dream for Chintu. No one ever received more than a fragment; intact visions were far too precious a resource to expend on any one naga or nagini. A gift like this marked the union of the two clans as the momentous occasion it was.

Shutting out all the hungry stares on him—how many friends and hangers-on did Asha and Chintu have?—Venkat produced the opal vial. Colors scintillated in its facets, a spectrum as wriggly as any serpent. "On behalf of the nagaraja and nagarani," he said, smiling, "the office of the court historian presents you with a betrothal gift: a complete mortal dream."

Hisses of shock susurrated through the space. Even Asha angled her head, uncertain.

"So *that* is why you refused me the other day!" Chintu declared.

"I see now." Releasing Asha, he grabbed the dreamstone and took hold of the cork. "How, pray tell, does this work?"

Their friends gaped at him with appalled curiosity, eyes and scales glistening in the vial's radiance. "You cannot do that here!" said a girl with a haughty expression worthy of an apsara.

None of the other people Venkat had given dreamstones to had experienced the contents in public. It was a solitary act. Still, taboos aside, he couldn't pass up the chance to see a dream being savored.

"Chintu," his uncle chided. "Save it for later, yes, beta?"

As if he'd known what was transpiring, Nayan strode into the room, his scarlet dupatta draped over his shoulders like pinions. Without trying, he cast the other guests into shadow, and they turned to take him in.

"Normally, yes, our tradition calls for restraint," Nayan agreed. "But tonight is about new beginnings and the bonds between us. What fortune meets your prince and princess, good or ill, befalls each of you as well, making this a gift for all to enjoy."

Chintu twisted the cork from the vial.

The dream drifted free, caressing his face, then came to rest on him. His cocky expression faded as his eyes fell shut. His friends swarmed him, jostling for the best view. Even Venkat shared their wonder. As a dreamsmith, he could only ever stand apart, analyzing and mining the elements from outside. But here was someone lost within the reverie.

Chintu's arms shot up, striking the people who stood closest to him. He began mumbling nonsense in a disturbing singsong that set the hairs on Venkat's arms prickling.

Then Chintu's incoherence culminated in a tragic wail. "That is *my* fork!" His invisible fork speared the correspondingly invisible object he'd grabbed from the air. "Give it back!"

The other nagas and naginis couldn't have been any more enthralled, judging by how they slithered even nearer. Nayan, like Asha and Madhu, looked amused.

Venkat stifled his own snicker. Sometimes doing your job came with unexpected benefits.

As Chintu kissed the air with wet smacking noises, he settled in to watch. For research purposes, of course.

11

Tanvi hovered anxiously a few feet from the palace exit, her fingers securing the bag of dreamstones on her shoulder. She'd never come here before, never had any reason to. Dream runners were supposed to stay hidden when they weren't harvesting. Her skin hurt at the thought of being on display like this, even if everyone assumed she was just another nagini in human form.

A large, boisterous family slithered past her and into the courtyard. Tanvi balked at the wide-open night and the masses of people celebrating in it. So many nagas. So many diyas and lanterns. She'd be too exposed.

But this was her one chance to carry out her plan, while Venkat was off at Asha's engagement party.

Jai's empty room plagued Tanvi's thoughts, a warning of what was at stake. She couldn't get caught dreaming. She wouldn't.

All she had to do was find one buyer for one dream. Just one.

Tanvi picked at the waistband of the chaniya choli she'd found in her wardrobe. There'd been a few outfits like this, actually, along with some simple jewelry. Probably Asha's castoffs, dumped there in some misguided attempt to get Tanvi to play dress-up, but she'd never seen them until tonight.

Not until Asha had pointed them out.

Tanvi scowled. She couldn't wait to forget them again.

When the next group of nagas came by, she slipped into it. The guards on either side of the doors wished her a merry festival, and she forced herself to smile at them. Any second now, a hand would be seizing her wrist. She knew it.

In step with the oblivious strangers, she passed over the threshold. Her nerves screamed that she was making the worst mistake of her life.

And then she was outside. In Bhogavati proper, where no dream runner belonged.

The group kept going, but Tanvi couldn't.

Her knees quivered. And here she'd thought the main corridor was big.

The palace grounds extended across the horizon, and she had to avert her eyes and glance back up as she walked. Avert her eyes and glance back up, until the overwhelming hugeness of it all receded.

But it didn't recede. Instead, all at once, Tanvi's senses activated.

The horizon wasn't just a horizon, she realized—it was an infinite black sky with a crescent moon and way too many pale stars.

She shook it off and started walking. It didn't matter. It didn't. Once she invoked the boon, she wouldn't notice anything like that ever again.

Tanvi didn't dare approach any more groups, but maybe she

didn't have to. Watching naga after naga cross the bridge over the river, she decided to try there. The shade of the bridge seemed like a good place to set up shop.

As she headed toward it, the fluorescent colors all around set her eyes on fire: decorations and lanterns in lurid scarlets, tangerines, hot pinks, neon greens. The barrage of fireworks bruised her brain: *boom*, *boom*, *boom*. A whiff of hot, syrupy jalebi choked her until she almost retched.

And the nagas *liked* this?

Every green and blue leaf on every tree and flowering bush stood out like it wanted to slice her open. The deluge of candle flame from the Navratri celebrations slammed over her like water from a fire hose.

No. The word pierced her sore-to-the-touch skull. *Like nothing.* She hadn't harvested any dream about fire hoses recently, if ever.

Tanvi tapped her wrist where her bracelet would go, tracing the shapes of the charms on her skin, but not even that could banish the details—or the fear.

Giving up on the bridge, she retreated to a copse of champak trees near a fountain. It smelled really sweet, and flowers kept flying through the air, but at least it was quieter, with much less to see. All she needed was one person to come through and buy one of her dreams in exchange for a single boon.

Then she could put this whole awful night behind her and start making up for the harvest she'd missed.

A pair of perfumed naginis strolled through the grove, arms around each other. The constant "sssssss" of their conversation made Tanvi want to claw out her eardrums.

Just get it over with.

She stretched her mouth into a smile and stepped forward. "H-hi! Want to buy a dream?"

The friends or sisters or whatever they were exchanged glances. Even Tanvi, who very much did not want to notice, could tell how sophisticated they were in their matching lilac-and-rose-petal saris.

"Certainly," one of the sisters said, "but I was under the impression that dreams are only brokered through Lord Nayan's office?"

"Oh," said Tanvi. "Um, this is—" Then she had it. "This is a Navratri special."

"A special. How lovely!" The second sister beamed, making Tanvi's vision smear.

"Here." She shoved ametrine and cat's-eye vials at the sisters. The dreams within pulsated. "Two for the price of one boon. What a bargain."

The sisters shared another look, this one despondent. "We have no boons," the first one said. "But if you would permit us to compensate you in gold—"

Tanvi shook her head. How would that help? Not even her gold bracelet could fix her problem.

The sisters offered her regretful smiles and moved on. Tanvi made a face at their graceful backs. Their loss. Someone else with more sense would snap these treasures right up.

A few minutes later, a middle-aged naga with a bulging purse came by, and Tanvi tempted him with a tanzanite vial from Jai's cabinet. It held an adrenaline-packed dream of a white pickup truck in a high-speed police chase, the driver sailing through red lights and even colliding with a silver minivan. "You won't be able catch your breath. I guarantee it."

The man opened his purse to reveal gold coins. "How much for such a marvel?"

"I only take boons," Tanvi replied.

"Surely just this once? I can pay quite generously."

"No deal." Her throat convulsed around the words. What if no one but Venkat had boons?

The man bowed his head. "As you wish."

Left alone again, Tanvi paced in the shadows between the trees, her eyes screwed almost shut so she didn't have to see anything except the bracelet in her mind.

She had to get hold of a boon. But what if she didn't?

What if she couldn't stop noticing things?

What if she couldn't stop dreaming?

What was she going to *do*?

Tanvi had almost talked herself into leaving the trees and trying her luck in a crowd when a naga around Asha's age wandered toward her. His diadem of lit sparklers was too intense to look at, so she darted her stare past him.

"Dreams for sale!" she called with desperate cheer. The boy contemplated her. She held up a moonstone vial. "Just one boon. That's probably less than a coin."

The boy frowned. "Venkat said nothing about anyone else distributing dream fragments." He examined her more closely, and the corners of his mouth turned up in triumph. "You are one of the mortal dream runners he keeps from us, are you not? Why have you hidden yourself in the trees?"

Tanvi felt like every cell in her body dried up right then. This boy knew who she was? "I'm helping him," she lied.

Her confusion must have shown, because the boy pointed behind him. "Venkat is back there, with Princess Asha and Prince Chintan. If you are helping him as you claim, why are you not with him?"

The names taunted Tanvi, smacking her in the face with how badly she'd misjudged this entire scheme. She tried to retreat, but it was too late.

"Venkat," the naga with the stupid crown called, grinning, "I have located one of your errant runners!"

Venkat appeared at the edge of the trees. "What is it, Karan?" His face went tight with shock. "*Tanvi?*"

"Why couldn't you just buy the dream?" Tanvi cried. She almost threw the vial at Karan's sneering face, but the jerk didn't deserve a free dream. When she dropped it into her bag, it clacked against the other unsold dreamstones, driving home her utter failure.

"Because this is so much more entertaining," he hissed so only she could hear him.

The spite in Karan's voice was more than she could deal with. Not when she was so tired, and Venkat was about to punish her.

But Venkat stopped a few feet away. "Tanvi," he said again. This time, it was an acknowledgment.

His gaze hooked onto hers, and she flinched. Something stirred in his expression, a sort of wondering, like he might be surprised, but not because she was here in the trees.

His eyes—they were so soft. They looked . . . worried? For her?

Something shy behind her ribs tickled at that, and she found herself openly looking at him. Letting her eyes rest on his. They were brown, warm. Nice. And they didn't hurt no matter how much she looked at them, not the way all the other details she couldn't block out did.

Tanvi could have stayed there for at least another minute, just looking.

Karan, though, moved closer, watching them intently, and she snapped back to reality. What was *wrong* with her? Who cared what someone's eyes were like?

She stared, rankled, past Venkat. There was only one thing she should ever be noticing, and that was her bracelet.

Venkat smiled his smooth, professional smile. "Thanks for finding her, Karan." He turned the smile on Tanvi, and she felt how impersonal it was, exactly as it should be. "Looks like Asha forgot to tell you we finished giving out the dream scraps last night. Sorry about that! But if you hurry, it's not too late to go harvesting."

She still wanted to punch Karan, and she didn't know what to make of Venkat—why was he giving her an out when he'd seen her talking to a naga who wasn't Asha or Nayan in public?—but she was too exhausted to care.

Fighting not to think of anything at all, Tanvi took off toward the palace.

12

The amrit gleamed up at Venkat, reflecting his bewildered expression in liquid as golden as the sapphire-and-emerald-studded goblet clutched in his sweaty palm.

Why in the worlds was Tanvi wandering the palace grounds? If he hadn't been there when Karan found her . . .

Venkat scanned the remaining guests by the light of the sparklers flashing and the diyas flickering everywhere. Now that the party had migrated outside for fresh air, the others had scattered, some to the bridge, some to the aquamarine fountain flowing with amrit and the nearby carved marble benches. But aside from Karan—and Asha, who'd witnessed the whole thing from a safe distance—no one else appeared to have spotted Tanvi. Good. For his part, Karan was busy flirting with two of Asha's friends.

That didn't buy Venkat much time, though. He didn't believe for a second that Karan had lost interest in what he'd seen, any more than he'd bought Venkat's feeble excuse. Venkat still didn't know how he'd been able to cover for Tanvi to begin with; stumbling onto her amidst the trees like that had thrown him. She'd looked so lost and vulnerable in her violet-and-silver chaniya choli and borrowed—stolen?—jewelry, a human girl completely out of her league.

He gripped the goblet tighter. Among the nagas, wasn't she?

Venkat headed back to the palace, weaving his way through the clusters of people enjoying the night. With any luck, he could catch Tanvi before she left for Prithvi.

The other day, when she'd shown up unannounced in the appraisal room, haunted him now. He'd known something had been off, with how slow she'd been to respond after he'd asked about her dreamstones. Like her attention had gone somewhere else.

He shouldn't have written that off. Venkat's heart squeezed. Tanvi and Jai were the last of their cohort, and burnout was just a matter of time.

Venkat glanced furtively around again, in case either Nayan or Madhu was nearby. It was silly, and he knew it. Even Nayan couldn't read his thoughts.

A hatchling swayed across his path, much more graceful than a human toddler. Venkat paused to let the small boy by. The miniature scales in his cobra tail aligned seamlessly, each iridescent section perfect in itself but also a fundamental building block of something larger and magnificent, like the elements of Venkat's dreamsmithing project.

If Tanvi was burning out, too, Venkat knew he couldn't hide it. He had to tell Nayan.

Except, he thought, half mesmerized by the hatchling's tail as it rippled away, Tanvi hadn't acted like Jai. Jai had been fixated on

111

the idea of selling his dreams, obsessed with the boon that would get him his beloved tricycle. Venkat could have asked him about anything—how he'd slept; going camping as a kid; the best kind of cake—and Jai would have turned the conversation right back to the boon.

In contrast, Tanvi had been strangely absent. Vague, even.

Anxiety pressed down on him, dark and heavy. If she wasn't burning out, what was wrong?

Venkat stared at the palace, its golden domes and jali balconies aglitter in the gentle blue-green halo. Whatever was happening to Tanvi felt like a piece that belonged to a different puzzle than the one he'd been painstakingly assembling all this time, and he had no idea what to do with it.

Asha appeared at his side, breezy as a spring day, and clinked her goblet against his. "Drink and smile, you sssssstubborn thing," she hissed under her breath. "They are watching!"

Venkat started to answer, but she dug her elbow into his ribs. "Ow!"

"You owe me a toast. Am I not the blessed bride-to-be?"

He glared but raised his goblet. "Every good thing to you, Princess! May your scales shimmer like a rainbow all your long reign." Then, remembering she'd kept her news from him, he whispered, "A rainbow trout, that is."

"And may all the thick, luscious strands of your hair grow pale and fall from your withered scalp by the thirtieth anniversary of your birth," Asha retaliated, a devious grin spreading over her fine cheekbones.

They tipped back their goblets. While the amrit might be a poor substitute for the actual nectar of immortality the nagas had lost to the garudas, it still tasted amazing, like honey made of sunlight. Venkat savored every drop.

Asha brought her mouth to his ear. "My foolish Venkat, do you know nothing at all? If you run to her so soon after without so much as a farewell, Karan will take note. Be assured of that."

"Fine," he said. "But you better get me out of here fast."

"Perhaps you are possessed of a grain of sense, after all." Asha preened, then looped her arm through his and walked him over to where Karan and her other friends were standing. "Look who I have brought to say good night!"

"It is early yet!" a girl said, her slit-pupil eyes as brilliant as her powerful copperhead tail. "Surely you will join us for some refreshments?"

Nayan had wanted Venkat to practice navigating the court, but that could wait. "No, no, you go ahead," he said, doing his best to sound casual. "I wouldn't want to intrude."

"Oh, but it is hardly an intrusion!" said Karan. "Right, Asha? For so long, you have kept him from us." His mouth bent in a mocking grin. "It is only fair we get to know him, too."

The rest of Asha's friends chimed in. They were beautiful, excessively so, in a way Venkat had grown numb to. Now he couldn't unsee how very not human they were. He wouldn't forget that again.

It figured the nagas wanted him around *now*, he noted dryly, when all he wanted was to leave.

"I suppose I can stay for a minute," he said, locking gazes with

Asha, who gave him a minute nod. "Then I have to get going."

Karan pouted, though his stare never left Venkat. "But—"

Chintu, of all people, came to the rescue. "That was incredible!" he announced, rolling his neck in circles. As his friends turned to him, the last wisps of the dream dissolved, returning to the ether from which they'd sprung. "When can I have another?"

His friends, including Karan, all broke into questions.

Thank Mansa Devi. Venkat would have to leave her an offering in the morning. He could only hope Tanvi hadn't left yet.

"I ate *pie*!" Chintu's fangs gleamed as he grinned. "Rhubarb apple pie."

"What sort of apple?" demanded the nagini with the copperhead tail. "Sweet? Tart? Crunchy or soft? We must have every detail."

"I will do my best."

Asha scoffed. "While the rest of you might well be content with dream desserts, I find myself peckish once more. It is grueling work, entertaining before one's own nuptials." She flipped her gleaming black locks over one shoulder. "While you tell them," she told Chintu, "I will find a snack."

He nodded, already deep into a description of his first succulent bite. "Such a flaky, buttery crust . . ."

On any other day, Venkat would be taking careful notes on Chintu's experience of the dream. Not now, though. Not when he couldn't stop picturing Tanvi among the trees. She needed help.

"Come," Asha ordered, gripping Venkat's elbow. "I need food, and you will help me find it."

Then they were off, speeding as only a naga could. Even with

Asha's magic carrying him along, Venkat's body vibrated like a car whose speedometer had gone into the red.

Ignoring the passersby calling her name, Asha rushed Venkat toward the carved golden double doors of the palace's courtyard entrance. The familiar medallion with the device of the nagaraja and nagarani, tails corkscrewed around each other, greeted him from the center of each door before Asha led him through the scalloped archway and into the palace. She scarcely acknowledged any of the guards they surged past, only stopping when the two of them stood alone before one of the many benches dotting the pearl-and-emerald hallway. "This is not good, Venkat. You must find her."

He fought to catch his breath. "I know," he said at last. "What are we going to do?"

Asha pursed her lips. "I will do my best to shield her." With a quiet sigh unlike the ones she put on for show, she murmured, "I do wish Chintu would choose his alliances more carefully."

"We all should," Venkat agreed. When Asha didn't reply, he added, "What about you, Princess? Are you okay?"

"Why would I not be?" Her wan smile might as well have been propped up on stilts, but her chin lifted in its usual defiance. "We have no time for your silliness. Go now and find her."

He didn't have a chance to answer before she undulated away, the diamonds in her hair sparking under the elaborate sconces like extensions of her fury. She looked like the queen she'd one day become—Venkat had no doubt who the true ruler in *that* marriage would be—but he wasn't sure whether that was a good thing.

Karan leered in his thoughts as Venkat hastened toward the runners' quarters. Well, Asha would certainly be better than that. She was right; Chintu had terrible taste in friends.

The future would have to take care of itself. For now, Venkat had to find Tanvi.

13

Back in her room, door tightly shut, Tanvi tried to breathe. She was falling to pieces, just like Jai.

An awful ticking had started in her chest. It echoed in her ears, and with each tick, she saw the girl in the street. She heard Asha saying that name.

Then Venkat's expression flashed in Tanvi's mind, that weird recognition when he'd looked at her in the copse of trees. Acid pooled in her stomach. Did he know what had happened to Jai?

Did he—did he think she was next?

One step into her closet, and she knew that wouldn't do anything to relax her. The image of the bracelet wouldn't even come into focus.

Her skin smarting, she lurched back into the room. Right away, things started harrowing her: A fussy cushion in the corner. The pale pink champak garlands on the walls. A tricolored rug at the foot of the bed. None of that had been there just this morning. Had it?

What if this was another dream?

No. No, no, no. Tanvi tossed the cushion under the bed along with her bag of Jai's harvested dreams. This had to stop. She would *make* it stop.

Everything had been fine until she'd gone to Philadelphia and run into that girl. If she could figure out why, maybe then she'd know what to do.

Tanvi changed back into her Prithvi outfit and tied on her pouch. If she stayed here, she would only freak out.

"Tanvi?"

She almost hit the ceiling, and the dreamstones in her pouch clacked together.

Venkat filled the doorway, all the peacock tones of his kurta arresting against his brown skin and black hair. Even avoiding his eyes, she saw that he was much more noble than Karan or whatever his name was could ever be. Of course, that bar was so low a baby could crawl right over it.

Focus. She grabbed another dreamstone and wedged it into her already-stuffed pouch. *Show him there's nothing to worry about.*

"Are you okay?" he asked, then laughed a little. "Sorry, I just feel like I've been asking that a lot tonight."

Tanvi finally met his gaze. Instead of the anger she'd expected, concern warmed his rich brown eyes as they skimmed her face.

She took an instinctive step backward. The walls felt like they'd shrunk until there wasn't even space left for her. He couldn't know that actually, she was anything but okay.

Three long strides, and Venkat stood in front of her. "I need to talk to you." When she didn't respond, he touched her arm, his fingers brushing just below the sleeve of her T-shirt. "Tanvi. Are you listening to me?"

She shied away, trembling. No one touched her, except Asha when she wanted Tanvi to hurry up. How could anyone *stand* this? It was so intense, *too* intense, sensation crashing through her a hundred times harder than even the colors and smells had. She could handle Venkat yelling at her for trying to sell her dreams, but not this electric feel of his fingertips lingering on her skin.

Tanvi hissed like Asha would. It didn't help, and that only made her more frantic. She didn't want to think about how Venkat was only inches from her, or why his familiar face had become strange, with that thoughtful consideration. Or about those expressive eyes that terrified her.

"Get away from me," she ordered as harshly as she could.

Venkat stared at her as if he felt like she did: like the universe had flipped inside out. Then his face shuttered, the warmth smothered. "Not until you tell me why you were trying to sell your dreams to Karan."

Your dreams. Did he suspect she'd been dreaming, too?

She had to distract him. "Where's Jai?" she demanded. "What'd you do with him?"

Venkat swallowed hard enough that she could see his Adam's apple bobbing. "He's with Nayan. Why?"

The dejection at finding Jai's room empty struck her again, and she lashed out. "Maybe you should be more worried about that instead of partying with the nagas."

Venkat was supposed to protect the dream runners. It was his job to keep her from dreaming. From her bracelet having to take a back seat to things that shouldn't matter. "It's your fault he's gone," she stressed, "and don't you forget it."

Then, tying up her pouch, she stalked past him and into the tunnel.

Dawn had broken by the time Tanvi got to Philadelphia.

Being exposed to the sun of Prithvi like this—with no shadows to jump into—felt sinful. She should be in her room right now, surrendered to oblivion.

But it would be worth it if she could find the answer she needed.

Tanvi tromped toward the intersection where she'd met the girl with the headband, passing stores and restaurants and people. So many people, so many odors and noises and textures. Even the air tasted of exhaust and stale frying oil. It was hard to breathe, and more than once she had to stop so her weary legs wouldn't give out.

A wall covered in street art stung Tanvi's eyes until she had to wipe away tears. An older, brown-skinned woman in a crown stared out from a swirl of blue, yellow, and orange, and the rainbow bubble letters under her spelled out ♥ ONE PHILLY, ONE LUV ♥.

Squinting, Tanvi raced around the corner. Why were there so many *colors*? Had the entire world made a deal to splash its paint over this one city?

When she dared to look again, the building behind the mural came into view. Big cartoon decals grinned at each other from the windows. Something about them was familiar in a way that scraped at her insides.

120

Tanvi hadn't meant to move, but suddenly her nose was at the nearest window. Beyond it, she glimpsed sunny yellow walls. And there, near the entrance, something purple and green—an open book large enough for a smaller girl to hide in.

The made-up museum from her dream. It couldn't be.

According to the sign by the doors, the museum didn't open for another three hours. Not that Tanvi had any intention of checking it out. Not ever.

She backed away and jogged off.

The shining mica chips under her feet switched to cracked concrete, and the concrete switched to cobblestones. The lumpiness of the cobblestones, the shock of almost tripping in a gap between them—it felt like someone pulling on her sleeve. Entreating her to stop and think. She ignored it. All she had to do was find that girl with the headband.

Mirror-shard mosaic walls reflected bits of her, broken up, as she ran past. That same awful itch of missing something obvious nagged at her, but she kept going. The crosswalk wasn't far now.

As the sun climbed into the blue sky, the tiny alley of a street where she'd recently been appeared. Tanvi didn't mean to, but she turned into it.

Her feet carried her to Sameer's row house with the pineapple knocker.

Queen Village. She'd been heading here the entire time. Her feet had known, even if her brain hadn't.

That thing in her chest, the thing Tanvi absolutely did not want, thrummed to life again.

"Stop!" she moaned, not sure who she was talking to. She parked herself on a stoop two doors down from Sameer's house, not far from a shredded garbage bag dumped by the curb. Chances were good he'd see her, but what difference did it make? She'd already flouted every other dream runner rule.

Her head thumped with the mess of dreams and half-sprouted memories churning inside. If only she could stuff them into the vials she'd brought. Never mind trying to sell them. She'd throw them away, right in this garbage bag. Shriveled-up orange peel, yellowed chicken bones, and black gunk oozed from the slashes in the plastic onto the reddish brick sidewalk. The whole thing stank of sickly sweet rot, making her throat close.

Why couldn't she shut all this out?

She'd lost count of how much time and how many pedestrians had gone by when a rat sprang from the garbage bag. Tanvi threw up her arms, but the rat wasn't interested in her. It fled a garter snake undulating in pursuit, and the two disappeared into a crack in the house's foundation.

Adrenaline shot through her veins at the sight of the snake. The nagas. Jai. Jai's empty room. What if that happened to her, too?

Someone was still asleep within the house behind her; Tanvi could just barely sense him dreaming. She pushed her inner radar for the usual details like degree and depth, but she didn't get more than a weird buzz.

Shrugging off the rising dread, she swallowed a lozenge and slipped inside the house. She was still a dream runner, and Venkat had told her to harvest. She might not have found the girl with the headband, but she could do this.

The family was in various states of preparing for the day: making breakfast, showering, scrolling on their tablets. Since she didn't have a lot of shadows to hide in, Tanvi made straight for the master bedroom, where a middle-aged man snored on top of the covers, still in his work uniform. *Perfect.*

She placed her hands above his head.

The man leaned over a railing, his fishing line dangling in the creek below. Cotton-ball clouds rolled through an emphatically cerulean sky, and a wall of fragrant pine trees spread to the horizon. Tanvi hadn't felt this unstressed in days, and she smiled with the man as a prize trout, as big as a toddler, bit.

He had only begun to reel it in when a voice interrupted.

"Honey? Sorry to bother you, but I can't find—"

The dream tattered, and Tanvi whirled around to see a woman staring at her. She groped for a dreamstone, coming up with a champagne zircon.

"Who are you?" The woman jabbed her finger at the wisps still billowing through the air. "And what the hell is *that*?"

Shame and panic clogged Tanvi's throat as she rushed to guide the loose wisps into the vial. But she'd waited a beat too long, and they dissipated even as she grabbed for them.

The woman elbowed her aside. "Stan?" she cried. "Stan?" She glowered at Tanvi. "What did you do to him?"

The man's eyes opened. "What's going on?" he slurred. "Marie?"

Swearing, Tanvi ran for the exit.

The woman's shouts had been enough to draw her children into the doorway. When Tanvi tried to force herself between them, the boy snagged her arm, and Tanvi had to kick him in the shin before he let go. In the process, she dropped the vial, and the girl snapped it up.

There was no time to fight her for it. The unwanted *thing* in Tanvi's chest pounding, she dashed down the stairs and back outside.

Everything was breaking. Everything. Not only had she been seen mid-harvest—by *four* people—but she'd let the dream get corrupted and even lost a dreamstone.

Her fantasy of returning to Bhogavati and resuming her normal life evaporated, just like the wisps of the man's dream. Tanvi ran and ran, desperate to put Sameer's street behind her.

Every house and restaurant and store felt like a mosquito biting her, injecting her with colors and signs and architectural flourishes that raised little itchy bumps of almost memory. Bumps she could feel but couldn't reach to scratch.

Tanvi was halfway to Penn's Landing, resigned to her fate, when another detail floated up. A memory.

She'd ended up at Sameer's door, but that wasn't the right one. The door in her memory was red.

The red door. It was real, and Tanvi knew where to find it.

The taxi idled, waiting for Tanvi to get out, and she muttered her thanks before handing over the promised diamond. First she hadn't been able to find a taxi, and when she finally did, it took her three tries before one would accept a dreamstone instead of cash to drive her out to Mount Airy. And here she'd thought mortals really liked these cold rocks, as if they meant anything without a dream inside them.

Her breath skittered. She didn't have to do this. She could give the driver another vial to turn around. Except everything had gone wrong since that night that girl had called her the wrong name, and she still hadn't found out why.

The driver grimaced at the diamond. "How do I know it's real?" he challenged yet again.

That decided her. "Only one way to find out," she shot back, then hopped out of the car.

The engine's rumble subsided, leaving her to confront the big gray stone house with the circular stained-glass windows on the second floor.

And the red door from her dreams.

Tanvi was going to throw up. Dread soured her guts, and the thing in her chest galloped fast enough to take on a racehorse. Every part of her screamed for her to run, to go home. Dream runners didn't have families. They didn't care about the past.

Every part—except the one that unclenched at the sight of the red door. The thing in Tanvi's chest, her heart that should have gone dormant for all time.

A bird had made a nest in the magnolia tree in the landscaped front yard. The tree promised more unknotting of memories she didn't want, now or ever.

Just like the azaleas, both pink and red, lining the side of the house. But not like that pinwheel garden stake or those solar lights on the railing—those were new.

Tears pricked at her eyes for the second time this morning, and she rubbed at them with her knuckles.

You don't have to do this. This isn't your world.

So what if her mind kept playing that name? She could keep ignoring it until it went away.

Except, her heart beat out, there was no going back. That door was closed, and the one before her waited to be opened. She had to know.

Tanvi had never felt sicker or more scared.

Something shot out of the bush by her feet, writhing across the grass and somehow leaping onto her arm. Tanvi shrieked and tried to shake it loose. The cobra only wound itself around her like a deadly vine until it glared up from her wrist. It opened its mouth wide, baring its fangs and throat. Its forked tongue flicked in and out; its green-gold reptilian eyes glinted accusingly at her.

Tanvi stared at it. She'd never had any reason to fear snakes until now. All it would take was one bite . . .

The cobra hissed and blurred. The next second, a mostly human Asha in a pretty silver dress appeared next to Tanvi. Her unnaturally golden-brown eyes were the only possible giveaway that she was more than what she seemed. "Well, good morning to you, resident troublemaker. Venkat is deeply fearful for you, poor boy."

Tanvi checked to see if anyone else had noticed the cobra on her arm or the girl materializing out of thin air. Luckily, they were alone. "Wha—what?" she finally managed. "What are you doing here? Are you trying to scare me to death?"

"You sssseek death perfectly well on your own, it would sssseem to me." Asha pointed to the nest in the tree. "That is no ordinary nest," she went on, mercifully ditching the exaggerated sibilants. "That is an *eagle's* nest. Luckily for us, the eagle in question is absent."

Tanvi didn't get it. What did nests have to do with anything? Then she remembered the garter snake chasing the rat. Asha could take any serpent form she liked. "Wait, did you *follow* me?"

"Someone had to keep watch over you, running all over town and exposing yourself as you are so foolishly doing. Harvesting dreams in broad daylight? Truly?" Asha studied her, then added in a guarded tone, "Tanvi, why did *you* come here?"

Tanvi didn't say anything, and Asha's canines sharpened to wicked points. "If you do not tell me, I will bite you, and I promise you will not enjoy the experience."

"Do you do that to Sameer, too?" Tanvi asked, trying to divert Asha as much as herself. The large house continued to loom over her, and it scared her even more than Asha had.

"Naturally. What is the point of being a nagini if I cannot enjoy myself on occasion?" Asha grinned. "It is hardly my fault you mortals are so easily frightened. Now"—she flashed her fangs again—"tell me!"

"No," Tanvi said. She waited for Asha to argue, or maybe to bite her. Even naga venom couldn't hurt as much as the fear in her chest.

Asha gave the house a calculating once-over. Then she tilted her chin toward Tanvi like she was waiting for something.

Tanvi shook her head. "I said no, didn't I?"

Asha sighed heavily. "Stubborn to the end." She morphed into a blue tree snake and leaped onto Tanvi's wrist, where she molded herself into a delicate bangle.

Whatever that meant. Tanvi didn't really think Asha would bite her. Or at least, she didn't think it was likely. But it was worth the risk if it meant she didn't have to do this all alone.

She slogged up the pebbled path, each step bringing her closer to the house. Someone had drawn a chalk rangoli with daisies and lotuses in jewel tones on the driveway. Asha lifted her head to inspect the artwork, her tongue testing the air.

Tanvi could swear she'd seen something like the rangoli before. Something about the daisies. Her temples ached.

The holes in her memory were like moth bites taken out of a wool sweater, inviting in the bone-biting chill. She shouldn't be here. She should leave.

But she'd arrived at the red door. It had a doorbell, and doorbells were for ringing. Tanvi's finger reached out, independent of her doubting head, and pressed the button.

The door opened almost immediately, and her own face stared back at her. A million different expressions flitted over it: incredulity, relief, joy, anger. "Tanvi?"

Say it, Tanvi commanded herself. "Nitya."

The girl with her face set down the camera she'd been holding and yanked Tanvi into a bear hug. It felt suffocating and gross—but it also felt like something Tanvi knew. Despite everything, she relaxed into it.

"Tanvi," her twin sister breathed. "You're alive."

14

Venkat pushed his blanket away. The tiny mirrors embroidered along the soft, sea-toned cloth snared the first rays of Lord Surya's chariot as it crossed the sky and flung them over him. He glimpsed his own eyes in the glass—sad and worried, with hollows beneath.

He'd tossed and turned for what little remained of the night, one ear primed for Asha's trademark hiss. Waiting for her to let him know Tanvi was okay. *I shall keep her safe*, she'd promised, and he'd had to accept that. *Go and rest.*

Tanvi's question about Jai ate at him as he traipsed through his suite of rooms and down the winding stairs to the carved jade tub. How did sending the dream runners back to Prithvi in a state of burnout, their hearts still silenced, actually solve the problem? Maybe Nayan could overlook that in the name of the greater goal, what with everything he had to juggle.

But having seeing runner after runner burn out, Venkat wasn't sure anymore that *he* could.

He rushed through his too-hot bath, scrubbing harder than necessary, like he could slough off the guilt along with the grime. Where was Asha? Why hadn't she returned with Tanvi yet?

The memory of Tanvi's pretty face glowered at him, accusing. He hadn't missed the absolute despair scrawled on her cheeks when he'd found her packing in her room, let alone the panic in her gaze—and it was all wrong. Dream runners weren't supposed to feel anything but the urge to harvest.

What could possibly make her panic like that?

Venkat grabbed for a towel from the selection arrayed in the linen cabinet. He shouldn't have let Tanvi go. He'd scared her off when he should have made her feel like she could tell him what was going on. He was failing all of them—his runners and Nayan both.

His heart hurt. He would never forgive himself for not having worked harder to help Jai. To save him. And now this.

That was it. He had no choice but to tell Nayan what was going on.

Once he'd dried off, Venkat headed to his wardrobe. The early-morning sunlight buttered everything in the suite, illuminating the colorful murals on the teal walls, scenes of the nagas through history, their scales rendered in iridescent mother-of-pearl and their jewelry and crowns done in delicate applications of gold leaf. Where it passed through the perforated designs of the jali borders separating the small rooms, it left a thousand four-pointed suns scattered in its wake.

Everywhere Venkat looked, opulent gem-studded lanterns glimmered gold like celestial bodies, vibrant torans hung over windows, and colorful embroidered poufs peppered the floor. More couches and chairs with ornate frames and sumptuous fabrics than he could ever need sat spaced at aesthetically pleasing intervals, their ocean-green and violet hues reminiscent of dreamstone vials. He even had two custom-made marble bookcases with a motif of tiny gilt elephants, one on either side of his bed, each crammed with volumes and volumes of stories.

The suite was a haven, a place any noble would happily retreat to from the cares of court life.

But none of it made him feel any better, any more than it had when Nayan first set eight-year-old Venkat up here, stressing that any member of his house deserved only the best. Than it had when Venkat cried himself to sleep alone every night, sobbing for the parents and brother he would never see again, until he'd eventually learned to find consolation in stories.

Even if the silver-gray kurta pajama he pulled on now was sized for an adult, he felt as powerless now as he had back then, too small to fill such a big role.

He'd dreamed, he remembered suddenly, just before dawn— the old nightmare: the afternoon of the earthquake, when he'd lost his first family. Over and over, as the theater crashed down, Papa begged him to save them, and over and over, Mummy screamed that he'd failed them. That *he* was the one who deserved to die.

Maybe, Venkat thought, the old self-loathing coating him like rubble from the collapse, *I do.*

He hadn't let himself think that way in years, but then, he hadn't had that dream in years, either, not since the parade of books had replaced it. Shame, raw and scorching, rekindled in his chest, threatening to suffocate him, the same way he'd watched his family suffocate.

You failed us, his mother's long-dead voice chanted, like a corrupted mantra. *You failed us, you failed us, you failed us.*

Someone banged at the door, jolting him out of the dark spiral. Asha. Finally.

Just like Nayan had taught him, Venkat locked the memories away in the invisible chest in his heart. "Took you long enough," he called, schooling his mouth into a pleasant smile.

But it wasn't Asha.

Instead Madhu stood there, wrapped in a cardinal-red sari, her thick white bun threaded through with strands of gold. The matching red bindi between her eyebrows dipped as she glared at him. "Lord Nayan wishes to see you before your appointments."

Venkat's smile sagged. "He does?"

"Jyotsna and Anand have delivered your breakfast to the archives." Tiny bells on her golden ankle bracelets tinkled as she moved. "Come; Lord Nayan awaits."

Nayan never sought Venkat out so early in the day. Was it Jai? Was it *Tanvi?*

Madhu didn't say a word as they hurried to the archives, which didn't help.

She barely waited to throw open the double doors, each with a pull in the shape of a praying nagini, before announcing, "I return to you the absent child, uprooted from his own fancies!"

"Ha, ha." Venkat entered after her, braced for Nayan to take

132

one look at his face and work out everything that had happened yesterday.

Nayan was seated at his desk, washed in the pale blue-green glow from the skylights. The ledger lay open before him, and scrolls tied with silk cords sat piled to one side. In his heavily embroidered cobalt sherwani and surrounded by the vast shelves of gilt-bound volumes and vials of previously mined dream fragments, he seemed aloof, the court historian engrossed in other times, other places.

The single incongruous object was the table set beside the desk. Two chairs ringed the table, and two golden plates bordered by emeralds and sapphires matched the covered platter gleaming tantalizingly at the center of the table.

Venkat's stomach rumbled at the aromas drifting out from beneath the domed cover, a pointed reminder that he never did pay his second visit to the buffet last night. But the thought of what he had to tell Nayan crushed his appetite.

"Good morning?" he tried as Madhu served the food.

"Thank you, Madhu." Nayan rose and pulled out both chairs. "Sit," he told Venkat.

Venkat sat.

Madhu poured them each a glass of jewel-fig water and stood back. "Enjoy."

The palace chefs had prepared Venkat's favorite foods: crispy masala dosa, pongal garnished with ghee, pillowy idli, and steaming sambar. Though obviously not like the Prithvi equivalent, it all looked and smelled fantastic, a rich combination of spices and hues and textures to rival any feast he'd extracted from a dream.

But Venkat didn't want to waste another minute. "I'm not really hungry."

He'd forgotten who he was talking to. Madhu cocked her head at him, the wrinkles deepening around her severe gold-brown stare. "Enjoy," she repeated.

"How often do we have the chance to break our fast together?" Nayan put in.

Never, Venkat said silently. That was exactly what worried him.

He tore off a piece of the masala dosa and dipped the bite into a dish of jewel-coconut chutney. It was tangy and savory, and the fresh idli was spongy enough to sleep on, but the entire meal might as well have been unseasoned khichdi. All he could taste was dread. Had Madhu seen? Did Nayan already know?

While Madhu hovered, eager to swoop in with more food, Nayan recounted his conversations from the night before. Venkat only half listened until he heard a familiar name. "Asha will need to be vigilant. Chintan's friends leave much to be desired." Nayan's baritone laugh rang through the chamber. "Would you believe that scoundrel Karan imagined he might ingratiate himself with me by alluding to his friendship with the prince?"

Madhu snorted. "I do believe it."

Venkat coughed hard and gulped the cool jewel-fig water. "What did you say to him?" he choked out between spasms.

Nayan's tone grew sharp. "I suggested he tread with care when trading on authority not his to claim."

Madhu smiled, and that simple but predatory twist of her lips left Venkat's palms damp with sweat. Anyone who thought she was a harmless old grandmother deserved what came to them. "Indeed."

He'd never had any illusions about what it took to hold down an office like Nayan's, with all the upstarts and opportunists and people blatantly out to wrest some power for themselves, but it was rare that he saw this side of it. Nayan really did keep him shielded. And Venkat didn't want to be on the receiving end of anything like that.

Which was why he had to speak up.

He shoveled more food into his mouth while doing his best not to think about Jai or Tanvi. With Madhu monitoring him, however, the last thing Venkat wanted to do was eat. It was hard enough not to fidget. Under the table, where no one could see, he tapped out a rhythm on his leg.

Nayan swallowed the last of his dosa and wiped his fingers on the napkin Madhu offered him. He turned an inquiring gaze on Venkat. "Would you like anything else?"

Venkat's cup clattered on the table in his haste to put it down. "No, I'm done."

"Good." Nayan waited for Madhu to clear their dishes away before continuing. "I trust you enjoyed yourself at the party last night?"

Venkat nodded cautiously.

"I am glad. I hear you were quite the hit among Asha's companions." Nayan smiled again, the proud smile that usually left Venkat glowing inside and eager to work even harder. Then it dimmed. "Until you left, that is. Rather early, as opposed to what we had discussed."

Venkat was almost relieved. Nayan knew. Of course he knew.

"I'm sorry," he blurted. "Last night I went to look for Jai. And he wasn't there." That wasn't true—Tanvi was the one who'd gone to look. His heart hammered in alarm; he never lied to Nayan.

But his mouth refused to form the right words. Refused even now to admit that Tanvi had run away.

"You are a son to me, Venkat," Nayan said, "and it pains me to see you suffering. Yet it must be said: everything has its cost, and no dream runner can endure indefinitely. You know this."

If only Venkat could be as calm as Nayan. "I do, but—"

But it still hurts. Venkat remembered the clever but cold boy Asha had rescued from neglectful parents, remembered how well Jai had taken to running dreams, and how each granted boon had invigorated him from the inside out. *We should have saved him.*

I should have.

Nayan and Madhu watched him steadily. "And you feel responsible," Nayan stated.

Venkat hung his head. "Yes."

"Let me show you something." Nayan unfolded from his chair. "Old mother, please leave us. I would speak to Venkat alone."

"You are being foolish." The exasperation in Madhu's pursed mouth was unmistakable. "He is not ready!"

Nayan's brows drew together. "Enough," he thundered. "I permit and even welcome your counsel. But do not forget who answers to whom."

Acrid resentment smoldered in Madhu's eyes. She made no attempt to look away, as if she meant for Nayan to catch it. Venkat had seen them clash before, but not like this. The air between them crackled with unseen lightning as Nayan held her stare.

At last Madhu lowered her head. "Understood."

"Good." Nayan dismissed her with a wave. "Then go about your affairs, and leave us to ours."

Madhu joined her palms before her averted gaze. Without another word, she turned and stalked from the archives.

Venkat could still feel the tension, leaden and oppressive. "What was that?"

Nayan beckoned for Venkat to follow him into the lift. "Madhu has her own conception of how things should be run, and I have mine. It occasionally leads to friction, but I much prefer that to the useless fawning of a sycophant."

Once they were in the workshop, Nayan stopped before a finely wrought but easily missed gemstone tiger nestled amidst one of the murals. Nothing about it suggested the animal was more than a pricey decoration. Only when Nayan applied a matching key to the tiger's amber eye would the treasury reveal itself.

"What am I not ready for?" Venkat asked, coming up beside him.

"I will show you." Nayan produced the key, which featured a roaring tiger in midair, and touched it to the amber. The mural melted away, unveiling a nondescript recess in the wall barely wide enough to admit two people.

Together, they stepped into the now-visible treasury. Nayan pressed a spot on the wall, one Venkat had never noticed before, and something like a stacked cube organizer appeared. It reminded him of the shoe storage compartments he'd seen in the lobbies of mandirs on Prithvi. Only instead of shoes, each cubbyhole was filled with strange objects—a deflated soccer ball, a video game console, a chapter book, a plush bunny, a golden charm bracelet.

Nayan pulled one out. "Surely," he said, his voice wry, "you do not need me to tell you what this is."

"No," Venkat agreed, his throat closing, and bent to examine the original tricycle Jai had brought with him and had always been striving to get back to through boons.

The yellow frame was dinged and scuffed, chewed-up gum was stuck to one of the tires, and something had scored a rip in the seat. It was what his grandmother would have called well loved.

In contrast, the tricycle he'd seen Jai purchase with his boon had been perfect. Immaculate and unmarked, something that had been idealized in nostalgia so many times that it turned into its own story.

"Why didn't you give it back to him?" Venkat demanded. At the very least, Jai could have had his beloved tricycle again.

Venkat should have pushed for the details long before now. He should have asked where Nayan was storing the runners' precious objects. He should have insisted on accompanying Jai back to Prithvi. He'd been a coward, and this was the result.

"Oh, I offered it," Nayan said. "He rebuffed me."

"What do you mean?"

Though Nayan spoke kindly, he couldn't disguise his pity. "He preferred the comfort of the illusion."

Venkat remembered how lovingly Jai had re-created the tricycle, the stand-in for the mortal life he'd given up. The comfort of the illusion—when the pleasure of pursuing the truth, over and over again, was better than the actual truth. An addiction.

The insatiable drive to earn boons. Nayan and Venkat had made that happen.

"Belief is a powerful force, my son. It can be a delusion to hide behind, or it can serve as the solder that holds one's purpose together. A dream is only as strong as the dreamer's belief in it. Break out of that belief, and the dream becomes a tool. Or, to view it from a different angle, we all spin the story we wish to be true. Remove that belief, and . . ."

Venkat glanced from the tricycle, now just a hunk of garbage, to the bracelet shining softly in its compartment. He'd messed up with Jai. And with his family, too. Clearly, he didn't know how to help anyone.

"Venkat," Nayan murmured, "where is Tanvi? It was too late for Jai, but we may yet save her. I know she was attempting to sell her wares to the nobles."

Of course he'd heard. Why had Venkat expected anything else?

But he had a second chance with Tanvi, and he'd do whatever it took to keep her safe.

"That was my fault," he lied. "I made her think she was supposed to help Asha and me. Once we got that sorted out, I sent her to do her harvesting."

A pernicious scum coated his tongue and his heart. Before today, he'd never lied to Nayan, and now he'd done it twice in the past half hour. It felt disgusting. But so did all of this.

His chest aching, he waited for Nayan to condemn him. To see through the deceit he couldn't believe had just left his mouth.

Nayan nodded. "It is a strange time." He replaced the tricycle in its cubbyhole. "Shall we get to work, then?"

Tanvi was being hugged. Hugged so tight she couldn't really breathe. Nitya's hair—her sister's hair, her identical twin's hair—smashed against her cheek. When she tensed, Nitya squeezed tighter, like Tanvi might disappear if she let go even a little.

Daisies, Tanvi thought randomly. Those daisies in the rangoli. She couldn't say how, but she knew Nitya had drawn them.

Then Nitya jerked away, almost shoving Tanvi in the process. In two seconds, she'd gone from wide-eyed amazement to flat-out rage. Her mouth had contorted into something frightening. Her hand hung suspended in the air, inches from slapping Tanvi across the face.

Tanvi's heart tumbled in her chest, and her own hands shook. She would give anything for this to be a dream, one she could sell off and forget about.

You're afraid, her pulse thrummed, *she's going to tell you to go away again.*

Nitya stood framed in the doorway for another second, wheezing like she might pass out, then stormed into the house. "Well, come in!" she bit out over her shoulder.

That fury. Tanvi had felt like that once herself. The feeling bubbled up now—a vivid, undeniable memory, though she couldn't remember anything else. Her head was so patchy. She hated this, all of it.

Turn around, she ordered her legs.

They must not have been listening, because they kept pace with Nitya, who kicked off her shoes and left them in the closet. Old habit taking over, Tanvi did the same.

All through the foyer and into the family room, scraps of recall attacked her, spiky and unforgiving. She *knew* that second-floor cathedral ceiling, knew she'd stood beneath it, danced beneath it, thrown tantrums beneath it. So many flashes in time haunting her.

Portraits on the walls screamed for her attention. Tanvi stared at the carpet instead.

Except it was gone. Hardwood floor had replaced the soft beige surface her feet had padded over, back and forth, back and forth. Somehow she knew she'd gotten in trouble for spilling a drink— grape juice?—that had left a stain. But the details stayed out of reach.

Nitya lingered by the couch, like she was waiting for Tanvi to sit first. At least the couch was the same, cream colored and overstuffed. But her body remembered nestling into the cushions to watch movies or get lost in a book, and she couldn't do it. She plopped down where she was on the floor instead.

Sister. Tanvi rolled the word around in her mouth like a sour piece of candy. *Twin. My twin.*

Nitya perched on the recliner across from her. Without taking her gaze from Tanvi, she smoothed out her shiny charcoal skirt.

It was petty, but Tanvi felt like she'd scored a point. Too bad she didn't know what the game was.

The ghost version of the room floated in her head, at odds with the reality in front of her. She shifted, hunting for a comfortable position that would let her scope out the furniture. Hadn't there been two recliners before, not one?

Nitya shot up from the recliner. "Don't you dare leave!" she cried.

The terror in that command hit Tanvi harder than Nitya's hand ever could have. She stared at her sister's desperate face. "I wasn't going to!"

Nitya dropped down beside Tanvi and grabbed her wrists roughly enough to hurt. She tried to wriggle away, but Nitya only dug her fingers in.

This was too much, too weird. Her sister should still look the way she did the last time Tanvi had seen her, baby fat clinging to her cheeks, the underlying bones hidden, not angular like this stranger's. Her black hair should only hit her chin, not hang almost to her waist. Her careful eyeliner and plum lipstick turned her into a sleeker version of Tanvi. Plus, her suspicious glare, like Tanvi was an intruder, was all wrong.

Nitya's eyes went wide again. Her words came through gritted teeth. "You're alive. *How?*"

Tanvi didn't know what to say. She didn't remember leaving this house. All she knew was her life in Nagalok.

"Did someone kidnap you?" Nitya's voice got shriller and shriller with each word. "Did they hurt you? How did you get away?"

The rapid-fire questions made Tanvi want to shout back. "Stop it!" she forced out. She still couldn't get enough leverage to pry Nitya's fingers loose. "Nobody kidnapped me. I don't think."

This house, this living room, felt like a movie set. She knew it so well, except she didn't. Those leaf-patterned window sheers in the kitchen hadn't been there. And the velvet toran with the silver bells hanging over the entrance to the living room—it had been sky blue, not chocolate brown. Tanvi was sure of it. It must have changed color from years of sunlight streaming in through the bay windows, years she hadn't been here. Even the silver mandir on the side table seemed smaller than she remembered.

Nitya pressed so hard she was actually cutting off the circulation in Tanvi's wrists. "You don't *think*? Where were you?"

"Let go of me!"

"No." Nitya's voice wobbled. "How are you even here? How are you not *dead*?"

"You thought I was dead?" Tanvi laughed, though none of this was funny. "I was in Bhogavati."

Nitya gawked at Tanvi like she'd never heard anything so stupid. "Of course we did!" she snapped. "You've been missing for *seven years*. Seven. *Years*."

"I wasn't missing. I told you, I was in Bhogavati."

"Is that some sort of cult?"

"You don't know what Bhogavati is?" Now Tanvi was the one gawking. "The capital city of Nagalok?"

"Nagalok?" Nitya scoffed. "That's just a story."

Just a story. Something about Nitya's tone, maybe how derisive it was, made the old pain of that day rush back in one violent surge.

"You laughed at me!" Tanvi yelled. "All of you!"

Nitya's grip finally slackened. "What are you talking about?"

"Our birthday party." Tanvi spat it at Nitya, the girl who shared her face, the girl who'd once been her best friend and biggest rival. Right then, she resented Nitya for that. For not being the sister she should have been. For chasing Tanvi off. "You know, when we turned ten."

She braced herself for Nitya to say she was making it up.

But Nitya didn't. "Mom and Dad called the cops when you never came back. The whole neighborhood was out looking for you!"

"*You* told everyone I wet the bed!" Reliving the humiliation felt like a scab being torn off too soon. It hurt so much. Nitya should be feeling the wound, too, Tanvi decided, how it bled and stung.

"*That's* why you disappeared." Nitya laughed bitterly. "You're kidding. You ran away because I was mean to you at a party?!"

"It was our *birthday* party!" Tanvi couldn't access the details, but it didn't matter. "And you were *always* mean to me! Always ganging up on me with everybody."

The pain had been branded into her. The betrayal. The knowledge she'd always, always be on the outside of everything. Even her sister, her twin, didn't care about protecting her.

She scowled. That awful feeling was all the memory she needed.

145

"Tanvi," Nitya said, picking at the hem of her top, "you *left* us." Tears shimmered in her eyes. "We thought you were dead! For seven years. Do you understand that?"

I'm not, though, Tanvi almost said, before a small blue head lifted slightly from her wrist, green-gold eyes alert. It was a wonder Nitya hadn't gotten bitten.

The room went wavy. Asha. Hadn't . . . hadn't Asha said Nitya's name to Sameer? Hadn't she brought Tanvi to his house?

That meant she'd known whose house this was, too.

Since Tanvi couldn't tear into Asha with Nitya looking on, she channeled all her wrath into her glare.

Nitya must have thought the glare was meant for her, because she rushed to say, "Don't look at me like that! Tanvi, we thought you *died*. Mom said you needed a little time to yourself, but when you didn't come back for an hour, we all went to look for you. . . ."

She explained how they'd searched and searched, and eventually the guests had left, but Nitya and Mom and Dad kept searching. No matter where they tried, no matter how many times they called Tanvi's name, no one answered.

The neighbors reported having briefly seen Tanvi outside, and no one had had any leads after that. The cops hadn't been any help, claiming she'd show up on her own. Of course, she never did.

"Do you know what it was like, wondering every day if you'd come home?" Nitya visibly vibrated with outrage. Her tears spilled over, and Tanvi wished she didn't have to see them or listen to any of this. "To wait for the day someone found your body? I couldn't sleep, Tanvi. I kept thinking I should have done something differently.

146

That it was my fault you ran off."

It was, Tanvi thought, but doubt chewed at her. She'd never stopped to think about how her parents, her sister, would have felt when she vanished. What it would have been like for them to imagine she was dead.

Or if she had, she'd forgotten after the initiation. She'd forgotten everything except this kernel of bitterness at the center of her heart. And the link to her sister, the thing that had made her dream.

Why? Why did Nitya mean anything to her?

"And now you just show up on the doorstep like nothing ever happened?" Nitya asked abruptly. "Why now? I mean, you let us believe you were dead."

Tanvi started to answer, but Nitya didn't let her. "I don't know you anymore. The Tanvi I knew never would have let us suffer like that. Do you know we had a *cremation* for you?"

"I was in Nagalok!" Tanvi protested. "How was I supposed to know?"

Nitya watched while she stood and picked up a copper giraffe figurine from the glass-topped coffee table. Recognition jolted through the nerves in Tanvi's arm, and she set the giraffe back down. Her hand *knew* the feel of it, like she'd picked it up a thousand times before.

She tore around the room, studying the framed pictures she'd avoided before. Mom, Dad, Nitya, and her, all posed in Indian clothes against a blue background. There were a couple of portraits like that.

Then they changed, only three faces where there had been four.

And finally Nitya alone: Nitya at tennis camp, Nitya graduating middle school, Nitya in a group with friends. Tanvi recognized some of them, but there were new people, too. The timeline of snapshots took her from the past where she'd once belonged to the present, where she might as well be a phantom.

This had been her family. She knew that, but the images of the four of them together refused to gel into any kind of memory. Almost as if it was someone else's life, and she was just peeking in.

Maybe, her heart accused, she didn't know how to be human. Maybe she never had.

"How could you leave like that?" Nitya demanded. She'd been trailing Tanvi the whole time.

"I already told you," Tanvi said, trying not to let her crabbiness show. There were other pictures she still had to look at, prints of roses and mushrooms in forests and carnival rides. One had a blue ribbon attached: *First Place*.

Nitya had been holding a camera when she'd answered the door. "Did you take these pictures?" Tanvi asked.

But Nitya wasn't listening. "I'm honestly not even sure this isn't a dream," she said. "Is it?"

Dreams. Tanvi didn't miss the irony. This entire trip felt like a dream.

"You know what I think?" Nitya didn't wait for Tanvi to reply. "I think you ran away, and something bad happened to you, and the only way you can cope is by making up a story about nagas."

Guilt, fuzzy and strange, spread over Tanvi. Nitya expected something from her—she could tell that much—but whatever it was, she doubted she could give it. Anyway, *she* was supposed to be the one getting answers.

She flashed back to the rangoli on the driveway. To her bracelet. "Daisies," she blurted.

"What?" Nitya's expression was one huge question mark. "What about them?"

"The daisies," Tanvi tried again. "On the driveway." But Nitya only looked more confused.

Tanvi had made a mistake coming here. There was nothing for her in this house, no solutions to her problem, no matter what her dreams had to say about it.

This wasn't her world. It never would be. If anything, it would be better for this family if they didn't know she'd come back. "You're right, it is a dream. Just forget you ever saw me."

Mom, she thought, her stupid heart pinching. *Dad.* She turned to her sister. *Nitya. I'm sorry.*

Then she headed for the door.

Nitya was faster. She stepped directly into Tanvi's path. "Where are you going?"

"Leaving, obviously." Tanvi glanced past her, but when Nitya wouldn't move, she faced her sister head-on.

All Nitya's coldness had thawed, and she looked like a scared kid. Not the person who always did everything right or even the one who had been so frosty just a minute ago. "You can't," she pleaded, and suddenly Tanvi's hands were in hers so tightly that bones were being crushed again. "You can't. I don't care if this isn't real."

"It's not," Tanvi said. "I told you, it's just a dream." Except the missing recliner still bothered her. "Where're Mom and Dad, anyway?"

Nitya looked ill. "You don't know, do you?"

Alarm bells clanged in Tanvi's mind. *Don't ask, don't ask, don'tdon'tdon't.* "Know what?"

"Dad." Nitya, who had been gaping at her ever since she'd gotten here, couldn't meet her eyes. "After you . . . left, Dad— Well, he couldn't handle it. Mom and he kept fighting all the time, and then they split up."

Tanvi felt dizzy. The soles of her feet tingled like she was standing on a cliff.

"They got a divorce. Dad moved back to Winnipeg."

Things Tanvi shouldn't know how to feel overwhelmed her now, an endless ocean of feeling. It had been so long since she'd had to deal with human emotion and contradictions, and there was nothing to hold on to as the riptide pulled her into its depths.

She was going under.

"Ow!" Nitya yelped. "Your bangle bit me!"

Tanvi took advantage of Nitya's shock to pull away, but like before, her traitorous feet stayed right where they were. She couldn't make her mouth say anything, either.

The world had moved on—her family had moved on—and she didn't know what to do with that.

"Lazy," Nitya asked, her words hushed, "what happened to you?"

Auntie Busy and Auntie Lazy. The reference to their childhood skit dissolved a lump deep within Tanvi. They'd been a team.

Sisters and adventurers. The specifics were a blur, but she *felt* them.

Auntie Clover and Auntie Daisy.

The secret names carved themselves into her chest. For no reason, her mouth kicked into high gear. "Do you—do you even still have the bracelet?"

"What bracelet? If this is part of your story, that's fine. It's okay that you have a story. Just don't go," Nitya begged. "Please. Please don't go. Not again."

Stop, Tanvi ordered her throat, her tongue, her lips. "The charm bracelet Dad gave you. With the daisy charm."

Where was this coming from? Of course the bracelet wasn't here. Tanvi hadn't bought it yet.

Her temples throbbed, and her vision blinked in and out. Like a lamp being switched off and back on—*click, click.* Her thoughts turned to static, fading around the only one that counted: the bracelet.

Nitya blinked a few times, then smiled nervously. "Oh! The one from when we were kids? Gosh, I don't know. Dad was supposed to fix it, I think, but then you disappeared, and everything turned upside down."

An entire universe yawned open between the two of them. Nitya dwindled into the background, taking the hallway with her, while the bracelet towered larger and larger in Tanvi's vision. It was so gold, so bright. Seven charms, all for Tanvi. All for her.

Nitya could say what she wanted about it. Tanvi knew better. She reached past Nitya for the doorknob.

"If you like bracelets so much," Nitya babbled, "I'll find you another one. I promise. All the charms you want." She glanced at the hallway clock. "Crap, my ride will be here any minute. You know what? I'll tell her I'm too sick for school. Please just stay."

Asha's tongue flicked in warning, but Tanvi didn't care. The bracelet was waiting.

Ignoring Nitya calling her name, Tanvi grabbed her shoes and left.

PART TWO

*O*nce, long ago, so long that the nagaraja and his brothers themselves might startle at the sheer expanse of unspooled time, there lived a nagini maiden. Her slithering hips were swift, her cobra scales shining, her amaranthine lips rich and round as any swollen jewel-currant. When she combed the fragrant waves of her tresses, they gleamed black and liquid like hematite, an invitation to bury one's fingers in their depths.

She had many sisters, this maiden, and while they were content first to frolic and then to seek lovers among their people, her own heart grew restive. It lies in the blood of a naga to care for precious metals, yet even in that the maiden felt alone: the cyclical waxing and waning of Lord Chandra in the sky above captivated her far more than all the gold and silver in all the wondrous palaces of Nagalok. It was the silver of the night, not the earth, that crooned to her, the song of the moon on the surf, and she often fancied she was a whispered spell of the star-speckled heavens mistakenly fallen into a serpentine body.

The maiden was but a hatchling when she first traveled to the beach with her family, and while the others made crowns of shells and gleefully splashed one another, she sat on the shore, the sand crunching beneath her coils, entranced by the play of the sun's light on the surface. It seemed almost to open a path of gemstones the color of crystallized honey into the horizon, a path that promised fiery adventure for the brazen. For her sisters, perhaps.

But that was not a path for her.

That evening, while her family feasted, the maiden slipped out to the sea and looked on as the moon ascended into the sky. His silvery radiance danced down, and where it met the water, the beams cracked into countless silver-white shards.

There. That was it, the path she sought, a trail of subtle moonstone rather than conspicuous topaz. She traced the jeweled path with her gaze as a veil of clouds drew across Lord Chandra's half-full visage. The path wavered, then vanished, leaving behind only the dark waters.

Not yet, *murmured the waves.*

The maiden returned home to Bhogavati with her family, the experience buried deep in the most secret parts of her heart, where fairy tales unwound into the stuff of dreams, and dreams transmuted into mystical enchantments. Where hope was born.

Years rolled by, and between bouts of the refined life expected of her at court, the maiden strolled the night-cloaked beach. Like infinitesimal galaxies in the shadowed sand, seashells glowed at her tail, at her toes, but while the path occasionally appeared, it dissolved just as quickly. She glimpsed the moon's face, curious yet remote, before it retreated behind its veil once more.

Not yet, *murmured the waves, again and again until it became a* chorus.

At last, when the maiden was in the full bloom of womanhood, the path appeared once more. This time, no clouds marred the sky. Moonstones blended into a silver ribbon, reflecting the plump moon's refulgence. Around him, his bevy of stellar wives sparkled with silvery flame.

It was so beautiful the maiden sobbed.

Now, *said the waves.*

She dove into them and swam more swiftly than she ever had toward her love and her home in the heavens.

Yet no matter how far she swam, the path eluded her. Lord Chandra cast her a glance—who was this strange maiden, so ardent and steadfast in her devotion?

The maiden knew she had but this one chance to woo her beloved, and so, though the horizon grew no closer, though fatigue spread like malaise through her body, she swam toward the luminous path. "I am coming!" she cried.

But his interest soured to indifference, for the maiden was no star, and the path dispersed even as she undulated toward it. The heavens, too, began to brighten as she watched, her eyes stinging with both tide and tears.

"No!" she begged, forcing herself onward. "Wait a moment, and I will be with you."

Lord Chandra, however, did not care to wait. Turning his attention from her, he forsook her to the sea.

Then Lord Surya rode forth in his chariot, his bold rays scattering the last lingering notes of the night. Gone was the delicate and dreamlike moonstone path. Gone, too, was the maiden's hope.

Nothing remained but the uncaring surf.

Its waves washed the maiden's unresisting body ashore. There, on the glimmering sand outside Bhogavati, she wept. Her blood might have turned to brine, for the sorrow that trickled from her eyes found no end.

The tears pooled and pooled until they formed a lake, and it soon drew to it all the tears of all the lost lovers in all the worlds. Eventually, sunlight itself could not resist the pull, and where it touched the surface, it splintered into innumerable golden gemstones.

Sometime later, the moon, too, looked down upon the lake, curious to see what had so fully absorbed even his celestial counterpart. In that instant, his own radiance was ensnared.

Every night since, the moonlit path appears without fail.

It is rumored that any who venture onto its silvery stream risk being swept away by Lord Chandra, perhaps for rapture, or perhaps for revenge, while those who keep to the grief-suffused shore will learn the song of their own lonely hearts.

—FROM *THE NAGA PURANA:
A FLORILEGIUM OF FOLKTALES,*
PROPERTY OF THE OFFICIAL ROYAL
LIBRARY AT BHOGAVATI

16

Tanvi balled herself up in the back of the cramped rideshare car. Her body ached for her bracelet. Next to her, Asha fiddled with her phone.

As they pulled away from the curb, the driver turned and smiled. "Beautiful morning, isn't it?"

I have a twin sister, Tanvi thought in reply, *and a mom and a dad, and now they know I'm alive, and I just want to turn my brain off, please and thank you.*

One glare from Asha, and the driver shut right up. Tanvi was pretty sure she glimpsed fangs and slit pupils. The driver must have, too; he blanched and nailed his gaze to the road.

Tanvi squeezed her own eyes shut and retreated into the haven of the bracelet. Once she got home, she'd never have to think about today again.

Golden warmth enveloped her, erasing everything else. The frenzied knocking in her chest faded. She could already feel the occupied dreamstones in her cabinet, ripe for trading in.

Asha elbowed her. "You are missing the view."

Tanvi reflexively opened her eyes just enough to take in the concrete-and-glass buildings and sports team logos flying past. A blue sign announced they were heading east on Interstate 76—*the Schuylkill*, her jerk of a mind noted—into Center City.

She knew this view. She'd seen it more times than she could count, driving downtown from the house with the red door. Nitya's house.

The image of her sister's distraught face—*Tanvi's* face—punched through the increasingly raggedy gilt cocoon. *We thought you died*, it accused.

"You knew whose house that was, didn't you?" she challenged.

Asha bit her lip, then stroked two fingertips over the back of Tanvi's hand. "Perhaps I did."

Even that slight touch made Tanvi's sensitized skin scream. She ripped her hand away. "Is this a joke to you? You *knew*, and you still let me go there. Do you even get how awful that is?"

Asha recoiled, her irises sparking. She shifted into a cobra and slithered under the driver's seat.

Tanvi peeked up front, but luckily, the driver didn't dare even glance at the rearview mirror. "What are you doing? He could've seen you!"

Asha hissed, so faint that only Tanvi could hear it, and her forked tongue darted in and out from beneath the seat.

"Be mad, then. What do I care?" Tanvi leaned her too-heavy head against the window and closed her scratchy eyes. She just wanted to go home. Home to her room in the dream runners' quarters, where she could sleep and sleep and never dream again.

Tanvi must have dozed off, because the next thing she knew, Asha, in human form again, was helping her out of the car. Asha deposited a gold coin on the empty seat. "Come, Tanvi. We have arrived."

The relief Tanvi felt at not having dreamed vaporized when she looked up. Instead of Penn's Landing, what had to be an American high school loomed ahead, one big, ugly hunk of brick and concrete.

Oh, Asha was so dead. Tanvi couldn't believe her nerve. "What happened to taking us back?"

"It will be but a few minutes," Asha promised, tapping at her phone, "and then we will leave. You have my word."

Tanvi toed a crack in the sidewalk. No one else was around, but she couldn't shake the feeling of being watched. All this being out in the daytime was unnatural. Wrong. "You keep saying that. Can't you see your little boyfriend without me?"

"Soon I will be immersed in wedding preparations and all the duties that follow," Asha told her phone before tucking it in her pocket. "I would enjoy a chance to say good-bye before being consigned to my royal cage, lovely as it may be."

Tanvi had expected some glib nonanswer, not this. She turned to look at Asha.

It still hurt to do that, but she made herself examine the sleek contours of Asha's cheeks and her perfectly smooth skin. All effortless in a way even the best makeup artist could only aspire to. Her lush ponytail, lustrous as a strand of black pearls, could have been cut from the night sky.

She might have long legs and blunt teeth right now. She might be wearing a cute dress. But Asha could never really pass for a teen girl, not to anyone bothering to pay attention. She was an other-worldly princess whose rhinestone flower clips sat on her head as regally as any crown, and her destiny, one she hadn't asked for, was calling.

It was probably just the guilt from Nitya's accusation clinging to her like dream residue, but Tanvi gave in. "Fine," she said. "Let's get this over with."

"Did you pack your lozenges? The doors are locked to outsiders."

"What kind of runner do you think I am?" Tanvi checked again for any prying eyes, then downed a lozenge from her pouch. "Aren't you going to glamour me?"

"I did not think to bring my vermilion." The barest trace of embarrassment showed on Asha's face before she perked up again. "I suppose we will simply have to chance it. How fun!"

"For you, maybe," Tanvi muttered. Side by side, they slipped into the building.

Inside, they passed an awards display case and electronic signs announcing the day's agenda and made a right turn into a corridor full of army-green lockers. The air smelled like harsh cleaners, and the fluorescent lighting sent forks of pain through Tanvi's eyeballs.

Worse, the knowledge of her missing memories wouldn't leave her alone. It was her brain trying to fill in the gaps and failing no matter how many times she ordered it to stop.

You left us. The Tanvi I knew never would have let us suffer like that.

The bell rang, spooking her, and students poured out of classrooms. A boy with fluffy curls and a violin case gestured wildly to a girl in a yellow headband.

Tanvi felt like she'd swallowed a pinecone. The girl with the headband. The one who'd first confused Tanvi for Nitya that night and put this whole horrible thing in motion.

Just a couple of hours ago, Tanvi had wanted nothing more than to find that girl and ask about the mix-up. Now she only wanted to flee.

That girl being here meant *Nitya* was here. Hadn't Sameer said something about going to school with her?

If only Tanvi had a lozenge that would let her melt through the floor.

"Hey, Nitya," the boy said to her. "Hitesh was looking for you earlier. You should text him."

Tanvi strained, her mind blinking on and off again, but couldn't come up with anything better than, "Uh, thanks."

Asha struck a pose. "Hello! I am Asha, Nitya's cousin."

The boy looked too awed to answer, but the girl with the headband introduced herself as Mai. Meanwhile, other people were crowding around them: friends of Nitya's, from how they kept greeting Tanvi.

Had Asha completely lost it? Coming here was bad enough, but impersonating Nitya and her cousin was begging for trouble. Not that Asha cared. She'd known this was Nitya's school, and she'd brought Tanvi here, anyway.

It felt like a bad dream—except she couldn't just cram it into a vial.

"Can't wait to see your portfolio today," Mai said. "I'm so glad I don't have to share mine until next week."

Tanvi made a strangled sound.

Mai laughed. "Oh, you're always too hard on yourself. Your photography is amazing, and you know it."

Another bell rang. "We're going to be late!" the boy said.

"I thought going to an arts school was supposed to mean less work," someone else complained.

"Not in Collins's class . . ."

"Well, we can't all be good at everything like Nitya," Mai teased.

Wishing she could stuff Asha inside one of the lockers, Tanvi forced a smile. Nitya must have arrived by now, too. The last thing Tanvi needed was for everyone to see them together.

She had to get out of here.

Asha, of course, was too busy telling some joke to catch Tanvi's murderous stare.

A few of the students, including Mai, herded Tanvi and Asha into a classroom with charts of the periodic table on the cinderblock walls. Before Tanvi knew what was happening, she was squashed into a chair with an attached desk.

It suddenly hit her that if things had been different, this might have been her school, too. Those kids in the hall, her friends. The sense of being in a dream heightened, growing even more muddled and surreal.

Looking positively ecstatic, Asha shimmied into the desk right by her. "There are at least two elements mortals have not yet discovered deep within Prithvi's crust," she confided. "We nagas have known about them since the beginning. Shall I inform the teacher?"

Tanvi's vision cleared. She'd had it all backward. Asha was the one dreaming. A stupid, completely selfish daydream about surprising a human boy at school. "Are you—"

"Hey, where's your stuff?" Mai asked. "Do you need to borrow a pen?"

Belatedly, Tanvi realized everyone else had notebooks and pens and tablets. She shrugged. "I forgot?"

Mai gave her a funny look as Sameer walked into the room. He did a triple take. "Asha?"

Asha practically sparkled at him, her smile was so bright, and pointed to the neighboring desk. "Sameer! Sit with me."

On her other side, Tanvi almost screamed. Any second now, he'd catch on that she wasn't Nitya. What was Asha *thinking*?

Maybe Tanvi should just make a break for it. Asha could fend for herself.

Sameer, who looked like he didn't know whether to be happy or freaked out, sat down and leaned over. "I told you *not* to come here!" he said under his breath.

A pale man in glasses tapped the whiteboard at the front of the room. "I hope you all studied hard for today's exam. It's a full third of your grade for the semester, and no, I will not be grading on a curve, so don't bother asking." Ignoring the grumbles, he started checking off roll call.

He hadn't gotten three names in when Tanvi glimpsed Nitya's shocked face staring at her through the window in the door. *Great.*

Nitya ducked out of sight, but not before someone muttered, "Did you see that?"

Sameer definitely had. He glanced suspiciously from Tanvi to the door, and she could see the wheels turning. He texted something from beneath his desk.

"Asha!" she hissed. *"We have to go."*

Asha winked at her, then stood. "Good morning, Mr. Collins," she sang out, sashaying to the front of the room. "As a token of my gratitude to you for permitting me to visit your class today, I wish to tell you a story."

Tanvi gaped at her. So did Sameer. And the rest of the class.

Mr. Collins raised his eyebrows. "Who are you, exactly?"

"Asha, Nitya's cousin from India."

"Nitya," Mr. Collins said, "I didn't receive any notice from the office about you bringing a guest today. Did you forget we have an exam?"

Nitya might have had the perfect response, but the best Tanvi could manage was a hesitant "No?"

"Oh, but I am certain you will enjoy this, sir," said Asha. "Back home, my family is celebrated far and wide for our riveting narratives." She patted the gold cobra-shaped bajuband on her upper arm. "I won this for my performance in a recent competition. And now to regale you with the prizewinning story, an epic tale of hope and the struggle for survival."

"Uh-huh. I don't suppose it's related to this?" Mr. Collins pointed to the whiteboard, where he'd written, *For extra credit: What do PVC, Kevlar, and Teflon all have in common?*

"There was a man." Asha surveyed the entire classroom, drawing out the suspense. Her voice dropped in pitch. "And there was a tiger."

"Here for it!" someone behind Tanvi exclaimed. "I hope he gets eaten."

Mr. Collins crossed his arms. "*I'm* still waiting to hear how this relates to synthetic polymers. Or even basic chemistry."

"Go," Asha urged Tanvi, who leaped up, along with Sameer.

He threw his backpack over his shoulders. "Uh, family emergency!"

That's one word for it, Tanvi thought. Before Mr. Collins could argue, she flung open the door.

"There was a tiger," Asha finished with a wily grin. She glided out after them.

"This way," Sameer said, leading Tanvi and Asha down the hall and through a set of heavy doors to a deserted quad outside. Someone had lost a red scarf on the pavement. Tanvi squinted; the color was jarring against the mass of gray clouds moving in.

Sameer and Asha settled at one of the tables, while Tanvi leaned back against a potted tree. The feeling of being in a nightmare had returned, and with it the sense of being spied on. "Asha," she said, trying not to yell, "we really need to go."

"You're not Nitya." Sameer frowned at her. "I know, because she texted me to meet her out here. Which means—"

Nitya burst into the courtyard. "Sameer, I said the *east* quad." A cool mask had replaced her tornado of emotions from earlier, and when she addressed Tanvi, her voice was level, with just a hint of impatience. "Why didn't you tell me you were coming here?"

"*You* didn't tell me your sister's *alive*," Sameer said, sounding like he couldn't believe the words coming out of his mouth.

Nitya scowled. "I didn't even know until two hours ago!"

The guilt bulldozed Tanvi all over again. She would give anything to forget this.

"Dude, what's going on?" a boy with Vietnamese features interrupted. "I got your texts. Right before Ms. Kovner gave me a demerit and confiscated my phone."

"See for yourself." Sameer motioned from Nitya to Tanvi.

The boy glanced between them, then whistled. "*Tanvi?* I thought you were dead."

"Binh." Sameer sighed. "Come on, man."

The other boy in Sameer's dream. Tanvi remembered now. She shuddered.

"I can't get over this," Binh said. "Where were you?"

Sidestepping the question, Tanvi pointed to Asha. "*She* made me come here." Asha waved. "We're supposed to be back in Nagalok already, but she just had to see you first, Sameer."

Nitya advanced on Asha. "Who *are* you? And what are you doing with my sister?"

"She's the one who took me to Nagalok," Tanvi said. An impression pierced the memory static in her mind, and her hands started trembling. A cake. *Their* cake.

"Wait, you kidnapped Tanvi?" Nitya repeated. Each word was as cold as an icicle. "What's wrong with you?"

"Yet we are all here together, are we not?" Asha said proudly. "Now you may talk to each other as sisters do. Go on."

Both Tanvi and Nitya shot her *are you kidding* looks.

"Stop it, Asha," Sameer said. "This is so messed up." His lip had curled in disgust. "How could you do this? And then act like you didn't know?"

"But am I not amending that now?" Asha protested. Her chin quivered.

Nitya gave her a naga-level dark glare. "Do you even get what you did? You destroyed our family!"

No one spoke. Sameer avoided Asha's stricken eyes, and when she tried to take his hand, he yanked it out of reach.

"Where did she take you, Tanvi?" Nitya pressed. "Tell me the truth."

"I told you. Nagalok," Tanvi said.

Nitya spoke gently, almost patronizingly. "Nagalok's not real."

"Yes, it is."

They stared at each other, Tanvi and the twin she shouldn't have, and her heart thumped hard against her ribs. None of this should be happening. None of it.

"I see," said Asha, her shoulders slumped. "Tanvi, let us depart."

As she pushed away from the table, something screeched above them, loud enough that Tanvi plugged her ears.

A flock of at least fifty gold-feathered eagles circled overhead, blinding against the gray-white sky. They were huge, much bigger than any birds on Prithvi had a right to be.

"What the hell?" Sameer and Binh demanded in unison.

The giant eagles keened again and dipped until Tanvi could see the malice in their cunning stares.

No ordinary eagles looked like that. They were garudas.

"We need to get out of here!" she shouted.

Thunder roared across the sky, and the clouds abruptly opened up, dumping their water in huge sheets and dropping visibility to almost nil. A garudi broke through the rain to dive-bomb the spot where Asha stood before soaring back up to her comrades. Her wings were the shade of pomegranates, like the scarf on the ground.

"Tanvi!" Asha cried.

Tanvi ran toward the sound of Asha's voice.

More garudas swooped down, isolating the two of them from the others. Tanvi heard Nitya scream, but there was nothing she could do.

"Princess!" a severe voice called. "Runner! To me, now!"

Madhu appeared behind Asha. She wore lean human legs, her fangs jutted dagger sharp from her mouth, and the rage radiating from her threatened to sear holes in the garudas' plumage. Her hand clamped down on Asha's shoulder. "We must leave *now*."

Tanvi barely had time to blink before Madhu seized her arm and brushed a pendant of interlocking snakes.

The blue-green of the water dimension appeared around the

three of them, forming a translucent veil. Keening, a few of the garu-das hurled themselves against the barrier, but they ricocheted off.

"Tanvi!" Nitya pleaded, already leagues away. "Don't go!"

Tanvi pretended not to hear.

As Madhu pulled them down, Tanvi's body yielded to the rhythm of the waves. She didn't even mind how intense the blues and greens were this time.

Soon she'd be home, back to the way things should be.

17

Yet another messenger, his satin dupatta billowing out around him, approached the entrance to the archives, where Venkat had been stationed. Venkat suppressed a groan.

"I am told Lord Nayan has been detained by urgent matters at present," the messenger said, making no effort to conceal his own pique, "and my liege would never deem to impose during such inopportune circumstances. Nevertheless, as time *is* at a premium, she bade me inquire if he intends to reopen trade for the day?"

Venkat flashed his best understanding smile, which, under such *inopportune* circumstances, felt about as supportive as a snake for the eagle that wanted to eat it. "I'm afraid Lord Nayan is still unavailable; however, I hope that will change shortly. For now, please accept our apologies for the inconvenience."

The messenger didn't look at all satisfied, but he bowed his head and left to relay the update.

Venkat was going to kill Asha.

She'd promised to find Tanvi and return as soon as possible—but had neglected to mention her back-to-back wedding-related consultations scheduled after breakfast. When she never showed up for the first one, and discreet inquiries failed to place her anywhere on palace grounds, her parents had come to Nayan.

Leaving Venkat no choice but to claim she'd gone to Prithvi on an unauthorized scouting mission.

He was sick of lying, but how else was he supposed to look out for Tanvi?

Though Nayan's mouth had thinned, he'd stood by Venkat and pacified Asha's parents, even welcoming them to wait in the archives. Then he'd dispatched Madhu to retrieve the princess.

All Venkat could do now was wait and try hard not to chew off his nails.

Behind him, Nayan's voice boomed. "Well done locating them so swiftly, Madhu. We can rest in the knowledge that our princess is secure among us once more."

"Yes, our heartfelt esteem to you," Asha's mother said. "I have been so worried!"

They were safe. Venkat's stomach unclenched, and he said a quick prayer of thanks to all the gods.

He sped around the shelves to find Asha trapped before the large desk, penned in by her parents on their cobra-patterned coils. Though they wore auspicious colors, vivid purples and yellows, their faces were grim. Tanvi hovered outside the elegant triangle like an afterthought.

A slow smile of satisfaction curled over Madhu's wizened cheeks. Tanvi's pendant twinkled in her grip. "I am merely performing my duty."

"What is the meaning of this, beti?" Asha's mother demanded. "Is this why we have permitted you such free rein, that you run off without a word to the mortal realm and bring shame down on our heads? You are no longer a child!"

Venkat waited for Asha to object, but she didn't. His stomach resumed gyrating as he searched her face, then Tanvi's.

Both girls seemed dimmer, like diyas glimpsed through a heavy curtain. Not even the glowing dreamstones or the gentle radiance from the skylights could compensate for it. Asha appeared oddly chastened, while Tanvi seemed on edge, not detached like a runner should be.

"Are you all right?" he asked, joining Nayan and Madhu. Tanvi's gaze flicked to his, and the unhappy bent of her mouth hurt his heart. Nayan, meanwhile, silenced him with a look.

"We have been offering excuse after excuse for your missed appointments all morning, beti, telling everyone you stayed up too late after the party and needed your rest," Asha's father said. "How do you think this makes us appear?"

Asha huffed. "Everything is so dramatic with all of you! 'The garudas will find us.' 'The secret will be revealed.' 'The world will end.' So on and so forth."

The wrinkles around Madhu's eyes deepened. "Have you already forgotten the battalion of garudas attacking you when I arrived? Had I not rescued you in time, you would be in their clutches as we speak. I would scarcely call that 'so dramatic.'"

Garudas had attacked them? Venkat thought his heart might rupture where he stood. From what he'd read, a casual brush of a garuda's talon was enough to cleave through bone. He fought the urge to hug Tanvi and Asha close and focused on calming his breathing instead.

A muscle convulsed in Nayan's jaw, a single twitch, before his features smoothed out again. Venkat knew how much he disliked being caught unaware. With Asha's parents there, Madhu wouldn't have had a chance to fill him privately in on the specifics.

"A garuda battalion! By Mansa Devi, are you trying to end me before my time?" Asha's mother's tail lashed the floor violently enough to knock someone over. She stared at her daughter in disbelief before wheeling on Nayan. "She travels to Prithvi on *your* authority!"

"You dare address Lord Nayan in such a manner?" growled Madhu. Nayan quelled her with an upraised finger. Her nostrils flared at the reprimand, but she bowed her head. "My apologies, my lord."

Nayan clasped his hands behind his back, in that moment wholly the remote and austere lord whose counsel King Vasuki himself sought out. "Dear lord and lady, we are all deeply dismayed by this matter, but I swear to you that Asha did not receive my consent to travel this morning."

Asha flipped her long ponytail over her shoulder. "It is not as if I asked the garudas to chase me down!" She sounded defensive rather than nonchalant, and she darted an anxious glance at Tanvi.

If Asha couldn't even manage her usual imperious tone, she was in bigger trouble than Venkat had realized. What exactly had happened out there?

"Be that as it may, you have evidently flaunted yourself enough on your trips to Prithvi that they knew to await you," Nayan said. "What if they had harmed you? If they had tracked your return path and breached the palace? A game this most certainly is not."

Her parents exchanged a meaningful stare before her mother reached forward and undid Asha's ponytail. "And what is this foolish playing at being mortal? It has gone on far too long. You are a *princess*!"

"But I *must* scout! We need a new dream runner candidate." Desperation bled from Asha's tone.

"Perhaps we should table this for now," Nayan suggested, "and revisit it after the wedding. You may even find your new responsibilities leave you no time for this old role."

If he weren't also a naga, Asha's glare would have poisoned him as surely as her bite. "You would take this from me, too?"

Her mother hissed, long and menacing, her slit-pupil eyes ablaze. "Enough. You will come with us now and attend the remainder of your fittings and consultations. Each and every one."

Even Asha, who Venkat had never seen back down from anyone, dropped her gaze.

"Don't worry," he said as cheerily as he could. "I'll take care of the runners."

Her parents joined their palms in acknowledgment to Nayan, then ushered her out. The archives, with its many shelves of books and dreamstone vials, seemed to balloon in their wake, and Tanvi made a forlorn figure against its backdrop.

"You can't punish her," Venkat said as soon as the doors had closed again. Tanvi picked at her wrist like she was grabbing for something he couldn't see. Her bracelet.

The guilt gnawed at him. Even if she wasn't burning out, this addictive behavior was Jai all over again. And Venkat had made it worse each time he'd reinforced her need to earn boons.

Nayan regarded Madhu's smug grin with impatience. "You must control your temper in public, old mother." She muttered an apology. "Go now and call an emergency meeting of the council. Their Majesties must be apprised of the situation."

"As you wish," Madhu said, and left.

Nayan took so long to speak again that Venkat wondered if he'd have to repeat himself. "Whom should I not punish?" Nayan asked at last.

"Either of them!"

Nayan turned a contemplative expression on him. "Your compassion is what sets you apart. Without it, your dreamsmithing would suffer. Yet with it, *you* suffer. A conundrum."

He plucked the quill from the inkwell on the desk and twirled it around. Unlike Chintu, he didn't spill a single drop of the golden ink. "Think of it not as a punishment but as a correction. Asha must learn that there are greater things than her own desires. She represents not only herself but also the people of Nagalok."

"But what if she doesn't want to?"

"Few of us choose our duty," Nayan said coolly. "It is instead chosen for us."

Venkat wanted to keep arguing. That wasn't fair at all. But Tanvi needed him, so he changed the subject. "I have a request."

"Ask, my son, and perhaps I may even grant it."

Venkat motioned to Tanvi, who startled, her lips parting.

"So do not punish this one?" Nayan half smiled. "Interesting. Go on."

Dreams and boons. "You handled Jai, and I respect that." The words stuck in Venkat's throat like barbs, and he had to push them out. "But let me take care of Tanvi. Please." He rushed ahead before Nayan could reply. "I know, I know; we have to stay focused on ending the war." His voice cracked. "But . . ."

"I will think on it. For now, escort her back to her room and prepare yourself for the council meeting."

"The council meeting?" Venkat *definitely* hadn't expected that.

"Indeed. Your attention has wavered of late, and it is time to return it to our greater mission. All else, while diverting in its way, is ultimately a distraction."

Venkat nodded. "Point taken."

He knew Nayan was right. He could best help his runners by staying focused on helping everybody.

But once Nayan had turned away, Venkat hurried to Tanvi's side. She was drooping like a plant no one had watered in weeks, so obviously worn out and terrified that he couldn't ignore it.

"Let's get you some rest," he said. "Can I walk to you to your room?"

She sized him up warily. Then, to his relief, she nodded.

As Venkat walked Tanvi through the gloomy tunnels, he kept waiting for her to say something. She didn't.

In her room, he guided her to the chair, then poured her a cup of water. When she didn't take it, he set it down on the table.

"Tanvi," he said cautiously, pulling the cotton coverlet from the bed and draping it over her shoulders. "What happened to you? Can you tell me?"

She didn't answer, only fidgeted. It was subtle, a rubbing together of fingers, yet he saw it.

Venkat needed to leave for the council meeting, but the thought of abandoning her here alone after whatever she'd been through sickened him. He knelt by her side. If giving her space to feel safe enough to talk made him a little late, so be it.

He'd never realized just how bare the dream runners' quarters were. The shelves in his apartments were stocked with enough books and scrolls to keep him entertained for weeks, and every room contained furniture for five people. Tanvi, on the other hand, had a twin bed, a cabinet—at least painted—a simple table and chair, and a spartan wardrobe.

At some point, however, Asha must have suffered one of her periodic spurts of generosity, because a delicate golden vase shone from the windowsill, and an embroidered cushion in red, blue, and green peeked out from beneath the bed. A pink-and-copper lotus-patterned rug glimmered on the floor, collecting dust. Trust Asha, Venkat thought wryly, to hang garlands on the walls and believe the runners would appreciate her efforts at beautification— or even notice them.

He knew he couldn't stay much longer, maybe another minute or two. "I just want to know if the garudas hurt you," he said. "If you need anything."

Tanvi picked at her wrist again. He winced and had to stop himself from laying his hand over hers.

You don't need it, he wanted to tell her. *It's just another dream.*

Instead, he let the seconds tick past, hoping.

Tanvi cocked her head at him, and the awareness in her brown eyes, a gloss the other runners lacked, confirmed what he'd already suspected. He'd never heard of this happening, but he couldn't deny it. Pain kindled in her face, pain and confusion. Things that no dream runner ever felt outside a dream, let alone showed.

There was no question now. She might be straining to hold herself together, but it wasn't because she was burning out.

Tanvi grabbed the cup of water he'd poured. After gulping down every drop, she said, "They didn't hurt me."

Venkat couldn't have been more relieved. "I'm glad. But are you okay?"

She nodded, then shook her head. "I don't know?"

"Want some more water?"

She shook her head again, this time with certainty.

"I have to go. To a council meeting," Venkat said, not sure why he was explaining. But the way she watched him, vulnerable and so present, made him want to tell her.

"I'll have some food sent to you," he added. He wanted to offer her something so she knew she wasn't alone.

"I'm a dream runner," Tanvi said, and she touched her wrist

again. "But Madhu took my pendant."

"You're a great dream runner." Venkat smiled extra hard, since he couldn't do anything about the pendant part. "Your wares are always top tier."

Tanvi pressed her lips together, then smiled as well, a shy, uncertain thing. It twitched and crumbled almost instantly.

But she'd *smiled*. At him.

Venkat hardly dared to breathe, let alone move. He held her gaze, which was anything but detached.

"I'll be back soon," he promised. Then, with hope swelling in his heart, he headed out to the council meeting.

Tanvi stared at the door Venkat had closed behind him. His voice echoed in her head, caring. Attentive.

She'd done her best not to let him see anything, to act like she was the dream runner she'd always been, but she was so tired.

Her eyes were so dry and scratchy they kept sticking to her eyelids, and every time she blinked, it felt like ripping away strips of skin. Her hold on the bracelet, already so slippery, gave way once and for all to Nitya's face—first irate, then cold. Tanvi's own face, but wrong.

A blister of memory rose up and burst, patchy and dim: Nitya fighting with her in the kitchen over the last piece of good Halloween candy. Nobody wanted the fake Twizzlers—so gross.

Then another, all faded panic and fear: Nitya tattling on Tanvi for watching a horror movie on TV.

Tanvi squeezed her cup until her palm went numb. She really needed to sleep, but if this was happening now, when she was awake, who knew what she might dream?

A third blister erupted: s'mores melting in a campfire in the woods.

Tanvi pummeled it back down. No sleep, then. She pinched herself as hard as she could all along her arm. She'd stay up no matter how much it hurt. Remembering hurt more.

Another memory: Sameer's pet rock collection, adorned with Sharpie mustaches.

The panic flared again, red and hot, scalding her stupid heart. She really was breaking.

Pulling the blanket tighter around her shoulders, Tanvi concentrated on her cabinet. Her harvest still sat there, waiting. She just had to make it until Venkat returned.

She pinched herself and pinched herself. Soon, finally, she'd get her boon and buy her bracelet, and everything would go back to normal.

Tanvi pinched herself. . . .

Nitya and Sameer sat in front of the giant TV in his family room, playing video games. "I miss her," Nitya said, tears trickling down her cheeks. "How could she leave like that?"

"I miss her, too." Sameer punched a button on his controller. His character, a mage, shot green fireballs at a shopkeeper, who turned to ashes. "Maybe she got lost. Maybe one day, you'll come home, and she'll be back."

"I'm right here!" Tanvi shouted, but no one heard. Her skin felt creepy, like no one could see her, either.

Nitya grinned wickedly. "Want to know a secret?" Sameer nodded. "I don't really miss her at all. I hope she never comes back."

183

Her character, a burly warrior, chopped down a bush with her sword and collected fifty coins. *Ding, ding, ding!*

Sameer laughed. "Me, too. Nobody liked her."

"*Especially* not Mom and Dad!"

The two of them cackled like cartoon witches.

"Mom's ordering pizza," Sameer said. "Let's go!"

He and Nitya skipped into the kitchen, and Tanvi realized she'd never existed at all.

Tanvi woke, crying out, to the afternoon sunlight slanting through the window. Had that actually happened? Or was it a dream?

Her room, so small and dismal, pressed in on her, and she couldn't get comfortable no matter how she turned. Dream or memory—it made no difference. She wanted to delete it from her brain.

She clutched her sweat-damp pillow tight as if it could anchor her. She wouldn't wind up like Jai, she swore. She wouldn't.

The slimy residue stuck to her like scum on the surface of a pond. If only she could harvest her own dreams, just bottle them up in a vial . . .

Tanvi heaved the mess of sheets aside and sat up. What if she *could*?

The residue of the nightmare still lingered; hopefully that would be enough.

Seconds later, Tanvi stood at the cabinet—had it always been painted like that?—reaching for a vacant dreamstone. The first one that came to hand was rose quartz. She uncorked it and set it on the table, then dug her fingers into her temples.

Until now, she had only ever imagined getting her boon and buying her bracelet, wallowing in the promise of how good it would feel. How satisfying. She wasn't sure she even knew how to visualize anything else, but she had to try.

Her nerves firing with fear and hope both, Tanvi pushed past the usual likenesses of the bracelet and Nitya's face. Then she tentatively opened to the new picture: reaping this newest nightmare. Freeing herself.

She'd only been on this side of harvesting once before, during her initiation. The memory unfolded now, and she welcomed it—a girl named Parul following Nayan's instructions as Tanvi nodded off, sent under by the sleeping brew Asha had portioned out for her.

Parul had never actually touched Tanvi, but as she drowsed, she'd felt the harvesting energy like a magnet, tugging.

Tanvi screwed her eyes shut and homed in on the slimy residue. How it felt, letting it draw her back into the dream. It hurt at first, like stretching a muscle she never used, but then it transported her.

Nitya . . . the video game . . . Sameer . . .

Nitya laughing, glad she didn't have a sister anymore.

Fire shot up Tanvi's fingers and into her head. She yelped, her hand cramping, and only realized a second too late that she'd broken the connection.

The nightmare was gone.

No. Tanvi refused to accept it. She'd been so close to getting rid of all that for good.

One of the blisters rippled back up, more sketched in this time. Nitya, age six, scrawling in the mustaches on Sameer's rock collection after Tanvi dared her to.

No. No, no, no. Tanvi flailed, hair whipping around her, until it abated. That wasn't her past. It couldn't be.

Gulping hard, she eyed the open vial. So she couldn't harvest her dreams herself. But another runner could.

Maybe if Tanvi promised Indu her next boon, Indu would agree to do it for her. All those names, all those faces would be scrubbed away. She'd be free again.

It would mean waiting longer for the bracelet, but what choice did she really have?

No more memories. No more dreams. None of these distracting vases and rugs and smells and colors clamoring for her attention. Just a job she knew how to do with a reward she understood.

Her fingers drummed out a *rat-tat-tat* on the table. Daytime meant that the dream runners were resting.

Which meant Indu would be in her room.

And *that* meant Tanvi had no time to waste. She threw on her shoes and ran.

In the corridor, she passed closed doorway after doorway, none of which had any decoration or even identification. She'd never noticed that before. Or how dusty it was. How dim.

Her heart panged, and Tanvi promised herself that she'd forget all these details soon enough.

There. Indu's room. Tanvi marched inside.

Everything in it was so simple, so impersonal. All utilitarian furniture, plus a mirror-work wall hanging and a pair of sheer curtains over the window slit. The room didn't feel lived in, despite the dozing girl mostly swallowed up by the white-blanketed bed.

Though Indu slept, she wasn't dreaming. Her round face was too blank for that.

Tanvi wanted that peace back so badly. For her own heart to be silenced again.

Glancing around, she spotted the tray of half-eaten food on the table. Of course Indu hadn't bothered to finish it, since food was nothing but fuel to her. Just something to fill her stomach so she could keep harvesting.

Tanvi's stomach grumbled, a reminder that she hadn't eaten in way too long, and Venkat had promised he would have a meal delivered to her room.

Venkat. Her shoulder suddenly warmed with the remembered weight of his hand. His mouth had gone soft and vulnerable, like he'd been on the verge of confessing a secret.

Quit being stupid, she ordered herself. *Think of why you're here.*

But she couldn't bring herself to wake Indu. Instead, she went to investigate the closet. Unlike hers, this one was a mess. Used towels and sheets lay strewn over the floor, and two soccer balls sat on top of the heap.

Two?

She knelt to pick one up.

"Don't touch that!" someone snapped.

Tanvi pivoted to find Indu standing behind her. "What're you doing here?" Indu asked, her eyes flat.

That impassive gaze unsettled Tanvi more than it had any right to, considering that was probably exactly how *she* used to look—and hoped to again. "You want a boon, right?"

Indu's apathetic tone brightened. "Are you going to give me one?"

"Sort of," Tanvi said. "Can I see your dreamstones?"

With a shrug, Indu padded to the cabinet and opened it.

Three of the dreamstones in the front row shone out from the rest. "They're the best quality," Indu boasted. "Once Venkat sees them, I'll get my ball."

She already has *a ball, though. She has two.*

It didn't make sense. Tanvi hadn't even gotten her first bracelet, and she was seventeen. How had Indu already earned two boons?

Tanvi had never wondered about anyone's age before, but now she guessed Indu must be around thirteen, that gawky age of being stretched out and gangly while trying to figure out how to finish growing up.

More doubts sprouted like vines in Tanvi's head. How long had Indu been here, then? She hadn't been in Tanvi's cohort.

"So," Indu demanded, "are you going to give me the boon now, or can I go back to sleep?"

Tanvi tried hard to imitate the easy, encouraging smile Venkat had whenever he'd bought her wares. "I can trade you dreams that are even better than the ones you have—if you help me with something."

"With what?" Indu almost sounded curious.

The thought of the plan burned like a fire ant's bite. Tanvi shrank from it. As long as the words didn't come out of her mouth, she was a dream runner just like Indu.

But as she examined Indu's wooden expression, she saw all the

188

people Indu had left behind on Prithvi. All the people who might still be mourning her. Nitya's grieving face floated before Tanvi's eyes. Her panicked plea not to go hummed in Tanvi's ears. What if Indu had a sister, too? One she'd played soccer with?

Fury igniting in her, Tanvi shoved the ridiculous worries away. That was not her problem. "I need you to harvest *my* dreams."

The interest that had sparked in Indu's face when she'd thought boons might appear guttered, then died. "Dream runners don't dream." She turned back to the bed.

"I do, though," Tanvi insisted. "Listen to me."

Indu climbed onto the bed.

"Don't you *want* your boon?" Tanvi tore her dreamstones from her pouch and waved them at Indu. "See? These can get it for you."

But Indu had already checked out; her expression was as tranquil as a doll's and every bit as remote.

"What happens if you can't sell your dreams?" Tanvi went on, not caring how desperate she sounded. "If you don't get any more boons after this one? Then what?"

Indu crawled under the coverlet. "Then I get replaced. Every dream runner's only as good as their harvest."

"Doesn't that bother you?"

"You're weird." Indu snuggled into her pillow and closed her eyes, unhesitatingly falling into that indifferent slumber.

Tanvi could only stare in a mixture of horror and envy. Had she really been like that, too?

Two soccer balls. Two. A pair.

"Indu?"

No reply.

Tanvi had no blanket, no pillow, but she lay down on the floor next to Indu's bed and aimed her glare at the ceiling.

At least neither of them had to be alone.

19

"I do not suppose we can consider a peace offering?" Himanshu of the clan of Maniakkhika said, delicately selecting a piece of spicy dhokla from a silver tray and popping it into his mouth. A scribe perched on a stool to the right of the great table, her arm forming huge, looping motions as she recorded every word with the zeal of someone hoping for a promotion. Never mind, thought Venkat, drumming his hand on his knee, that the council had been having the same argument for the past hour.

From the dignitaries and diplomats of each of the Eightfold Clans to Asha and Chintu to Nayan and the nagaraja and naga-rani themselves, the wide rectangular conference table represented nearly every major court official Venkat had seen at events. They looked completely at ease in their onyx-and-emerald chairs, which had been artfully carved to resemble miniature versions of the royal thrones.

Venkat, however, still wasn't sure what *he* was doing here in the council chamber, the lone human surrounded by paintings of ancient naga-and-garuda clashes interspersed with deadly curved talwaars and heavy round shields salvaged from those same skirmishes. He'd never swung a sword in his life, and so far, he hadn't even persuaded Nayan to spare Tanvi. The only thing he could really offer was his dreamsmithing, and that was a secret.

If all that wasn't enough, two life-sized portraits of the nagaraja and nagarani gazed imperiously down from the golden walls. No matter which way he turned, their critical green-gold eyes drilled into him.

He shifted yet again, feeling like a little kid in the too-large chair with its grandiose cobra-hood corona. Nayan shot him a side-long glance full of reproach. *Show no weakness*, it said.

Venkat pushed himself upright and tried his best to look solemn.

Trishala of the clan of Kauravya made a miffed noise. "How many times must we re-tread this same ground? Garuda already enjoyed his victory. He robbed our people of the amrit. If that is not enough to appease his bloodlust, what is?"

"The last breach cost eleven lives," Sunaina of the clan of Virupaksha called out.

Eleven lives? Venkat hadn't known that. He stared at the velvet table runner, tailored to create the effect of a serpent slithering through grass, and felt ill. Had the victims been children? Some-body's parents? Husbands and wives? His heart ached for the people they'd left behind.

Nayan's project *had* to work.

"Eleven lives," Sunaina repeated. "And I sense they were merely toying with us."

"I also sense that," Nayan agreed. He pointed to a painting in which Garuda, monstrous and shrieking, gouged a scimitarlike talon into the broad chest of a mace-bearing naga soldier. Blood sprayed liberally across the soil. "From all we have seen, it is clear Garuda has no interest in peace offerings."

Trishala's plump lips thinned, and she hissed at Himanshu. "We must reinforce the troops guarding the borders and fortify their armory. If the council insists on dithering, perhaps the clan of Kauravya must take matters into its own hands."

The susurration of heated hisses and the flashes of fangs battered Venkat until he had to tune them out. He thought of Tanvi, alone in the sad room where he'd left her. Her smile, so unexpected and pretty, more precious for how quickly it had vanished, warmed him even now. He should have given her a book to read. Something to keep her company since he couldn't.

"The time before, it was six deaths. What if this time, it had been the princess?" inquired a sly voice. "I do not believe she has clarified why she was on Prithvi to begin with."

Karan. The type of naga who gave snakes on Prithvi their bad reputation. Exchanging a glance with Nayan, Venkat caught a flicker of displeasure beneath Nayan's cultured façade.

Asha's father, on the other hand, made no attempt to hide his vexation. "Princess Asha's affairs are of no consequence to you."

"I disagree; she placed all her subjects in danger," said Sunaina, and Karan could not have looked more pleased with himself.

Venkat fought down the urge to argue. Asha still owed him an explanation, and he wouldn't be surprised to learn the reason the garudas had found her was because she'd been indulging one of her unauthorized whims again. But that didn't mean Karan could just offer her up for his own ends.

And Asha didn't let him. She met his derisive smirk with her beaming menace. "I do not mind recounting for the sake of clarity," she said, sweet as champak perfume. "As a future monarch, I took it upon myself to investigate the current security of our dream running operations on Prithvi. As you may imagine, however, I did not anticipate being attacked while on my mission."

Not bad. Venkat would give her that. She'd certainly gathered herself, to the point he would never have guessed how shaken she really was. But that didn't mean her cover story would hold. All someone had to do was poke a hole in it—like Nayan wondering why she had been with Tanvi. During the day, no less.

And then taking a closer look at Tanvi and realizing her condition had nothing to do with burnout.

"This is unacceptable," Falgun of the clan of Takshaka announced. "You present a singular target, and yet you act as though this were all for sport!"

"I fully admit it was unwise to have gone alone," Asha agreed, and despite everything, Venkat bit back a laugh. Asha never troubled herself about what she should do, only what she wanted to do. "My haste was born of care for the people I serve."

"If you truly cared for your people, Princess, you would have abided by the travel ban. You fail to comprehend the gravity of the perils you court with such alacrity," Sunaina said, her mouth puckering. "Perhaps you are too young to move forward with this betrothal."

Chintu hopped up and laid an arm around Asha as though claiming his trophy. "There is no need to worry about that." She didn't resist, even permitting him to draw her down into her seat, but Venkat cringed, anyway. "I will see to it myself that my betrothed is always well guarded."

"More than that," Asha's father added, "she will restrict her movements to Bhogavati. You have our clan's word on this."

Asha bowed her head in acknowledgment. Beside her, Karan spoke in hushed tones to Chintu, whose frown gave way to a smug smile.

Himanshu wasn't having it. "And what of dreams? With so few of them to go around, my people grow agitated!"

Nayan held up a hand. "My apprentice"—he gestured to Venkat—"will be addressing this matter."

Dharmesh of the clan of Apalal, who'd kept his own counsel for most of the meeting, glowered, first at Nayan, then at Venkat. "You would entrust this to a mere mortal? A child at that?"

A mere mortal? Who was this guy to question Venkat's capabilities? He might not have been able to defend Asha, but he wasn't about to stay quiet now. Sitting up taller, he met Queen Naga Yakshi's intrigued eyes. "By your leave, Majesty, I would speak in my own defense."

She inclined her head, her crown catching the light. "Then do so."

Venkat took a long swig from his goblet, collecting his thoughts. The rest of the table watched him with various degrees of skepticism and curiosity. Nayan, however, nodded encouragingly.

"I might be human, yes," Venkat said, careful not to let the hot, angry defensiveness creep into his words, "but Bhogavati is my home, as it has been for the last ten years. I've trained under Lord Nayan's careful eye all that time." He smiled proudly. "Every dream you purchased, every runner who harvested that dream—I was behind them. I manage the runners, and I sort and sell their wares. I know my trade better than anyone else in this room. Better than anyone else in this city."

That might have been a little too arrogant, but he didn't care.

"This scarcely serves to address my query," Himanshu protested. "What of the dream supply?"

Nayan didn't miss a beat. "If you are done interrogating my apprentice, I believe we should return our attention to the actual topic," he said with a firmness that brooked no dispute. "We are here to discuss the garuda assault on our princess."

"Lord Nayan speaks truly."

All heads swiveled toward the nagarani. She rarely entered debates, preferring instead to abstain and then converse in private with her husband. Venkat had heard that the final decisions on so many subjects affecting the kingdom were often hers; even King Vasuki deferred to her wisdom.

She made no move to rise from her chair, just one more member of the council. A quiet confidence radiated from her, as soft but powerful as her immense beauty. More ballads had been written of Vasuki's greatness than of hers, and Venkat got the impression she liked it that way. He appreciated that; he, too, would rather stand on the sidelines and work his magic in the shadows.

"Lord Himanshu," she said firmly, "you know the accessibility of dreams is hardly a priority at this time. No one would wish otherwise more than the nagaraja and I, yet we may only act in the realm of what is, not what we wish were so." She turned to Asha. "As for you, Princess, no matter how confinement grates at us all, it is vital you remain within our borders if we are to shield you."

There it was again, Asha's brittle smile. She reached for a cobalt-honey cake and fed it to Chintu. He smiled, obviously gratified, as he chewed. To everyone but Venkat, it must have seemed a sweet moment between lovers-to-be.

"As for how we should proceed," the nagarani went on, "it seems to me that we must curtail all travel beyond our realm, at least until the wedding is past." She looked at Nayan. "I am afraid that includes even your runners, my lord Nayan."

The assembly broke into roars. "How are we to get along without dreams?"

"Of what relevance are dreams when the garudas wish to drink our blood?"

"If the borders cannot be secured, the clan of Maniakkhika will not remain here to be slaughtered!"

"The clan of Takshaka is prepared to reclaim Prithvi for our people, with or without the rest of you!"

Venkat could only think of his runners. It made sense to keep Asha in Nagalok, but why did they have to suffer, too? What would they do if they couldn't harvest?

"Enough!" King Vasuki called. He had to repeat himself twice before the council settled down once more. "I have always tolerated

197

and even welcomed dissenting opinions. What I will not endure is this lack of unity. That is what permitted the garudas to regain a foothold among us."

The other nagas offered apologies, some more reluctant than others.

"Naturally, the borders will be secured," said Queen Naga Yakshi, steel underlying her mellifluous tone. "We have already tripled the number of troops safeguarding the portals. In addition, as I have already said, there will be, effective immediately, no more travel of any kind between the realms. I am certain all of you can endure a few weeks without fresh dreams."

"In the meantime," Nayan said, "the scholars continue to research potential solutions to the garuda threat."

"And how goes that?" asked the nagaraja.

"Work continues apace, Your Majesty." Nayan was the essence of equanimity, a boulder untouched by the turbulent waves all around. "I remain certain a breakthrough is imminent. We must but cultivate patience."

In contrast to his calm, the mutters grew in intensity. "You, former insurgent, who were once against the crown, believe we are to heed you?"

Venkat blenched, but Nayan nodded. "It is better to put speculation to rest, is it not? You have all heard the rumors—so permit me to tell you a story." He glanced from the nagaraja to the nagarani. "With your leave, that is."

"Certainly," said King Vasuki.

Nayan rose and circled the table, surveying each member of the council. His clothes were crisp and finely tailored; the gold circlet on his forehead gleamed as richly as his firm stare. "The young always imagine they have all the answers, and that the old are fools who have forgotten to care. It is endemic among societies. I was no different."

He smiled at Venkat, rueful.

"I was a firebrand among firebrands, keen to prove myself. After all, was I not King Takshaka's youngest nephew, desperate to break free of his all-encompassing shadow? Takshaka, the reckless warrior. Takshaka, the mighty ruler. It took little to light me up—a single spark too often resulted in a bonfire."

Venkat tried to reconcile the meticulous advisor he knew with the headstrong boy Nayan was describing. They felt like two different people.

"In my single-minded conviction, I saw no reason why the nagas should limit our dominion to Nagalok. Why not found an empire in the manner of the mortals?" Nayan shook his head. "Fool that I was, I declared war on the throne."

The courtiers gasped, Venkat loudest of all. He'd never heard this part.

"Indeed you did," Queen Naga Yakshi said, mildly mocking, "and how swiftly we put you down."

"Fortunately for my wayward nephew," King Vasuki said with a chuckle, "rather than exile him outright, I approached a mortal sage who had strayed from his duties with a bargain he had no option but to accept."

"The rishi was as overjoyed about this as you might imagine," said the nagarani, "yet the terms were clear: either the world would learn he indulged in drink, spent time with women not his wife, and gambled away his money . . . or he would take Nayan into his tutelage." She grinned, impish. "I suppose they became clearer still once we promised him a boon in return for his 'freely rendered' services."

Nayan picked up the thread. "I was no happier to be thrust into exile. I put out his fires, destroyed and hid objects in his hut— everything I could to provoke him into chasing me away. And perhaps he would have, boon or no boon, except one day, I fled into the forest and encountered a fellow wayfarer who wished to hear my tale."

He circled the table again. "To my astonishment, not only did this person reprove me, but he stated that if I persisted in my foolishness, I would lose everything I claimed to fight for. He convinced me so thoroughly, in fact, that when I returned to the hut, I prostrated myself before the sage and implored him to teach me."

"That must have been quite the lecture," Trishala said. "What happened then?"

"At last he deigned to instruct me in the art of meditation and mastering one's impulses. Over time, my blood cooled, and my awareness expanded. I remained with him until his last breath, which he used to invoke his boon. As you might expect, he asked for his own rejuvenation."

"Naturally," said Dharmesh. "What else?"

"We parted ways and returned to our respective lives, but with opposite roles. The sage went off to enjoy his second youth, and I, having matured, rejoined the naga court." Nayan took his seat.

"And that is my tale," he concluded, placing a hand on Venkat's shoulder. "But it is also a single chapter in *our* tale, the ongoing saga of our people. If I could learn humility and to work in harmony with those I had once believed to be holding me back, you may all avail yourselves of this opportunity to set aside your machinations and maneuvering and stand together for the greater good. It is your choice: How do you wish this chapter to end?"

More hissing ensued as the other representatives of the eight clans deliberated amongst themselves, but this round left Venkat more optimistic.

Minutes later, one by one, they joined their palms before their faces, each repeating, "My clan and I stand with you, Your Majesties."

"We must mark the occasion. I propose a celebratory picnic on the Lake of Lovers' Tears," said Asha's mother. Her eyes flared gold with enthusiasm. "It is tradition to host such a picnic in honor of the intended, and all Bhogavati will be welcome. The clans must see a future in our standing together as one."

Of course it had to be another party. Of course. Venkat stared askance at the table runner. Did the nagas even know how to do anything else?

At least she'd picked a good location. Venkat had only been to the lake once, but he'd never forgotten it. The legend of how it came to be sang to him as strongly as when he had first learned it.

"In our combined strength, there is hope," Chintu's uncle chimed in.

"Excellent!" Chintu grinned, and a smattering of agreement sounded from around the table. Only Asha stayed quiet, but Venkat could imagine her disdain. "Is it not, Asha?"

"Splendid," she agreed, and her sunny smile could have rivaled even the glint of the topaz over the Lake of Lovers' Tears.

As the rest of the council departed, Nayan motioned for Venkat to stay behind.

"Impressive," Venkat said admiringly. "I didn't think anything could get them to quit fighting."

"My son," Nayan replied, "everyone enjoys a good story. It gives them both an umbrella to unite beneath and a role to play."

As they walked out into the corridor, he smiled. "You have won me over with how well you stood up for yourself in there. You request permission to care for Tanvi? Consider it granted."

20

Tanvi had fallen asleep, of course, and dreamed again. Images of Nitya and Dad in their garden in Mount Airy blended with snapshots of Venkat and Asha outside the palace. Tanvi grabbed the trowel from her father's grasp and uprooted the daisies from Nitya's raised bed, the daisies Nitya had planted herself. It didn't alter a thing; Nitya only picked other flowers, and Dad dug with his hands.

A soccer ball soared past Tanvi's head, landing at Venkat's feet. The palace glittered behind him, a mirror for the burning sun. He punted the ball back to Asha. "Come play!" they urged, and Tanvi raced toward them. But before she could get there, Indu appeared and bumped the ball with her head. In response, a trio of garudas swooped down from the cloudless sky and swallowed the three of them. All Tanvi could do was watch, helpless, as Asha, writhing in snake form, disappeared into a vicious golden beak. Abandoned on the grass, the ball cloned itself. Then both balls deflated.

When Tanvi woke, her mouth parched and gross, Indu's bed sat empty, and the sky had darkened to the color of squid ink. Tanvi practically guzzled the entire jug of lukewarm water, but no matter how much she drank, she couldn't wash away the ugly feeling in her chest.

Those stupid two soccer balls. They'd even been in her dream.

She sneaked over to Indu's closet to stare at them some more. Plump and too real, they gleamed at her, the black and white patches spotless like they'd never been tracked through dirt or scuffed by shoes.

How could Indu have two balls while Tanvi didn't have a single bracelet?

She heard the muffled echo of her conversation with Nitya, when Tanvi had asked after the bracelet Nitya couldn't possibly know anything about.

My bracelet. The one Tanvi was still waiting to buy with her boon.

No. This was skirting way too close to dangerous territory. As long as she didn't go any further, what Nitya had said—what Tanvi herself had asked—didn't exist.

In her head, Tanvi tried to retreat from the soccer balls and Nitya's words. She just wanted her bracelet—and the emptiness that surrounded it.

Instead, she backed into what felt like a school of vengeful jellyfish, tentacles tipped with spotty memories: a younger Nitya building a castle out of cardboard paper towel tubes, their parents complaining that the bowls in the dishwasher were still crusty, a summer meal of sweet-and-sour mock duck chased by raspberry water ice. Each one stung Tanvi's heart, demanding that she look at it. That she remember.

Tanvi was cracking like an egg. Little fissures were forming all over her, and she would dribble out, drop by gooey drop, until there was nothing left. These awful dreams, these memories—it was all their fault.

She screamed, loud and long. It shredded the lining of her throat, making her cough. *From the diaphragm,* a familiar voice, but one she couldn't place, floated up in her thoughts. Something about . . . singing?

Tanvi screamed again, this time from her belly, and again. She screamed her resentment and uselessness, the confusion and pointless feelings shoving through her, at this depersonalized room that could have belonged to anyone at all, at how ridiculous these unwanted, half-cooked recollections were. More than anything, she screamed at herself for being stupid enough to care.

Her head threatened to pop like a kernel of corn. She needed to get out of this box and talk to Venkat.

Tanvi had never gone to the appraisal room at night before. Night was for harvesting. She couldn't be sure Venkat would even be there. How long did council meetings run? But she didn't know how else to find him.

You don't know much at all, do you?

Baring her teeth at the thought, Tanvi slunk out of the dingy passage and into the room. It was so small, like a jail cell. She shivered. The spell of the memories still lingered, and all she wanted was to be outside.

Well, that and not to be dreaming, let alone remembering.

She waited awhile, but when Venkat didn't show up, she inspected the room. There was a small panel she'd never noticed before. Curious, she opened it a crack. Voices sounded from far off.

Maybe one of them was Venkat?

The passageway was totally different than hers, amply lit with sconces shaped like praying nagas and filled with colorful carvings. Her eyes watered, forcing her to squint as she hurried through it.

At the other end of the passageway, two massive gold doors with the royal emblem towered over her. Tanvi didn't remember standing here before—or did she? The tangle of memories in her head pulsed, throbbing, throbbing until she pushed the question away.

The voices sounded again. Voices, plural. She couldn't just mosey on in.

But maybe, she allowed, eyeing the doors, she didn't have to.

Tanvi fished a lozenge out of her pouch and downed it. She flowed right under the doors and into the archives.

The fancy shelves of books and scrolls, the dreamstones for decoration—she'd seen them all before. She might not remember the doors, but she'd definitely been here. It was where Nayan had initiated the runners. Except then, instead of the silver-white sliver of moon against a starry black sky, waves of aquamarine light had poured in from above, straight out of a cartoon set underwater.

And that giant desk, with its registry Tanvi had tried to read . . .

A fragment of memory bubbled up now. Ignoring the horrible jellyfish stinging, she gave in to it.

The dream runner initiation. *You all know what comes next,* Nayan had said. *Madhu and I will permanently release you from the pain.*

Waiting in line for her turn, with the pretty teal light and glowing jewels everywhere, Tanvi had felt like a mermaid under the sea. She'd bounced on her toes and hummed to herself.

One by one, Nayan stilled the candidates' hearts, silencing them so they could never hurt again. Tanvi watched their faces change when they came out of the little appraisal room. They stopped crying and hitting one another. It seemed like a great thing.

But the shorter and shorter the line got, the more nervous Tanvi became.

Even if Nitya was the Worst Sister in History, did Tanvi really want to forget her for always?

So she'd distracted herself by tiptoeing over to the registry. It was such a big, pretty book—Tanvi knew its gold-edged pages must be packed with fairy tales about unicorns and flying horses and magic wands. She wanted to read every one of those stories. Not just that—she wanted to *be* in them.

A hand had come down hard on her shoulder. Sharp nails pierced her sleeve.

Madhu had looked so scary, a witch in a grandmother's skin, like the wolf that ate Little Red Riding Hood's grandmother and then put on her frilly cap and nightgown. *Get back in line,* Madhu had snapped, and for a second, Tanvi was sure she'd rippled, her contours going blurry. Like a mirage that had sprung out of the registry. *Or go back home.*

You're mean, Tanvi retorted, scooting toward the line.

But Madhu had already moved on by.

That decided things. If this was how people were, Tanvi was done caring about them. Done letting them matter. She didn't need her stupid heart.

When Nayan waved her forward, he asked one question: *Do you choose this?*

Yes, she'd said, totally sure. Yes, she did.

Then come, he'd said, and led her into the tiny room.

The memory cut off there.

Nausea roiled in Tanvi's stomach, and she grabbed for the edge of the desk to keep from passing out. She missed and crashed to the cool marble floor. The sound reverberated through the huge hall.

The voices she'd heard somewhere deep in the archives broke off, and suddenly Madhu fumed before her in full human form. "What are you doing here?" she asked, her contempt a whip flogging Tanvi's ears. "Have you not done enough damage already?"

Tanvi had to go. Now. But she stayed sprawling where she'd fallen. Moving wasn't an option.

Because Madhu wasn't alone.

Looming behind her were two garudas and a garudi. Their brawny arms ended in golden talons long enough to skewer even the most massive naga. And their feral brown-gold eyes settled on Tanvi from over curved beaks that might as well have been meat hooks.

As one, they smiled—rapacious smiles that cornered her.

Reduced her to prey. Tanvi's muscles turned to pudding. If they wanted to kill her, she couldn't do a thing to stop them. But at a signal from Madhu, the garudas returned to the pots of vermilion they held. As Tanvi watched, petrified, they glamoured themselves into naga servants and stole out through the archive doors.

"You will not utter a word of this to Lord Nayan," Madhu said, having shifted into her own serpentine shape, and now her tone matched it, low and dangerous enough to pass for a naga's enraged hiss. Her eyes constricted to gashes, deepening the grooves in her face.

She looked, Tanvi thought, like a peach pit come to life. A terrified squeak escaped her: "Why not?"

"I know where your sister lives."

The air leaked slowly out of Tanvi, like a balloon that had been untied. Asha had seen an eagle's nest in the tree at Nitya's house. At Tanvi's house. "You were spying on us?"

Madhu only laughed. "You comprehend nothing, runner. And Asha should have known better than to select a twin to begin with. Close connections prove the most difficult to eradicate."

"Leave her alone," Tanvi muttered, pushing herself to her feet. She didn't know how else to protect Nitya, but if there was a chance Madhu might listen, she had to take it.

Madhu's long white braid lashed like a serpent in midspring. "Then keep still. This need not affect you."

It hit Tanvi like a slap. *You were spying on* Asha. *Not on us.*

Madhu and she stared at each other, locked in a contest Tanvi knew she'd already lost.

209

The doors opened, and Venkat entered. He made her think of a dreamstone in his chrysoprase-green kurta pajama, the way he was radiant from the inside out. What possible reason was there to be happy?

"Remember," Madhu whispered, "no one must know. If they do . . ."

Tanvi's heart thumped fast enough to make a hummingbird jealous. If only she could blur herself and fly away, too.

"Madhu?" Venkat's voice was such a welcome contrast to Madhu's sinister hiss. "Tanvi?" He glanced between them, his forehead wrinkling in apprehension.

"I was looking for you," Tanvi mumbled.

Madhu scowled. "You should have your runners better in hand, apprentice. Imagine if she had been recognized, loitering about the palace at all hours."

Venkat's worry flattened into his usual placid smile. "Your concern is noted. I'll speak to her."

"And I will be speaking to Lord Nayan." Madhu shot one more glance at Tanvi, and the voracious tilt of her head, like one of her garudas scoping out a target, rooted Tanvi where she stood.

No wonder the garudas knew where to find Asha. They'd had a spy the entire time in the highest levels of the court, someone Nayan trusted to help run his operation.

And Tanvi couldn't say anything. She didn't doubt for a second that Madhu would follow through on her threat.

There was a man, and there was a tiger. There was a tiger.

Asha had never intended that as a serious lesson, but Tanvi knew what happened when you tangled with a tiger—and presumably with a garuda, too.

Why hadn't Asha taken her own advice and followed the rules? Now Tanvi was stuck. She didn't want to have to worry about Nitya or anybody else.

Madhu beamed, then swaggered across the floor. "After all, we must not delay retiring our unruly runners."

"He already told me *I* can take care of Tanvi," Venkat called after her.

Her tone frigid, Madhu replied, "We shall see about that."

Once she was gone, Tanvi and Venkat stared at each other. She wasn't sure what to say.

"What happened?" he asked. His gaze was kind, the total opposite of Madhu's. It made her *want* to tell him, so very much. She wanted so very badly to hear him say he could help her.

Tanvi especially wanted to warn him that Madhu was a plant, that she'd hoodwinked Nayan and everyone else all this time. She'd put Asha right in harm's way. Tanvi would never forget the garudas' hateful glares as they'd borne down on Asha at Sameer's school. Annoying as Asha could be, there was no excuse for that.

Not to mention Tanvi's own fate being up in the air. Really, she had every reason to turn Madhu in.

But Nitya.

"Don't worry about Madhu," Venkat said when Tanvi didn't respond. "Nayan told me to take care of you, and I will." He smiled again, this one as lucid as the slice of moon watching from above. "I know she's on one of her power trips, but she doesn't get a vote in this."

His smile was so sweet, so comforting. Tanvi wanted so much to dismiss the past few days, to hide in being a dream runner with no other worries but the harvest. She was so tired. So hungry. Her body exhorted her to tell him. He could take over. It would be so easy.

"I'm going to make sure you're all taken care of, I promise," he went on, and the temptation to believe him almost undid her. Let it be somebody else's problem.

Except she couldn't, not when he didn't know what she knew.

Tanvi didn't dare go against Madhu directly, but maybe she could hint at the truth? "How—" she stammered. "How did they meet? How did she, you know, start working for him?"

Venkat did a funny thing with his mouth, like he was trying to think back. It might have been cute if Tanvi's attention hadn't been eaten up by what she'd just seen. "I don't know; she's always been there. Why?"

The cracks in Tanvi started to widen. Too much had happened too fast. Exhaustion, despair, and a string of unwelcome memories all swelled up in her, and she couldn't subdue them any longer. A sentence she'd never imagined saying flew out of her mouth. "I'm dreaming."

The pressure inside her eased, and Tanvi pressed her lips shut. He didn't need to know anything else. Not about her memories, and definitely not about her side trip to find Nitya.

Venkat considered her, confused. "I'm sorry, but I don't get it."

Did she really have to say it twice? Tanvi mustered the shreds of her courage. "I'm dreaming. I've *been* dreaming. . . ."

With that confession, she'd thrown her future in the trash. Venkat's smile would go dark and freaked-out, and there would be no more running dreams for her.

So she didn't look. "And I want you to make it stop."

21

The words assailed Venkat with their sheer impossibility. *I'm dreaming.*

All he wanted was to disappear into the shelves of stories behind him. No matter how out of control their situations got, those heroes and heroines never quailed. They always knew what to do.

Venkat, on the other hand, had never felt more lost. He kept swallowing as he stared at Tanvi, her scowl half veiled by her glossy hair. "Dreaming?" he finally choked out. "You?"

"It's awful," she said, scowling harder. "Take it away."

How was this even possible? "I don't understand," he began to repeat, then caught himself. Making her say it a third time wouldn't change anything.

Venkat dragged his gaze from Tanvi's huddled form and flicked it around the archives, taking in the gold-and-sapphire settees for reading, the scalloped niches with meticulous maps of the naga kingdoms, the carved lanterns and lit sapphire-and-emerald sconces—details he rarely even noticed anymore.

He tethered himself to them, each one a reminder. He was Nayan's apprentice, and this was his domain. "How was the food I had sent?" he asked, slipping into his professional calm like a coat. "Was there enough?"

Tanvi hunched farther into herself. "I never got it."

Feeling like the ground had stabilized under him, Venkat picked up a tray of snacks he'd requested earlier from the kitchens. "I can fix that."

He ushered Tanvi to a pair of chairs tucked between the first and second aisles of shelves. A few of the more zealous scholars occasionally dropped in to do some late-night research, and he couldn't risk her being seen. She looked uncomfortable, squirming against the chair's ornate carving and silken teal upholstery, but once he offered her the tray, she attacked it like she hadn't eaten in a month.

Venkat watched her keenly, noting the relish with which she inhaled and chewed. She was actually smelling the salt and spice of the potato and onion pakora, actually tasting the sweet tartness of the tamarind chutney. Actually savoring them. Even if it shouldn't, that made a contrary part of him glad.

He fisted his hands in his lap, biting back the question until she'd polished off the last crumbs of fried batter. "What do you mean, you're dreaming? What kind of dreams?"

The hint of pleasure in her expression faded. "Does it matter?"

Maybe it didn't. Wasn't it bad enough she was dreaming?

When she'd first arrived in Nagalok, Tanvi's fiery temper had intimidated him. But it had moved him, too. He'd hated watching

215

that be stripped from her, even if she'd chosen it, chosen to join the stable and leave behind the miseries of mortal life.

That choice, Nayan had always said, meant everybody benefited. Both the nagas of Bhogavati and the children Asha spirited away could find their balm in escape.

Now, though, Venkat wondered if that wasn't quite right. Not if dream runners could dream again. "What do—"

"Don't ask me that," Tanvi blurted, her head whipping up. Her glistening eyes bore deep into his, and his pulse stuttered. A fierce light radiated out of her face, as if all the dreams she'd harvested in the last seven years were concentrated behind her undeniably aware expression.

He couldn't pretend Tanvi was anything but awake. As he studied her, his incredulity darkened into suspicion. Had Asha noticed anything like this? And if so, why hadn't she said anything to him?

The two of them were certainly going to have a chat as soon as possible.

"Don't ask," Tanvi repeated. "It hurts."

The anguished plea rent him down the middle. Venkat put his hand on hers, hoping she'd fathom what he was trying to say—that she wasn't alone.

Something crackled between them, bright and electric, and Tanvi twisted away. "Don't touch me!"

"I— I'm sorry," Venkat said, but it was automatic. His nerves still tingled. *What in the worlds?*

"I just need you to help me stop this." Her legs kicked under her chair. "That's all. Then I'll leave you alone."

How was he supposed to do that? "I can't help you if you won't tell me anything."

Tanvi shook her head. "Just—just fix it. And you can't tell Nayan, and definitely not Madhu."

"I won't."

Though she glared at him, her chin quivered. "Promise me."

Venkat didn't know if that was a good promise to make, but fresh guilt filled him, gray and heavy. Failing the dream runner initiation meant he'd skipped all this. It meant he'd lived a pleasant life in Nayan's house, playing with stories and dreams, while Tanvi and the others suffered. And he didn't have even an inkling of how to make it better.

"I promise," he said earnestly. "Just tell me what's going on."

Tanvi touched her temple. "It *hurts*." She wailed. "Make it stop."

"It's okay," Venkat soothed, though sirens were going off in his own head. "It's okay."

It wasn't okay, of course. It was really bad.

Ire sparked deep in his chest. Why hadn't Nayan told him this could happen?

Then the spark went cold, extinguished by a worse question. *What if he doesn't know?*

How was Venkat possibly supposed to fix this on his own?

A handful of hours later, marginally rested and dogged by his own version of dream residue, Venkat set about visiting his stable of runners. The nagarani was right; they couldn't be out harvesting if the garudas were on the prowl. He still couldn't believe they'd struck in broad daylight. The problem was, confinement to their quarters would leave his runners at loose ends, trapped with no purpose and irritable.

At least, he thought with a touch of irony, they wouldn't pick up on his own bad mood.

He'd never been to most of the runners' rooms, and Indu's was as good a place to start as any. The few touches of color among the serviceable furnishings and bare white walls merely drove home how little she had. Venkat balked at the soccer balls dumped in her closet, while Indu stared vacantly at her cabinet, her hair matted in snarls that must have formed while she was sleeping.

This isn't right, insisted a voice deep within him.

"Show me your wares," he said, feigning clinical disinterest and Indu, lighting up, pulled them from her cabinet.

Pretending to examine them, Venkat looked her over for signs of Tanvi's strange alertness. Luckily, Indu appeared as hyperfocused on boons and the soccer ball she would buy as always.

"This is boring!" she complained, but it was flat, lacking the passion of Tanvi's anger. The life in it. "When can I go harvesting again?"

"Soon," Venkat assured her. "But you have to stay here in your room for now, okay? You can't go anywhere until I say otherwise. It's important."

When Indu nodded, Venkat pointed to a vial of chrome chalcedony. "I'll take this one." He handed her a fraction of a boon in exchange for a dream about a girl tutoring a horde of bloodthirsty green dinosaurs. But for once, he couldn't care less how that dream might be useful in his work.

Indu's face grew even rounder with joy as the boon disappeared beneath her skin. She was so young, Venkat thought miserably. Just a kid.

He wanted to say something to let her know he was there for her, to comb through her tangles, but all he could offer was a pathetic, "See you soon."

Indu had already turned away, absorbed in the soccer ball to come. Venkat quietly closed the door behind him.

The same scene played out again and again with the other runners, until the visits blurred into one. The only things that changed were their faces and the objects of their obsession.

Bharat, his video game controllers partially obscured by a blanket. "Is it time to harvest?"

Srinivas, his plush bunny abandoned in a corner. "I want a boon."

Mona, her chapter book open to a folded page and forgotten. "How much for this dream?"

And on and on. Each conversation carved out another hole in Venkat's heart. He wanted to drop to his knees and give them all a hug, but he couldn't.

Jai's room, of course, was empty.

So far, Venkat's runners appeared healthy enough, free of Tanvi's symptoms. That was something, he figured. They'd even accepted that, for now, they were restricted to their rooms, and Venkat would be coming to them for their appointments.

But of course they had. Pursuing boons became its own addiction. As long as they could keep doing that, who cared about the particulars?

This couldn't go on.

Venkat had saved Tanvi for last.

She lay against her pillow, and when she gazed up at him, he knew he'd definitely been reading too many stories, because his first thought was that she looked like a character in one, the maiden whose night-sky tresses had spilled all around her in "a spray of silk and shadow." Or maybe it was her curious expression, so present and rich with feeling.

Promises to her aside, the right thing would be to go to Nayan and fill him in. Venkat knew that, and his stomach writhed with self-reproach. But, he reasoned, not until he had a better grasp on the situation. Madhu was already scheming to get rid of Tanvi, and Asha's little stunt had only made things worse for all the runners.

His heart pounded, sluicing him with waves of fearful heat.

Shaking it off, he pulled the chair over to Tanvi's bed. "How'd you sleep?"

Her shoulders sagged. "I dreamed. And dreamed. And dreamed some more."

Until then, Venkat hadn't admitted to himself he'd been hoping it was all a fluke. Some type of monumental misunderstanding. "Do you want to tell me about it?" he asked. "Maybe it'll help."

"No." Her voice grew thick, and her face crumpled like she might cry. "I mean, maybe. I don't know."

Dread ate into him, caustic and awful. He'd seen those same tormented features only hours before, swimming through his nightmares—not only Tanvi's face, but Jai's, too, smeared with a film of blood and tears.

The ghost images returned now, just as injurious and impossible to escape. Both Tanvi and Jai had accused him of forsaking them, and then, eight years old again, he'd watched as the collapsing theater crushed his family over and over, leaving only a stew of red pulp. Every shard of bone, every scream had inserted itself into his skin as forcefully as Mummy's and Papa's accusations had insinuated themselves into his soul. It was all his fault. All of it.

Venkat scrambled for the book he'd grabbed from his bedside table, a purple volume with garlanded nagas embossed on the cover. He'd planned to give it to Tanvi later, after he'd shown her what she needed to see, but the dream was poisoning him all over again. "Can I read you a story?"

She sat up, her sorrow sharpening into suspicion. "Why?"

He flashed his cheeriest smile. "I've had this book since I got here, almost. There's a story in it I used to read over and over when I was lonely. I thought you might like it, too."

"I'm not lonely."

"No, but I bet you miss harvesting, and a dream's a type of story, right?"

Tanvi stared at the book. "Can you help me?"

Could he? He didn't even really understand what was happening to her.

"I don't know," he said honestly. "But I'm going to try."

Tanvi nodded, then rested her chin on her knees. "You can tell me the story," she said. "I used to really like books. I think." She winced. "It hurts to remember."

Venkat heard the part she left unspoken. Pain aside, she shouldn't be remembering at all.

He settled into his seat and began reading aloud, occasionally adjusting his angle so Tanvi could see the illustrations, too. Although Venkat knew the story of how Princess Uloopi, a lonely widow, became enamored of wandering Prince Arjun so well he could recite it by heart, it still never failed to draw him in as deeply as the first time he'd heard it at his grandmother's knee.

He'd needed this distraction, but now he wanted to give Tanvi the same comfort that memory gave him.

At some point between Uloopi bringing Arjun down through the Ganga River into Nagalok to spend a day and night together as husband and wife and Uloopi's subsequent journey to Prithvi so her new son could live alongside Arjun's human bride and their son, Tanvi dangled her legs over the side of the bed. She sat close enough to lean her chin on Venkat's shoulder if she'd wanted to. When she blinked, he tried not to notice how long her lashes were.

What was he thinking? Just because this was a love story?

Venkat threw himself back into it. Arjun's human son Babruvahana had been cursed to kill his father on the battlefield, and only Uloopi knew the truth of that curse. Despite everyone else's horror, she coaxed Babruvahana into going through with the unthinkable deed. Then, once Arjun lay slain, she brought out a nagamani and rejuvenated him.

"See?" he finished. "Everything worked out."

Tanvi assessed him, her gaze shrewd. Venkat should be alarmed by that, at least disturbed.

He wasn't.

Worse, he *liked* the glimpses of her curiosity. The flares of her passion. She was too animated for this lifeless room, too vital to be hidden away. Maybe it was selfish, but the thought of dousing that spirit a second time made bile rise in his throat.

Get up. His pulse ticked faster and faster, a clock counting down the minutes until he'd need to head to the archives and unlock the doors for the public. *You have to show her.*

Just when he'd almost convinced himself, Tanvi reached for the book. Relieved, he gave it to her.

She ran a finger over everything but the embossing, like the nagas might sprout fangs and attack. "Do you think there's a nagamani for fixing dream runners?"

Funny, Venkat thought. *All these dreamstones, and not a single wish-granting gem.* "If there is, nobody told me."

For so long, he'd yearned to forget his own past. He'd envied the dream runners, who'd passed the initiation and had their hearts stilled. Their pain stamped out. They couldn't be hurt.

Watching Tanvi now, desperate to forget whatever it was she refused to tell him, Venkat considered not showing her. Letting her stay oblivious like the others.

But even if he did, burnout was coming. He couldn't freeze time.

"Tanvi," he said, "tell me what you remember. I can't help you if I don't know."

223

"None of that matters. Initiate me again," she pleaded. "I know you can."

He had to fight against the lump in his throat. "Do you know why I ended up here?" he asked. "My family died. In front of me. And I couldn't do anything to stop it."

Tanvi watched him, so wretched it tore at his heart. "Wouldn't you want to forget that if you could?"

Wouldn't he?

"No," Venkat said slowly. "I wouldn't. If I don't remember them, it's like they never lived at all."

She buried her face in her hands. "I just want my bracelet," she whimpered.

That settled him. She had to know. "Tanvi, did you ever *get* your bracelet?"

"Of course not—I never got to sell my last harvest. If I had, I'd have the bits of boon I need." A beat passed, and she added, full of frantic hope, "Do you want to see my wares? I can get them."

Something knotted in the pit of Venkat's stomach. He tried to ask it nicely, but the question felt like spitting knives. "How long have you been a dream runner?"

"Asha brought me here when I was ten, and I'm seventeen now, so seven years?" Tanvi chewed on her bottom lip. "Why?"

"Why would it have taken you seven years to earn one bracelet?"

Her body grew stiff, her shoulders rising around her ears, and the skin around her eyes pulling tight. "What are you talking about?" she whispered.

As sick as he felt, Venkat plowed ahead. "How long does it take you to earn a boon? How many dreams?"

He could see her mentally doing the math. "No," she said finally. "No. That— No. Just no."

"How many bracelets should you have by now?" Venkat asked, resigned. He had to be the biggest jerk in all the worlds.

"No," Tanvi told the air. "You're wrong."

But she sucked in a breath.

This was the worst victory Venkat had ever won. His voice came out hoarse and exhausted. "Do me a favor. Go look in your closet. If I'm wrong, I'll give you all the boons you want."

His chest hurt. It would be so easy to keep shielding her from this, but he couldn't. She deserved the truth.

Her eyes trained on the plain white blanket, Tanvi nodded. Then she got up, giving Venkat a wide berth, and approached the closet.

22

Tanvi hesitated outside her closet. Venkat was wrong; all she had to do was prove it.

But her feet wouldn't move.

She could feel Venkat's gaze drilling into her spine. How was she supposed to do this with him watching? "Quit looking at me," she snapped.

Paper rustled behind her, followed by the squeaking of chair legs. "I can wait outside," Venkat offered.

Tanvi nodded and took in the entrance to the closet. There was nothing to be afraid of.

Stupid, she told herself. *You know what's inside. You saw it just . . .*

Now in her line of sight, Venkat edged toward the exit.

At least two days ago? Not possible. Sitting in the closet was her daily ritual. She couldn't get by without it.

Her head threatened to go foggy again, but she shook it hard. Nothing could have changed in that time. The box would still be there, awaiting the moment she could lay her perfect charm bracelet in its velvet-lined nest.

That moment would be today.

Venkat turned the knob.

"N-no," Tanvi stammered. "Don't go. Just—just don't watch, okay?"

Keeping his back to her, Venkat closed the door again. "Okay."

Now she had no excuse not to take those last steps into the closet. Her foot twitched a half pace forward.

Two. The number hounded her. Two days ago? Like two soccer balls?

What had Nitya said?

I don't care, Tanvi insisted.

Hadn't Indu—

I. Don't. CARE!

She glanced around the room, at all its familiar blankness and the absurd, out-of-place decorations that Asha must have given her. Asha, who had known about Nitya and maybe thought this was a way to make up for it. For having separated the sisters in the first place.

Tanvi didn't *want* to understand Asha's motivations. She didn't want to see anything except her dreams and her vials.

Please don't leave. Nitya's frightened voice, her stricken face.

Tanvi's hands trembled, each finger its own earthquake. She didn't feel them, though. She couldn't feel anything except the straitjacket of nerves contracting around her heart.

She'd only felt that way once before, when she'd downed three cups of burnt coffee from a convenience store in Bangkok to wait out her night owl of a dreamer and reap her harvest. When she'd smugly presented her wares to Venkat the next morning, her body had felt brittle, like blown glass. It had absolutely been worth the trouble—she'd netted a full three-quarters of a boon, her biggest triumph to date.

The nausea burned. If what Venkat was saying was true, had it been a triumph at all?

You don't have to do this, she told herself. *Just go back to sleep. The dreams have to go away sometime.*

But she did. She had to prove Venkat wrong. So what if Indu had two soccer balls? So what if Nitya had said . . .

Before Tanvi could change her mind, she marched into the closet.

Her immaculate wooden shelves greeted her, with the velvet-lined enamel box as their crown jewel. The empty one primed for its bracelet.

Empty.

Tanvi breathed in the familiar air of the space, then exhaled hard, letting the panic drain out. She was safe and at peace here in its four walls. Venkat had really scared her for a second, true. But he didn't know what he was talking about. He wasn't a dream runner.

She crouched in front of the shelves and regarded them the same way she always had. Soon there would be a bracelet to fill the space.

But there wasn't one now.

"See?" she called, whirling around. "I was right!"

Venkat looked as exhausted as she felt, but he met her in the closet. She strode forward, on the brink of demanding the boon he'd promised.

Gold glimmered in his eyes, a reflection in his brown irises. So much gold.

Tanvi spun around again.

The pink velvet–lined jewelry box gleamed with gold. So did most of the surrounding shelves. Bracelet after bracelet with charms dangling from the links.

Not one bracelet. Multiple bracelets. So many she couldn't begin to guess the number.

Her thoughts blinked in and out. Her hand inched forward on its own. It took hold of one of the bracelets, then another.

They felt so solid. Tanvi's hand brought them closer to her face. Her eyes, though she hadn't told them to do that, either, scanned the charms. All seven pristine, perfectly formed dangling shapes on a delicate gold chain. Just as she'd always imagined.

No. No, no, no!

Tanvi flung herself at the other bracelets, scrutinizing one, then the next. A small, messy pile of gold loops accumulated on the floor, identical in every respect. She stared at them, then stormed past Venkat.

The accusation blasted out of her, almost loud enough to give voice to the backlog of screams in her chest. "What did you do?"

Even as devastated as she felt, as lost, she didn't miss Venkat's abashed pose, his shoulders and neck hunched over. He raised his head, and the sadness she saw there made her pause. "I traded you boons for your dreams. And you bought bracelets with them." When he smiled, it was as bitter as that first cup of coffee from Prithvi. "Over a hundred, I believe."

"No," Tanvi said. "You *lied* to me. You let me believe this—at least a hundred times!" Just like Asha had known about Nitya and led Tanvi by the nose in her stupid, conniving games. As if Tanvi was a doll to wind up and move around.

The pile of discarded bracelets in the closet sparkled in her thoughts, cruel, compelling. She had to go look at them again.

This time, when she touched the shimmering pile, she knew they weren't right. They didn't *sing* the way her real bracelet should. No wonder she'd thrown them down.

Get lost, she thought impulsively. *I don't want you.*

As if they'd heard her, they did, coming apart in a gale of golden particles that grew dimmer and dimmer until they disappeared altogether.

"They're just copies," Venkat said, though he sounded baffled. "Even so, they shouldn't have vanished like that."

Tanvi felt so small. Smaller than the smallest of the charms. She wanted to be as numb as Indu.

She thought of how Venkat had read her that story, of how close they'd sat, taking in the drawings together. How she'd liked that.

She could have punched him. None of that should have happened. None of it.

"Where's the real one?" she managed. "I know you have to have it."

Venkat jerked, clearly startled. "The real one?"

The shock in his voice almost felt good. Like she still had some control. "I said it, didn't I?" she countered. "Take me to my bracelet. Please."

Venkat escorted Tanvi from the lift and into what looked like a giant dreamstone vial. "Welcome to my workshop," he said. "Only Nayan knows it exists. Well, and now you."

Tanvi almost ran back to the lift, her already-dazzled senses overloading. Incredible crushed-jewel blues and greens and purples blazed out from the equally incredible serpent and sea murals on the walls. The aerial view of the kingdom from the balcony made her feel like she was flying, and the shelves and shelves of dreamstones could've been a witch's cupboard.

A feeling of recognition swelled up. This was everything her ten-year-old self had ever wanted.

But she didn't care about that. She couldn't afford to. Just like she didn't care about all the guards they'd had to dodge on the way here—there really were a lot more roaming the halls now—or how much nicer Venkat's tunnels were than the runners'. She only cared about her bracelet.

Venkat glanced shyly at her. Her cheeks got a little warmer, and she wished he'd look elsewhere. "This is where I use the dreams you bring me," he said, sounding self-conscious. "The ones I don't sell. I make things."

Make things? She didn't answer.

With a sigh, he took out a key and tapped it against one of the murals. A mini storeroom appeared in the wall. "That's our private treasury. Coming?"

Relieved, Tanvi hopped in after him.

Cubbyholes lined one side of the cramped treasury. She scanned the nooks, her belly doing somersaults. A dented tricycle, a video game console, a deflated soccer ball—her stomach lurched. Indu's soccer ball.

Tanvi had expected the real bracelet to be displayed on a velvet shrine like the box in her closet, not slotted in among random odds and ends. She'd been sure it would beam even brighter, so bright it washed out everything around it.

There. Her heartbeat quickened to warp speed. A gleam of gold peering out from the dimness.

"Do you want to get it," Venkat asked, "or should—?"

Tanvi scooped the bracelet off the shelf before he could finish and stepped back into the sunshine. Her bracelet, finally. She'd waited so long for this.

She closed her eyes, afraid to believe it was real. Gold flashed behind her eyelids. The solidity of the cool metal in her hand—*this* was what all the nights of running dreams had really been for. She understood now.

Her limbs stiffened with anticipation.

Slowly, so slowly, Tanvi opened her eyes and gazed down.

The bracelet sat in the cup of her palm, a thin gold squiggle like a snake. Tanvi gobbled up the sight of it, dying to saturate herself with every single detail. She was actually holding her bracelet. The only thing she wanted.

Fireworks burst in her chest.

The glittering charms. The tiny, delicate links. The gold, the brilliant, beautiful gold . . .

Her breath hitched. Something wasn't right.

The metal was dull, even scratched in a couple of places so grayish nickel showed through. Nickel? It should be twenty-four-carat gold, the kind a princess would wear.

And the charms themselves were clunky, not really defined. She took a quick inventory: the carousel horse, the quarter note, the toadstool, the unicorn's head, the open book, the intertwined hearts. Where was the daisy?

The jump ring where it should be hung broken from the tarnished chain.

Tanvi's euphoria clouded over, and her throat rebelled. This wasn't at all how she remembered the bracelet. It was supposed to be pristine, like the ones the boons had granted her.

But it was still her bracelet. She pasted on a rubbery grin. As long as she had it, Asha and Venkat and especially Nitya could never hurt her.

She rubbed one of the remaining charms between her fingers and thumb—the rearing unicorn's head.

It just felt like a piece of metal, and the rusty tang stung her nose.

Where was the delight? Tanvi gripped the bracelet tighter. The completion that was supposed to fill her until there was nothing else?

Doubt needled her. Why was the daisy missing?

Dad was supposed to fix it, I think, but then you disappeared.

Leave me alone! Tanvi squeezed the charm, desperate to smother the voice. She squeezed harder, until the metal cut into her skin. Then harder still.

The charm stabbed her, and she cried out.

A drop of blood, so red against the junk gold, bloomed on the unfinished edge of the unicorn's stumpy horn. Tanvi wiped it on her thigh. It didn't mean anything. She shouldn't have pressed so hard.

She draped the bracelet around her wrist and waited. The joy would come now. It had to.

Nothing. The scratch on the quarter note only mocked her.

Hot tears pooled in her eyes. The bracelet was a lie, just like everything else.

This "treasure" she'd spent her life yearning for? A cheap toy among other cheap toys. A worthless trinket her ten-year-old self had reimagined as a talisman.

Against all the colors of the gemstone workshop, under the unforgiving spotlight of the sun, the bracelet looked like the piece of trash it was, something to be thrown out without a second thought.

The all-consuming hope that had raged in her, driving her from harvest to harvest—and apparently from copy of crappy bracelet to copy of crappy bracelet—fizzled out, and in its place the now-familiar gloomy gray fog descended, so heavy she wanted to curl up on the floor and disappear beneath it.

It wasn't *fair*. She stomped her foot. She'd sacrificed everything for this. Everything.

From a universe away, as she ripped off the bracelet and thrust it at Venkat, she heard him say, "I'm sorry, Tanvi. I really am."

Another memory tried to unfurl and fell apart in the middle, but not before she saw Nitya's face at the moment the garudas attacked. The mirror Tanvi didn't want. *You owe me*, it charged. *This is your fault.*

Tanvi collapsed onto Venkat's work stool. She had to erase all of this. "Reinitiate me," she demanded.

"You still want to do that?" Venkat's voice was hesitant, and he laid a hand on hers. She didn't have the strength to push him away. "You don't have to."

Yes. The word sat on the tip of Tanvi's tongue. The dream-stones on the table before her formed a fairy ring, enticing her to step inside and forget.

Venkat waited, and the mix of worry and softness in his face, like he really cared what she would choose, snagged on something in her chest. If she said yes, she wouldn't remember that, either.

"I'll do it if it's what you really want," Venkat said. She could hear his reluctance, but the choice was hers.

All she had to do was agree. If she did, nothing would ever make her cry again.

But her finger still stung, and that little spot of blood wouldn't let her be. How did she know Madhu would leave Nitya alone? And their mom?

Plus, Venkat didn't even know about Madhu. What if she hurt him?

"Before you decide, though," Venkat stressed, "I have to ask you something. What are you dreaming about?"

Tanvi went cold all over. She should have known this was coming.

Her temples thrummed with the memory of Nitya pleading with her not to go. The missing daisy charm felt like a vise clamped tight around her head. Something about that charm—about that day—was important.

"What's so awful that you have to erase it? Help me understand," Venkat said.

"A girl," she blurted, too tired to resist. "She looks like me. Her name is Nitya."

Venkat nodded. "Okay . . ."

"I can't stop dreaming about her." Tanvi knew she should shut up and run, but the words kept coming. "She won't leave me alone."

"Tanvi . . ."

"She's my—" Tanvi's courage foundered. "I don't want to dream anymore," she said weakly.

Venkat's hand tightened on hers. "Your what? You can tell me."

She had to forget: the bracelet, Nitya, all of it. Her heart, stupid beating thing, refused to let her. *The garudas,* it drummed. *Your fault.*

"My sister." The words shot out before she could muzzle them, and Tanvi wanted to smack herself.

Why had she said that? Now he'd change his mind about reinitiating her. After all, hadn't he just said he'd never want to forget his family?

She heard his sharp intake of breath. "Wow. I—"

Tanvi yanked her hand out from under his and ventured to the

236

balcony railing. She stared at the sky and the sun, at the palace and people below. She turned back to the vials and mosaics in rainbow hues, so intricate only magic could have made them. After the plain darkness of her own room, it was all an assault on her senses.

So many colors. So many scents—the jasmine and champak and jewel-fruit floating in from outside. So many sounds—Venkat's low voice and that awful, accusatory pulsing in Tanvi's chest. Her skin still bristled everywhere the bracelet had touched it.

A tear trickled down her cheek, and she impatiently swiped at it. "You're not going to help me now, are you? Because you think me remembering her makes up for your family or whatever."

She'd meant for him to get mad, too. To yell like she was yelling. Instead, Venkat watched her with so much sympathy she could scream. Why was he being so *nice* about this? "Are you sure that's what you want?" he asked quietly.

What did she want? To sleep again, without dreams and memories. Without waking to see any of this. Without knowing the truth about her bracelet.

And without the dense thicket of stupid feelings rubbing her raw. Most of all, without that guilt, bitter and tipped with talons and feathers, the guilt that insisted Nitya deserved to be safe from the garudas and would be if Tanvi and Asha hadn't led them straight to her door.

Tanvi's shoulders slumped. The guilt was too strong. "I want you to reinitiate me, but . . ."

Venkat looked so hopeful she couldn't stand it. "But?"

"But not . . ." She tried one last time to hold out. "Yet."

Relief brightened his face like the sun burning through mist. "Good," he said, and he squeezed her hand again. "And not just because of my family."

Tanvi squirmed. Why did he even care what she did? And why was he looking at her like that?

She glanced down to where Venkat's fingers were wrapped around hers. It felt warm and safe. Almost comforting. She didn't know what to do—was it okay to stay like that?

Their eyes met, and Venkat must have realized he was still holding her hand, too, because he suddenly let go and started fiddling with the nearest vial. An amethyst, its violet as rich as the dream it must contain.

Her neck heating, Tanvi bobbed her wool-stuffed head in an approximation of a nod. "I'm not promising anything. Only that I'm not doing it right this second."

Venkat smiled at the dreamstone. "I'll take that."

23

For Venkat, the next day passed in a flurry of meetings, curating elements for his project with Nayan, and fending off the line of anxious customers that seemed to triple in size each time he looked up. Word of the runners' hiatus had spread faster than a serpent could slither, and suddenly everyone who'd ever flirted with the idea of experiencing a mortal dream was turning up in the archives.

Who cares if you get to dream? Venkat could've demanded. What if *he* didn't have enough scraps left to move into the next phase of the project? Or to help Tanvi and the others?

Instead, he smiled politely and explained again and again that dreams needed to be rationed, and surely the ban on travel would be lifted soon, allowing the runners to resume their harvest. He smiled and smiled: at Nayan, at the courtiers, and especially at Madhu, trying to feel her out.

Madhu returned amiable smile for amiable smile, going so far as to praise Venkat's handling of an unusually aggressive customer, as if she'd never threatened to report Tanvi to Nayan. That only worried Venkat more.

He longed to escape into his experiments, but he settled for checking on the sky-faring sofa. Like the scissors, it showed every sign of enduring. He should have been excited, but he just felt irritated. A doll-sized flying couch wouldn't solve his problems. The runners were counting on him, whether they knew it or not.

Tanvi was counting on him.

He hadn't even had a chance to ask Asha what really happened to the two of them on Prithvi.

That night, determined to clear his head, Venkat climbed under the covers with his favorite volume of naga folktales. But he kept reliving Tanvi sitting beside him, chewing on her lower lip as he read from the purple book and hugging herself tighter at the tense parts.

Not only that, but then she'd held his hand and told him about her sister. She'd scorned the fake bracelets and insisted on the real one. Unlike Jai, she'd turned down the illusion. Did that have anything to do with why the copies had disintegrated?

Piecing together what had woken her might be the key to preventing burnout.

Venkat's pulse sped up. She'd been *awake*.

How could he possibly put her back to sleep?

The next morning melted into a haze of yet more meetings, the first of which began at dawn and left him no time to check on the runners. Venkat's mind buzzed with chatter—the location and placement of extra sentries; the menus for the picnic at the Lake of Lovers' Tears and the wedding feast, including delicacies from each clan's region so none of the royal guests felt snubbed; his own consultations with the official tailors—but once he and Nayan set foot in the workshop, he pushed all that aside.

Now that they were alone, he had to find out what, if anything, Madhu had reported to Nayan.

"I thought today was never going to end," Venkat said as breezily as he could while lining up the dream elements he'd curated for Nayan's latest request—grief crossed with sweetness—on the worktable. "It's exhausting being you. How do you stand it?"

Nayan raised an eyebrow. "Well, someone must be me," he said in a perfect deadpan, "and I am arrogant enough to believe I am best qualified to fill the position."

Hoping his nerves didn't show, Venkat laughed.

Nayan strolled around the table, assessing the array of elements: a jar of crystallized tears, the isolated chanting of a choir, and the honeyed but acerbic nectar from a silver crabapple. For extra sweetness, Venkat had selected a bristle from a broom the dreamer's grandmother had passed down through the family line.

He knew he'd chosen well, and yet he held his breath.

"But you are certainly worthy of being my successor." Nayan's stern visage dissolved into a proud smile. "Such an eye for detail! I could not ask for a finer dreamsmith."

"Thank you," said Venkat, spotting his opportunity even as pride cascaded over him. "I suppose that means you want to know how my experiments are going?"

"I do, indeed." Nayan's eyes crinkled with mirth. "That saves me the trouble of asking."

Venkat busied himself fetching the sofa experiment from its shelf in the treasury. Somehow, even as he got better and better at his craft, showing Nayan what he'd forged on his own time never failed to reduce his nerves to a bundle of sparking wires.

"After your success with the scissors, I am certain to be impressed," Nayan said, all business again.

As chuffed as Venkat was with his whimsical little couch, he wasn't sure it could meet that high bar, sky-faring or not. He had to convince Nayan he was on top of his job, not give him another reason to listen to Madhu.

With clammy palms, he offered up the sofa.

Nayan examined it with slow deliberation. His expression remained an impenetrable mask. Once he'd finished, he asked, pointedly, "Is that all?"

"What—what do you mean?" Venkat stammered.

"I expected more." Though mild, Nayan's tone conveyed a realm's worth of disappointment. "Certainly you have had enough time to turn out multiple pieces since we last discussed your progress. Did I not make it clear we have a deadline?"

Venkat heard the unspoken censure all too loudly. He'd let his attention splinter, singling out one dream runner, when it should have been fixed on his craft. On their project, which would, at least in theory, solve the problem of the garudas and make dream running irrelevant.

242

"So you talked to Madhu," he said, striving to sound conversational.

"I did." Nayan sighed. "My son, what is it you seek to achieve here?"

Venkat could tell Nayan he'd been planning to try forging calibrated potions next, until he'd seen the life restored to Tanvi's face and heard the emotion in her voice, and how that had inspired another idea.

He saw her plaintive eyes again, begging him to help her. The shy smile when she reached for her bracelet in the treasury.

A warning bell went off in his brain. No, he couldn't say anything about that.

If Nayan even suspected she'd been here in the workshop . . .

"She's burning out," Venkat blurted, and something in him broke. "I can't lose another runner. I'm sorry."

Lying. He was lying yet again to the person who'd taken him in and given him a home and a craft. Who'd seen potential in him no one else had.

Nayan regarded him for a moment before speaking. "I see."

Venkat braced himself for a lecture. After all, he'd broken a cardinal rule by letting things with Tanvi get personal, never mind sharing secrets that could put their entire operation in jeopardy. Even if Nayan didn't know that part, the fact that Venkat was hiding things just made it all worse.

He should tell Nayan. He should.

But he couldn't forget the pain in her voice, the grief in her eyes.

"I realize you feel an attachment to the girl," Nayan said kindly, "and that you are invested in her well-being. Indeed, the fullness of your heart is what grants your dreamsmithing such power. But I have entrusted you with a tremendous responsibility, and what I ask of you in return is respect."

Venkat bowed his head. "I know. But I can't let her go. Not yet, anyway."

Please, he chanted, *please don't say it.* If Nayan suggested they send Tanvi back to Prithvi like they'd done with the other burned-out runners, Venkat didn't think he could keep from arguing.

Nayan motioned toward the shimmering spectrum of dream-stone vials covering the shelves. "If it brings you a measure of peace to attend to her, then do, but not at the cost of the fruits of our labor. Our history is fraught, pockmarked by the scars of war and constant siege. A revisioning, as it were, is in order—but I cannot do it alone."

Revisioning. A new vision. That was as good a name as any for dreamsmithing. "I know," Venkat said. "I'm sorry."

"I have no need of an apology." Nayan sighed. "I merely wish to know that you are not losing focus. We are a partnership, Venkat, a team. If you cannot trust me, and I cannot trust you, how can we revision things for our people?"

Shame flooded Venkat. Why couldn't Nayan have just yelled at him?

"All I want from you, my son, is the truth."

Venkat groped for the dream elements on the table. He had to change the subject before that truth came barreling out. "Didn't you say something about grief and sweetness?"

244

The trance slipped over him like a shining coat, and he vanished into its embrace. Eddies of color and feeling danced all around, and he wished he could stay like this always. Lost to the worlds, a compliant vessel for whatever new concept wished to come forth.

A thousand possibilities bloomed in his thoughts, but he let them all fall away like petals from a shedding flower and concentrated on the intersection of grief and sweetness. His hands traced the path his spirit laid out, trekking from the familiar, gutting devastation of his family's deaths to a new image of Tanvi and Asha on Prithvi, eating too-big scoops of ice cream in a park with Asha's mortal boyfriend, who sat outside the frame. That had never actually happened, of course, but it made no difference. The imagined conspiratorial smiles were sufficient fuel, and the swing of emotions drove his hands as he combined and sheared away.

All too soon, the trance released him, and he looked down, panting, to see a new section that glowed with promise. It featured a dawning sun and what looked like an assortment of variegated golden eggs. Many, many eggs, at least a couple thousand.

Eggs. Dreamsmithing never failed to astound him with what it could generate when he got out of the way and let the elements guide him.

"A fine symbol of renewal and hope," Nayan remarked. "And this is why I have not yet filled you in. If you have expectations . . ."

"I wonder how many omelets that would make," Venkat mused, still out of breath. "I bet they'd be delicious."

Nayan let out a surprised laugh. "I daresay a multitude of

omelets!" He clapped Venkat on the back. "I am proud of you, my son. Your craft shows assurance and inventiveness both. And the resolve you soldered into your latest pieces—including the sofa—will sustain their integrity, ensuring they last. Without a doubt, you have come into your own these past few weeks."

Venkat couldn't help the grin spreading over his face. "Really?"

"More than that," Nayan continued, "you have thrived under pressure, and we are well on the way to completing our project on time. What we are doing here involves healing. The rejuvenation of our people."

"You're finally going to tell me what we're doing?"

"I know how frustrating it must be to wait for the specifics, but bear with me just a little longer. At present, I would tell you a story."

As desperately as he wanted to hear everything—after all, this was his project, too—Venkat bit down on the urge to protest. He'd been lucky to get off with a scolding, and he wasn't about to risk Tanvi's safety.

"A story I have, until today, never told another person." Nayan led him onto the balcony, where another table had been set up. The completed sections of their project glistered over its surface, phantasmagoria that shifted with each blink. Nayan must have assembled them while Venkat was in his trance.

Faint music drifted from below, as merry as the ringing peals of laughter that accompanied it. It all felt so surreal to Venkat, that anyone could be so carefree while he was trying so hard not to disappoint everyone who depended on him.

"Have you ever wondered where dreamsmithing originated?" Nayan asked. "Or how I knew what to look for in you?"

"Of course!" When he was a kid, Venkat had badgered Nayan with exactly those questions and received no answers. Now it appeared he might actually get them.

"The wanderer I met in the forest while in the sage's hut was not the only person to mold my view of the world, you see." Nayan adjusted his dupatta around his shoulders and tilted his head up to the teal-toned heavens. "I loved a woman once, and though circumstances forced us apart, my devotion to her remains true. She was brave. She was virtuous. She loved me truly. Alas, she suffered dreadfully at the hands of cold-hearted tyrants, and in her name, I swore I would find the means to bring justice to us all. Our people have waited long enough."

A lover? Venkat wondered what kind of woman could catch Nayan's eye and hold it for so long.

"As my hostility cooled, I began to observe mortals and their magic. Their inclination toward narrative. How they defined their world through perceived cause and effect. It is a power as potent as any spell; entire universes can be found along that arc, all formed of belief. And so I sought to harness and bring it to the nagas. After a little experimentation, I discovered that mortal dreams are as pliable as clay. But only if another mortal forges them."

He turned to Venkat with a soft cast to his patrician features that, in anyone else, might have been wistful. "For so long, we have all been spoon-fed a tale of enmity. Imagine that we could give rise to the conditions in which peace might bloom between our peoples.

Imagine, too, that we could even entertain such an outlandish idea. *That* is what we hope to achieve here, you and I."

Venkat recalled the representative from the clan of Maniak-khika, who had suggested peace talks at the council meeting and been shouted down. "But what about the garudas? They're still attacking us."

"Indeed. They would also be part of this revisioning. We all fail to see beyond the pain of our collective past."

"And you think *I* can do that?" Venkat almost laughed. "I think your faith in me is a little misplaced."

"When I call you my son, I do not do so lightly," Nayan thundered. "I recognized your inherent ability when you came to me, and I have nurtured it since. Do not dismiss that honor with false modesty!"

"Okay, okay." Venkat held up his hands in surrender. "So what exactly does this mean—*if* you can tell me, that is?"

"You and I will bring true healing, one section at a time." Nayan gestured to the table. "Behold, the entirety of our collaboration thus far."

The sections didn't match, scraps of varying sizes and textures as random as remnants of fabric pieced together, but the emotion from each one struck Venkat in the heart. He'd forged every one of them, and he could feel how seamlessly they might fit together. How, if they did, they would create something immense enough to heal the scars of endless strife.

The nagas had taken him in when he'd had nowhere else to go.

248

Nayan and Asha had become his family. If he could give them such a huge gift, of course he would.

For all his dreamsmithing ability, he couldn't imagine a more noble goal.

"A revisioning," Venkat said. "I like it. Tell me what I need to do."

24

Of all the reasons Tanvi wanted to go back to being a dream runner, boredom had never counted among them. Her body twitched with jitters. Two days of being confined to her room with nothing to distract her from her dreams and memories but Venkat's occasional visits, the purple book he'd left behind, and the food that appeared before her door, though, had her raring to jump out the nearest cracked window.

She thought about sneaking out, but where would she go? Madhu still had her pendant.

Instead, she'd scribbled a note for Asha and left it with her dinner dishes: *I need to talk to her.* If it actually reached Asha, she would know who Tanvi meant.

Tanvi even tried flipping through the purple book, but the memories, never further than a blink, continued to blister and spike.

Agonizingly distinct recent ones: the unbearable revelation of the bracelet; the feel of Venkat's hand on hers that had her flushing in ways she didn't understand; Nitya's accusing words and their bee sting. Older ones riddled with moth bites: Nitya giggling in their blanket fort; Mom praising Tanvi for locating a lost earring; something about Dad, two rows of tiles, and a Scrabble board?

Tanvi could hear the giggles, could see the tiles, could feel the rosy sheen of Mom's pride. She felt even sicker. If she hadn't run away seven years ago, she might have those things plus a million more now.

What was she supposed to *do* with all these huge, dizzying feelings? Even the plain white walls of her room made her frantic, never mind the closet that had been her sanctuary. Just glancing toward its dark mouth was enough to gouge more holes in her stupid heart. She'd been lied to, and the anger and despair threatened to strangle her.

Assuming this jail cell of a room didn't crush her first, that was. How could she break out?

She needed help, and Asha still hadn't answered. Maybe, a voice deep within urged, she *should* tell Venkat everything.

On the third day, Tanvi jolted awake from a nightmare. *Rain,* she recalled, the dream's tentacles still convulsing around her.

Even now, she saw the chilling ashen light filtered through noxious clouds. She saw a face like hers, but distorted by revulsion. She heard a sentence as serrated as a blade: "No one wants you." She felt hands shoving her into a downpour, and talons sinking into her skin. It was what she deserved.

The gray feeling, as bleak and sodden as the cloud-stained sky in her nightmare, settled over her, draining her like an open wound.

Tanvi got up and inspected the mirror over her sink; hollows shadowed her eyes. She looked lost.

Were the other runners deteriorating, too, caged in their rooms like this?

Eventually Tanvi bathed, dressed in the purple-and-silver chaniya choli Asha had gifted her, and brushed her hair. It wasn't to impress Venkat, of course, she informed her pretty reflection. It was so he would take her seriously. Then, after forcing her breakfast down, she waited.

The sun rose higher into the sky beyond her window. At last, a knock came at the door, and Tanvi let Venkat in.

She couldn't believe how relieved she felt at the sight of his familiar face. It made no sense, since he was the one who'd conned her into working for fake bracelets he'd probably made himself— and then stolen away.

"How are you?" he asked, his eyes soft and sincere.

"Bored. It's awful in here."

"I figured as much." Venkat sat down on the floor and motioned for Tanvi to join him. "Asha's picnic got me thinking."

She stayed standing. Asha and Venkat, the two people she'd trusted. Suddenly she really needed him to know how much he'd hurt her. "You *lied* to me."

Venkat bowed his head. "Tanvi, I'm really sorry about the bracelet. I am. At least let me do this much for you."

"Do what?"

"I can't let you out of here, as much as I wish I could." Tanvi could hear his regret. "But I can at least try to help with the boredom.

How would you like to go somewhere?"

"You just said you can't let me out of here," she pointed out, suspicious.

"Well, I can't, not exactly. But it'll *feel* like we left the palace." Venkat set down a pair of rime crystals, one in the shape of a key wreathed in pale green ivy and ice-blue lotuses and the other a matching door. "Ta-da! I just forged these. Want to try them out with me?"

Tanvi thought about that. A chance to escape her cell and forget the last few days? "You mean, like dreams? I'm doing enough of that already."

"More like lucid dreaming. You know, where you take control of the dream? Except we'd start out that way, and no one else would see us."

She almost said no. Dreaming by choice felt like chugging a goblet of poison for fun. But . . . "And I'd stay in control?"

"Just like you are now," Venkat promised.

"Okay," Tanvi said finally. That part did sound nice. Besides, Venkat already looked so discouraged. "But you'd better take me somewhere really cool."

"Deal." Venkat offered her the key. "Ready?"

Tanvi took it. He held up the door, and she turned the key in the lock.

Tanvi couldn't recall ever having seen much of Bhogavati before. Everything was so rich, from the showy people in their heavy silks to the *this could buy entire countries on Earth* bungalows and villas with their scale-shingled roofs to the groves of juicy jewel-fig trees. It was like a wedding cake on steroids. No, an old-time fairy-tale painting in shades of stained glass.

Her brain, which had spent seven years tuning out anything unrelated to dreams, felt like it was going to short out. Too much stimulation, too many worries running in circles like a rat in a cage. They'd done that experiment in school, she remembered out of nowhere, putting a white rat through a maze in exchange for treats.

Desperate to go blank again, Tanvi squeezed her eyes shut. But she could still feel the rat's supple fur under her fingers—she'd gotten in trouble for sticking her hand in the cage, while Nitya, scared of the rat's beady gaze, stood back—and for a minute, she couldn't tell whether she was there in the classroom on Earth or here in Nagalok.

She was dissolving, and like dream wisps escaping their vial, soon there would be nothing left.

Something cool pressed into her palm. "Drink," Venkat said from nearby. "It'll help."

Hisses suggested at least one naga slithering around, but she tried hard to ignore the sounds. To ignore the aromas of the food stalls mere feet away. The music that sneaked into her heart, seeking to seduce her along its journey.

She took a sip from the goblet and almost swooned. It tasted like the nectar of the gods to her parched tongue—sweet, frosty, and totally refreshing. "What *is* this?" she asked, opening her eyes to see she held a silver rose. A clear liquid shone in the depths of its satiny petals. "Amrit?"

Venkat laughed. "Water."

Water. Plain water. Tanvi swished the liquid around in her mouth. "I can't handle this. It's all . . . all . . ."

And that brought on another memory: the day she'd made her own soda. Mom and Dad wouldn't let her have more than half a can, so she'd added water to it. But when she tasted the "cola," it was flat and flavorless. All she'd done was ruin the good thing she already had. "I can't."

"It's okay. We'll take a carriage from here, and you can relax." Venkat pointed to the gilded traffic going by: pedestrians, carriages, even a line of royal palanquins. "Not those—they're here for Asha's wedding."

Tanvi scrunched up her face. She didn't want to think about Asha and Chintu, or Sameer. And she definitely didn't want to think about Nitya.

Her side tingled, nerves alive with awareness again. Venkat stood inches from her, as close as they'd been in her room—all she had to do was reach out, and she'd touch him.

Her cheeks on fire, she pointed to the nearest carriage. "That one!"

Venkat followed her to the pearlescent scallop-shell carriage. There was no driver, but four swans drew it on thin golden chains they carried in their beaks. "Sounds good to me," he said, and together Tanvi and he climbed onto the turquoise-and-gold velvet seats.

She'd expected a long, leisurely ride over the ground, but before she could get situated, the swans, feathers glimmering, soared into the sky. Not even thirty seconds passed before the carriage sailed high over the landscape, which resembled a gemstone mosaic.

A watery shape appeared below them, a cosmic looking glass reflecting Lord Surya's radiance. "The Lake of Lovers' Tears," Venkat announced. "It's really more of a lagoon, seeing as how it opens onto the ocean, but I guess that didn't have the same ring to it."

Tanvi couldn't take her eyes off the numerous topaz shards cresting the surface. How many tears had been shed across the worlds, only to end up here, transformed into jewels by the sun's rays?

But she forgot the question as a wave of black-and-orange monarch butterflies descended on the lake, devouring the chunks of topaz. The black veins and dotted borders of their wings lit up with a lemony halo as they flew away again.

She didn't even notice that their carriage had touched down on the shore, not far from the butterflies' feast, until Venkat nudged her. "This way."

They hurried barefoot to the far side of the lake. Lavender grains of sand like decorative sugar wedged themselves between Tanvi's toes, and she glanced at Venkat. "Where are you taking me?"

"I want to show you something," he said, his eyes crinkling with mischief. "Almost no one ever comes back here, because they all want to see the monarchs. But that's not the only beautiful thing here."

They headed toward a group of lambent moonstone boulders. "You want to show me rocks?" Tanvi asked. "I already have dreamstones." But there was something weird about how the light hit the boulders. "I see it!"

Venkat grinned. "You and I may be the only people who ever noticed."

Without thinking, Tanvi grabbed his hand. "Well, come on!"

He glanced sharply at her, but didn't say anything when she pulled him forward.

There, tucked away in a niche in the rocks like a secret, was a carving of a woman in a snake-scale sari. A nagamani flamed from the circlet set across her forehead, and her cupped hands held out a crescent moon. The boulders were near enough to the water that, with each reunion of sea and shore, spray frothed around her feet.

"I think this is for Lord Chandra," Venkat murmured, his remark almost lost to the salty wind.

"But is she praying," Tanvi asked, "or rejecting him? The moon, I mean."

Venkat squeezed her fingers, and his appreciative smile was the sweetest thing she'd ever seen. "Good question."

As the wave receded, delicate script came into view on either side of the carving. Tanvi reluctantly dropped his hand and bent to look closer. "It's a poem. 'The Nagini's Night Song.'"

Venkat knelt beside her, not seeming to care that the water was soaking into his nice clothes, and read the inscription aloud.

Silver-stained surf my robe
Liquid silk, my tears
Trimmed in foam, so delicate
A maharani's discarded pearls
I wear them well

How bright, how alien
This sea breathes
My skin, salt and seaweed
Aphrodisiacs from other days
I inhale

At the mention of silver stain, Tanvi could see another body of water, this one beneath a star-strewn sky, its waves all grays and blacks except for a slight overlay of lunar lacquer.

Weave my breath
With crashing tides
O my heart,
Strum your sitar strings,
Call out the moon

Another ocean, each of its waves an unfurling sari of dark swells edged with foam-pearl lace. They lapped at her feet, at her ankles, in search of the night bride who would swathe herself in them and be claimed by Lord Chandra, the moon.

Venkat's voice came from far away, an incantation excavating the memory. The words of the unnamed poet wove in and out of the vision, a braid of light and shadow against a nocturnal seascape. Tanvi only caught fragments of the verse, but they were more than enough.

My skin alone stretched too tight
Over this cage

Each bone a steel bar
A pause between crashes
A pause between breaths
A pause between lives
A single sigh—

I pray the ocean swallow me whole
Drowning is the sea's way to fly

Two groups of charcoal rocks bordered the expanse of sea. There, the nagini paced, waiting for Lord Chandra to appear. And as the half-moon emerged from his cloak of clouds, silvery beams splashed down onto the water. They turned to shards of moonstone, creating a silver-white path leading to the sky.

Kohl-dark ocean kisses my knees
Thief! You who steal my breath!—
Who stroke my sari with bold, wet fingers
Who seep, unrepentant
Into my flesh

Her palms grew hot and prickly. The nagini definitely wasn't rejecting Lord Chandra. She wanted to be his night bride.

"I think he has something like twenty-four consorts?" Venkat said, frowning. "No, twenty-seven, all sisters. And he loves Rohini best."

Tanvi laughed. "It doesn't sound like he had room for anybody else."

"Oh, that never stopped him. Before he married these sisters, he ran off with Tara, who was already married to Brihaspati, got her pregnant, and almost started a war in the heavens. And later, favoring one wife among all twenty-seven got him in big trouble."

Venkat grinned again, and his tone took on a storyteller's resonance. "They say that Chandra's father-in-law, Daksha, repeatedly warned him to treat all his wives the same, and when Chandra didn't, Daksha cursed him to fade away. But Lord Shiva, knowing the world would suffer without a moon to illuminate the darkness, intervened. Daksha was right, he said, and there did need to be some consequences for Chandra's favoritism, but what if they could strike a compromise? For fifteen days each month, Chandra would fade to nothing, and for the other fifteen, he would grow into fullness. Daksha agreed to the terms, and that's how we got the lunar cycle of waxing and waning."

"That's really sad," Tanvi said.

"I don't know; at least we have a moon."

She pointed to the woman in the boulders. "No, her. She wanted him, but she never got him. I saw it while you were reading."

Venkat didn't say anything, but she could see she'd captivated him.

Each time the nagini had tried to step onto the moonstones, Lord Chandra had disappeared behind the clouds, and the path vanished.

Though she'd waited, kneeling in supplication, until daybreak, he'd never returned.

Tanvi kind of hated the moon for that.

"Hey," Venkat said softly. He nodded at her, his eyes even warmer than usual, a complete contrast to the coolness of the moon in her vision. "Are you okay? We can go back if this is too much."

"Why did you . . . ?" she began.

He wandered closer and took his hands in hers. "Why did I what?"

Her mouth dried up again. His grip was strong, solid. She couldn't help noticing how nice his deep purple kurta looked against his brown skin. The way he was gazing down at her made her belly turn a flip. "Why did you bring me here?"

"I promised Asha and Jai I'd look out for the rest of you, and I wanted to say I'm sorry."

Tanvi stared at him. But what did that have to do with this place?

"You're so brave, Tanvi. Braver than me. I wanted to give you a good story, something special." Venkat sighed, releasing her. "But that doesn't fix the problem, does it? Asha's still going to have her picnic here and get married to that dud of a prince, and you're still dreaming."

Tanvi couldn't stop thinking of the night bride Lord Chandra hadn't wanted. She was just as clueless. Nitya was right; she was totally stunted. She'd grown up without a heart, and she had no instincts to trust.

"But I'm going to help you," Venkat finished. "I promise."

The tension in her arms went slack. Help was exactly what she needed.

When Tanvi turned to him again, Venkat was surveying the

261

water. "I want you to know you can trust me," he said.

She and the spurned night bride might have been the same person, both overflowing with a child's hope for the impossible. Tanvi wanted to trust Venkat.

Yes, she'd tell him about the memories. About meeting Nitya and needing to keep her safe.

Maybe he would even understand.

Before Tanvi could stop herself, she said, "I need my memories back. All of them."

"Apprentice!" Madhu's voice invaded Tanvi's room like an encroaching army in pursuit of Venkat a second before she marched over the threshold. "What is the meaning of this, playing games when there is work to be done?"

Venkat been so thrown by Tanvi's pronouncement that he'd accidentally terminated their dream journey to the lake. Of course Madhu had to show up now. Madhu, who never visited the runners' quarters.

He slapped on his blandest smile and stood. He had to seem composed, like he didn't care she was obviously checking up on him. Like he wasn't replaying Tanvi's plea on loop: *I need my memories back.*

What memories? Was she remembering her sister? The rest of her family? Even who she'd been?

Tanvi cowered on the floor, her fingers tangled in a lock of her hair. After what she'd shared with him, he wasn't about to let anything happen to her.

"Just making my rounds with the runners," he said lightly, pocketing the crystals before Madhu could get a better look at them. "You know, doing my job."

"Nonsense," she snapped. "It is your job to support Lord Nayan." To Tanvi, she added, "You try my patience, runner. I should report you to the lord for inciting the others."

Inciting the others?

Fear shot across Tanvi's face, and she rolled into a ball. She'd been so bright and alive in the dream version of the lake. So present.

Venkat's smile warped like old wood, and it was only his years of practiced diplomacy that kept him from telling Madhu off. "What can I do for you?"

Madhu examined the door to the room from both sides. She was as out of place as a peacock in the drab corridor. "Locks. I see none. Why have they not already been installed?"

"Forgive me, but why would we need locks?"

She turned an expression on him that was both grin and glower. "You mean to say you did not know your own beloved runners have been loose in the palace? And here I thought you were doing your job!" She crooked a finger behind her, the wrinkles in her cheeks deepening with delight. "I found one roaming the archives this very morning and am returning him to you. Bharat, I believe his name is?"

A blank-faced Bharat trotted into the room.

Bharat had done *what*? It took every ounce of self-control Venkat had not to react. "Thank you for handling the matter," he said evenly, though he wanted to scream.

Madhu nodded, a crisp, decisive motion. "The lock must be on the outside." She gestured for emphasis.

"Got it," Venkat replied. The thought of locking the runners in made him ill. Weren't they already trapped as it was? "I'll take it from here."

"Lord Nayan's work is far more significant than you could possibly fathom." Madhu's cobralike gaze bit into him, molten with the promise of paralyzing venom. "He would not wish me to tell you this, but someone must: despite his many burdens, he has chosen to keep you, tiresome foundling, close. To award you a place of honor at his side." She spared a scathing glance for Tanvi, who clung to the back of the wooden chair and stared at the purple book on the table as if hypnotized. "One might believe you would acknowledge that honor by striving not to compound his troubles."

Venkat swallowed hard. She was right, and he couldn't argue. Not with that, anyway.

"I will not report your laxness this time," Madhu went on, "so as not to disturb him, but if you fail to keep your own runners in check, do not make the mistake of assuming further leniency." She jabbed a finger at the door. "Locks on the outside. Do not forget."

Then she was gone, her footfalls echoing down the corridor.

The unexpected reprieve only made Venkat more nervous. Madhu wasn't doing him a favor. She was reminding him how Tanvi's presence here—maybe even his—was at her whim.

"Wait here," he told Tanvi, who'd finally sat up, then led Bharat back to his room and reiterated in detail that the runners had to stay put. Whether it got through this time, Venkat couldn't say.

Everything was slipping through his fingers like lakeshore sand.

When he found Tanvi again, a thunderhead of terror and gloom had swept over her features. She was blinking rapidly, like she couldn't focus.

Venkat didn't think he'd ever been as angry at anyone as he was at Madhu right now. What she'd said was only half true: Yes, Venkat owed Nayan a huge debt, one he'd never be able to repay. But Tanvi had a claim on him, too. She needed him, and Madhu had no right to scare her like this. No right to try to control Nayan's operations, and especially not Venkat's own.

He imagined Tanvi alone in this dismal place, descending again and again into the loss of her bracelet, falling into nightmares with no one to wake her. Forget books—she deserved all the enchanted things he could forge for her, all the time and help he could offer. She and the other runners deserved him. *I'm sorry,* he thought, like an incantation. *I'm sorry.*

"The door and key are for you. My gift." None of his experiments were supposed to leave the workshop, but he didn't care. "Just, uh, let me work out the kinks first, okay?"

Tears glistened in Tanvi's eyes, turning them into chocolate opals, and he couldn't tear his attention away. Despite all her efforts to make herself small, her heart, her fire, blazed in those eyes.

It was wrong, and he knew it, but suddenly all he wanted to do was cross the few feet separating them and crush her close, burying his face in her beautiful hair.

Tanvi watched him, the tilt of her head almost a challenge.

"Tanvi," he said, the syllables sparking like a damselfly born of a diya's flame.

Before he could take a step toward her, an ominous rattle rang out from the hallway, accompanied by a theatrical hiss.

Tanvi ripped her gaze from his and plunked herself down on the bed, her arms crossed tight.

Asha, Venkat swore, had the worst timing in the universe, worse than even Madhu.

A rattlesnake zipped across the floor in a wave of undulations almost too swift to see and stopped at Tanvi's feet, where it transformed. If Madhu had looked bizarre beside the tiny room, Princess Asha was a fanged streak of lightning hurled down from the sky, all high-voltage energy and coruscating scales, with a store of amusing comments on hand for any occasion. Normally Venkat would have welcomed that.

At that instant, however, he had never wanted to see her less.

"At lasssssst!" she exclaimed. "I was certain I would *expire* by the time she left."

Burying his frustration deep, Venkat shut the door. "How kind of you to join us, Your Highness."

"Count yourself fortunate I could steal away at all," Asha rejoined, daintily settling herself next to the bed. "Either Madhu or one of her sycophants harries me day and night, ensuring I never have a moment to myself. And if not them, then Chintu or my parents." She gave a haughty sniff. "Do you know how *exhausting* it is, pretending to care for a buffoon?"

Venkat thought, but wisely didn't say, how exhausting it was pretending to keep up with *her*.

Asha hissed at Tanvi, her jewelry tossing golden sparkles around the room like one of the palace's chandeliers. "And you! Why could you not sssssimply *wait* rather than seeking me out so publicly?"

"It was just a note!" Tanvi yelled. "It's not like anyone knew I was talking about Nitya."

There was a note? Venkat wasn't following.

"If you had waited but a few more hours, I would have come of my own volition." Asha's mouth curved in a parody of a smile. "When you are beset at every turn by the ceaseless joys of nuptial preparation and assuaging the fears of the people, carving out quarter hours for clandestine rendezvous rather becomes a luxury, you see."

Tanvi looked at her askance. "What does your wedding have to do with anything?"

"Perhaps," said Asha, "it is not the wedding I care for, but rather avoiding additional scrutiny when Madhu and Nayan Uncle already suspect us? Come, Tanvi. Surely you are smarter than that."

Venkat moved closer to the bed and held up a hand. When Tanvi and Asha continued to glare at each other, he added, "Tanvi. What are you remembering?"

Tanvi fiddled with a loose thread on her choli. "Memories." She shrugged, and her hair shimmered, framing the misery in her cheeks and mouth. "I guess from before?"

"Which memories?" he pressed. "When did this start? With the dreaming?"

He'd expected her to resist, for any confession to be like wresting a too-tight cork from its vial. Instead, the answer burst out of her in a hasty staccato. "My head's like Swiss cheese. I remember stuff, but it's all full of holes and broken. If—if I think about it too hard, it *hurts*."

Venkat parsed the torrent of words, trying to find the sense in them. "Okay. Why didn't you tell me before, though?"

We cannot have secrets between us, he thought inanely in Nayan's voice.

Tanvi grabbed his arm hard enough to hurt. "You can't say anything to Nayan. Or Madhu!"

She was terrified, he realized with a jolt. Really and truly terrified. What had Madhu done to scare her like this?

That question would have to wait. He wiggled his wrist and, when Tanvi didn't get the hint, said, "Could you let go? I promise not to tell."

Though she narrowed her eyes, plainly not believing him, she loosened her grip. He started to rub the spot where her fingers had dug in, but thought better of it. "I promise," he said again. "Just tell me what's going on."

Tanvi exchanged a glance with Asha, who waggled her head. "Go on."

"I didn't just dream about my sister," Tanvi mumbled. "I met her. The other day, I mean. We went to her house."

It was Venkat's turn to stare. "You did?"

"The garudas know how to find her." Tanvi dabbed at her face with the edge of the blanket, leaving wet spots on the white fabric. "Because we went there!"

"She speaks truth," Asha announced soberly. "I myself took her to the house."

Asha had done *what*? Venkat was being mauled from every angle. Tenderized.

"When I ran away and let Asha spirit me here, I hurt her. I hurt my whole family. My parents got divorced because of me." Tanvi sobbed so hard that the back of the bed vibrated against the wall. "I did that."

Venkat's breath snagged in his throat. "You can't think that's your fault," he managed to get out. *It's Asha's and mine.*

"When I saw her, she told me they thought I'd died."

"Tanvi . . ." Venkat didn't know what else to say. Her anguish buffeted him, too, almost palpable in its intensity. It was too big for either of them. Even Asha looked beaten down, her hand clutching something at her hip.

"In your story," Tanvi continued, her tears drenching her choli, "Uloopi gave up being with Arjun for the good of everybody else. I can hold off on being reinitiated until I know my family's safe. I owe them that."

"Wait, that wasn't what I—"

"I keep remembering stuff, but it's not enough. I can't— The memories, they're killing me. It's . . . it hurts, so much. I *have* to remember, but I can't, not totally." Her voice ramped up in speed and pitch, as if she couldn't restrain it any longer. "They're tearing me in half. They won't leave me alone, so I need them back. I need to remember. It's the only way. Please, Venkat, you have to help me."

He'd known she was struggling, but not like this. "Oh," he said, because he had to say something.

"I have to protect Nitya and my mom until Asha's wedding," Tanvi finished, and collapsed back against her pillow, panting like she'd sprinted across the palace.

"Yesssss," Asha sibilated. "Until my wedding." She thrust whatever she'd been holding at Tanvi, who unthinkingly plucked it out of the air. "Here. Now I must go. I have already overstayed."

"Oh, no, you don't," Venkat said. "You owe me an explanation, *Your Highness*."

Asha waved him off. "And you will have it. But not now. They will be searching for me even as we speak."

Tanvi eyed the folded piece of paper like it might detonate. At least her tears had subsided, replaced by distrust. "What is it?"

Asha was already shape-shifting. "You wish to speak with your sister, do you not?"

Both Venkat's and Tanvi's heads snapped toward her. "How?" Tanvi demanded. But Asha, now in cobra form, slithered off as abruptly as she'd arrived.

And then Venkat was alone with Tanvi again. He didn't know what to do, what to say.

"Can you just go, too?" she asked, eyeing the note.

Venkat still felt dazed. He still had so many questions. And he was dying to hear more about Nitya and find out what that note said. But he couldn't deny Tanvi's requests, not either of them.

He nodded, running through his inventory of dream elements,

271

considering the forged pieces that, so far, had endured. He'd come up with something.

He had to.

"Yes," he said, on his way to the door. "I'll help you get your memories back."

26

The paper in Tanvi's hand was starting to soften where she gripped it. She didn't know whether to read it or throw it out. Had Nitya gotten in touch with her? How? *Why?*

She ran a fingertip over the royal seal. The paper seemed innocent enough, the paisley pattern in blue, green, and purple as pretty as any of the other things Asha had left here. Pretty like the rest of the palace. Asha had probably never owned an ordinary thing in her life.

But, Tanvi asked herself, head pounding again, how had Asha gotten a note through when the borders were closed? Didn't she know how dangerous that was?

The greedy patrols were bad enough, but Madhu, with that hard-eyed, calculating stare and her secret garuda allies? It made Tanvi want to retreat under her bed.

Madhu, who had promised to hurt her sister if Tanvi dared open her mouth, had stood here. In her room. Brashly ordering a lock for her door. Venkat might believe Madhu had only been bringing Bharat back, but Tanvi knew the truth. It had been a warning:

she was being watched, and she would never get around the palace unnoticed. For all she knew, Madhu was monitoring her right now. Expecting her to unfold the note.

What if, by reading it, Tanvi ended up hurting Nitya even more?

The poisonous fog pulsed, pulsed, pulsed behind her temples. Tanvi wished, just a little, that she hadn't told Venkat to leave. That they were still together at the lake, watching the waves.

A memory bubbled up: Nitya's voice, drowning out everything else. *Let's be dragons. We can burn anything that tries to hurt us.*

Nagas were kind of like dragons, right?

Asha always hissed at anything she didn't like. It wasn't hard to imagine flames whooshing past that forked tongue.

Okay. Let's be dragons. Half delirious with pain, Tanvi tore the royal seal off the paper.

It wasn't a note. It was a packet.

A few small brown-green ovals fell out and rolled all over. Tanvi lowered herself to the floor and started hunting.

It took some frenetic groping, but she found all five. She held one up between her thumb and index finger. A bead. It looked like lichen-wreathed mud.

Where was the message from Nitya?

Tanvi glanced back at the paper. Two sentences had been scrawled there. *Water and feed. Single use only.*

No, she corrected herself. Not a bead. A *seed*. She had to water it.

She scoped out the room and seized on the pitcher. Empty— she'd drunk it all down. But maybe Asha's gold vase of flowers on the shelf, the one that had seemed so pointless before, had a purpose, after all. Tanvi dipped a finger in the liquid and sniffed. It hadn't been replaced even once that she knew of, but it still smelled fresh, like the pink blossoms blooming out of it.

She flashed back to the stagnant, oil-slicked puddles in Philadelphia, a total contrast to the sterile monotony of this room, before dumping out the flowers. After a deep breath, she dropped the seed in the pitcher.

It plopped through the leftover water, twinkling like a dreamstone as it vanished beneath the surface. She hoped it wouldn't need much in the way of sunlight, because with the inverted naga pupil she had for a window, it wasn't getting any.

Then she waited, afraid to breathe, but nothing happened, good or bad. Maybe Madhu *wasn't* spying. Or maybe Asha was playing her cruelest prank yet.

Nothing, and more nothing, and still more nothing. Tanvi got itchy.

More memories spiked, aching like a rotten molar, until her brain seethed and her stomach knotted. If Venkat couldn't help her, Tanvi swore she was going to bash her head against the wall.

The bracelet. It would soothe her.

Tanvi was halfway to her closet before she caught herself.

Whatever happened when—if—the seed sprouted, she thought, before the pain swallowed her in a stupor the exact tarnished gold of her bracelet, it had to be better than this.

Tanvi came to on the floor, her mouth disgusting. She'd been dreaming—something about a garden of miniature girls in sweet-scented flowers?—but the vision faded, insubstantial as the ether it had come from. The part of her that was still a dream runner hated to lose the dream before it could be properly harvested and stored in a vial. Another part, the one that screamed for reinitiation, couldn't wait for it to be gone. It hadn't really been hers, anyway. Just mental clutter passing through.

And the third part, the part that had agreed to be a dragon, wondered how it all ended.

Trying to quash that traitorous thought, Tanvi aimed her attention at the white walls, the plainness of the furniture. This room was meant to be a way station, she realized. A place to recharge before heading back out. If it felt like a home, she might start to think she was someone she wasn't. Someone who not only dreamed but also cared about those dreams.

She should have gotten rid of Asha's annoying gifts a long time ago. Every single one, starting with the gaudy vase of flowers.

The vase. The seed! Had it sprouted?

Tanvi raced over to the shelf. A plant had sprung from the water while she'd slept, green enough to be sculpted from emerald. No, blue as star sapphire. Wait—was that the violet of sugilite?

A plant that thought it was an opal. Tanvi wondered if she was still dreaming.

As she watched, a lone leaf bud sprouted from the color-changing stem. She gingerly prodded it. It shivered, unfurling like a fiddlehead fern, but instead of a leaf, rows of green barbs splayed in a graceful shape, one she recognized. A peacock feather.

What in the worlds did this have to do with Nitya?

The plant shivered again, and the feather tumbled onto the shelf. The rest of the plant dissolved as if it had never been.

Oh, gods. What if Asha had given her the wrong thing, and she waited here like a fool, and meanwhile the garudas ripped her family to gory shreds?

"Nitya?" she whispered, as mortified as if the feather's eye were judging her. "Um, are you there?"

Silence.

Tanvi had never felt more ridiculous, but the sooner she knew Nitya was safe, the sooner she could be reinitiated and forget this entire mess. "Nitya," she tried again, louder. "Hello?"

She didn't know what she was expecting. It wasn't like Nitya was going to jump out of the feather. And there weren't any strange whorls or symbols that might have been a message.

It was just a feather.

Tanvi grabbed it off the shelf. She'd chuck it into the vase and then toss the whole thing out the door. What was wrong with her, believing for even a second that Asha might care about anyone but herself?

If only that didn't make Tanvi's heart sting so much. She clenched the feather tighter. Why were feelings so *stupid*?

The tip of the quill sliced into the meat of her palm. Tanvi flinched, but before she could drop the feather, the cobalt-and-turquoise eye at the center blinked open, revealing a screen.

Nitya's relieved face appeared there. "Tanvi?"

"Nitya?"

"There you are. I was starting to think you'd never call."

Tanvi felt herself gawking. "What?"

"I made Sameer tell Asha to get hold of you. He didn't want to, but I told him I'd leak his film footage if he didn't." Nitya sounded triumphant. "I guess he believed me."

Tanvi didn't have the first clue what to say. Worrying about Nitya was one thing, but now that she had her sister here, her brain might as well have gone to Prithvi without her. "How do you think I'm calling you?" she asked, hesitant. That seemed safe enough.

"My phone, duh. Don't be weird." Nitya frowned, and it was so controlled, a slight lowering of her eyebrows. "Tanvi, *what* is going on?"

"Didn't Sameer tell you?"

Nitya shook her head. "Of course he did, but magic? Nagas? Like, do you get how weird this is?"

"So what were the garudas that attacked us?" Even Tanvi could hear her own aggravation. "You saw them, right?"

"I saw . . . eagles?" Nitya allowed.

"Eagles that *attacked* us. That attacked *you*."

Nitya didn't say anything.

Exhaustion made Tanvi's whole body heavy. Why bother? "I'm glad you're safe. I'm gonna go."

"Wait!" Nitya said. "Please. Look, I just— I don't understand. You're *really* in Nagalok?"

"Really."

Nitya gnawed on her thumbnail. "You need to come home. You know that, right?"

Tanvi's hackles went up. This whole dynamic felt familiar,

Nitya bossing her around, and Tanvi pushing back. Had that been their pattern? Whatever it was, she didn't like it. "I have to go," she repeated.

How do you hang up a feather? She really hoped she didn't have to poke the eye.

"Tanvi!" Nitya made a frustrated noise. "No. Please. This is . . ." She sighed, and Tanvi could actually see the fight drain from her face. The face that should have been recognizable or else a stranger's, but wasn't either, that drew Tanvi in and drove her away at the same time. "I don't know, okay? This is really weird. We thought you were dead."

The guilt snapped at Tanvi, so she automatically turned its teeth on Nitya. "Well, I'm not!"

"I know. That's not what I mean. It's just—" Nitya took a breath deep enough that Tanvi could hear it. "You're my sister, and you're still here. Wow. Also, how? I'm super confused, but really happy?" She offered a tentative smile, and Tanvi felt herself mellowing in response. "What I'm trying to say is, I don't understand any of this, but I want to. Okay?"

"Okay," Tanvi said. Then, because this was too serious, too mushy, and she felt itchy again, she added, "I'm talking to you on a peacock feather."

Nitya giggled. "You're what?"

Tanvi folded the feather over so Nitya could view it. "See?"

"Whoa," said Nitya. "Double whoa. I was already going to kill Sameer for keeping this a secret, but I'm going to have to think of something even worse."

"I harvest mortal dreams," Tanvi blurted, not sure why she was telling Nitya that. Or why it mattered if Nitya was impressed. "It's my job. I sell them to the nagas. I mean, I sell them to this human guy named Venkat—he's the broker—and *he* sells them to the nagas."

Nitya watched her with rounded eyes. "Oh. Um. I take pictures? Of typical things in fresh contexts?"

They stared at each other, and Tanvi was pretty sure she'd never felt more awkward in any of her memories. But at least she didn't want to hang up anymore.

"It's actually pretty cool here," she said. "Venkat just took me to this lake where butterflies eat topazes that used to be tears."

"Uh, right." Nitya didn't sound pleased, and Tanvi realized her own mouth had turned up in a smile, like when she'd been in the surf with Venkat, listening to him read that poem.

Too late, she tried to backtrack. "It wasn't real, but it was."

Nitya only looked doubtful. "That sounds . . . nice, I guess?"

How did Tanvi keep saying the wrong thing?

"Crap, I have to get to class," Nitya said after what felt like five years. "I don't want to!" she rushed to explain. "But I'm happy you called."

Tanvi nodded. She didn't know whether to be relieved or disappointed.

"You'll call again, right?" Nitya's expression had gone remote, but the hope in her voice tore at Tanvi. "And tell me more about Nagalok?"

"If you don't tell Mom about me. I'm serious." No way could she handle that.

"I won't, I promise."

"Then yes," Tanvi said, and oddly enough, she meant it. "I promise, too."

Venkat had had to monitor Asha's schedule closely for two days before he managed to corner her. She'd been walled away behind a never-ending roster of wedding preparations, many of which didn't even pretend to be anything more than a glamorous excuse to keep her under constant surveillance. He felt like the hero of one of Bharat's video games, trying to dodge all the sentries, attendants, relatives, and even friends who'd been enlisted to sequester her and ensure her safety until after the wedding.

The guard barring the doors to Asha's apartments, a nagini in the equivalent of her twenties, scowled at him. Her armor clinked as she changed position. "The princess is not taking unscheduled visitors."

"I'm here on behalf of Lord Nayan," Venkat said smoothly. "He wishes for me to look in on Her Highness during what must be an intensely stressful occasion for her."

It wasn't exactly a lie; Nayan had instructed him to be Asha's support, hadn't he?

"Then why did you not send a messenger earlier?" the guard asked. Judging from her dubious stare, she was going to report this to Madhu.

Let her. Venkat had his excuse: he was worried about his friend.

"You question Lord Nayan's motivations?" He paused long enough for the accusation to register, then declared, "A quarter hour will be more than sufficient."

"Fifteen minutes and not a moment more," the guard snapped, "not even for Lord Nayan."

Venkat rewarded her with his most charming smile. "You do us a kindness, indeed. Lord Nayan never forgets that."

The guard's dour face softened a degree, and she even inclined her helmeted head before unlocking the suite and gesturing to the attendant waiting there. "Fifteen minutes."

"Her Highness can be found resting in her sitting room," the attendant announced. "I will accompany you there, but mind you do not tax her strength."

Venkat nodded and followed her.

Asha's apartments were grand even by palatial standards, with their gilt-trimmed mosaic ceilings, ornate decorations, and gold-and-silver-worked fabrics in every shade of the gemstone spectrum, and Venkat had always enjoyed his visits here. Today, however, they felt like an endless warren, made worse by glimpses of ladies-in-waiting sorting through her clothes, organizing her jewelry, and other tasks as mysterious to him as dreamsmithing would be to them.

No wonder Asha relished her trips to Prithvi so much. They were the one time she could truly be alone.

Venkat and the attendant finally reached Asha's sitting room. The attendant rapped at the doorjamb. "Your Highness, you have a visitor. Shall I admit him?"

As promised, Asha lounged on a divan in the center of the floor, languidly sipping from a golden goblet whose stem had been sculpted to resemble a pair of intertwining serpents. Resplendent in apricot silk spangled with seed pearls, she might have sprung from one of the copious champak blossoms garlanding the room. "You may let him by." She set down her goblet and blew Venkat a kiss.

If it had been just the two of them, he would have mocked her for hours.

"I shall be right outside if you need me, Your Highness," the attendant said.

With your ear pressed to the door, of course, Venkat amended silently. *Don't forget that part.*

"Yes, yes," Asha said, with a minor tilt of her head. "As always, your help is greatly appreciated, Udita."

The attendant bowed her head and backed out of the room, shutting the door behind her.

"At lasssssst," Asha hissed, her relaxed expression falling away. She leaped off the divan and glided to the farthest wall, beckoning for Venkat to do the same.

He strode after her. "You owe me that explanation, Asha. Was seeing your boyfriend really worth all this?" His banked rancor heated from a simmer to a boil. "Do you *ever* think about anybody else?"

Asha drew in a breath. Fury radiated from her glowing eyes,

284

and her fangs emerged. "How dare you! At least *I* aided Tanvi in finding her truth. Can you say the same?"

"I'm trying to—" Venkat cut himself off. They didn't have time for this. He lowered his voice. "Never mind. Listen, Tanvi won't tell me what's going on. What happened that day?"

"Is she using the feather telephones?"

Venkat nodded. Tanvi had told him that much, at least. "Where did you even get them?"

"The Night Market." Asha examined a plum-and-cerulean enameled lotus ring on her right hand. "That pleases me. I would have supposed Sameer had talked Nitya into keeping her distance."

"So what happened?"

He couldn't believe it, but the proud Princess Asha, descendant of the nagaraja and symbol of the clans' unity, actually hung her head. "I grew curious. Most of the runners have no true family left to speak of; that is one of my criteria for selecting them."

Venkat waved impatiently. "So?"

"Yet Tanvi did—and does. She has a twin sister and parents who treated her properly."

"And you still took her?"

"She was miserable and desired to go," Asha said. "Would *you* have refused her?"

"Yes, Asha! Gods." Venkat could have shaken her. He settled for running his hands through his hair. "That's not a reason."

Asha harrumphed. "I know that *now*. In any case, I went back to see what had become of her family. Instead, I found Sameer." She sounded marginally abashed. "I had not planned to return after

285

that, but who knew mortals could be so endearing? He told me all about Nitya, one of his oldest friends. How Tanvi's disappearance had shattered their family."

"And so you decided to set things right—without telling me?" Venkat almost laughed. "Or thinking about how it would affect Tanvi?"

His heart ached again. He was so tired of this. Of everything.

"I do not know!" she cried. "They were all so sad. They believed she was dead, and I knew otherwise. I had to act."

"And you're sure Nayan hasn't figured it out?"

"I am not certain Nayan Uncle concerns himself with these things. His attention is firmly fixed on our realm." Asha's smile was melancholy. "Nor do I blame him. Madhu, on the other hand . . ." She hissed. "The garuda assaults have unnerved everyone, and Madhu glories in it. Under her direction, they lock me in here, their inestimable prize, and dog my every step."

"You think *you're* a prisoner?" Venkat held out his arm to encompass the luxury of the sitting room. There were more jewels and priceless objects strewn on one table than most humans would ever see in their entire lives. "What about Tanvi, stuck in her cell? You know, if you hadn't basically advertised her to the garudas in the first place, you wouldn't be dealing with this now!"

"That was hardly my intention." Asha pressed her lips together. "I merely longed to see Sameer's world again before I wedded Chintu. It seemed my last chance."

Venkat wished he didn't understand, but he did. "Okay, but you had no right to drag Tanvi into it."

Asha examined her reflection in one of the decorative mirrors dotting the wall. "Judge me as you like. I will never regret reuniting her with her sister, and if two objectives could be accomplished at once . . ."

"But what actually *happened*?"

"What ever happens when fire meets water?" Asha lifted one corner of her mouth, then the other, as if considering her better angle in the looking glass. "They argued—rather dramatically, I might add—but during it all, I observed Tanvi. Despite the initiation, she had never completely forgotten Nitya, nor Nitya her."

Venkat recalled Tanvi telling him she'd dreamed about a girl like her. No, he grudgingly conceded, he couldn't be sorry she knew about Nitya any more than Asha could.

"If anything, I wish Sameer would let me apologize," she murmured, then turned back to Venkat. "And you? How are your days?"

The simple question caught Venkat off guard. All the secrets he'd been carrying alone sprang up, eager to pour out of him—the dreamsmithing, his project with Nayan, his failures over and over again to forge something that could help Tanvi. He hungered to share his burden, even with Asha. But of course he couldn't.

"I'm drowning," he said instead. "Juggling the runners, everything with the council, Tanvi. She wants her memories back now. How am I supposed to do that?"

He'd expected Asha to commiserate, but she *tsk*ed and tapped him on the head. "Oh, silly dream broker, forever overcomplicating things." She extended her hand, one of her rings twisted around so the cluster of rubies sat there like a dreamstone. "Tell me, what will you give me for such a rare vision?"

A boon! Venkat could have kicked himself. "You're amazing. Thank you."

She treated him to a pretentious grin. "It *is* my task as future queen to be of service."

His amusement faded at that, and he clasped her still-upturned hand. "You don't have to do this, Asha. Getting married, I mean. It's not too late to say no."

"The entire kingdom will be in attendance, Venkat. Many of the guests are already here. Have you not been paying attention?" The set of Asha's jaw was dignified, even stern, and she pulled free of his grasp. When she spoke again, it was a whisper. "I could not withdraw now if I wished to."

"Do you?" Venkat moved closer. "Maybe I can't help, but you can still talk to me, you know."

Asha beheld him with the proud bearing of the monarch she would one day be. No trace of her earlier emotions showed. "Certainly not. This is my duty to all of you, and I do not shirk my duty."

After a perfunctory knock, the attendant stuck her head inside the room. "I am afraid your time is up."

"Thank you for the message, Venkat," Asha said, all bright scales and sunshine once more. "Please convey my parents' gratitude to Nayan Uncle." Aiming a perky glance at the attendant, she pointed to her goblet. "Udita, would you be a dear and procure more jewel-lychee cordial for me? I find I have quite the thirst."

Venkat took his cue and left.

"I would like to see you add more harmony throughout, a subtle yet pervasive sense of concord." Nayan trailed his fingers down through the air. "Like the drifting of a leaf in the wind that, though unseen, bears it across an entire city."

A week ago, Venkat would never have supposed making things from scratch could feel like a chore. It had always been his art, his secret joy. Now even his beloved beautiful workshop failed to lighten his mood.

But then, he supposed, reaching for the dreamstone vial containing a piece of bark from a shalabhanjika's tree, he'd never forged as fast or as much as he had these past few days. The water in his well of inspiration, almost tangible in its strength, had run dry. All he could think of was getting Tanvi a boon to restore her memories.

How was he supposed to do that with the dream trade on hiatus and the runners no longer selling their wares?

"More harmony it is," he said, uncorking the vial before the qualms could show on his face.

Nayan paused his stream of directions. "You seem out of sorts, my son. Is something amiss?"

Venkat forced a laugh. "I don't know how you do it. This is exhausting, and I feel like I've barely slept all week."

He didn't add that, when he had, he'd dreamed of his grandmother and her gold elephant necklace, and he'd woken with tears drying on his cheeks.

Nayan offered him a sympathetic nod. "It is not easy, and I have asked a great deal of you these last few months. I do know this. But when we bring peace to our people, the strain will have been worth it."

Nayan's quiet conviction, steadfast and unshakable, had always been enough to carry Venkat along. Now, however, he needed more. "Can I ask you something?"

"Always." Nayan patted his shoulder. "What is it?"

"Aren't you worried? We don't have much stock left to sell, and the runners are bored out of their minds."

He steeled himself to hear that Madhu had reported Bharat in spite of her promise. Or that she'd complained again about Tanvi distracting Venkat from his true work.

Tanvi. The sensation of her hand suddenly enfolding his while the monarch butterflies feasted on their banquet of topaz tears, both shocking and warming him, surged through Venkat like the incoming tide, and he had to wrestle back a smile.

He couldn't risk exposing her.

Nayan contemplated him for a moment. "Ah. You are young, Venkat, even in mortal terms. Though they may loom large to you, the gripes of a few overly privileged nobles are nothing to fear. Once Asha's wedding is upon us, and our project complete, there will be no need for the dream trade. You know this."

"What about the runners?" Venkat countered. "The nobles can wait, but what if *they* can't?"

A note of irritation entered Nayan's voice. "My son, I have been patient with you, but your insistence on continually internalizing the state of our vessels grows wearying. They are a means to an end, and your energy would be far better spent on our actual mission."

A means to an end. Venkat wanted to refute the ugly words, to deny he'd heard them. But Asha was right. For Nayan, caring for the nagas was paramount, and whatever it took to secure that, whether marrying off Asha or sacrificing the dream runners, it was a price he was willing to pay.

The emptiness yawned in Venkat's chest. Nayan had been everything to him: his foster father, his home. How had things between them changed so much? Or had it always been this way, and Venkat had never noticed?

This must be how Tanvi felt, like she'd lost everything twice.

Shame heating his neck, he remembered how Nayan had left Jai to wander the streets of Prithvi with just a purse full of bills and no family to greet him or memory to guide him. Why had Venkat ever thought that was okay?

"How?" he demanded, knowing it was reckless. "You still haven't even told me what we're doing. Healing. What are we healing?"

Nayan's brows drew together. "I think perhaps you are correct," he said, "and I have, indeed, waited too long to show you the truth. I was wrong in expecting you to share my perspective on this when you did not have the full story. Let us finish up here, and then I will explain."

They spent the next half hour completing the section, Venkat doing his best to concentrate. Though ice didn't exist as such in balmy Nagalok, the air between them had grown glacial. When the trance came over him, it was a relief.

Once he emerged from that other space, he'd created a forest hut, the kind an ancient rishi might have lived in. Another egg, too, this one enormous.

Venkat didn't even care. He gave Nayan no time to praise the results. "So? What is it we're doing here? Why are you having me make you eggs and huts and all the other stuff?"

His hands behind his back, Nayan began to pace. "Family has always meant much to you, has it not, my son?"

Venkat nodded. What did that have to do with anything?

"It does to me as well." Nayan gestured to the hut. "That is the dwelling place of Rishi Kashyapa and his wives. Do you remember their story?"

"The story of how the nagas and the garudas came to be?" Venkat echoed. "Of course I do."

"What we are doing here is recalling an era of harmony. Our people and the garudas have both forgotten that we were not always at war. Acrimony has become baked into our societies." Nayan sighed. "War has become our way of life. You and I will remind our people that it was not always so. Nay, not remind but truly *revision* our future—by writing in peace over the once-immutable imprint of hatred. If we do not, the fighting will never cease."

That was great as far as rousing speeches went, but Venkat didn't want a speech. He wanted to understand. "What does that *mean*?"

"There is only one way to end the war," Nayan said. "As you know, I have devoted centuries of study to the problem, and in time, it became clear to me that no measures we take in the present can stem the enmity between our peoples. It has become the story of who we are."

"Right . . ."

"We must go to the root of the conflict—the wager that pitted Kashyapa's wives against each other. That is where all the problems began." Nayan's eyes blazed gold enough to rival the sun. "We must revise the old story."

"You want to undo the wager." Venkat felt like someone had blown off the top of his head. The enormity of what Nayan was suggesting—the purpose behind Venkat's entire training—was almost more than he could process. *I could rewrite history. Something I made could do that.*

All their talk of stories made sense now. Nayan had been preparing him for this from the beginning.

"What do you think, my son?" Nayan asked, watching him expectantly.

Venkat's mind had gone on strike. Every time he thought he'd gained a handle on what revisioning really meant, the true scope of it fanned out before him once more. For all his imagining why Nayan had taught him dreamsmithing, he'd never even approached the reality.

Revising history. What in all the worlds?

Hoping to digest it, to come to terms with such a profound idea, Venkat rubbed his temples and limited his thoughts to the wager.

It did make a kind of sense. One rigged bet had led to so much cruelty. "I get it," he said cautiously, "but wouldn't messing with the past cause other problems?"

He didn't know how to feel about that.

Then he remembered the council meeting and the garuda

attack on Asha and Tanvi. Maybe there really was no other way to realize peace.

"A fair question, and one I have spent much time considering. There will always be difficulties in life, my son. Yet they need not perpetuate wholesale slaughter and endless strife between those who should be kin." Nayan's smile was serene. "Do you see now why I waited to tell you our true aim? If you had known sooner, you might have begun to question your capabilities."

"Yeah." It came out in a huffed breath. "Yeah, I do."

"Good." Nayan patted Venkat's shoulder. "In my haste, I spoke too harshly. Take some boon fragments for your runners. Nourish them. Let that ease your mind."

"Thank you," Venkat said, though he would never be able to forget that while he considered the runners worth nourishing, Nayan didn't. But at least Nayan had unknowingly given him exactly what he needed to help Tanvi. "I will."

28

Tanvi was down to her last two feathers. She'd pieced together fairly quickly what Asha had meant by "single use," since the first feather had crumbled the second Nitya hung up, just like the plant that had shed it. And feeding the feather—that was the blood. Tanvi's palm had three painful puncture wounds, ugly and scabbed over. Stupid vampiric feather phones.

The cost was worth it, though, even if her conversations with Nitya were hard and stilted. At least the two of them were starting to work past the awkwardness. Yesterday, after their tentative hellos and a long pause, Nitya had slowly opened up about coping in the wake of Tanvi's disappearance; about Mom, Dad, and her simultaneously coming together and drifting apart; about the divorce and how empty the house felt now; about what Mom was doing these days—apparently she'd resumed her Ganesh pooja *and* joined a roller derby league.

I told her she should do them at the same time, Nitya had said, rolling her eyes and laughing. *Shri Ganeshji on wheels! Can you imagine?*

Each word had been bait on a fishhook, reeling Tanvi's heart in. *Mom. Dad.* More and more memory blisters had swelled up in her head as Nitya went on about her friends, including names that pinged at Tanvi, each one as agonizing as a zit perched on a nerve ending. She should have asked Nitya to stop, but she didn't. She couldn't.

As the morning wound on, Tanvi idly twirled the remaining green-and-blue feathers, torn between wanting to hoard them and dying to know if Nitya and Mom were still all right. If the garudas were still keeping their distance. The daily updates, along with Venkat's visits, were the only things making being trapped in her room at all tolerable.

But Nitya was in class right now, and Mom obviously wasn't an option.

One of the quills abruptly jabbed Tanvi deep in the meat of her thumb. She gasped. Blood pooled around the cut, triggering the feather.

Mom's face, older than Tanvi remembered but still so familiar, appeared on the screen. "Hello?" She nodded at someone outside the frame. "Right there is perfect. Thanks, Bryonie."

Heart shrieking against her ribs, Tanvi tossed the quill away.

"Hello?" Mom asked again. "Is anyone there?" She must have hung up then, because the feather turned to dust in midair.

Mom. Tanvi had almost talked to Mom. Almost let Mom see her. *Too close, too close, too close.*

Whatever the nosy feathers might think, this was a job she was doing, nothing more. Tanvi wasn't looking to get roped into any emotional tangles. She absolutely, definitively, one hundred percent did *not* need to call Mom.

Not even if a secret part of her longed to hear her mother say her name.

Her shoulders tightened. Now she was down to one quill. One last call with Nitya.

It was going to be so hard to relax into forgetting when Venkat finally silenced her heart again.

Tanvi could feel the next batch of memories gnawing their way loose like worms, sending pain sparking through her. She had to head them off.

Unfortunately, Venkat wasn't due for another hour or so, and she'd already done her calisthenics and bathed. Reading his book wouldn't help; it just made her remember their trip to the lake and the tale of the poor night bride.

And the slow flutter of Venkat's lashes as he appraised her with the same careful consideration he would a dream for sale.

Suddenly too warm, Tanvi forced the picture from her thoughts. That was *not* the distraction she needed.

The other runners, she thought hurriedly. What was happening with them? They didn't even have a feather phone to help pass the time.

She glanced at the door, then at the now-empty jar Venkat had dropped off yesterday. *I'm sorry I haven't had a chance to tinker with the crystals yet,* he'd said, *but I hope this helps a little. It's from the Night Market.*

Last night, Tanvi had unscrewed the lid of the jar and let the glimmering contents soar around her bed while she slept, night-lights to keep bad dreams at bay. Even in the morning sun that squeezed through her slit of a window, the cloud of fireflies glowed a gorgeous yellow-green, converting the blank space with its assortment of random objects into a cave of wonders. Venkat had told her they were the hearts of those who'd searched for something they'd never found.

Yesterday, Tanvi had called that sad. Today, it gave her an idea.

The lock Madhu had ordered hadn't been installed yet. . . .

Tanvi lifted the empty jar, and as if by some silent pact, the fireflies all returned to it. She screwed the lid back on and stepped into the doorway, where she hesitated. Was she really going to do this?

But this might be her only opportunity, and besides, she couldn't take another second of being detained.

Praying Madhu wouldn't catch her like she'd caught Bharat, Tanvi carried her shining beacon into the corridor and then to Indu's room.

Indu lay in her bed, surrounded by a dozen occupied and vacant dreamstones. Her glazed stare was absent, like a doll's. Going by the empty tray outside her door, she was still eating and drinking, but who knew how long that would last?

Jai had burned out doing his job. This was worse. This felt like a gradual fading, a stripping away, until one day, Indu just wouldn't be there anymore.

Tanvi bent over her. "Indu, it's me. Wake up."

No response. Not even a blink. Indu hadn't even noticed, not that Tanvi could tell.

A lump rose in her throat. She didn't have a nagamani, and she couldn't exactly ask the nagarani to lend her one, but at least she could do this much.

She opened the jar and released a handful of fireflies. After all, Indu was seeking, and so were they. Maybe they could keep each other company.

The fireflies flew straight to Indu's head, forming a gentle peridot-colored halo. Indu didn't stir, of course, but her new friends weren't going anywhere. Maybe their magic would get through to her somehow.

"Stay with us." Tanvi hesitated, then clumsily stroked Indu's hair back from her forehead. She couldn't say why, except that, according to her thumping temples, it was what Mom would have done.

Trying not to throw up, both from the pain and from the memory, she fled—but only to Bharat's room. And then to the other runners', until all the fireflies had been given out. She didn't think Venkat would mind.

Then she lugged herself back to her own room, where, still clutching the empty jar, she flopped onto her bed and passed out.

By the time she wrenched free from blood-splattered nightmares about garudas beheading her mother, Tanvi's body and brain felt like someone had worked them over with a sledgehammer. Dizzy, she sat up and realized she still hadn't called Nitya.

Her last feather. What if Asha couldn't get her more seeds?

Gritting her teeth, Tanvi stabbed her hand for the second time that day.

Nitya answered right away. "I don't want to freak you out, but there've been a couple of eagles circling the house. They were there when I left for school and still at it when I got home."

Tanvi froze. She might as well have been an ice sculpture of herself.

Madhu. It was Madhu, reminding Tanvi she was watching. Reminding her what the price would be for not keeping her mouth shut.

Had Madhu seen her sneaking out to visit the other runners?

"Tanvi? You still there?"

Tanvi put her face close to the feather's screen. "Is—is Mom okay? Are you?"

"Yeah, we're fine. Don't worry; I haven't told her anything."

"Good. *Don't.*"

"I wasn't going to! Calm down." Nitya, who should have been the one freaking out, seemed to think her news was no big deal. "I thought about calling animal control, but last I checked, they still considered eagles acceptable wildlife."

Tanvi wanted to reach through the screen and throttle her. Nitya didn't get how bad this was, not even after seeing the garudas. "It's not a joke! This is serious."

"So what am I supposed to do, hide in the basement all day? There're bugs down there!"

Someone knocked at the door, two sharp raps.

Despite everything, despite knowing how stupid it was, a secret thrill streaked through Tanvi. Venkat was here. "Come in!"

"Is that him?" Nitya called.

"I'm sorry I'm so late." Venkat's hair was rumpled, and the shadows under his eyes alluded to a sleepless night. "There's been another breach. I should actually be at the council meeting right now, so I can't stay, but I had to come by and try this first."

His words cast a pall over her jubilation at seeing him. *Madhu*, she thought again. The breach was happening because of Madhu, and Tanvi couldn't tell anyone. "Nitya wanted to meet you."

"Me?" Venkat sounded surprised but also pleased. "Well, let her watch, then."

"Watch what?" Nitya asked from the feather, which Tanvi propped up against the vase on the table. "Are you going to help my sister? If you're as great as she says, you'd better be."

Tanvi glared at her. "I never said that!"

"You didn't have to."

Venkat smiled in the direction of the feather. "I'm going to try."

"Garba's this weekend," Nitya chattered. "Why don't you come back for it? Venkat, my sister needs to come home."

"I couldn't even if I wanted to. I told you, the borders are closed." Nitya hadn't pushed like this since their first call, and now Tanvi wanted to hang up on her again. "Also, people would *see me*. Do you get that?"

"Asha could glamour you," said Venkat, whose opinion no one had asked for. "I wish *I* could go."

"See?" Nitya looked smug. "No one would have to know. I like him!"

Now Tanvi's glare included Venkat. Unfazed, he pulled a boon from his kurta pocket, round and radiant like the moon in her vision at the Lake of Lovers' Tears. "Speaking of Asha," he said, "if this works, we'll have to thank her. She's the one who suggested it."

A boon. Tanvi's entire body flooded with recognition—with yearning. All her old lust for the bracelet crashed back over her in a tsunami of need.

It didn't matter that she knew the truth. She craved the boon all the same.

"Ooh, is that a moon lamp?" Nitya asked. "I have one."

"It's a boon," Venkat said.

"Like a real, actual boon?" Nitya managed to sound both awe-struck and dubious. "If you're handing them out like candy there, maybe I should go to Nagalok, too."

"What do you mean?" Tanvi asked crossly. Letting Nitya see any of this was a mistake. It was Tanvi's, just Tanvi's.

"In all the old stories, it took rishis lifetimes of meditation and prayer to earn a single one of those. Don't you remember?"

Nitya's tone was teasing, but Tanvi bristled. She exchanged a troubled glance with Venkat. "I'm going to go now, okay?"

"Come home for garba, Tanvi. We'll tell Mom together."

Nitya waited, her smile hopeful, but when Tanvi didn't reply, her face closed off and she hung up.

Tanvi and Venkat watched the feather decompose. "That was the last one," Tanvi mumbled.

A hundred reactions passed over Venkat's features, but he only offered her the boon. "Ask for your memories to be restored. I don't know why I didn't think of it."

She cracked up. "Of *course*." Trust Asha to put together what had been right in front of their noses this entire time.

But then, as the boon lit up her skin, packed with all the wish-granting potential of the cosmos, Tanvi went quiet. This was it. She was about to remember everything she'd tried to erase. About to fill in all the threadbare memories that had sawed at her brain for the past two weeks, all the memories that dream runners shouldn't have.

"Are you ready?" Venkat asked, touching his fingertips to the back of her hand. His deep brown eyes were affectionate as they took her in, and she shivered.

"As ready as I'll ever be." She sucked in a breath, then intoned, "The restoration of all my memories."

The half-formed memory blisters in her head thumped horribly but refused to cohere. In her hand, the boon continued to glimmer.

Venkat's forehead creased. "Try again, but say you invoke them?"

"I invoke the restoration of all my memories."

The boon's gentle shine mocked her.

Tanvi's back grew uncomfortably warm and damp. Something was wrong, really wrong. "I invoke the restoration of all my memories!"

The boon sat on her skin, useless.

A horrible thought hit her. *What if . . . ?* "I invoke a candle."

Still nothing.

"I invoke a milkshake. Any flavor. It doesn't matter."

The boon's clean white light was turning dingier and dingier with each failed invocation, or maybe that dirty yellow was the color of Tanvi's fury. She'd been cheated.

From the twitch in Venkat's cheek, he'd had the same thought.

"I invoke my bracelet," Tanvi spat.

Just as she'd expected, the boon wavered and dissolved. Seconds later, a perfect replica of the perfect bracelets once heaped in her closet materialized on her palm. Tanvi lobbed it at the wall, where it promptly disappeared.

Venkat fished another boon from his pocket. "I invoke Tanvi's bracelet."

The boon might as well have been Nitya's moon-shaped lamp.

If Venkat hadn't been there, Tanvi would have stomped right over to the archives and confronted Nayan. In the heat of her rage, she didn't even care what Madhu might do to her anymore.

But Venkat *was* there, and unlike her, he didn't look mad. He looked shattered, like something had broken inside him, something vital.

Tanvi couldn't stand seeing him like that. She moved to touch his arm, maybe even to hug him, but he was already careening toward the door. "I'm sorry. I just— I need to go."

"Venkat!" She had to tell him about Madhu. Together, they might find a way to protect Nitya and Mom.

The door slipped shut behind him. More memories blistered, bruising Tanvi's brain. She dropped to her knees and massaged her temples. It didn't help.

She was still trapped, and now she couldn't even check on Nitya.

This time, when the despair washed over her, Tanvi let it.

29

As the council meeting wound down, Venkat knew he'd put on a good face. For the past hour and a half, he'd sat next to Nayan, courteous and attentive. He'd backed up Nayan's smooth reminders that security for the upcoming picnic and wedding was well in hand. In response, the nagarani had graced him with a minute smile.

"These progress reports would indicate we are in an excellent position to move forward with our plans," said King Vasuki, "so unless there is anything else, Lord Nayan, your closing summary?"

The overall mood of the meeting was definitely lighter than usual. According to the reports, Asha's and Chintu's deliberately carefree displays of affection had gone a long way toward raising morale in the city and ramping up excitement for their nuptials. Not only that, but the increased safeguards at the borders had repelled the garudas' attack before a single naga soldier could be harmed, let alone a civilian, soothing the public unease. With the pressure off them, the majority of the council members now bowed their heads, indicating Nayan should speak.

Only Falgun seemed determined to keep squabbling. "Your Esteemed Majesty, pardon my candor," he said, scowling at Sunaina from across the great table, "but I find it hard to believe that the clan of Virupaksha means to perform any action that does not place its own interests before the common good."

Sunaina's face tightened. Before she could retaliate, however, Venkat jumped in. "Esteemed colleagues, let us all take a step back and reflect. This is precisely what the garudas want, to scare us into tearing one another down on their behalf." He smiled at each member of the council before continuing. "But we don't *have* to do their dirty work for them, do we?"

The others chimed in with their agreement until Falgun mumbled an apology. "Please go on, Lord Nayan."

Outwardly, Venkat shone—solid, confident, altogether Nayan's rising star. But underneath, he was wobbling.

Not once, not even when they'd gone into the treasury together, had Nayan bothered to admit the so-called boons were limited, or that the objects they produced didn't last. Venkat jammed his fingertips together under the table, forcing his shoulders to relax. His heart fizzed with anger. And after all the talk about no secrets between the two of them.

"As has been noted," Nayan put in, "guests from around the realm have already begun to arrive, the betrotheds have withdrawn in preparation for tomorrow's royal picnic, and with the newly reinforced magical defenses in place, Garuda himself could not hope to break through." When no one contradicted him, his steely manner mellowed. "In short, we have all earned a respite. I invite you now to enjoy the fruits of your labor at tomorrow's celebration."

Unsurprisingly, most of the dignitaries applauded at that. Venkat never could have predicted that. *Nagas and their parties.*

"I believe that is the entirety of our agenda for today," King Vasuki said. "Our thanks and gratitude to each of the clans for coming together as one in these trying times. As a result, we will not only endure but flourish." Beside him, Queen Naga Yakshi's enigmatic expression bore all the allure of twilight.

As the dignitaries rose and filed out of the council chamber, they paused to pay tribute to the nagaraja and nagarani, as was tradition. But Asha's parents first stopped to greet Nayan.

From behind them, Karan sneered at Venkat, then slithered off. Venkat could almost respect him for it. At least Karan didn't hide what he really thought.

Politics was a sham. Venkat had been wasting time placating self-important nobles that he could have spent on his experiments. Or at least on the project with Nayan, the one that was supposed to heal everything.

They were all pretending. All of them.

His bitterness had grown so strong he didn't know how the chamber wasn't submerged in it.

"I am saddened to learn you will be unable to join us tomorrow, Lord Nayan," Asha's father said, "but I recognize the burden of your many obligations. Take good rest, so that you are refreshed for the nuptials."

Nayan waggled his head. "I am deeply obliged for your kindness. The picnic is certain to be a lively event."

"To say the least!" Asha's mother said. "Well, Lord Nayan, your apprentice is certainly a credit to you."

"You flatter me," Venkat said politely, itching to hightail it out of there.

Asha's mother beamed at him, a perfect older version of her daughter. "Nonsense! You have been a kind and supportive friend to our Asha, who needs that more than ever."

Venkat nodded, but he was only half listening. Supportive friend. To whom, exactly? Asha didn't *want* the wedding he was working so hard to make happen. Tanvi? He gave a mental snort.

The truth had been there all along, if he'd only paid attention. Like Nitya had said, boons took years and years of dedication to obtain; it was a big deal for a sage to receive one. Yet Nayan had Venkat doling them out to the dream runners as pacifiers.

Where was the logic in that?

"You speak truly. I could not ask for a better apprentice or a finer son," Nayan said, and the cool composure he'd maintained throughout the meeting fell away, replaced by obvious pride. A father's pride.

Hearing that knocked Venkat right out of his rumination. As far as he knew, Nayan had never publicly acknowledged him as anything but apprentice before.

A sliver of warmth chipped at the ice in his chest. He'd been so mad, but . . .

Asha's parents exchanged surprised but intrigued looks, and

Venkat knew they'd be spreading this juicy new development the second they were out of sight. "I see. Well, we are greatly indebted to you and your son for all your diligent efforts these past few months," Asha's mother said at last, head inclined, and after another minute of pleasantries, the two of them left.

Then it was only Nayan and Venkat in the vast hall, surrounded by the weaponry and portraits of naga heroics.

Nayan turned to him, that paternal satisfaction still written across his features. "You performed admirably," he said, and the fondness in his voice left Venkat even more conflicted. "With each day that passes, you continue to reward my belief in you."

"Thanks." Venkat flashed what he hoped was a plausible smile, while inside him, everything frothed and smoldered. "I've been thinking. If I keep giving away boons like this, we're going to run out. Can you show me how to make more?"

Come on, he pleaded. There had to be some way to fix things between them. *Tell me they're not true boons.*

"Always on duty." Nayan's laugh was affectionate. "Yet a break is called for, my son, even for us."

"I—" Venkat shut his mouth. The question perched on his tongue, but he couldn't ask it: *When were you going to tell me about the boons?*

A lump formed in his throat. He couldn't ask it because he already knew the answer. Never.

"Venkat, listen to me." Nayan clapped him on the shoulder. "You have achieved so much already, and we are so close to the goal. This evening, my wish is for you to rest. Partake of our vast library, perhaps, or go for a swim beneath the stars. Refresh yourself, for we have much to do tomorrow."

"I was wondering why you wanted to skip the picnic," Venkat said lightly, even though each word felt like hefting a boulder.

"Precisely. We will have the entire day to work unimpeded." Nayan actually grinned, and despite himself, Venkat would have given a lot for a camera to capture the moment. "And then, once the wedding is past and our goal accomplished, you and I will enjoy an outing together. A stroll around the city and dinner at a riverside restaurant—perhaps even the theater."

Venkat couldn't remember when they'd last spent a single hour together that didn't revolve around work in some way. He could already see the colorful lanterns dangling over their table. The two of them would trade ideas and stories over delicious food like they used to, while around them lotuses glowed in the water like neon pink pedestals. They'd go not as lord and apprentice but as father and son.

Part of him wanted that so much.

But the rest of him thought of Madhu demanding locks for the runners' doors. It replayed what Nayan had said about Tanvi and Jai and all the others.

Nayan wanted to talk about family? The runners *were* Venkat's family, and he'd been feeding them lies like cakes of sawdust for the spirit. All because Nayan hadn't trusted him with the whole truth of his plan.

He let that longing show in his face.

Naturally, Nayan caught it.

"Soon," he said, gratified. "Just you and I. Tonight, however, you care for yourself. I do not want to hear of you anywhere near the archives or the workshop. Is that clear?"

"Got it." Venkat grinned, too, hoping he looked excited. Hoping the pain and confusion lancing through him like broken glass stayed hidden. Nayan had to believe he was still every bit the faithful apprentice.

"Good." Nayan laid a hand on his back and steered him toward the double doors. "I have already arranged for a meal to be served on your balcony, and the attendants have been instructed to provide you with anything else you might desire."

At the exit, Nayan smiled once more. "Now go and make merry. I will see you at sunup tomorrow."

Whatever adrenaline had been carrying Venkat through the day suddenly drained off, and he felt like a bag of bones with no muscle to hold them up. A dense fog shrouded his brain, and he yawned.

Nayan's gaze sharpened. "Rest. I insist."

"I guess it wouldn't be so bad to take a night off," Venkat allowed, yawning wider. "So I can be at my best for tomorrow."

Pulling off this ruse might have been the hardest thing he'd ever done. But, he told his guilty heart, Nayan had never answered his question about the boons.

Nayan was already pushing him in the direction of his apartments. "Good night, my son."

At first, Venkat did as Nayan had requested, feasting on his balcony and going for a nice starlit swim in the river before collapsing into bed. He even let himself enjoy four full hours of sleep, but that was as far as the night's luxury could go.

If Nayan wouldn't tell him the truth, he'd find it himself.

His weary body protested, begging for just thirty more minutes, but instead, Venkat got dressed and made his way to the workshop. Ransacking the inventory, he assembled the various fractions of "boon" left until a line of twenty-nine white orbs glowed at him like miniature moons.

Odd—that was the same number as there were current runners. Had that always been the case? Venkat had never bothered counting the boons before; there had always been more than enough to give out, and as far as he'd known, Nayan had replenished them as necessary.

But he'd never thought to ask where they came from.

In the ancient epics, when a rishi or a demon won a boon from the deities, it was a favor so powerful that Lord Brahma had to place limits on what it could be used to invoke. Immortality, which challenged the cosmic order, was strictly forbidden, but crafty petitioners had found loopholes around that: King Hiranyakashipu had used his boon to stipulate that he might die neither on land nor in space, neither in fire nor water, during neither day nor night, neither indoors nor outdoors; nor could he be killed by human, animal, demigod, or even a weapon.

The brutish buffalo demon Mahishasura, on the other hand, had kept things simple—and more misogynistic—merely seeking protection from death at the hand of any man or god.

Since both petitioners' demands technically adhered to the

rules, Lord Brahma had had no choice but to grant them, and of course, chaos ensued.

Both had been taken down in the end—Hiranyakashipu on a threshold at twilight by the claws of a lion-headed avatar of Vishnu, and Mahishasura by an incarnation of goddess Durga—but only after accessing magic so mighty they had almost bypassed death.

In contrast, Venkat recalled Tanvi trying to invoke her memories and the random milkshake just that afternoon. How only her bracelet appeared—and even it had instantly vanished.

He was willing to bet the other runners would only be able to invoke their own particular obsession, too. Like the "boons" were keyed to them as individuals.

What had Nayan said, something about the power of belief as solder for one's purpose? What if he'd meant that literally?

A dream is only as strong as the dreamer's belief in it.

Venkat peered through his jeweler's loupe at the orbs lined up on the worktable like a strand of illuminated pearls. Were they dreams, then?

The idea of slicing into one felt like sacrilege, but he had to know. He chose an orb that seemed thinner than the rest and grimly set about prizing it apart.

30

"Tanvi." The gentle voice cut through Tanvi's dream of dicing huge mounds of potatoes and carrots as fast as she could. Her persnickety kangaroo chef boss planned to use them as actual dice. "Wake up."

When she came to, the sky outside was a blend of evening blues and purples. She'd just meant to take a quick nap.

A warm hand touched hers, and she sat bolt upright.

Venkat crouched by her bed, smiling down at her. Moonbeams braided themselves into his inky hair, turning him as ethereal as a naga prince from a private lagoon of dreams. He was much cuter than the kangaroo, that was for sure. "Sleeping Beauty," he teased. "I didn't want to wake you."

Her stomach did a little backflip. His soulful eyes were such a beautiful shade of brown, as rich as maple syrup, and so curious as they slid over her face. So *beguiled,* the way they'd been at the Lake of Lovers' Tears.

Suddenly Tanvi understood the night bride. She forgot about

314

Asha, about Nitya, about the garudas. For a second, she even forgot to breathe.

It was just the two of them, and he was so close to her. She couldn't look away from his full lips. All she'd have to do was tilt her head up . . .

Then his mouth flattened into a line. "I'd love to let you keep sleeping, but I can't. We have to go."

Tanvi fought to focus. There was something she needed to tell him, but her woolly brain couldn't remember what. "How'd you get in here?" she finally ground out. "The door's locked."

A surly attendant had installed the forbidding metal rectangle that morning, so she hadn't even been able to check on the other runners.

"Not from the outside," Venkat said sourly. "Listen, the boons are just dreams, Tanvi. *Your* dreams. I think that's why that bracelet you made yesterday didn't last."

Tanvi's head spun. "What do you mean, I made it? I invoked it! Didn't I?"

He shook his head. "I'll tell you more later. Right now, we have to go."

She'd wanted nothing more than to escape this holding cell of a room, but Tanvi found herself burrowing deeper under the blanket. "But— I thought we can't leave here? I mean, Madhu's keeping tabs on us!"

She touched the spot on her collarbone where her pendant should have been. Madhu had taken that, too.

Madhu. That's what I was going to tell him. About the garudas.

"Asha's going to sneak us out," Venkat explained before she could. "But only if we leave right now."

Asha? Starting to wonder if this was one of Venkat's door-and-key dreams, Tanvi let go of the blanket and got up. Venkat turned away as she threw on her Prithvi outfit. Out of habit, she groped for her pouch. "Where are we going?"

"The Night Market. We would've gone last night, but I had to set it up with her first." With that, Venkat led Tanvi into the tunnels and through a back corridor she'd never known existed, which he said terminated right in the middle of Asha's apartments.

Tanvi rolled her eyes. Of course Asha had her own secret passageway. Rich carpets and intricate mosaics lined its depths, and sconces posted every few inches provided way more illumination than any troublemaking princess could possibly need.

Venkat must have caught Tanvi's expression, because he looked sheepish. "Asha used to use this tunnel all the time to get around the palace. These days, Madhu's minions keep a close watch on it, so we have to hurry."

Tanvi shivered at the thought of all those eyes on them. "What if someone sees us?"

"I promised you I'd get your memories back, and since it turns out we don't have any actual boons here, the Night Market is the only place I can think of." He smiled sadly. "Besides, it's the least Asha and I can do for you after . . . everything."

As they walked, he filled her in on his research. "I think the initiation took your ability to dream and filtered it into a fake boon. And since the last thing you had with you when you got here was the thing you"—he winced—"became obsessed with, that was the only thing you could dream of."

"Until I woke up, you mean."

"Exactly. There was one boon that was thinner than all the others. I figured it was yours, and I was right. It was so flimsy it dissolved the second I cut into it, probably because your ability to dream had already gone back to you." He frowned. "You were dreaming when I woke you up, weren't you?"

"Yeah," Tanvi admitted.

Venkat hesitated, then took her hand. "I'm not sure I *can* make you a dream runner again."

The implied question drifted between them: Did she even want that anymore?

She'd thought so, but the world had gone topsy-turvy while she wasn't looking. When the fake boon failed to restore her memories, it should have been a comfort.

Instead, Tanvi felt deprived of her past. Talking to Nitya had made her want to remember, to plug in the missing puzzle pieces, at least temporarily. Who had she been before? Who had *they* been?

All that was too much to worry about right now, so she nudged it into the waiting room at the back of her mind. "But why the Night Market?"

Venkat's shoulders dropped in obvious relief, and he squeezed her fingers. His hand felt so solid in hers. "You know how you shared the fireflies I gave you with the other runners?"

She nodded, wondering if she was in trouble.

"Well, it seems to be helping them. They're not getting better,

317

but they're not getting worse, either."

Tanvi chewed on her cheek so her glee wouldn't show. She'd helped the other runners!

"Anyway, those fireflies came from the Night Market. It sells all kinds of impossible things, so maybe there'll be a pill to fill in memories or something like that."

The tunnel stopped then, opening onto Asha's . . . wardrobe? *How very melodramatic of her,* Tanvi thought, and smirked in Venkat's direction.

But he was pushing through the racks and racks of clothes and didn't notice. Tanvi felt stupid and shy all over again.

The two of them stepped out into a chamber overflowing with rich fabrics and extremely expensive furniture. It figured; Asha lived in a jewel box while the runners rotted in their jail cells.

Before Tanvi could really take it all in, Asha loomed before her, dressed in what must have been her picnic finery.

"Karan suspects me. We must not dally." Asha grabbed Tanvi's right arm, since Venkat still held her left hand, and hoisted a cup of water.

Karan—that meant Madhu. The lush room pressed in on Tanvi from all sides.

She'd already waited too long, and Venkat needed to know. She had to say it now.

"Wait!" she cried.

Both Venkat and Asha stared at her. "What is it?" Venkat asked, his gaze full of concern.

That only made what she had to say worse. *Spit it out*, she told herself. "Madhu . . . Madhu'sworkingwiththegarudas."

"That conniving quisling!" Asha exclaimed. Venkat only looked dubious.

"Why would you say that?" he asked roughly, mistrust displacing his concern.

"I should have told you sooner," Tanvi said. "But it's true."

Asha cocked her head, and her tongue tasted the air. "The tale will keep. They are coming," she announced, and let a single drop splash down from her cup. Then she swept Tanvi and Venkat into the water.

31

Still clutching one another, Venkat, Tanvi, and Asha emerged from a puddle onto a sidewalk lined with closed shops. Venkat pitched forward, and Tanvi rushed to steady him. He was pretty certain he'd almost just drowned.

"Did I not say you need to leave Nagalok more often?" Asha chided. "This sort of travel requires practice."

Venkat spotted signs that bore names like *Sona Jewelers* and *Chowpatty Restaurant*. A few cars sat parked along the curb. He was somewhere on Prithvi, then—or as humans called it, Earth. When Nayan had brought him to the Night Market all those years ago, they hadn't come through this entrance.

Nayan. The boons. Venkat felt like he'd been shoved back under the water, his air choked off. And Tanvi's claim about Madhu and the garudas. How could that possibly be true?

If it was, what was he supposed to do with that?

Everything was falling apart.

A set of colorful tents and stalls hung superimposed over the stores on the street, all wreathed by a gilt haze as diaphanous as an organza curtain.

"This is it," Asha said, hauling Venkat and Tanvi before a gargantuan golden peacock that had coalesced out of the haze. She released her grip on both of them. "The Night Market."

"How do we get in?" Venkat asked, grateful to have a different conundrum to tackle. "It looks like it's in an alternate dimension."

As if in reply, the peacock blinked down at them. *Meh-aao!* it called, then lowered its head. Its dagger-sharp beak opened wide, revealing the Night Market in all its decadence. Venkat could almost smell the enchantment wafting out, lures set to ensnare the eager.

No one spoke.

"Fine," Asha huffed at last, throwing up her hands and making her bangles tinkle. "I suppose I will go first, then, you milksops. At least it is not a garuda's beak I must face down this time." She moved toward the peacock's head, closed her eyes, and slithered inside.

Tanvi, though, turned to Venkat. Her smile was weak but sincere. "I know I must've shocked you back there, and I'm sorry. I wanted to tell you, I swear! But she threatened me."

"Madhu?" he asked doubtfully, since Tanvi could just as easily have been talking about Asha. Madhu, a traitor? It made no sense.

Tanvi nodded. She'd folded into herself but seemed to catch it and stood up straight again. "She threatened to hurt Nitya if I told anyone."

Venkat's jaw twitched. She had? How could Nayan be okay with that?

"We just spent the day together, you know," he said offhandedly. As if they weren't standing outside the fabled Night Market of lore, its peacock portcullis eyeing them with a little too much interest. "Nayan and I. We worked on our project, and I pretended I didn't know about the boons. I pretended everything was fine. And it was . . . really nice. Despite everything."

He laughed, the sound as cheerful as a cremation pyre.

Frowning, Tanvi grabbed his hand. "I don't think Nayan actually knows. She ordered me not to say anything to him."

She was so pretty, with that determination, that *life*, in her face. Venkat wanted to tell her so, to rest his chin on the crown of her head, to show her how precious she was, but he didn't. "Tell me everything," he said instead. "From the beginning."

He listened, vacillating from disbelief to dismay as Tanvi filled in the gaps in her story, from being called by Nitya's name to finding her sister to the garuda attack at Nitya's school and seeing Madhu with the garudas. "It would have been my school. I can't stop thinking about that."

"You know what the worst part of this is?" he muttered. "Aside from finding out that Nayan's not the only one lying to me? Or that Madhu's selling us all out?"

"What?" Tanvi asked, inching closer. "What's the worst part?"

Venkat had been holding himself stiffly so he wouldn't break, not while they still had tasks tonight, but now he let himself sag against her. She felt so nice, so warm and strong and supple all at once. "I thought the work I was doing meant something."

"It does," she insisted, sticking her face in his. "I wouldn't lie."

322

"No, you wouldn't," he murmured, almost to himself, "would you?"

Then his knuckles were stroking her cheek, and her eyes were drawing him in, pools of darkest fire. Of curiosity. The curve of her mouth hinted at the passion simmering inside her, the fierce sense of justice and desire to set things right.

Tanvi. My beautiful Tanvi.

It would be so easy to bring his head down to hers. To learn what she tasted like, if her lips were as soft as they looked.

He started to bend toward her, then stopped. No. Not until she had her memories back. Then she could choose for herself.

Plus, the oversize peacock was still gaping at them. That definitely put a damper on things.

With a heroic effort, Venkat stepped away from her, even though it felt like abandoning a roaring fire to plunge headfirst into a snowbank. "I need to give you something." Her serpentine pendant glimmered on his palm. "In case we get separated, so you can get back to the palace. I should never have let Madhu take it in the first place."

Tanvi scarcely glanced at the pendant. Instead, she closed her hand over his. "You said you bought the fireflies here?"

"Nayan bought them, actually, but yes." What was she getting at?

She nodded, considering him. "And you really think we can fix my memories here?"

"I don't know," he said. "But if we can, are you sure you're ready for that?"

Tanvi nodded again. "I am. I'll remember, long enough to get my brain to quit blowing up and make sure Nitya's safe for good, and then you can initiate me again."

He stared at her, trying to read the cracks in her stony expression. "But Tanvi, *you found your sister.* Don't you think that changes things?"

The thought of losing her now, when they'd only just started discovering who she was, made his stomach hurt. Plus, after listening to her talk about Nitya, he didn't believe she wanted to forget again.

"Changes them how?" Tanvi snarled, finally tugging the pendant free and clasping it around her neck. She might have been an incensed nagini in that moment, all embers and sparks, her long hair lustrous in the multihued radiance from the Market. "Are you saying I don't know what I want?"

"No, I—" Venkat sighed. Where was a white flag when he needed one? "I think once you remember your past, you might want to stay with her. Not just until she's safe from the garudas."

Gods, how he despised saying that. It was all he could do not to seize her hand again and pull her close. But Tanvi had every right to return home to her loving family, the one he and Asha had stolen her from. What was left for her in Bhogavati, anyway—a junky bracelet? Burnout? War?

Tanvi glared at him like she'd gladly tear him apart if she could. "Are you trying to get rid of me? Is that what this is all about?"

Get rid of her? He laughed without meaning to. "No! It's just— If I could see my family again, that's what I would do. That's all."

"What does that have to do with me?" she asked, blunt as a board.

Venkat held up his hands before he could do any more damage. "Fine. What do *you* want?"

She glanced to the side, the flame in her abruptly cooling. "Let's worry about tonight," she shot back, before stalking toward the entrance.

Wow, that was pitiful. *He* was pitiful. He could soothe a roomful of naga nobles, yet one human girl had him tripping over his tongue.

But she was right. They did have to get through the night—and the Night Market—first.

As Venkat hurried to catch up with Tanvi, the peacock opened its beak once more.

32

So this is the Night Market, Tanvi thought. A filmy blue-black scarf of a sky studded with silver stars draped over gem-toned tents and lanterns. Magical.

But she couldn't stop dwelling on Venkat and their conversation. How he'd looked like she'd crushed him with her news about Madhu.

The bitterness in his voice ate a hole in Tanvi's chest, exposing the stupid, vulnerable fleshiness of her stupid heart. All the feelings she'd been damming up spewed out, violent fumes from an erupting volcano, raw and toxic enough to devour her. She wanted to find her sister and their mom, though she still didn't know what to say to Mom, and hide them in a closet until Madhu forgot about all three of them. She wanted to shake Venkat and ask why he wanted her to leave even after he'd smiled at her like she was more valuable than any dream she'd ever brought him.

And the other runners. Always the other runners.

She wanted to scream. How did people *feel* things all the time and just go on with their lives?

Asha moved to block her view. "Stay with me. We must find Grishmabai."

"Who's Grishmabai?" Tanvi asked. Dizzy from all the feelings, she'd almost forgotten where they were.

"The person we have come to see. From what I was told, she has been in a terrible mood for the past five hundred years, and we can only pray she will help us. Now come!"

The three of them dashed past stall after stall with stranger and stranger wares: featherlight bamboo flutes that could only be played by foxes, fresh lassis made of blue mangoes harvested from starry orchards in Svargalok, stone figurines the size of her thumb that softened into living animals if you watched them long enough. The tiny monkey chirruped at Tanvi, and in the space of a blink, it had bounded across the distance between them and landed on her shoulder.

"Shoo!" Venkat swatted at it. The indignant monkey made as if to bite him but hopped back to its tent.

"Potions! A potion for what ails you!" a rickety voice called. The voice's owner, an old man with far more wrinkles around his mischievous grin than teeth in it, displayed vials of striped healing salve: red, white, and black. He tapped a vial with a hairy knuckle. "Ground-up unicorn horn to mend all bodily wounds."

"No, thanks," Tanvi said. Her wound wasn't physical.

"I also have unguent of unicorn eye, if that is more to your liking." The man brought out a jar of glowing cerulean eyeballs suspended in a viscous jasmine-scented liquid. "Steeped from new moon to new moon for true insight into one's own shortcomings." He cackled. "Unless you are too afraid to know yourself?"

Tanvi already knew what a mess she was. She didn't need magic for that.

Venkat touched her arm. "Everything all right?" He smiled, his brown eyes seeming more golden, as if the haze surrounding the Market had settled inside them.

She nodded, making herself look away before the flood of feelings could knock her over again.

A stall down the winding path glittered at her, covered in keys of all kinds. Silver keys wreathed in white apple blossoms and green heart-shaped ivy; golden keys wrapped in fiery leaves in reds, yellows, and oranges; translucent keys made of icicles and tipped with ice-blue frost. Venkat's crystal door and key would fit right in here. "Open the door to autumn," the vendor cried. "Find your way to a fragrant, fruitful spring!"

"Serenade your ears with the music of the spheres!" proclaimed a middle-aged woman in a silver-blue-and-black sari as she uncorked a cut-crystal vial of miniature silver musical notes. They soared up and surrounded Tanvi and Venkat in perfect constellations, tinkling for the span of a few heartbeats before returning to the vial.

Venkat stepped closer to the retreating notes, entranced, but Tanvi flicked away the stray one by her ear. The Night Market was almost irritatingly full of temptations. Its magic diffused around her like a mist, wrapping her in its promise. Inviting her to forget why she'd come here. Inviting her instead to stay.

Asha glanced over. "Hurry," she urged. "If I must resist shopping for more feather seeds, surely you can resist everything else."

They raced around the Market through spirals and loops. It felt like every vendor they passed flashed a predatory smile, wielding enticements like weapons, but Tanvi had her dream runner single-mindedness to fall back on. *Nitya. Nitya. Nitya.*

And then Asha came to a halt before a small square garden of bleeding hearts that actually bled. A roomy tent stood next to it, flamboyant yet intensely creepy. Butterflies in many colors served as its trim, occasionally abandoning their role and flying off. The only source of light inside the tent was a single floating bulb, burning through the layers of gloom like a lost star.

A scowling old woman rose from a chair within the tent, grunting as her knees creaked. "These bones are not what they once were." She turned her glare on Tanvi. "So you are the reason for all this to-do? A waste of my time."

"Grishmabai—" Asha began, but the old woman clapped sharply.

"Urvashi! That silly apsara is never around when you need her."

Venkat squinted at Grishmabai. "You look like my grandmother," he said warily. "But—"

The old woman cackled. "Child who once wished so fiercely for a deadened soul, I look like everyone's grandmother. Who speaks for this girl?"

Venkat and Asha answered in unison. "I do."

"Then the cost is doubled. From you, nagini princess, a scale; from you, lost boy, a story. The story of your heart, the one you take solace in. No, you will not tell it; you will *give* it to me."

"No!" Venkat stared at her like she was asking him to trade the sky for the sea.

Grishmabai cast him an antagonized glance. "Do you wish my help or not?"

"I already gave it to her," he said, with a nod at Tanvi.

Tanvi remembered him reading to her. How dare this mean old woman? "What about *me*?" she cut in. "I can speak for myself."

"Tripled, then," said Grishmabai. "From you, the first taste of your grief."

What did that even mean? Tanvi shot apprehensive looks at Venkat and Asha, but she didn't see any other choice. "Fine."

"Hold out your hand," Grishmabai instructed.

Tanvi reluctantly obeyed. Grishmabai's long nails cut into the flesh as she ran them over Tanvi's palm. Then she gasped.

"What?" Tanvi demanded. Was her past really that horrifying?

Grishmabai dropped her hand with a snort. It was a coarse, phlegm-ridden sound. "You humans are always so easy to fool. So quick to panic."

"Grishmabai, please," Venkat said. "You can have the story. Just help us."

Tanvi started to tell him to shut up. That was his favorite story. Except, she realized, *she* could read it to *him*.

"Naturally shed nagini skin." Asha removed a length of molted scales from her bag. "As I hear you are constantly seeking for your spellcraft."

The butterflies fled as one, and now the bulb's harsh white

glow exposed a lilac flag fluttering in the breeze. The fabric stilled, revealing a disembodied brown thumb juxtaposed against a bow and arrow. Blood as dark as garnets dripped from the thumb's ragged base in eerie contrast to the neon blue OPEN sign flashing on the door below.

"Customers!" a voice sang out, drifting toward them as unhurriedly as the fluff from a dandelion. An apsara joined them from the recesses of the tent, and the entire space lit up with colored lights. "Welcome to Eklavya's Thumb."

"About time, Urvashi," Grishmabai barked. "I was starting to think I might actually have to help these interlopers!" She vanished into the back of the bar that should never have fit into the tent. Shelves of bottles filled with fantastical beverages blinked into view.

But everything dimmed in comparison to the bizarre conversation piece perched on a high table: a hacked-off brown thumb bleeding in a jar.

"You put his thumb in a *jar*?" Venkat squeaked.

Even Asha looked taken aback.

The jar jolted a memory loose in Tanvi, and the resulting burst of pain made her gag. *Eklavya*, she recalled between pulses of nausea. In the *Mahabharata*, he'd wanted to study with the sought-after Guru Dronacharya, who'd shaped Prince Arjun into the finest archer in all the land. But Drona had refused.

Instead of giving up, Eklavya had sculpted Drona's likeness in clay and sat at the statue's feet until he gleaned the knowledge to master archery. Word of his incredible abilities spread fast. Jealous Arjun hadn't taken that well, and Drona had reminded Eklavya that students must pay their teachers for their tutelage. He'd then forced Eklavya to cut off his own right thumb as payment, effectively ending his archery career.

Some guru dakshina. Not that that made this particular memorial any less grotesque. Mythical beings were, Tanvi decided, seriously *weird*.

"Indeed." Urvashi ran a finger over the shelves of jewel-colored liquors. "Someone must remember his sacrifice. Now, what will it be? Fluid flame? A sip of the sea? Rainbow in a bottle? Or chandini, the elixir of illumination?"

She gestured to a crystal decanter. The incandescent orange brew it held spat and crackled like fire. No, it *was* fire. The bottle beside it barely contained the blue-green waves crashing within.

Where was the rainbow in a bottle? Tanvi could already taste it. She needed it. Would each color have its own flavor?

But that would have to wait for another day. She was here to remember. "Chandini."

Urvashi reappeared a minute later with a glowing bottle and a single tumbler.

No matter how many times Tanvi blinked, the bottle still brimmed with something frosted and luminous, like the moon on the Lake of Lovers' Tears. The color of mercury, it was translucent but not liquid, and it shone softly. Distilled moonlight. Silver wine.

The moonstone path. It had found her again.

She dipped a wary finger into the wine. Her skin didn't melt off, at least. Instead, a cool, refreshing sensation like the caress of menthol spread from her fingertip into her body. She could almost see the stream of silver seeping into her veins.

Was she about to discover she'd done something awful before Asha had spirited her away? That *she* was awful?

"I do not have all day, mortal girl." Tutting, Urvashi pointed to the line of customers that had built up behind Tanvi. Human and mythical being alike looked aggrieved. "What is your decision?"

"So irksome!" grumbled a brown bear on his hind legs. He might have been part of Hanuman's army back in the days of the *Ramayana*. She stared up at him, startled at his bulk—and his claws.

Venkat put a hand on her shoulder. "You can do it," he whispered.

Tanvi brought the tumbler to her lips. As the chandini touched her tongue, her taste buds seemed to dissolve. *Pop, pop, pop . . . ahhh.*

The silver wine slid down her throat in a slippery waterfall of stars and crescent moons. They devoured time on their way into the darkness. It was exactly like sipping the moon. Like drinking the night sky. Or the universe itself—constellations, galaxies, black holes.

The wine sighed through her blood, and her chest cavity expanded, opening to encompass everyone and everything in an enormous golden web. Within it, Tanvi touched those she'd loved, those she'd hated, those she'd never known. There was no place to hide from the web's overpowering light.

The web extended outward and outward and outward until Tanvi knew she would die, or at least vomit. It would continue growing until it hit the edges of the universe, except she could feel there were no edges, only infinity. The beauty of the cosmos was terrible and compassionate at once, whittling away the oblivion she'd worked so hard to maintain, leaving her bare. So bare.

Tanvi. Her mother's voice. *Happy birthday, dikri.*

Tanvi started to shake.

When she raised her head a million years later, she sat alone in her dining room, surrounded by unicorn party plates and napkins, pink and purple plasticware, and a thawing marble ice cream cake with twin unicorns on top, one with a pink mane, the other with purple. Mom had left the twenty candles—ten in pink, ten in purple—next to the cake, along with a book of matches with an insurance company logo on it.

Mom had even given them matching swirly pink-and-purple unicorn bathrobes, with a pink hood for Nitya and a purple hood for Tanvi.

Tanvi inspected her hands. They were small, with short fingers, and on her right hand, she wore the rubber decoder ring she'd fished out of a cereal box a couple of weeks ago.

It's my birthday. Our birthday. And she knew the reason she was sitting alone.

All their friends from school had wandered off into the backyard to play in the hot tub while Tanvi was in the bathroom, and no one, not even Nitya, had bothered to come back for her. Even Mom and Dad hadn't noticed she wasn't outside.

She knew what Mom would say: go join them instead of feeling sorry for herself. Tanvi got up and opened the sliding door. Fine, she'd go outside, but she'd feel sorry for herself, too.

Then she heard it: "She still wets the bed? Are you kidding?"

Her breath froze. Nitya had told them Tanvi's secret.

The humiliating thing Tanvi still couldn't admit happened the other night after she'd woken from a bad dream. She'd been afraid to go to the bathroom—monsters crawled in the dark—but she couldn't hold it, either.

Dad had washed the sheets, and Mom had put in a night-light and promised it wasn't a big deal. But Tanvi was still so ashamed.

The betrayal gutted her, splaying her insides everywhere. It left her furious and hurt and confused and so small. Why would Nitya do this?

"Oh, my God," someone yelled, "I would *die*!"

"What a baby!"

Tanvi waited for Nitya to defend her. To tell those "friends" they were being jerks.

"I know, right?" Nitya giggled, then lowered her voice. "But you can't tell anyone, okay? I mean it."

Something in Tanvi broke.

She glanced over at the pile of presents on the card table Dad had set up a few feet from the regular one. Presents should be exciting. She should be thrilled. But all she could think of was how her supposed friends were laughing at her.

The whole school would know by Monday. Sooner if they were already texting.

The sound of more giggles and shrieks filtered in from the backyard through the open sliding door. Tanvi wanted to slam it shut, but that would only get her in trouble.

She settled for clawing out a chunk of the cake with her bare hand. It felt sticky and wrong and awesome. Then she crammed the cake into her mouth.

Gross; of course she'd gotten the vanilla part. Why did Nitya insist on a marbled cake just because their friends liked it? It was *their* cake, no one else's.

Tanvi went to wash her hands in the kitchen sink. Something on the counter caught her eye. Nitya's charm bracelet.

The jump ring on Nitya's new daisy charm had broken that morning when Dad tried to attach it to the bracelet. He'd promised to fix it before the party. But he hadn't gotten around to it, which meant Mom would probably be breaking out the needle-nose pliers soon.

Nitya loved that bracelet. She wore it everywhere.

An idea seized Tanvi by the shoulders, so good she couldn't resist. She palmed the bracelet and, before she could think better of it, ran out the front door.

Barely waving back when the neighbor mowing his lawn called out a greeting, Tanvi made for the woods at the end of their cul-de-sac. She disappeared through the little gap for hikers. Everything was in that last bloom of summer, bright green and dark green and pale green and smelling like freedom. Like magic. Like a yaksha might appear at any moment.

Tanvi had planned to dump Nitya's bracelet out here, where her sister would never find it. It was only fair that Nitya feel as bad as she'd made Tanvi feel on their birthday.

How was Tanvi supposed to face anyone after *that*?

But as she ran, twigs jabbing her bare feet, doubts started to sneak in. They felt as slick as shadows, attaching themselves to her until she couldn't shake them loose.

Maybe this wasn't such a great idea. Nitya really did love her bracelet. Tanvi was the one who'd surprised her with the charm of two hearts intertwined last year. She'd had to save weeks of her allowance for it. "It's us," Nitya had said, beaming.

Tanvi's real heart twisted. Why couldn't things always be like that, where they were each other's number one? Where they didn't need words to talk about the important things?

Why did everything have to *change*?

She ran until she came to a pond. That was weird. The woods weren't big enough for a pond—unless they went back farther than she knew?

Maybe, she thought with a rush of inspiration, there was another path nobody had ever discovered until now. A path where she might meet a real unicorn. Maybe it would even let her ride it!

Plus, the water reminded her of a sapphire she'd once seen on TV. It was so blue it looked fake, like food coloring.

As she neared the pond, a snake with diamond-patterned scales appeared out of nowhere, making squiggles across the path. Tanvi screamed, and the snake reared up, revealing a flared hood. Its fangs glistened in the afternoon light dappling the forest, and its tongue flicked at the air, tasting it.

A king cobra!

Tanvi floundered and fell in the mud. The bracelet flew out of her hand. She didn't dare blink until the cobra relaxed and slithered off into the water. Were cobras even native to Pennsylvania?

Probably not. Maybe some pet owner had released it into the wild. Or maybe it had escaped the zoo.

She thought through theory after theory until her breathing slowed down. Then, careful not to make any sudden moves in case the snake was still around, she started digging for the bracelet.

It was gone.

Tanvi scrabbled in the mud, desperate to find it, but no matter how much she got under her nails, no matter how many pebbles scraped her, the bracelet stayed missing.

She finally got to her feet and brushed off as much mud as she could. No one would know she'd taken the bracelet. She could go back and rejoin the party. Mom and Dad would be mad about the cake, but they wouldn't say anything in front of the guests.

No, she couldn't. Everybody knew she'd wet the bed.

Tanvi hesitated. If she didn't go back, what if they forgot about her? Maybe they'd already lit the candles and let Nitya blow them all out, and everyone was opening presents, and Nitya got them all . . . while still laughing at Tanvi!

It made her so mad all over again. Now she wished she could find the bracelet just so she could throw into the pond and watch it sink forever.

The air started to shimmer. The trees danced, their leaves shushing and swishing in the breeze, and the pond glowed like a jewel. Tanvi could feel magic thick in the air.

"I hope you were not looking for this," a silky voice said. "Because once an offering is given, it belongs to us."

Tanvi looked up to see a beautiful teenage girl with a snake tail holding the broken bracelet. A nagini! She'd only ever seen them in illustrations before, and this girl made all those drawings look like chicken scratch.

Her long, thick black hair would have made Mom so jealous; Mom was always scrubbing her scalp with a fine-tooth comb to stimulate her follicles. The girl's big, kohl-lined eyes gleamed with mischief, and she bared her fangs when she smiled. Maybe that should've scared Tanvi, but it didn't. Of course a nagini would have fangs.

"I like your fangs," Tanvi said. "I bet you get to bite people when they annoy you."

The girl smiled wider. "Why, thank you. I suppose you wish you had sssssome, too."

"Who are you? What are you doing with my sister's bracelet?"

The girl tossed the bracelet into the water, where it disappeared on contact. Just like Tanvi had wanted to do, which won the girl at least fifty points. "My name is Asha. As for your other question, you summoned me with the offering you made." She held out her hand. "Now let me pose a query of my own. Tanvi, will you come away with me and leave this realm of misery behind?"

The pond parted to expose a set of circular steps, like a snaky staircase cut from jewels. A staircase to another world.

No more fighting with Nitya. No more trying to be noticed. No more getting disappointed.

Tanvi had read enough fairy tales to know the nagini was asking to spirit her away to a magical world where she could have everything she'd ever imagined. She also knew this invitation would only come once.

And besides, a spiteful little voice pointed out, the other girls would just die if they knew.

Tanvi held out her own hand, the rubber ring spattered with mud. "Let's go."

33

Watching Tanvi gulp down the chandini had been hard enough, but seeing her now made Venkat feel so nervous he thought he might be sick. His heart was a frenzied moth beating its wings against the glass prison binding it.

She rocked back and forth on the floor, her eyes closed. He wanted more than anything to go to her. Instead, he swapped worried glances with Asha. Had they done the right thing?

Urvashi continued puttering around the bar, perfectly untroubled. She didn't offer them anything to drink, and Venkat was glad. He might have taken it, and Tanvi needed him sober.

Tanvi shot upright. She blinked a few times, looking as shell-shocked as Venkat felt, and let out a little cry, a kind of gasp of despair.

Now Venkat did rush to her side. "What happened?" He was dying to take her hand, to hug her and brush back her hair.

Asha undulated over and put her arms around Tanvi. Her usual bubbly expression was nowhere to be seen. "You are trembling. Tell me what you saw."

Venkat held out his hand, just in case. He couldn't believe it when Tanvi took it and squeezed tight.

"I saw—" A shudder ran through her. "Everything. Every memory. I saw my parents. I saw my friends. I saw the day I ran away." She wriggled around in Asha's embrace to face her. "I saw you steal me away!"

Asha at least had the grace to look embarrassed.

"How do you feel?" Venkat asked. "It must be a lot, suddenly remembering your entire life."

"Horrible. Shaky? Like I wish I hadn't done it, but also really glad I did?" Tanvi pressed her lips together. "I . . . I remember everything. Everything! How I used to hide goldfish crackers in my room. How Nitya and I were always fighting over books. How—" Her face filled with pain. "I remember the initiation."

Venkat felt like someone had kicked him in the stomach. He'd stood by and let her entire memory be erased and her heart be silenced. How could he have ever thought that was okay?

"My heart—it won't slow down." Tanvi touched her free hand to her chest. "I can't breathe."

"Shh, shh," he soothed. "Hold your breath." Tanvi did. "Now breathe out."

They repeated that for a few minutes until Tanvi's hand in his stopped quivering. "What do I do now?" she asked, leaning against Asha, who stroked her hair. "I don't know what to do. It's so much. Too much."

Asha smiled then. "I am cccccertain," she hissed, releasing Tanvi and rising up on her coils, "that you *do* know. You wish to see your sister, and I wish to see Sameer. Ergo, *we* are going to go to garba and dance with them."

Urvashi, who'd been unabashedly eavesdropping, smiled, too. "I happen to know a purveyor of fine garments right here in the Market. . . ."

Venkat and Tanvi stood outside the mandir in their newly purchased enchanted outfits. Tanvi wore a set of rich orange-pink chaniya choli whose fabric had been snipped from a sunset and embellished with satiny cloth-of-sky ribbon and matching cerulean sequins. Her gold tika and earrings complemented the nose ring she already had.

In the yellow light splashing out from the mandir's entrance, she looked prettier than Asha and even Urvashi, who was renowned for her charms. Venkat arranged and rearranged his dupatta so he wouldn't give in to the urge to hug Tanvi some more. Or try to kiss her. Or maybe run off into the night with her.

The vendor had dressed him in matching colors: an indigo kurta with the same design and trim, and that same sunset fabric lining his jacket. None of the people milling around the entrance could begin to compare to either his or Tanvi's sartorial splendor, but that didn't make him feel any more confident.

He was starting to think this detour had been a mistake. The longer they were on Earth, the more likely somebody back in the palace might notice they were gone.

Plus, if Tanvi was right about Madhu, they were in more trouble than he'd realized.

But Asha had already disappeared inside to search for Sameer. At least she'd glamoured Tanvi first so no one but Nitya and the two of them would recognize her.

Even so, with her entire backlog of memories settling in her head like sediment, Tanvi claimed she wasn't ready to go in. "I feel drunk? But totally aware at the same time," she said. "It's really weird."

"Sounds fun?" Venkat joked. "You can wait for Nitya out here, you know."

Tanvi clutched his arm so hard it hurt. "Don't go anywhere. Promise you won't."

As antsy as he felt, he didn't have to force his smile. "I'm right here, as long as you need me."

She let go, darting a glance at him before looking down. "I like that blue on you," she mumbled.

He stepped toward her. "Tanvi, you—"

Nitya appeared at his elbow, and Venkat swallowed the rest of his sentence in a frustrated gulp. She was the reason they'd come here—well, and Sameer—but he still wished she'd waited one more minute to show up. Just one. Was that so much to ask?

"You actually came." Nitya's tone was reserved, and Venkat couldn't tell whether she was glad or irritated. Both, maybe. "They're doing aarti right now, but dandiya raas hasn't started yet."

"Are you okay?" Tanvi asked anxiously, looking her sister over. "Is Mom?"

"Totally fine." Nitya hesitated, then added, far too casually, "I'm glad you came."

They might share the same features, Venkat thought, but seeing them side by side, they weren't identical, not truly. It wasn't just the variations in their cosmetics and accessories, or that Tanvi's hair hung a few inches longer than Nitya's. Tanvi's face was like a kitten's, full of raw emotion that stormed, unchecked, to the surface. Whatever she felt *showed*, and she moved like she was always on the verge of pouncing or fleeing. Nitya's face, on the other hand, was like a vigilant elder cat's, her narrowed stare coolly gauging. She held herself close, as if nothing passed her lips without being thought through at least twice.

Had they always been so different, or was it the years apart, living such different lives, that made them that way?

"I remember all of this," Tanvi whispered. "Not these exact people, but I remember coming here. Eating the second the prasad got laid out. Doing aarti. Dancing with you."

Venkat had never been to a Gujarati garba, but he'd certainly gone to his share of festivals with his family. This was the first time he'd been back on Earth since the day his family died. Listening to Tanvi, he felt his old grief spasm in his chest, incongruous in this spirited celebration.

Tanvi must have noticed, because her mouth turned down, and she reached for him.

He held his breath, anticipating the feel of her fingers on his.

"You do?" Nitya sounded skeptical. "I thought you said that wasn't possible."

Tanvi nodded. "Turns out I just needed a little help from the moon." Her arm fell to her side, and her voice rose in panic. "Is Mom here? You have to hide me."

"You're glamoured," Venkat reminded her, pretending he didn't miss her touch. "She won't know it's you."

"It's not like she'd bite you, but fine," Nitya said, with something like cautious amusement. She ran her gaze over Venkat, evaluating. "You're the guy who helped her in Nagalok and sells dreams. That's so wild."

"It's pretty cool," he agreed.

"I guess?" Tanvi shrugged. "It's all I know. Well, all I knew."

Nitya's jaw worked, and Venkat could practically feel her weighing how to respond. "You wanted to know I'm okay. I am. So what do you want to do now?"

Quit playing this stupid game! he burned to tell them. *Just admit you need each other.* His family was gone, but theirs had a second chance.

"Right now?" Tanvi asked. "I want to go inside and see how much it looks like my memories. It's all so . . . so much?"

"Fine by me." Nitya led them inside. Venkat got the sense she was relieved. "Great clothes, by the way."

The chanting from the main room came to a close as they entered. The aarti Nitya had mentioned.

They doffed their shoes in the vestibule and left them in the mess of other loose shoes on the floor. "Hopefully we can find them later," Tanvi said, "though I'd rather go barefoot, anyway."

346

Nitya snorted. "Not in Philly, you wouldn't."

The band launched into what sounded like a traditional tune, and Tanvi's face lit up with recognition.

"Raas is starting!" Nitya said. "Come on."

"I don't know if—" Venkat began.

Nitya pulled Tanvi into the crowd, leaving him to trail after them.

An altar had been set up in the middle of the room, featuring lit diyas and marigold-and-rose-garlanded portraits of Ma Durga in brilliant colors. Dancers ranging from small children to grandmothers and grandfathers had formed two concentric circles around it, moving in time to the band singing and playing onstage. As Venkat watched, each dancer, facing their partner in the opposite circle, held up a pair of dandiya—some plain wood, others wrapped in ribbons—and struck them against their partner's pair. Then they stepped back, twirled once, stepped forward, and struck their partner's dandiya again before each circle shifted one pace to its respective right, where the cycle started over with a new set of partners.

The music had started out slow, but every so often, the band increased the tempo, until finally everyone who hadn't dropped out was sweating and panting as they danced faster and faster.

Around Venkat, adults gossiped about who had bought a house where for how much and who let their children run wild. The uncles were only too happy to entertain him with opinions about skyrocketing malpractice insurance costs and whose children would be going to Harvard and who had to settle for Penn.

Venkat wanted to shout at them to count their blessings. Their families were all together. They hadn't lost everything twice, and they didn't have to worry someone they'd trusted might be sabotaging all they'd been working for. Instead, he turned back to the dancing and picked out Asha, then Sameer, then Nitya, and finally Tanvi.

His mouth went dry. By Mansa Devi's wings, she was so pretty. The rich sunset salmon pink gleamed against her brown skin, and the cerulean sequins on the cloth and the gold of her jewelry brought out the sparkle in her eyes. When Nitya executed a flashy move with her dandiya, Tanvi raised her eyebrows but copied it without hesitation. Her cherry-red lips were so soft and appealing as she laughed that he had to restrain himself from finding a pair of dandiya and joining in. Whether she knew it or not, she looked right at home in the dance.

As the circles moved again, Tanvi came face-to-face with a boy in an elaborate gray kurta. She held up her dandiya to meet his. Then she smacked his knuckles instead and opened her eyes wide in feigned apology. The boy scowled at her. When the moment arrived to strike their dandiya together a second time, he jumped out of range.

Venkat chuckled. Dancing with sticks had its dangers, it seemed.

The band eventually wound the music down, and the dancers scattered to find water and air. Radiant like she'd won the lottery, Tanvi plunked her dandiya down on the table behind Venkat. "Apparently I'd been waiting seven years to do that. Who knew?

And it was even better than I'd hoped—even if Hitesh didn't know it was me."

Venkat had a million questions but decided they could wait. "Where's Nitya?"

"She went to the bathroom." Tanvi pushed damp hair off her forehead. "Whew! It's hot in here. Let's go outside."

It had definitely gotten humid in the hall. Sweat trickled down Venkat's own back. "Sure." He put his hand on the small of Tanvi's back to guide her through the crowd.

She startled and looked up at him, but the expression on her face wasn't upset or disgusted. It was thoughtful.

They hurried through the doors and into the much cooler night, where Lord Chandra in his crescent form bore witness to the parking lot full of chattering people. Phones lit up the landscape like blue-flamed torches.

Venkat spotted Nitya before Tanvi did. She stood under a streetlight with a group of kids her age, including the boy in the gray kurta. He had his arm around her, and Nitya laughed at something he said. "You're so *bad*, Hitesh!"

"Yuck," Tanvi said. "I guess they like each other now?" She sighed. "You know, when I ran away that day, I don't think I really understood that life would go on without me."

Venkat nodded. "I think you and I are the only two people right now who get that." The whole *world* had gone on without him, and he didn't even have a family waiting for him to return to them.

"What . . . ?" She considered Nitya, then tried again. "What was I like when I got to Nagalok?"

He grappled for words. "You had a fire inside you," he said at last, "like you weren't going to let anyone tell you what to do. I liked it."

Tanvi caught the inside of her lip between her teeth and glanced coyly up at him. "What about now?"

Venkat's heart palpitated wildly. "Definitely now."

With her breath calming and her sweat cooling, and Venkat gone to find Asha, Tanvi realized she and Nitya were out in the open in a dimly lit parking lot bordered by trees. So many light poles and branches garudas could spring out from. She felt like an exposed rabbit, all twitching nose and terrified heart.

They'd already stayed a lot longer than she'd intended. The point had been to see that Nitya was safe, and so far, she was.

Nothing else was keeping Tanvi there. *Right?*

She hazarded a glance in Nitya's direction. Nitya waved her over, and Tanvi strode across the parking lot to her sister's side.

"There you are," Nitya said, hooking her arm through Tanvi's. "This is Chitra. She's a family friend."

Chitra. For a second, Tanvi had expected Hitesh and the others to recognize her. To wonder why there were two Nityas again. But of course not. She was glamoured.

Nitya introduced her friends, and their names rolled right off Tanvi. Even Hitesh, who glared at her, wasn't the same person from her memories. The boy she remembered was a shadow. He'd gotten older. All these people had. They'd grown past her. Some had never even met her. It felt like the hole she'd left when she'd run away had been filled in and built over.

But it wasn't all terrible. Tanvi could still hear the garba singer's throaty voice calling out the folksy lyrics, something about "cash today, credit tomorrow." She could still feel how the beat of the drum had set her blood alight with the need to move. How her body had recalled what to do with her dandiya, how to spin and leap. She'd missed that so much, even if she had forgotten until tonight.

She still had anchors if she wanted them.

Did she?

"Can I talk to you alone?" she asked Nitya, once the conversation had shifted away from her.

"Sure," Nitya said. She excused herself, and, arms still linked, they wandered to a patch of grassy earth off among the trees. It was so isolated, far from the mandir entrance.

Tanvi wanted to protest, but she didn't. She'd said she wanted privacy, after all.

"You're not worried about messing up your clothes?" she asked as Nitya sat down.

"That's what dry cleaning's for." Nitya leaned back on her elbows. "Venkat's cute, huh?"

The way he'd drunk her in earlier, like he wanted to consume her, sent a rush of heat through Tanvi's belly. "I guess," she said, plopping down next to Nitya. "I don't want to talk about him."

Nitya shrugged. "Okay." She gestured with her chin toward her group of friends. "So what do you think?"

"They seem nice. Is Hitesh your boyfriend now?"

"Yeah, right." Mirth danced over Nitya's face like the flames from the diyas, then dimmed. "I'm just . . . not interested in that, you know? With anybody, and I don't think I'll ever be. Only Mom knows."

"Oh." Tanvi toyed with her serpentine pendant, which lay flat against her collarbone beneath the silk of her choli. Why would Nitya confide in her about that and not Sameer or Hitesh?

She sensed Nitya's disappointment, her annoyance, even though her stoic expression didn't waver. Looking closer, Tanvi saw the strain underneath.

Why did this have to be so *hard*?

She couldn't stand how stilted being here felt, like she and Nitya were strangers, even as the memories she'd regained whirled around and around on a carousel in her head: day camp together. Watching anime together at Sameer's house. Picking blackberries in the woods near school together.

Nobody had known them better than they'd known each other.

"I hate that you left," Nitya said in a rush. "I hate that I don't understand any of this. I've been trying." She scooched closer to Tanvi. "Tell me about Nagalok. What's it like?"

"Um," said Tanvi. "Okay." She tried to think where to start. Then she dipped into her pouch, which had been tied at her waist and hidden beneath her filmy cloth-of-sky dupatta. "Do you still like pink?"

Nitya looked confused. "Not really. I'm more into green these days. Why?"

Tanvi paused with her hand on a reddish-pink rhodonite dreamstone. It was supposed to be a surprise. So much for that. Why had she bothered having her memories restored if even Nitya's favorite color had changed?

"I'm going to guess you still like purple, though," Nitya said, patting the fabric of her red-and-purple chaniyo. "I do, too."

Warmth seeped through Tanvi, banishing the letdown, and she switched out the rhodonite for a blue kyanite vial. The dream within glowed like foxfire in the gloom. "Here," she offered, ducking her head. "It's not green, but it's got Sameer's dream. Maybe you can give it back to him."

Nitya took it without a word.

Tanvi's heart went cold again. Nothing she did here would ever be right. If actual magic couldn't get through . . .

Nitya swiveled the vial between her thumb and index finger, admiring the powder-blue glimmer that tinged the air and highlighted her clothes. "No battery pack. No wires. No on/off button. Wow. So Nagalok is *real* real. Not just a story."

"*Real* real," Tanvi agreed. Nitya believed her!

"Hmm." Nitya brought the dreamstone to her face and peered into its facets. "Sameer's dream, huh? Is it really embarrassing?" She began to uncork the vial.

"Wait!" Tanvi cried. "I don't know if I can put it back in once you open it."

Nitya grinned, impish as a pixie, and let go of the cork. "You know, I think I'll hang on to this. I'm sure I can find a good use for it." She gave Tanvi a one-armed squeeze. "This is so cool. Thanks."

"Yeah," said Tanvi, stunned. Nitya *liked* it? Enough to hug her?

"So," Nitya prodded, leaning against her, "dreams? What's the story there?"

Tanvi gathered her breath and the glut of words she'd never thought she'd share with anybody. To her astonishment, she wanted to say them as much as Nitya wanted to hear them.

There, on the secluded patch of brown grass, she described getting to Nagalok and the initiation and what it was like to harvest dreams. She talked about the other runners and how they needed help. She explained how worried she'd been about Madhu's threat.

Everything but the reason she'd run away.

As she was finishing up, Nitya's phone buzzed. She fished it out of her tiny beaded-elephant purse and tapped at the screen. It buzzed again, and she typed another lightning-fast reply. "Mom's asking where I am. I told her I'm with a friend."

Tanvi inspected the now-empty parking lot. "Everybody really cleared out." Something hooted above, reminding her she'd seriously overstayed. Other, much more dangerous birds might be circling, too. "Maybe we should get going."

"Just so I'm clear," Nitya said, "Nayan's the one who had Asha steal you?"

"Yeah." It sounded so stark put like that, but it was the truth.

"And the other kids are still there?"

"Some of them." Tanvi thought of Indu. Of Bharat and Jai.

This had been great, but it couldn't last. She got to her feet. "I know you want me to stay here, but I can't. I have to help them."

Nitya stood, too, holding up the kyanite dreamstone like a lantern. "Then I'm coming with you. What do you think I was just arguing with Mom about?"

"What?" Tanvi couldn't have heard right. "You said you didn't tell her about me!"

"I told her I was sleeping over at a friend's."

A shout tore through the night. "For the fiftieth time, Sameer, I have no wish to wed him. It is my duty!"

"Yeah, and what am I supposed to do?" Sameer retorted. "You show up when you want, you disappear when you want, and now you're getting married. Why'd you even come tonight?"

Their voices drifted over from the side of the mandir. Tanvi glanced at Nitya and saw her own worry echoed there. "Stay here," she ordered, then broke into a run.

When she reached them, Asha and Sameer stood glaring at each other. A few feet away, Venkat seemed ready to throw something, maybe at them.

"Come on, Asha, let's just go," he insisted. "We're probably already in trouble. Didn't you say Karan suspected you?"

Ignoring him, she glowered at Sameer. "How many times must I repeat myself? You refused my calls, so I returned here to apologize. To see you one last time, yet even now, you do not listen. Do you know that if I had my choice, I would choose you?"

"Then why'd you quit calling?"

"Because, you preposterous creature, I gave Tanvi my remaining feather-telephone seeds!"

Tanvi hadn't known that. She felt strangely shy again.

Behind Venkat, two more figures emerged out of the darkness, their features unmistakable. Madhu—and Nayan.

Tanvi's joints went watery. Nayan had come himself instead of just sending Madhu. Oh, this was bad. She was going to ram Karan's sparkler crown down his throat, that self-serving little snitch.

Venkat practically shriveled before Tanvi's eyes as he looked between Madhu and Nayan. She wanted to run to him, to soothe the defeat in his face.

"I told you, my lord," Madhu said, her wrinkles deepening in triumph. "You thought you could trust them, and they have been lying to you this entire time."

If only Tanvi could grab some steel wool and scour that oily smugness right off Madhu's face—the more abrasive, the better. *You're the one working for the garudas!*

But then she remembered Madhu's threat and peeked over her shoulder. They never should have come here, no matter what Asha said.

Nitya wasn't anywhere in sight; had she listened and stayed put, or better yet, left?

Durga Mata, Tanvi prayed, *I'm so sorry I skipped aarti, but if you're listening, please keep Nitya and Mom away.*

"So I see," Nayan said. His fierce expression left no room for argument. "A very touching performance, Princess, worthy of an award, but it is time to return home. Because of your antics, the garudas might have infiltrated the palace or even captured you

357

again. Was once not enough?"

Asha lowered her head, but not before Tanvi noted the mutinous twist to her scarlet mouth. Next to her, Sameer looked like he'd quit breathing.

"Do you truly think I did not know of your seeds? Of your infatuation with this mortal boy?" Nayan thundered. "We have all been far more than lenient with your thoughtless stunts, yet you continue to put the entire realm at risk."

Nayan had known about the feather phones? Tanvi shivered. Did he know Asha had given *her* some of those seeds?

"She just wanted to help," Venkat said.

Nayan rounded on him. "I expected better of *you*, my son," he said. "You know precisely what is at stake here, and yet you disobeyed me."

Venkat winced. "It's my job to take care of the runners. That's what I was doing."

"By flouting the travel ban and cavorting behind my back?" Nayan's formidable gaze could have withered entire forests. "Whatever you believe you are playing at, it ends now."

Blinking hard, Venkat opened and closed his mouth. "I—"

"You nothing," Nayan said, his voice precariously close to a growl. "I have labored much too long for you to undermine all my efforts."

Tanvi shivered. With his fangs bared and his muscular coils of cobra tail lashing, he made Asha look like a child playing at being a monster. At any moment, he could rear up to strike.

Thank the gods he didn't see Nitya. Tanvi prayed again that her sister had more sense than to come investigate.

Nayan's reptilian gaze slid coldly over her before turning back to Venkat. "Where is the runner?"

"She ran off," Venkat lied, the slightest tremor in his words. "I thought if I fixed her memories—but the burnout must have gotten her after all."

Tanvi didn't dare breathe, terrified Nayan would look again and see through her glamour. How had it worked on him even this long?

"A waste of our time," Madhu said. Loathing rippled over her features. "Obstinate whelp!"

Tanvi dug her nails into her palms to keep from telling Madhu off.

Nayan raised a hand. "I will handle this." To Venkat, he said, "I appreciate that you cared for her, but one runner is hardly worth besmirching the trust between us. Perhaps Madhu is right, and I erred in placing my faith in you."

"Uncle!" Asha protested.

So many emotions muddled together in Venkat's expression Tanvi was sure he was going to be sick.

"Oh, look." Madhu grinned, her fangs glinting. "It would seem your runner has changed her mind. Perhaps some part of her remembers you."

The tiniest vestige of alarm surfaced before Venkat stifled it, but it was enough to confirm Tanvi's fear. *No.* As slowly as she could, she pivoted to find Nitya watching with a blank expression.

Go, Nitya mouthed, so small only Tanvi would see it.

Tanvi wanted to shake her. Why hadn't she just *listened*?

"We might as well leave her here," Venkat said. "She'll only run away again."

"Absolutely not," snapped Madhu. "We do not know the scope of her recall. The garudas may well find a weakness to exploit. Besides, you will scarcely be able to focus on your work if you are worrying about her."

I'm her hostage, Tanvi thought, the shame hot and bitter. She could see from Venkat's rigid jaw that he knew it, too.

All she'd wanted was to make sure Nitya was safe, not deliver her directly into the garudas' talons. Somehow Tanvi had to get her out of here. But how?

She perused scraps of plans: grabbing Nitya's hand and making a break for it. Offering herself up in exchange for Nitya. Taking Venkat as her own hostage until Madhu agreed to leave Nitya alone. They all ended in the same place—with both sisters carted off to Nagalok.

No. No, no, no. The realization crashed over Tanvi like an avalanche.

She couldn't say anything. She couldn't do anything. If she gave herself away, they'd both get caught, and then she'd never be able to help her sister.

"Madhu speaks truly. Tanvi returns with us," Nayan declared. "As for you, Princess, I will brook no more of your nonsense. We leave now."

Madhu's eyes bored into Sameer, then Tanvi. "Surely neither of you will be foolhardy enough to repeat anything you overheard here. If you are, well . . ."

"N-no," Sameer stammered. "Of course not." Tanvi could only shake her head.

"Oh, *fine*. No need to be so stodgy, Uncle." Asha flicked her fingers dismissively at Sameer. "It was entertaining for a time, but I have no more need of you or your little friends. Go home and make your little movies." Smirking, she glided toward Nayan and Madhu. "Perhaps one day you could even make one about me."

Tanvi seriously doubted that Nayan bought the sudden reversal, but Asha had given her an out, and she had to take it. She nodded at Sameer and backed up, step by step by step. Then she sprinted all the way around to the front of the mandir.

Sameer thudded after her. "What *was* that?" he asked when they reached the doors. "Who are you?"

Tanvi felt as deflated as Indu's real soccer ball. "Tanvi. Listen to Asha and go home," she told him tiredly. "You're better off, believe me."

Alone in the dark of the mandir's parking lot, Tanvi almost sobbed. She'd never felt more broken, sifting through her memories and realizing how much she still didn't grasp.

Worse, Venkat had been right; now that she remembered everything, she couldn't even cut the memories loose. She didn't want to. Definitely not for any bracelet. They were what connected her to Nitya and her mom.

Despair, storm cloud–gray and bleak, descended over her. She wasn't a dream runner anymore. She wasn't anything. Just a failed sister and daughter and friend.

It was her fault this had happened, and not only because she'd come here tonight. If she'd never left with Asha all those years ago, Nitya would be safe now, tucked snugly in bed.

They all thought Nitya was Tanvi, so what would Madhu and the garudas do to her?

Worse, they blamed Tanvi for distracting Venkat. What if, to punish him, Nayan put *Nitya* through the dream runner initiation? If they'd worked out the rest, they must know Tanvi had woken up, too.

She remembered Nitya and the dreamstone, how its supernatural radiance had briefly transformed her twin into a pari. How awed Nitya had been. How she'd trusted Tanvi with her own secret.

Slowly, the sky-toned light of the memory burned off Tanvi's fog of despair.

She and Nitya couldn't recover what they'd lost, but who said they couldn't build something new in its place?

Tanvi traced her fingertips over the familiar contours of her pendant. Venkat and Nitya might think they were being noble, giving her a chance to go home for real, but they'd misjudged her completely. Venkat especially, if he believed she'd turn her back on all of them and disappear into Nitya's life.

After all, he'd been the one to return her pendant.

Sneaking past the sentries was going to be hard, but she could manage that. And then she'd puzzle out the rest. She had to.

At least, Tanvi thought, examining her filmy dupatta's subtle, kyanite-like shimmer, she was already dressed for Asha's wedding.

PART THREE

*O*nce, so long ago even the wisest of rishis himself, the eminent Val-
miki, could not determine when, a brother and his dutiful sister
came into possession of a handheld looking glass. The mirror, as clear as
polished crystal, gleamed from a round golden frame encrusted with vines
of emerald, blossoms of ruby and sapphire, and curving onyx thorns. A
beatific serpent spiraled about its handle, each scale lovingly rendered. It
was a gift designed to enchant its recipient.

It happened that a multiplicity of gilded mirrors already graced the
family's hall, for it is a simple truth that all nagas are a joy to behold. As
a result, the siblings were scarcely strangers to their own winsome beauty:
the boy knew well his finely etched cheekbones and roguish smile, and his
sister had, in stolen moments, glimpsed the sparkle of her gemlike eyes.

Yet the girl, soft of speech and manner, found herself ever obscured by
her elder brother's ebullience. She was the faint moon to his effulgent sun,
echoing but the slightest portion of his light. Eager for another reflective
surface in which to see herself, to know she had not been erased, she reached
for the unexpected gift.

Her brother, however, snatched it up. His expression promptly darkened. "The glass grows misty!" he groused. "What manner of gift is this?"

He cast aside the useless mirror and glided toward the door. "Come, our companions await," he urged, impatient to join the games in the metallic fields of gold and platinum, silver and palladium, where he would be applauded and adored.

Her cheeks aflame, the girl trailed behind. Of course the gift had been for him. How foolish of her to imagine otherwise.

Thus the looking glass languished where they had abandoned it, forgotten.

For years it was so, the siblings frittering away their days in picnics, tournaments, and rambles in the coral woods. Always where the brother boldly led, the sister meekly followed.

In time, they matured, as hatchlings will, and the young man yearned for glory. Abiding by his sister's sage counsel, he soon garnered great renown as a wanderer of worlds. How fervently the masses now vied for his favor. How fully his radiance eclipsed that of his reserved sister, whose prudent guidance had propelled him to this peak.

It was, perhaps, inevitable that he then no longer saw fit to acknowledge her.

Her brother's disregard reduced the young woman to sheerest shadow, a never-ending new moon. Yet even the mildest of moons may in secret burn to swallow the arrogant sun.

One evening, while hunting for a misplaced trinket, the young woman chanced upon the looking glass in a drawer. Something shimmered up at her from its depths. Strange; should it not have misted over, as her brother had said? Gathering her caution, she grasped the serpentine handle.

The image gazing back from the glass wore the young woman's face. Its hair and jewelry, too, were hers. Yet she did not recognize its diadem of multicolored roses, nor did she possess a choli the deep gray-green of a hurricane-tossed sea. And although she stood in her bedroom, the peculiar light of a gibbous moon glimmered behind her double—an invitation.

As the young woman watched, bitterness yielding to bewilderment, her reflection plucked a bunch of turquoise jewel-berries from a nearby bush and popped one into her merry mouth. She winked one kajal-lined eye.

I see you.

The young woman's tail rippled in wonder. The looking glass had never been meant for her brother at all!

It soon became her sole source of pleasure. She drank in every detail as her double lingered with lovers, cavorted at carnivals, and dazzled crowds during storytelling duels. Such adventures her reflection had; such a luxuriant life she lived!

Always the young woman had slithered along in the grooves carved by her brother's coils. Yet in the realm beyond the glass, she shone like a pearl at the center of a pendant.

If only she could climb into the mirror and claim that life.

When her brother returned from his voyage, he chanced upon her clutching the looking glass. His lip curled at the sight of his sister's double. "What is this?"

Ever dutiful, the young woman shared her discovery with him.

"That is not you," he declared with a frown, attempting to pry the mirror from her grip. "That is a bhootini, perhaps a demoness. Give up this foolishness at once!"

The young woman and her reflection exchanged smiles rich with meaning. "See for yourself, then," the young woman challenged her brother.

In his vanity, he could not resist another glance into the looking glass. When he saw he still had no reflection, no double, he roared his wrath.

The young woman waited. Unlike her brother, she had befriended patience.

He thrust a fist at the mirror's beclouded surface, yet instead of smashing it, his hand penetrated into the world on the other side. Swift as a snake in the grass, the young woman's double tugged him through.

His sister had no desire to witness what transpired next. She tucked the looking glass back into the drawer, securely locked it, and set off on the first in an assortment of adventures beyond counting.

The brother no longer leads, and the sister no longer follows. Instead, the full moon shines bright and cool as silver, and that is why you may sometimes note its glint as you pass a mirror at night. It is Lord Chandra in his chariot, bearing the young woman's tidings to her heart's reflection.

—FROM *THE NAGA PURANA:*
A FLORILEGIUM OF FOLKTALES,
PROPERTY OF THE OFFICIAL ROYAL
LIBRARY AT BHOGAVATI

35

The day of the wedding dawned like a dreamstone mosaic: a sky of ceruleite and greenish-blue tourmaline, gardens ranging from Panjshir emerald to pale green prehnite, with a spectrum of blossoms in the deepest garnet to the brightest lavender quartz. Lord Surya himself was a blazing topaz no amount of coin could ever buy.

It was a perfect jewel box for a perfect royal couple.

Except the bride didn't want to marry the groom, and Venkat was locked in the workshop with Nayan, soldering together the final sections of the revisioning. He would have finished it yesterday, if he hadn't gone to Prithvi with Tanvi and Asha instead.

Outside the mandir, he'd seen the baleful way Madhu had stared at Nitya, whom she'd believed to be Tanvi, and all his doubts dissolved. She *had* been arguing with Nayan, and after last night, it didn't take much to imagine her conspiring with the garudas in revenge, orchestrating the breaches when his back was turned.

Nayan needed to know. But Venkat didn't have the slightest

notion how to bring it up. He didn't even think he could ask where Nitya was. Or how she was.

At least, he comforted himself as he molded the last of the solder, Tanvi was safe.

It almost made the chill in Nayan's demeanor bearable. Almost.

In all their years together, Nayan had never frozen him out like this. The charged silence between them, harsh and unforgiving, was shredding the already-unraveling gossamer threads of their relationship. It hurt more than Venkat could have expected, and it infuriated him, too. He wasn't the only one who'd broken their trust. What about that?

"There," he said, standing back to survey his work, "done, just in time for your wedding gift."

Pride swelled in him. The sections had come together to form a three-dimensional tapestry, one forged of dream elements rather than textile and ready to be invoked, just like a real boon. It depicted sage Kashyapa and his wives outside their hut, surrounded by a thousand opalescent naga eggs and the much larger golden egg containing Garuda, marking the short-lived peace before the sisters' rivalry would come to its destructive head.

The creek behind the hut burbled; the clouds overhead coasted lazily by. A butterfly, wings the pink-violet of a jewel-fig fresh from the palace orchards, soared through the scene.

Unlike his earlier trials, this tapestry would hold. Venkat had soldered in all the resolve he could, all his desire never to rely on dream runners again. The only thing left to do was to activate it once he and Nayan stood before the nagaraja and nagarani.

"*Our* wedding gift," Nayan corrected, perusing it.

"Still think your faith in me is misplaced?" Venkat asked, unable to keep the bitterness at bay.

"I spoke in anger," Nayan admitted, his words low and gruff, all the apology Venkat was going to get. "You have produced a masterwork. The absolute epitome of my vision; I could not ask for better." He paused. "And yet it is not complete."

"Not complete?" Venkat gestured at the tapestry. Even he couldn't believe how lifelike it was. Power wafted from it in tangible waves. What could possibly be missing? "Don't tell me; there's a thread out of place." He hated the snark, how it felt in his mouth and sounded in the air, but he refused to walk it back.

Nayan glanced up, and his closed-off expression yielded to affection. "We have spoken of family, yes?"

Venkat just stared at him. After everything, did Nayan really think that was appropriate?

"Though your behavior of late has tended toward the impulsive," Nayan said, still smiling, "I have not forgotten the credit you are due. This is your day as well, Venkat. You will see."

Venkat didn't really need to be lauded in public by the nagaraja and nagarani, but there were worse things. Like betrayal. Looking at the tapestry he never could have created without Nayan's guidance, he knew he had to try.

"Nayan," he said, "I need to tell you something."

"I am listening."

"Madhu's a spy. You can't trust her."

Nayan's smile turned quizzical. "Forgive me, my son, but is this another of your clever stories? It must be—a suitable topic for a jest it is not. I have taught you better than that."

"It's not a joke," Venkat said. "Tanvi saw her talking to a bunch of garudas in the archives."

The second the name left his lips, he realized his mistake.

"Tanvi saw?" Nayan cocked an eyebrow. "Tanvi, who is unwell?"

"I trust her," Venkat insisted.

"I know you do. She was one of the runners in your care. Nevertheless, you must not allow yourself to become carried away and lose all perspective."

That reasonable tone, that cool guidance. Why couldn't Nayan just get mad and yell? Venkat felt himself losing his grip on the situation, already so slippery.

"I know how it sounds," he said, "but all those attempted breaches?" He waited until he had Nayan's attention before continuing. "I think Madhu was behind them, and she's going to bring her garudas to the wedding. It's the perfect time, with all the clans in one place."

"Such a vivid imagination you have." What should have been a compliment from Nayan stung like a rebuke. "It is the sharpest tool in your dreamsmithing arsenal, but you must learn to master it, not permit it to rob you of your perspective."

"It's *true*." Venkat fought to keep his voice in check. If Nayan only knew about Nitya. About Tanvi's mother. "Madhu threatened Tanvi if she told anyone. And—"

What was he saying? No, Nayan couldn't know about Nitya. Not while he trusted Madhu.

"And yet Tanvi told you," Nayan observed. "That seems counterproductive, does it not?"

Venkat had no answer for that.

"A spy," Nayan repeated, amusement leaching into his words. "I selected Madhu myself. I have kept her close for centuries. If there were even the least hint she wished to betray me, surely I would have noticed by now."

He spoke like he was deconstructing a council member's unreasonable demands. Like they both knew Venkat was being childish, and he needed to be brought back into line.

It was easy enough for Venkat to forget before, but now, with nothing to distract him, he saw it. Nayan was a lord. He was accustomed to being right. His aristocrat's features had hardened into their remote lines, and it felt to Venkat like his heart had slammed shut, too.

"But . . . ," Venkat started, then gave up.

What was the point? The only proof he had was Tanvi's secondhand account. A rogue dream runner was hardly what anyone would call a reliable witness.

"But nothing. Let us leave the matter there," Nayan said tersely. "Now go and prepare yourself. At noon, before the ceremony begins, we will present the bride and groom with our gift of long-overdue healing."

"As you say." Venkat bowed his head. "But if I may, I want to give the runners back their toys. After today, we won't need them anymore, right?"

"Now that, my son, is a fair and compassionate suggestion, and one it pleases me to hear," Nayan said. He opened the treasury, and Venkat loaded his arms with everything but Jai's tricycle. It was too bulky, and there was no one to return it to, anyway.

Before he could succumb to the melancholy again, he left.

As Venkat hurried toward the dream runners' quarters, he wasn't sure what he'd find waiting for him. He hadn't told Nayan about dissecting the "boons"—only repaired them when he was through investigating. All but Tanvi's, that was.

Tanvi had been able to fully wake up, but what of the others? Or would he hurt them even more without knowing it?

Venkat could only hope that if he showed them their original objects, they would wake up and recover, too.

And, of course, he still had to pinpoint where Nitya was. Somewhere in the palace? Surely heavily under guard.

Nayan clearly thought his public acknowledgment of Venkat as his son would fix everything. That it would give Venkat what he'd been searching for since he'd lost his own family on Prithvi. And before, even a few short months ago, that would have been true.

It wasn't anymore.

If Nayan couldn't see that, then his acceptance of Venkat didn't mean much at all. Maybe the runners were only ever meant to be tools, maybe erasing their sense of self was meant to be a mercy, but Venkat didn't believe that. He couldn't, especially now that he'd gotten to know Tanvi, to see her alive and alert, the way she should have been all along.

If she'd truly known what lay ahead for her, would she have

gone with Asha? Would any of them have?

They weren't tools. They were innocent kids who had been tricked out of their childhoods, even out of their basic personalities. They deserved so much more than these dingy halls and sterile rooms and brief lives that inevitably ended in burnout. Venkat couldn't undo the past, but at least he could give them some kind of dignity now.

He started with Bharat's room. He knocked, then reached for the key protruding from the lock.

It had already been turned. The attendant must have forgotten to lock the door after delivering Bharat's breakfast.

No one was inside, though the fireflies had clustered by the ceiling, blinking on and off.

A black hole opened in Venkat's stomach. He checked inside the closet, then under the bed. "Bharat!"

No answer came.

He thought of how Tanvi had tried to help Indu. Had Madhu done something to the runners to punish her? Or had *Nayan* played some trick? He'd just granted Venkat permission to give back all the toys. . . .

Venkat dumped all the trinkets on the neatly made bed and rushed out. With each room he tried, his heart sickened more. They were all unlocked, all empty.

Finally he reached Indu's room.

His mouth foul with dread, Venkat pushed open the door.

36

"Q uit eating my ants!" demanded a kid named Srinivas, his once-blank face screwed up in rage. He wouldn't stop accusing another runner, an older girl named Mona with curls that hung to her shoulders, of stealing his chocolate ants.

Which made no sense—unless he'd been dreaming of chocolate ants.

"Shh!" Tanvi admonished. "Somebody'll hear you."

Who knew the other runners could be so *chatty*? They fired off question after question, as if they'd only just realized their vocal cords worked: Why were they here in Indu's room; who was Tanvi really; where was Venkat; what happened to their dreams?

Her glamour hadn't worn off, either, which made it harder to convince the runners to listen to her.

"My head hurts," Indu whined. She'd closed her eyes and sat huddled with her knees to her chest.

She wasn't the only one in pain.

Twenty-two kids, all younger than Tanvi, all confused and

possibly dreaming, all crammed too tightly into this tiny cell. They fought, they cried, they clung to dreamstones. Between the vials and their kurta pajamas and chaniya choli, this had to be the most color the sparse room had ever seen. What with all their shouting and complaining, the most action, too.

Herding twenty-three runners into a single room had been hard enough, and she'd lost one, a recent recruit. She'd asked everyone to hold hands in the hallway, but the boy had wriggled free and taken off, cheetah-fast for having such stubby legs.

If Tanvi had been alone, she might have chased him down. With twenty-two other charges to keep together, she'd had no choice but to let him go. Though she'd never met the boy before that moment, the thought of him ending up in a guard's clutches made her throat ache.

And what if he got them all caught?

Her plan had seemed so simple back on Prithvi: use the pendant to sneak into the palace as a wedding guest, round up the other runners, locate wherever Madhu had locked up Nitya, and devise a way to get them all out of there. Of course, now that Tanvi was here, listening to the runners bicker, she had to admit the second half of the plan was mostly wild hope propped up by wishful thinking.

"I didn't touch your gross ants!" Mona bellowed. She shoved past Srinivas. "Get out of my face."

"Worst babysitting job ever," Tanvi muttered. Her pulse beat in her temples, promising a headache as bad as the ones from the memory blisters.

Even if she could somehow get the other runners out of the

palace, where would they go? Didn't people on Earth need paper-work and money and things? They definitely needed their families, but how was Tanvi supposed to find them? Or Venkat, for that matter?

Stupid, stupid, stupid. She might have her old memories again, but they didn't change a thing. She still didn't know how to be a person.

Watching Indu now, Tanvi saw her younger self the day she'd run away. They'd both been talked into abandoning anyone who might have cared about them, any future they could have had, to run after meaningless objects. And now look at them.

She flopped down on the floor next to Indu. "Hey. It's me, Tanvi."

Indu glanced over, her gaze alert. "I miss the fireflies. Can you bring them back?"

The night-lights! Flustered by all the commotion, they'd scattered. But the jar was in Tanvi's room, and she didn't dare leave the others alone long enough to go fetch it. "I don't think I can. I'm sorry."

Someone knocked, and the door opened. Venkat appeared in the ocean of runners, clearly shell-shocked. "Tanvi?"

She straightened, a thrill running through her. "Uh, surprise?"

Some of the runners attached themselves to him, clamoring for boons. He smiled, though she could tell it hurt him, and gently disengaged from them before making his way over to her.

He leaned close, his mouth almost brushing her ear, and she shivered. "What're you doing here?" he demanded. "You're supposed to be at home with your mother! Safe."

"Then I guess you shouldn't have given me back my pendant."

"I guess not." Srinivas bumped into him, and he held up a finger to count the runners. Then he frowned. "There should be twenty-nine of you. Where're the others?"

Twenty-nine? Tanvi felt like someone had clubbed her in the stomach. Where were the five she hadn't known about? "We lost one," she confessed, "but that's all I know."

"Some old lady took Bharat away," Indu piped up. "The servant ratted him out for trying to escape. He told me the old lady already got some of us, and if we tried anything, we'd be next."

She didn't sound afraid, at least. More outraged. Tanvi figured she hadn't actually seen Madhu yet.

Venkat, though, fumed. "Who does she think she is?"

"I'm not afraid of her," announced a stocky boy named Rohan, who looked just a couple of years younger than Tanvi.

"Well, you should be," she said, furious. All he had—all any of them had—was her. "All of you should be. This isn't a game. That 'old lady' wants to hurt us."

But, lost in their own dreams and delusions, her fellow runners had already stopped listening.

Venkat sighed. "I don't know if we should give them their things back now or not." He explained that he'd gathered their objects from the vault and left them in the corridor. "What do you think, Tanvi?"

The way he said her name, the way he looked at her—really looked at her, like he wanted to know her thoughts—made her shiver again. She put her hand on his, locking their fingers together.

"Ooh, is he your boyfriend?" Mona wondered from across the room. Tanvi tore her hand away. Of course Mona had noticed *that*.

It was too much. She felt too vulnerable. Tanvi didn't dare look at Venkat, afraid she might go up in sparks if she did. "Give them back," she rushed to say. "They've waited long enough already."

"You don't think it could hurt them?" But he was already getting to his feet.

"They're hurting right now."

Venkat nodded, then smiled, his eyes crinkling at the edges. Tanvi felt too warm, warmer than she could blame on the overcrowded room. "I'll be right back."

She nodded, too, enjoying how the silk of the Night Market kurta pulled taut against the strong line of his shoulders as he strode toward the door. How would it feel for him to hold her? Not just a quick hug, but actually hold her, like the night bride had imagined?

Whatever else happened, Tanvi hoped she'd have the chance to find out.

A minute later, Venkat reappeared, his arms full of the objects Tanvi had seen in the vault. Around her, the room went silent, as if the toys gave off their own gravity, pulling the runners into their orbit.

But they were just toys. Nothing special. Toys each runner would have grown out of and forgotten, just like Nitya had long since forgotten the charm bracelet, the one she'd sworn she'd never take off, not even for bed.

It hit Tanvi now—the runners had been robbed of being kids,

of having normal lives with friends and games and birthdays. Every single one of them had been robbed, both the ones who'd burned out and the ones who hadn't yet but would, if she and Venkat couldn't find a solution.

Venkat started distributing the toys. Indu was first, and he handed her the deflated soccer ball. Her eyes went wide, and she wrenched it from him. "My ball!"

Just as suddenly, her bottom lip began trembling. "But what's wrong with it? Why'd you break it?"

"It was always broken," Venkat said softly. "It was like this when you brought it here."

Indu stared at the flattened ball with its marks and dirt. "I don't believe you." She threw it down and stomped on it. "I hate you!"

Tanvi wanted to hug her, to tell her it would be all right, but she couldn't lie. Not about this.

Instead, she watched, her eyes stinging, as the rest of the runners repeated the cycle she'd gone through with her bracelet: utter joy that turned to bewilderment and finally to the bitter knowledge that it had all been for nothing. That ideal they'd been persuaded to give up their lives for didn't exist.

A few of them cried. Srinivas pitched his plush bunny against the wall. "No!"

Mona approached her chapter book and flinched away. "It's not right. Make it right!"

Others wrestled with what had to be moth-eaten memories, their eyes as glazed as doughnuts. The rest were silent.

Venkat put his arms around Tanvi and pressed close, as if he'd heard her question from earlier. "I'm sorry," he whispered into her hair.

"Me, too." Tanvi sank gratefully into him, feeling his warmth, his solidity. She eyed the unclaimed toys he'd left by the door, a silent accusation on the part of their missing owners. "But at least they know."

Venkat nodded before letting go, and again Tanvi felt the bite of tears in her throat. "We have to find Nitya," she said, shaking it off. No time for these huge, seriously annoying feelings. She gestured to the wreck of her fellow runners. "Do you think we can leave them here?"

He rubbed his eyes. "Your guess is as good as mine."

"I don't think we have a choice."

"Yeah." His shoulders drooped. "Too bad we can't just ask Asha to whisk them all to Prithvi."

Tanvi chewed the inside of her cheek. "Do you think Nitya's okay?"

"I'm sure she is," Venkat said bitterly. "They want me to show up, after all." He ran his knuckles over Tanvi's cheek, light as a damselfly's wings. She closed her eyes. "I'd better get going. I have to change into my royal tailor–approved clothes. Nayan wants us to present our gift at noon."

"What gift?"

"Remember I told you I can make things out of dreams?" Tanvi nodded. "We made something that Nayan says will fix everything. Tell a new story."

"That sounds pretty vague," she said, leaning into his touch.

"I can hear them," Indu intoned, lying on her back while drifting in and out of what had to be a dream. Her arms and legs scissored feebly like she was an overturned bug. She opened her eyes and looked straight up at Tanvi. "They say we need to run. Now."

"Who?" Tanvi asked. "Who says that?"

The door burst open, and guards swarmed in.

37

It was happening. Venkat could scarcely believe it. Asha was getting married—but not until he'd debuted the secret project he'd labored over for so long.

He stood with Nayan in a screened-off corner of the grand outdoor pavilion, waiting for an attendant to summon them. The two of them looked like nobles in their matching red-and-gold sherwanis, father and son, and Nayan held the silver tasseled tube containing the rolled-up tapestry. Today should be Venkat's moment of triumph; he was about to reveal his secret talent to the entire realm. Together, he and Nayan would undo the ancient mistake that had caused so much grief.

But all Venkat could think of was his poor dream runners—and Tanvi. He hadn't been able to stop the guards from taking the kids elsewhere, on what they claimed were Madhu's orders. At least Tanvi had managed to pass herself off as his personal guest for the wedding before the guards escorted her out.

But what if Madhu had figured out who Nitya really was?

Restless, Venkat peered out from behind the partition.

Guests in their finest silks and jewels milled about the pavilion, so many that they might have been their own city. Their anticipation hissed in the air like the uptick in wind before a storm, seemingly not disturbed by the phalanxes of armed guards shoehorned in among them.

Just beyond the pavilion, architects had constructed the mandap, its four golden pillars and rose-bedecked golden ceiling set atop a dais generously strewn with a variety of blossoms. Filmy red curtains had been tied back from each pillar, and two matching thrones sat at the rear. A patterned havan kund had been positioned in front of the thrones, primed for the sacred fire that would soon be kindled in it.

Asha rested in the throne on the left, impossibly regal in her scarlet wedding choli with its golden sequins and beads and gold ribbon trim. White dots arced over both her brows, surrounding her ornate ruby bindi, and a spiderweb-thin gold chain led from her hair to a large gold ring in her left nostril. Jasmine and marigolds wove through her loose bun like tiny starbursts, her large eyes had been outlined in kajal, and her lips were a spectacular rouge. Intricate mehndi patterns of serpents and leaves wound over her hands and wrists, peeking out from between the plethora of gold-and-red bangles, while each individual scale of her coils had been flecked with gold.

She was stunning, an ethereal beauty radiant with joy and flanked by loving parents.

Venkat, though, saw through Asha's brilliant smile to the

private sorrow beneath. She would do her duty as a princess, but her heart was with Sameer. Or at least off having adventures.

For his part, Chintu looked bored in his ivory-and-gold turban and cream-colored sherwani. He mustered a weak grin for the crowd, one undercut by his lazy slump against his lofty seat.

His parents, who stood to his right, mouthed something. Venkat wondered if they truly believed this union was the best course of action, or if, like the garudas, they just wanted power, too.

Come to think of it, did the wedding even need to happen? Neither Asha nor Chintu wanted it, and the revisioning would render it beside the point.

Venkat glanced off to the side, where Madhu and her contingent of sentries loomed, and his bad feeling returned. How did Nayan not see how duplicitous she was?

Moments later, bearers halted at a second set of ceremonial thrones installed on a dais a few feet from the mandap, where they lowered two exquisitely decorated palanquins. Handlers slid open the door of each palanquin and accompanied the nagaraja and nagarani to their seats.

In the wake of their arrival, the air felt electric with expectation, enough that Venkat had to resist the urge to rub the goose bumps on his arms. Despite his fury at Nayan and Madhu, exhilaration coursed through him. Everything was about to change.

From the position of Lord Surya's chariot in the sky, it was almost noon. Almost time. Venkat retreated behind the partition, his anxiety spiking.

"Be at ease," Nayan said, as steady as if they were merely chatting in their private workshop. "All will be well."

Venkat reflected on that with new cynicism. If Nayan cared so much, why hadn't he stopped Madhu from issuing that order? Why was he holding anyone hostage?

Undaunted, Nayan added, "Today is our day, my son."

An attendant peered around their screen. "Lord Nayan, it is time."

Nayan winked, then motioned for Venkat to come along.

Countless eyes pursued them as they sauntered, on foot and on tail, over the teal carpet leading to the mandap. The distance simultaneously felt interminable and like it would end far too quickly. Venkat had never had so much attention directed at him in his life, and the weight of it might have been the river sky itself pressing down.

"Welcome, Lord Nayan and Apprentice Venkat," said the nagaraja from his throne. "You wish to address us before the ceremony begins?"

"Indeed, my liege." Nayan moved to kneel before the cobra-hooded thrones, and Venkat followed suit, his palms growing clammy. Here it was, the moment of truth.

His stomach churned. Everyone would see his work. Would his craft hold up?

What if it didn't?

"Rise, Lord Nayan," said the nagaraja, "and speak."

"Time and again, our ancient feud with the garudas has brought grief and death to our doorstep. Even now, they seek their reprisal." Nayan stared out at the guests, letting the accumulated fear and rage settle over them. Letting them remember why they had all come here to be united under one banner. "You have requested a permanent solution to the problem, Your Majesties, and my apprentice—my *son*—and I bestow one upon you now."

At his signal, two attendants set a long easel before King Vasuki and Queen Naga Yakshi. Then Nayan, with a flourish, shook the revisioning from its tube, unrolled it, and spread its featherlight bulk across the easel.

At the sight of the tapestry, the audience broke into curious muttering.

Equally entranced, Venkat marveled at his masterpiece as if he were just another guest. The vibrant hues, the integrity of every detail, the sheer power radiating from it all floored him once more.

He really had forged something special, and after so many years of imagining, he was going to see what it could do.

"Your Majesties," Nayan said, "I present to you a tapestry of dreams. Of healing."

The nagarani nodded for him to continue.

Nayan pointed to the scene depicted in the tapestry. "Long ago, two sisters imprudently entered into a terrible wager, the consequences of which ripple out into our present day. It is that wager we must correct."

Something about his manner struck Venkat as off. Nayan's tone should have been benevolent or at least cordial. Instead, he sounded self-satisfied, even haughty.

"We have brought you all here to behold a reversal of fortune." The bent of Nayan's secretive smile set Venkat's teeth on edge. "You see, my son has been training in the art of smithing dreams. Of retelling stories. Together, we have forged a spell that will revise the mistakes of the past."

The audience was spellbound. Venkat heard its shocked whispers, but he was too busy trying to decipher what the tapestry was saying to listen.

Nayan had never been an extraordinarily large man, but now his body began to elongate and spread, growing to mammoth proportions. The muscles in his arms swelled to boulders. His body brightened to gold as his snake tail split into sinewy legs.

Screams, including Chintu's, erupted as the guests fled in every direction. Guards advanced on Nayan, but he ignored them.

Venkat must have fallen into a nightmare. What was happening?

Twin mounds like mountains sprang up from beneath Nayan's shoulder blades. He now stood as tall as the palace. "I believe we all hold cheating to be an abomination, do we not? An act so vile it cannot—must not—go unpunished?"

"Lord Nayan," demanded the nagaraja, towering on his coils, "what is the meaning of this?"

Nayan's aquiline nose rounded into a cruel hooked beak, and his face reddened to the scarlet of poppies. Talons like carving knives jutted from his fingertips. "Surely you remember me, *Cousin*?"

The tapestry. Venkat tore his gaze from Nayan's changing form and really pored over the image he'd forged. The scene came into focus: the birds, the village, the sage.

And at last he could see what he'd been missing.

There were two women, one with a boy on her hip and a giant egg at her feet. Venkat had seen enough illustrations in the books he'd read as a child to recognize her.

He squinted to be sure, but that woman was Vinata beyond a doubt. Younger, in her prime, vivacious. On her hip was Arun, who would later mature into Lord Surya's charioteer. Her sister Kadru stood beside her, surrounded by a thousand naga eggs. Venkat could feel the fleeting truce, a fragile pause in the sisters' age-old rivalry.

As he watched, the nagas hatched in unison. At the same time, the giant egg cracked, and a baby Garuda emerged.

Then the sequence shot forward to the bet.

"Guards!" Queen Naga Yakshi called. "Seize him!"

More sentries charged at Nayan. With lazy flicks of his taloned fingers, he flung them across the turf. "I do grow tired of violence, but if you insist, you shall have it."

No. Venkat dropped to his knees in the grass. He could finally hear what the tapestry was saying. Nayan wasn't just going to undo the wager. He was going to invert it.

The bumps on Nayan's back burst into wings, the legendary wings that had once blotted out the sun.

And in a final flash of gold, he was no longer a naga but a garuda. *The* garuda. Garuda himself.

Venkat's hands shook. How had he not realized?

"With this dreamsmithed tapestry," Garuda concluded, as though he were simply wrapping up a presentation, "I will go back in time and so restore justice. My dearest kin, it is your turn to know the pain your wickedness caused."

"Now!" Madhu shouted.

She gave a flip of her wrist, and the sentries around her transformed. Garudas and garudis all, they ambushed the retreating guests and naga forces alike.

In the same breath, a trio of garuda soldiers leaped toward Asha. Before Venkat could blink, two of them had incapacitated her bodyguards even as they raised their swords, while the third apprehended her.

Madhu's own skin grew smooth and taut, while her white locks darkened to a lustrous black. The planes of her face shifted into the bloom of youth, and like Garuda, her tail divided in two, until a beautiful human woman stood there, clad in a white sari of mourning.

"You're not Madhu," Venkat said. "You're Vinata. Garuda's mother."

Old mother, he thought bitterly. How many times had he heard Nayan call her that? *Of course*.

Gray clouds scudded across the aquamarine river sky. More and more garudas flooded in—so many that even the heightened security wouldn't be able to stop them. The nagas fought valiantly, but no one had foreseen this.

Venkat felt like a total fool. No wonder Nayan—no, *Garuda*—had dismissed his warning. Behind the scenes, Garuda and his mother must have downplayed the need for the naga army's reinforcements.

Garuda stooped and took Vinata's much smaller hands in his talon-tipped ones. Over his shoulder, he roared, "None of you are equal even to the ground this magnificent lady treads upon. Because of you, she cannot forget the horrors inflicted upon her during her years of unwarranted servitude."

Venkat staggered backward from the might of Garuda's voice. It was formidable enough to rend the skies themselves, as befit the creature who had once served as Lord Vishnu's mount. Vinata smirked.

"Now, Venkat," Garuda boomed, his words like a series of thunderclaps, "let us invoke our revisioning. Open your heart to justice."

"No." Venkat stared at the stranger who had left him completely scale-stripped. Garuda had even swindled him out of the person he'd loved and trusted—Nayan. And Venkat had gladly helped him pull off his schemes. "No, I won't."

"Ah, but you will." Garuda released his mother. "We are holding your runners captive, after all—but that is an incentive I am certain will prove unnecessary. I know that, deep in your heart, you still grieve. What if you could have those you loved and lost returned to you?"

"Jai's gone," Venkat said, not caring how sullen it sounded. "Or do you mean Tanvi?"

He glared at Garuda through a film of shock and tears. All their conversations, all their years of collaboration, all the riverfront dinners and strolls and gifts of home and position—even Nayan's praise and Venkat's pride—had been a lie.

There had never been a Nayan.

Garuda only laughed. "Think in greater terms, Venkat. You are a dreamsmith!" He indicated the tapestry. "There is power enough in what you have forged to restore your family to life. Their deaths would be but a bad dream, swift to fade upon waking."

Venkat opened his mouth, but nothing came out. "What?" he said at last, stupidly.

"When you first came into my care, you entreated me to help you. To revive your family." Garuda patted Venkat's shoulder, the touch surprisingly light. "I could not think of a greater gift to bestow upon you than providing you the tools to make that so. Death, too, need only be a story one revises in favor of a better outcome."

"I—" Venkat scrambled for the nearest chair. He had to sit down. "I don't understand."

That wasn't true, but it was as close as he could get to expressing the experience of having his grasp of reality blasted apart.

"What is it that you want from us, Garuda?" a baritone voice rumbled. "Call off your minions, so that we may parley."

Venkat turned to see King Vasuki and Queen Naga Yakshi gliding toward them through the chaos, the many hoods of their fearsome coronas hissing. The monarchs had expanded to match Garuda's massive stature, and the air thrummed with their dominion, driving the few nagas still upright to genuflect. Even Venkat found himself off the chair and kneeling. The garudas alone resisted the pull.

"I could create the illusion of boons," Garuda told Venkat, as matter-of-fact as if the leaders of his enemies weren't bearing down on him. "I could guide you through the process of forging our revisioning. But only you, with your mortal's grief-ridden yet compassionate heart, could actually forge it." Garuda's sharp gaze pierced through Venkat, skewering his doubts and laying bare the most secret part of him. "And now you must be the one to rectify the ills of the past."

Venkat felt like someone had shoved him outside himself. He'd wanted this chance so badly, so very badly he would have sacrificed anything for it, but he'd resigned himself long ago to the idea that it could never happen.

Suddenly that was no longer true. His family, alive again. With him.

Garuda smiled, a terrifying thing. "The elements we have chosen include a pocket of potential specifically for you to rewrite your own past. To undo your own tragedy. Tell me you do not want it."

The long-nurtured fantasy, securely stored in the vault of Venkat's heart, expanded now, merging into the tapestry, until they were one and the same. He couldn't say he didn't want it, as Garuda well knew.

"Both of us will benefit," Garuda said, as he faced the nagaraja and nagarani. "Justice will be served, and you will be reunited with those you love best."

Mummy. Papa. His grandmother. Everybody Venkat had lost appeared in his imagination, so richly alive, so close he could see the wave of a breeze dancing through their hair. He'd lost count of the nights he'd prayed for the privilege of being pestered by his little brother one more time.

Butterflies made of need fluttered against his rib cage, eager to be let out.

How many times had he wished his own dreamsmithing could bring them back?

And now, if Garuda was right, it would.

"You!" the nagarani spat. "We granted you succor in our land. Our court. How dare you?"

Another naga guard, somehow free, rushed Garuda, and he swatted the man as easily as crushing a beetle.

"How foolish are you, Cousins," Garuda mocked, "not to have registered my presence among you all this time? Thousands of years have passed for mortals, so you, too, fail to recall your own history? Or did you think I would simply forgive and forget?"

King Vasuki's coils twitched as if he were about to strike. Venkat prayed he would keep his head. Garuda's machinations had already led to the casualties on the ground, and all it would take was one foolish move for the entire scene to descend into carnage.

"Release the princess," the nagarani countered. "She is not part of this."

The tapestry spoke louder, urging Venkat to invoke it. Compelling him.

"Give me Kadru," Garuda said. "I wish to look her in the eyes as I subject her to her own cruelty."

All around him, small clashes continued—the nagas' swords and maces swinging and their arrows flying; the garudas' golden talons slashing and their beaks impaling—but Venkat hardly noticed. Nayan was gone, a fictional character, and with him, all Venkat had in the worlds. He was no one's son now.

395

Revise the story.

He couldn't be left with nothing again. He would shatter.

What did he owe the nagas, anyway? After all, hadn't they cheated in the first place? All Venkat would be doing was setting things right.

He had no desire to help Garuda, but he could help the dream runners—help *Tanvi*—and his own family if he went ahead with the revisioning.

Not to mention, the tapestry wanted to be invoked. Its enchantment crooned to him. He had worked so hard on it; shouldn't he see it through to fruition?

He could already hear his grandmother's voice again.

"You can halt this anytime you wish," Vinata said to him. "I will even see to it that the mortal girl goes free."

"You'll let Tanvi go. You swear it?"

Vinata waggled her head. "Why not? I have no further use for her."

Then he had no reason to refuse.

"Okay," Venkat said. "I'll do it."

38

Gold. There was so. Much. Gold. So many jewels, all cut and polished for decoration's sake. Tanvi had thought she'd been overwhelmed before, when she'd glimpsed Venkat's workshop. But this was oversaturation. Like eating too much candy, could someone get sick from seeing too many riches?

The palace went on and on and on, but worse than her funhouse dream, because this was real. Being dressed like one of Asha's friends gave Tanvi leeway with the overburdened staff, who barely spared her a glance, but it didn't do anything to help her navigate the labyrinthine corridors and endless flights of stairs. The lines of statues, the portraits and pools and fountains, even the mosaics all made her dizzy, like she was walking in circles. And maybe she was—she'd run into that servant carrying the giant platter of teal and violet jewel-rice once before, and she'd definitely gone by the steamed-up kitchens at least twice. No wonder Asha had so many attendants; without them looking after her, she'd fall through a remote chute and vanish. Hissing the whole way down, probably.

Tanvi couldn't even smile at that. The only parts of the palace she'd been to were the runners' quarters, the archives, and Asha's apartments. None of which she knew how to access from this stupidly pretty courtyard, and even if she did, who said Nitya or the other runners were here at all? Madhu could have stashed them anywhere in Nagalok. Or even wherever the garudas lived.

What if Tanvi somehow lucked out and located Nitya, only to find Madhu's henchmen had hurt her? Or the other runners? Tanvi couldn't handle the thought of Indu being tortured or worse.

And Mom. Tanvi's throat closed up. Mom already thought she was dead. Tanvi couldn't let her lose Nitya, too.

Nitya, she almost screamed, just for the relief of it. *Nitya, where are you?*

The silence echoed in her ears, and Tanvi's panic began to rise again. She was too small for this, too trivial. Hadn't her plan to help the other runners blown up in her face? Wasn't it her fault Nitya had been kidnapped?

Who did she think she was kidding, trying to help anyone?

So many feelings. They swamped her, and she couldn't escape. Screwing her eyes shut, Tanvi perched on the edge of a red enameled chair set with enough emeralds and gold to buy five of her childhood house. Her fingers grabbed the armrests like they could keep her afloat. *Deep breaths, just like Venkat showed you.*

Venkat. Her grip relaxed. She remembered their adventure at the Lake of Lovers' Tears. How good it had felt when he'd held her in Indu's room. How minding the runners together had warmed her reawakened heart.

She remembered how happy Nitya had been holding Sameer's dream. How she'd switched places with Tanvi so Tanvi could go home and live a normal life.

Even Asha, outrageous and totally annoying Asha, had just been trying to fix things.

Tanvi didn't want to escape her feelings anymore. She didn't want to keep struggling to do this alone, either. She needed backup.

With one more slow, deliberate breath, she opened her eyes and took stock. Ahead, a guard blocked the next passageway she'd meant to try.

Before she could talk herself out of it, Tanvi hopped up and approached the guard. "Pardon me, my lady," the guard said firmly, "but it would appear you have taken a wrong turn. This route leads to the larder. The wedding ceremony is outside, by the grand pavilion."

"Yes, thank you!" Tanvi gushed in her best impression of Asha. "I was to accompany my sister, but I think she went on without me, and now I am lost."

It wasn't a very good impression, and she knew it. Tanvi's fear galloped in time with her erratic thoughts, but as long as she was glamoured, no one could possibly suspect who she really was.

The guard sighed irritably. "I will show you the way out. Come with me." She strode forward, and Tanvi followed.

Tanvi touched her pouch of dreamstones for reassurance.

The guard led her back the way she'd supposedly come, but Tanvi couldn't recall a single detail about this corridor, not even the distinctive green marble floor with its wave motif like the sea.

Pressing her lips together, she tried to memorize everything in case she needed to return here later.

As they reached the exit, screams ruptured the air, accompanied by the ring of metal on metal. The guard cursed. "Stay here," she ordered, then unsheathed her sword and ran toward the noise.

Staring after her, Tanvi recognized the significance of the grayscale sky, a thing normally never seen in Nagalok. The garudas had arrived.

Tanvi's first instinct was to run, too, but she quashed it. Instead, she tiptoed forward. How weird that just days ago, every bone in her body had resisted going in public among the nagas. Now she couldn't stay inside the palace a second longer.

Hadn't Venkat said he had to present some gift he'd forged? What if he was out there, wounded? Or Asha?

Tanvi held her breath like the air in her lungs was a spell, an incantation to keep everything in stasis until she got outside. She froze when she spotted the guard from the hall, locked in combat with a gleeful garudi.

Bodies, too many, lay on the ground. Tanvi didn't dare look closely enough to see which ones had quit breathing. The pools of blood, ironically the same color as auspicious wedding red, told her way more than she wanted to know.

Please, she prayed, drifting between the various battles in a daze. None of this felt real. *Let them be all right.*

Arms that might have been fallen tree trunks filled her vision. She registered the quills next, gold and deadly. Then the red face, the exceptionally long wingspan. Garuda.

Tanvi had never seen him before, but she still recognized him. He dwarfed even the garudas that had attacked at Nitya's school. Power wafted from him like radiation from a supernova, altering everything it touched.

From somewhere far off, her brain shrieked at her to run. Her legs didn't budge.

Garuda stood facing two equally colossal nagas who must have been the nagaraja and nagarani. The three of them were hulking monsters, far too big for all the people in the vicinity. Tanvi shuddered. All the people they would trample in their rage. She felt as tiny and exposed as a bug.

The cousins sized one another up. Unfettered by his disguise, Garuda blazed with vigor. Even folded, his wings cast shadows over a good chunk of the space around him. And his claws and his beak were the sharpest things she'd ever seen, promising anyone unlucky enough to meet them a quick but vicious death. "Give me Kadru," he said. "I wish to look her in the eyes as I subject her to her own cruelty."

King Vasuki drew himself up on his tail, which was thick and muscular enough to asphyxiate an elephant. Though the stories extolled the depth of his compassion, Tanvi only picked up on his menace. His fangs gleamed with venom, and his green-gold eyes shone with fury. "What you are saying is unfeasible," the nagaraja thundered, "as convenient as it might be."

Beyond them was a human woman who looked nothing like Madhu, but Tanvi could place the bitter triumph etched in her face. Not knowing what else to do, Tanvi listened as Vinata promised to let her go—or at least the girl Vinata thought she was.

Venkat nodded. "Okay. I'll do it."

Whatever he'd just agreed to couldn't be anything good. Tanvi scanned the landscape, frantic to find help. There, on the mandap. Asha sat on her throne, bound in place by three garuda soldiers, their swords held to her neck and head. She hadn't looked so terrified even in the quad at Nitya's school.

The throne beside Asha sat empty. Tanvi idly wondered if the groom-to-be had abandoned her, then shook the question away. It wasn't important. Getting to Venkat was.

"I will gladly release the girl, but there is one more thing," Vinata informed Venkat, her voice pitched low. "A small stipulation." She smiled sweetly. "My son fails to comprehend the true capacity of a revisioning. Simply reversing the wager is not enough. We must erase the existence of this degenerate species. Only then will I know peace once more."

What? Too long steeping in old animosity had poisoned Vinata far more than naga venom ever could. That was abhorrent. Unspeakable, even. Tanvi knew Venkat would never agree to that.

No wonder Vinata as Madhu had threatened Tanvi if she told what she'd seen. Garuda would never have allowed it.

From Asha's horrified expression, Tanvi could tell she'd heard Vinata's condition and thought the same thing.

Tanvi stared as hard as she could at Asha until Asha snapped to attention. Luckily, she had the sense not to let on. Willing her to get the message, Tanvi kept staring.

"You will have your family," Vinata cajoled. "I will honor the terms of your original agreement with my son. I only wish this one adjustment."

The conflict had written itself on Venkat through his demoralized eyes and slumped posture. He was visibly wavering, one hand reaching toward a tapestry that sat on the easel. That must be the thing he'd presented, the thing Vinata wanted him to modify.

Tanvi had to get to him before he could say yes.

"You wish to parley?" Garuda asked. "Then tell us where you have hidden Kadru."

The soil itself quaked before the nagaraja's glower. "What do you want with her?"

"For her to bear witness. To know that her selfish betrayal is your undoing."

"I am afraid that demand must remain unmet," the nagarani said, her scepter raised high. "I will not permit you to harm her."

Garuda nodded. "I assumed as much."

Vinata shot the three of them an exasperated glance, then confronted Venkat. "You will begin now. Amusing as it would be, we do not have another minute to squander upon my faithless sister. She will learn soon enough the nature of the fate she has called down on herself."

Asha hadn't blinked once during her wordless consultation with Tanvi. *Go,* she mouthed now.

Then, so fast even her captors couldn't interfere, she morphed into a snake and shot away from the throne. The trio of guards raced after her, but she easily eluded them, only stopping when she reached Garuda. Next to him, even back in nagini form, she was a toddler at the feet of a titan.

It was the stupidest thing she could have done, and Tanvi desperately longed to hug Asha for it. If they survived, she would. For now, she got ready to run.

"Nayan Uncle!" Asha cried, projecting her voice so it carried across the grounds. "Garuda Uncle! Why are you doing this? I do not believe that you hate me."

It was now or never.

For the runners. Tanvi lifted her chaniyo and sprinted toward Venkat as fast as she could.

Garuda took in Asha's quivering mouth, her shaking arms. "I bear you no ill will, child," he said. "But these are matters much older than you could possibly fathom." He laughed. "Besides, I thought you would be pleased to have this wedding you do not want interrupted?"

"Release her," Queen Naga Yakshi commanded. She'd slithered to Asha's side, and even the garuda soldiers who'd pursued her and stood hovering didn't dare lay a hand on the nagini queen. "She has no part in this."

"Give me Kadru," Garuda said, "and I will."

King Vasuki's coils undulated faster. "I will not."

"Kadru. Now." Garuda's smile had vanished, and his wings began to beat behind him, sending thunder cracking through the air with each vast flap. In the next instant, King Vasuki's tail lashed out, taking down the garuda guards who'd originally captured Asha.

"Venkat," Tanvi gasped, a stitch forming in her side. She

grabbed his hands. "Listen to me."

From how wide his eyes got, she might have turned into a garudi. *"Tanvi?"*

If glares were weapons, the one Vinata leveled at her now would have eviscerated Tanvi. "What is this?" Vinata sneered. "You were the girl at the garba! What are you doing here?"

As if on a cue audible only to them, Garuda and King Vasuki lunged at each other. Snarling and stabbing, they wrestled. Garuda's hooked beak ripped a chunk from the nagaraja's shoulder. Blood spurted through the ruined fabric of his sherwani.

Vasuki hissed and whipped his head away before transforming into a giant serpent. He slipped from Garuda's grasp, only to wrap around his body again and again.

"Stop!" Venkat yelled.

His shout melted into the noise. Garuda and King Vasuki continued their brawl. His eyes glowing like jade, the nagaraja reared back, then struck, plunging his fangs into Garuda's neck. Garuda keened and fell onto his stomach, pinning Vasuki's head in his prodigious grip.

And to think Tanvi had ever been worried about Asha biting her.

"Do not embroil yourself in their little scuffle," Vinata said. "Once you have invoked the adjusted revisioning, there will be no troublesome nagaraja to goad my stalwart son, and therefore no scuffle about which to worry."

Tanvi dropped Venkat's hands and snatched up the end of her dupatta. She attacked her forehead with it, wiping away the vermilion Asha had methodically applied. The telltale flush began at

Tanvi's midsection, rapidly fanning outward.

"Guess you don't have me, after all," she taunted.

"Perhaps not, but I still have the other runners, you foolish girl." Sounding more amused than anything, Vinata moved closer. "Do it now, apprentice, or lose this opportunity forever."

"What opportunity?" Tanvi asked.

Venkat looked completely overwhelmed, like he was a machine about to shut down. "Nayan—I mean, Garuda—told me if I invoked this tapestry to fix the past and undo their wager, I could bring my family back to life at the same time." His soft, beautiful eyes beseeched her to forgive him. "They were all I had. I can't say no to that."

Anger so fierce it flamed white in Tanvi's vision spread through her, lighting up her veins. "Don't be a jerk. You have me."

Venkat let out an *oof* like she'd decked him.

Good. What a stupid thing for him to say. She scowled. "You don't think I'm scared? But I'm awake now, and you're stuck with me, and that's the way it is, okay?"

"Enough!" Vinata shoved the tapestry into Venkat's hands. At his touch, the images shimmered and writhed, as if they were trying to come out. "Invoke it!"

Tanvi jabbed a finger at the tapestry. "That's Kadru, isn't it? I see her!"

Sisters. Stupid rivalries. Had she and Nitya been like this, too?

Well, they weren't going to be like that anymore.

"Be still!" Vinata raised a hand like she was going to slap Tanvi. Tanvi, who'd had plenty of experience dodging Asha, pivoted aside.

Venkat needed to hear what she had to say, and no one was going to stop her from saying it.

Sweat beaded over his forehead, and his jaw had clenched. "I can't hold it back."

"Yes, you can," Tanvi insisted over the cacophony around them. "You made this, right?"

Venkat nodded.

"Vinata wants you to change the story. To fix the mistake she and her sister made. But she doesn't know what she's doing," Tanvi explained. "I didn't for the longest time, either. My sister hurt me, and I wanted to hurt her back. I thought I could erase her, too. But it doesn't *work*." She gestured to the pavilion that had become a battlefield. "This is what you get when you do that."

There was probably a much more sophisticated way to phrase that. But she had missed out on school and books and all the things that would have taught her how to convey what she meant, so this would have to do.

Venkat studied her with the same consideration he had in all their recent conversations. The muscle in his jaw relaxed. "Gods," he said. "You're right."

"This isn't our fight," Tanvi babbled. "Don't you see? They think we're toys or dolls or something they can jerk around. All of them think it, like humans only exist for them. But this whole mess? It's not our problem. The runners are our problem. *You and I* are our problem."

Vinata made another grab for her. "Still your prattle, you ignorant whelp!"

Tanvi's cheeks heated at the insult, and she wanted to hide, like she was back in the archives on her first day here and Madhu had lambasted her for peeking at the registry. But she didn't. "This is their problem," she repeated. "Even if you 'fixed' it, that wouldn't be the end of it. *They* need to be the ones to find a solution, not us."

Behind them, the fighting, large and small, went on.

"You made this." Tanvi touched the tapestry. "*You* decide what to do with it."

Venkat looked down at it, then at Tanvi, and finally at Vinata. "You want me to invoke this? Done."

39

Even with what he'd just learned, even with the chaos around them, Venkat relaxed. He had Tanvi.

She stood there like a warrior princess. She didn't even need a sword—the gleam in her eyes and determination in her face were weapon enough.

He glanced around once more, at the wounded, the dead, and the battles steeped in putrid hate. A hate so old, so incapacitating, it had yellowed and gnarled back on itself like fingernails that hadn't been cut for twenty years.

Garuda and the nagaraja still grappled, locked in their death embrace. It was so huge and so frightening that it almost became too much to process.

But Venkat still had Tanvi and the other runners.

"Well, boy," said Vinata, "do you want your family back or not?"

Venkat considered her. Nothing was stopping him from simply invoking the revisioning as Garuda had planned it—allowing Vinata to win as she should have. Hadn't the nagas and the garudas already endured enough, all because of one foolish wager their mothers had made in a moment of boredom? First the enslavement, then the retaliation. Again and again and again.

But Kadru's spite seethed from within the tapestry, a noxious brew that perfectly matched the hatred that had so embittered Vinata until vengeance was the only thing she cared about.

Like Tanvi had said, Garuda and his mother didn't even really understand what they were asking for. Kadru had wronged Vinata, so now Vinata in her righteous rage would wrong Kadru—and then Kadru would lash out again. The cycle would never break.

Plus, Venkat had no desire to carry out Garuda's bidding.

Tanvi watched him with undisguised hope, while Vinata sneered. She might be objectively beautiful, but Tanvi was the one with the light. In her single-minded search for retribution, Vinata had become hollowed out.

"I do," Venkat told her, "but I want something else more."

Brushing his fingertips across the tapestry, he let the trance come over him. It was hesitant at first, inconsistent—until Venkat realized the uncertainty came from him. He'd been waiting for Nayan to instruct him. To direct the flow.

But the Nayan he'd known, of course, had never existed.

In his mind, which filled with anguish like spikes and shards of broken glass, Venkat opened his fists and splayed his fingers. Raw power streaked through him, power so strong it threatened to devour him. It had been there all along, he saw, but Nayan—Venkat winced—Garuda had kept it carefully leashed. Defanged as one might do to a cobra. He had never let Venkat truly explore the extent of his dreamsmithing abilities. Even Venkat's experiments had been subtly reined in, because otherwise, he might have discovered that he didn't need direction and gone off on his own. He wouldn't have been so malleable, so easy to manipulate.

The wrath and sorrow blurred together into a conflagration of pure fury, blue-white like the hottest stars. Venkat pushed past it and toward the goal: a new story.

Garuda wanted a reversed wager. Vinata wanted to destroy her sister's progeny.

Well, Venkat was going for a third option.

What he tapped into now was on another plane altogether.

Power sang and sparked in every cell of his body. The only time he'd ever felt anything even close to the sensations singing through him was when Garuda had him construct the individual sections of the revisioning, but that had only been a crude approximation of this, a thumbnail sketch of what had been honed into brilliance so keen it could cut. No wonder Garuda had hidden the truth from him.

He was inside a prism, with every conceivable hue reflected at him in every possible image. He could smell every aroma, taste every flavor that was or would ever be. He heard every sound, horrific and honeyed both. He felt every texture from rough to soft to slimy and beyond. He swam among all those qualities while also holding them in his hand. He was the dreamsmith, and they were his tools.

Time itself had condensed into shining threads of gold and silver and copper, and Venkat could see how they all wove together. Sometimes they tangled; other times they cut off, but always the cosmic tapestry continued. Not even the knife from the Night Market could sever these threads.

His little tapestry was a trifle compared to that.

The tapestry. Garuda as Nayan might have guided him, but this tapestry was *Venkat's* work. Proud as he was of it, he hadn't forgotten the cost: the poor human children who'd been taken from their world and made into vessels. No matter how much Venkat might miss his family, no matter how much he wanted to have them again, he couldn't pay that price. Anything bought in purloined youth and burnout could only ever be tainted, no matter how well intentioned.

Some dreams were meant to be pursued, and others were mere mirages. A dreamsmith had to know the difference.

He hunted through the uncountable threads, searching for his mother. His father. His brother and his grandparents.

They manifested before him, their beloved faces alight with compassion. He hugged each of them hard. Even if they were nothing more than dream figments, they felt so real.

"I'm sorry," he told them, his eyes welling with all the tears he'd stored up. "I wanted to bring you back. But I can't."

His grandmother clicked her tongue. "What a horrible business," she exclaimed. "Don't you even consider it, my little one. Look forward, not back. You have so much yet to do in this life."

"Nothing ever ends, only changes shape," his grandfather reminded him. He began to glitter, and the others emulated him, until they had become distant comets trailing across the universe.

Then they dissipated, as soft and evanescent as dream wisps. Venkat knew that, imaginary or not, he'd never see them again.

412

He combed through the threads and located the boy from Nayan's origin story, King Takshaka's hotheaded nephew. Venkat watched, sick, as Garuda disposed of the boy and took his place. So much anger driving so much violence. It fed off itself.

That thread wove into the ones showing how Garuda as Nayan had initiated runner candidate after candidate until he found one with the potential for dreamsmithing—Venkat.

Venkat wanted to go in and rip out that last thread. It would be so easy. He wasn't sure he'd ever get over Garuda's deception. It threatened to destroy everything good about the past ten years. Everything he'd come to believe as secure and true.

But if he did that, he'd sever so many other threads, too. Shred the lives of people who'd never done anything to him. Like Tanvi.

His grandmother would never have stood for that.

Moving into the present, Venkat sifted through the threads one last time and tugged on one, then another. He mined, he gathered, he soldered.

He didn't even feel human anymore. He'd soared beyond that, his fingers deftly sorting through elements of dreams and combining them to create something greater. Inspiration *flowed* through him, almost as if the revisioning itself were guiding his hands.

Tanvi had shown him you couldn't just paper over mistakes and pretend them away.

And if she could be brave enough to face her sister again, then Vinata and Kadru could face each other. What happened after that was up to them.

When he emerged from the trance, the grounds around him

were silent. Garuda and King Vasuki were frozen in mid combat. The other soldiers, too, had stiffened in place, a gruesome tableau he wouldn't want anyone to see in their dreams.

As the tapestry dissolved, Kadru floated out of the sky and settled next to Vinata. "Hello, *sister*," she purred. "Did you forget to invite me to the party?"

"What did you do, you impudent boy?" Vinata cried. "You have ruined everything!"

She rushed at him, her timeless beauty contorted into a mask of fury. The expression Madhu had worn all too often, especially these last few weeks.

"Wrong," said Venkat, even as her nails gouged lines of fire into his wrist. His skin screamed, but he couldn't afford to get distracted. "You're the ones who did that." He concentrated on Tanvi, who nodded her encouragement. "So now you're going to be the ones to fix it—if you can."

Ignoring the pain, he sent his fingers dancing over the easel once more. A dome of colorless crystal arced up and around the sisters, shutting them in.

He watched as their eyes cleared. Their howls of outrage stilled as they gazed at each other.

"A moment of unclouded sight," he explained. "Also, that really hurt."

"Probably not as bad as being bitten by the nagaraja or nagarani," Tanvi said, and even that feeble attempt at humor helped. She swept her arm to include the immobile figures surrounding them. "What happens now?"

Venkat shrugged. "They'll have to talk to each other. Nothing's going to get healed overnight—and maybe not at all. But if they want to get out of there, they'll at least have to do that much. In the meantime . . ."

He marched over to Garuda and the nagaraja. The nagarani had enfolded Asha in her arms, and Venkat thought again how hard it must be to have everyone else decide your destiny for you.

"This has gone on long enough," he declared, and though they made no move to reply, he knew all four of them heard him. "You thought you could rewrite history the same way we wiped out the dream runners' memories. But you can't do that. You can't do either one. It's our memories that define who we are."

He heard Tanvi before he saw her. "You can't go back. Only forward. I should know."

"You wanted renewal and hope," Venkat said to Garuda. "Here you go."

Garuda made a sound of displeasure. "Do you truly believe this will end here? Come now, my son."

My son. Just two words, but they hit Venkat right in the heart. He still loved Nayan, never mind that Nayan was no better than a hallucination. The calculated creation of someone who knew how to act in order to get what he wanted. It didn't make any difference. Venkat would always love Nayan, and he would mourn him as much as he'd mourned the family of his birth.

"I thought you were my father," he said quietly. "But I was wrong."

Tanvi laced her fingers through his.

"Come here, Asha," he said, and suddenly Asha was shimmying toward them. "See, none of you get it. It doesn't matter *what* we do or don't do here. This is a problem that only you can resolve. You can't kidnap kids and have them harvest dreams for you. You can't throw magic at bad decisions and expect everything will be fine."

Garuda watched him with shrewd eyes. Venkat marveled that he hadn't noticed how avian Garuda's gestures had always been. He'd wanted so much to believe in the story of Nayan and him. "I don't know; maybe eagles and snakes can never get along. But either way, it's not our responsibility, and it's time for you and your army to leave."

"How do you propose to compel us?" Garuda asked. It sounded like one of the challenges Nayan had issued Venkat in the workshop. Pushing him to do more, do better. To flourish—but only as long as he didn't flourish too much.

Maybe that wasn't fair. Despite everything, Nayan had loved him, too. But Venkat was too tired to worry about what was fair and what wasn't. "Tell me where the runners are."

Garuda laughed. "The workshop seemed to me a logical place to hide them, but my mother had her own designs. Alas, it appears she is indisposed at the moment and unavailable for comment. But you have learned how to navigate puzzles; surely you will solve this one as well."

Venkat hadn't really expected Garuda to answer. He let it pass, then presented the object he'd forged while in his trance. He hadn't needed dreamstones; each element he'd drawn on had been right there.

"*This* is how I'll compel you," he said, and iridescent bubbles formed around the various garudas and garudis—all but Garuda himself. "You'll go back to Svargalok and Lord Vishnu, and you'll never come back here. It's up to you what you do after that, whether you find a way to make peace with your cousins or not, but you won't involve humans in your affairs ever again. If not, I'll trap you in a dream."

One by one, the bubbles and their inhabitants vanished.

Garuda could have leaped at him, and Venkat wouldn't have been able to lift a finger in time to stop him. But he didn't. "I cannot promise the other garudas and garudis will abide by this," he said, smiling. If anything, he sounded oddly proud. "You will need to invest more than that to stop a war."

Venkat nodded. "But *you* can abide by it. Show your mother it's the only way."

"If I were you," Tanvi called, "I'd agree."

Garuda glanced at his mother and his aunt in their bell jar. He smiled again, a wry yet chilling smile. Then he ascended into the air and flew off into the once-more jewellike sky, leaving Venkat behind.

40

After seeing to the fallen and wounded naga soldiers, the naga-raja and nagarani had sent attendants to scour the palace for Nitya. They'd searched for a full day, endless hours during which Tanvi gnawed her fingernails to nibs and refused to eat. What if Vinata had stuck Nitya somewhere no one would ever think to look? They still didn't know if she was in the palace at all.

Tanvi couldn't even go to Venkat for comfort; he was in yet more emergency meetings of the council, recounting everything he knew while they tried to establish order in the capital.

But then, of all places, someone checked under a mound of clothes in the laundry. Madhu had bound and gagged Nitya, then covered her with baskets' worth of royal garments waiting to be washed. Nitya claimed it was like being stuffed inside a pillow, but she wasn't any worse for wear. Just infuriated. And bored. *I missed all the excitement while I was buried in dirty laundry? Seriously?*

Good thing nagas don't sweat, Tanvi had replied, the relief at finding Nitya intact and breathing almost making her boneless.

The runners had actually been easier to track down—initially, anyway. Garuda's quip turned out to be a misdirection. Venkat had sighed when Tanvi and he had taken the lift up to the workshop and discovered their charges there in the sealed-off balcony. *I think that was Garuda's idea of me proving my mettle,* he'd said. *He knew I'd try here eventually, but the question was, how long would it take?*

Mythical beings really didn't think like humans, that was for sure. Tanvi couldn't believe it, but she was starting to feel nostalgic for what she remembered of life on Prithvi. It might take time, but at least she could figure out how to be a person.

The runners had been scared and exhausted, not to mention dehydrated and famished, but they were safe. It was only when Tanvi and Venkat began counting that they realized not everyone was present and accounted for.

Two of the runners—Bharat and Srinivas—had gone missing. And no matter how long or where anyone hunted for them, they stayed that way. Tanvi hugged Indu close and promised they'd never stop searching.

But the days passed in a tornado of tasks to check off and arrangements to sort out, and Venkat had to concentrate on helping the runners who hadn't disappeared. Some, like Indu, were demanding their parents, while most would need somewhere else to stay.

Despite all odds, Nitya and Asha had hit it off, bonding first over ways to needle Sameer and then over their love of artisanal pastries, the more elaborate the better. Tanvi had soon found herself being dragged to Asha's favorite bistro in the city so Nitya could try all kinds of desserts based in jewel-fruits, including a dish involving sweet, creamy kulfi and puran poli stuffed with jewel-mango and jewel-kiwi paste, all topped with spirals of gold and silver leaf.

Tanvi had hung back as they strolled along, soaking in the details of Nagalok, which she'd never had the chance to see before. No longer a dream runner, she supposed she was a tourist now.

Asha's parents, aghast at what had befallen their daughter, had called off the betrothal. It was more of a formality than anything, because Prince Chintan and Karan had already fled back to the lap of the clan of Anant Shesha. On hearing that, Asha had sniffed. *Fangless, that one. An embarrassment to his forebear. And to think he would have been my husband!*

Sneaky as ever, she'd capitalized on her parents' guilt and asked them to accompany Nitya and her to Prithvi. They would meet Sameer and then explain everything to Nitya's and Tanvi's mom and dad. Eventually, Tanvi would follow.

It was a good scheme, but Tanvi wasn't ready to go. Not yet.

Nitya hadn't seemed surprised, only wary. *I get it if you need a little more time, but don't make me have to come get you.*

And then suddenly she and Asha were gone, and it was just Tanvi and Venkat. She'd avoided him for a week, feeling strange. Not sure what anything between them really meant. Maybe he'd realized what a mess she was.

But the council in its infinite wisdom had decided the best course of action was to throw a gala in honor of Asha upon her return from Earth, because apparently that was all nagas ever did, and Asha insisted Tanvi attend.

Tanvi had reluctantly agreed. It wasn't like she'd be here much longer, anyway. She owed Asha that much.

And Venkat, a voice deep inside her had prodded, but she'd disregarded it.

And now Tanvi sat alone among nagas and naginis who kept studying her with fascination. It didn't help that aunties and attendants were dashing in and out and hissing directives at one another.

Fighting the urge to duck out, Tanvi sat on her hands. Her sari was hot pink like the chair. Maybe if she didn't move, she'd blend in with the upholstery.

"Wow." Venkat sidled up to her, and just like that, she didn't want to leave anymore. He looked so good in his burnt orange kurta. "You look amazing."

She quirked an eyebrow as she got up so her giddiness didn't show. "Yeah, right. I look like one of the servers. Someone even asked me to get them a drink."

"Did you do it?"

"It was Asha. I had to." Tanvi pointed to a small room off to the side. "That's how I can tell you there's a whole spread of snacks in there."

"Well, if it was Asha," Venkat teased. He lowered his voice and confided, "She gave Sameer one of the runners' pendants, and he's here."

"She did *what?*"

The nearby relatives cast disapproving frowns at them. Apparently the species didn't matter; human or nagini, all aunties had that same judgmental grimace.

But Venkat ignored them and smiled at Tanvi. "Speaking of snacks, I'm actually a little hungry. Join me?"

"I could eat," she agreed, and took his wrist to lead him past the watching aunties and uncles.

In the refreshment area, a wealth of spicy and savory and sweet aromas combined to create the promise of a luscious buffet she wanted to demolish bite by bite. Food, so much food.

Tanvi hadn't been ravenous like this in years, hadn't wanted food for its own sake. But now, she thought, salivating, she could devour it all.

Huge platters covered the available surfaces, some of which she couldn't identify. But the rest sang to her growling belly: mounds of ivory cashews and ivory pistachios; jewel-rice in teal, plum, and rose; plump spiced jewel-vegetables the envy of any farmer on Prithvi; glittering silver rose lassi; and dried copper jasmine petals.

She used her hip to nudge the door shut behind them. "Gimme."

Side by side, they helped themselves to plates and got to work loading them.

You're going home soon. Ask him.

"Why—" she started, then faltered. Why did talking when it mattered have to be so *hard*? It was just making sounds come out of your mouth in patterns other people recognized, and yet in some ways, it felt more magic than magic itself.

Absorbed in his food, he mumbled, "Why what?"

"Why *me*?" The words burst out of her. "Why do you care about what happens to me?"

Venkat glanced up at that, and his smile was so warm, a ray of sunshine she wasn't sure she deserved. "I like you, Tanvi."

"But why?"

Venkat put his plate down. "When Asha brought you here, you had a spark about you. A passion, like you wanted things, and you were going to get them. Even the initiation couldn't take that away, not really."

He bridged the tiny distance between them. "I hated seeing how sad you were," he went on, and she saw her own pain mirrored in his face. "You still have that spark." He tucked a lock of hair behind her ear. "It's so pretty, just like you."

So many feelings poured over Tanvi that the only thing she could do was drink in the sight of him.

"I'm so sorry all this happened to you. And for my part in it." Venkat pointed to her plate. "Aren't you hungry?"

She was, for many things. Especially the boy standing right before her, offering her kindness she'd been too shut down to appreciate before. More, besides, if she wanted it.

You still have that spark.

They were so close that all she had to do was lift her chin, and then there wouldn't be any space between them at all. A tiny universe, a self-contained circle of two.

No one knew what was going to happen once she went home. This might be her only chance to find out the answer to her heart's questions.

Do it, her heart whispered.

So Tanvi set her own plate aside and brought her face to his.

She heard his sharp intake of breath before Venkat cupped her cheeks in his hands. He gazed down at her like she was the most precious thing he'd ever seen. His dark eyes might have been tourmaline dreamstones, but filled with visions of her and only her. His long eyelashes brushed his cheeks as he blinked.

Heat pooled in her belly until she forgot all about the food, and she couldn't stop staring at his mouth. The air between them, around them, crackled, an electric current that she couldn't and didn't want to pretend away.

Want. She tingled with so much want, so much longing, she couldn't stand it. Her nerves fizzed, as if the silver wine still effervesced in her blood. She needed him to touch her. Needed to learn the scent of his skin, to taste the hollow over his collarbone.

"I've been alone since my family died," he said, his voice low and raw. "I thought I had Nayan. That I belonged here with him. But I have you."

Everything Tanvi wanted to say got knotted up in her throat. She sucked in huge lungfuls of air, trying to force the words out.

Venkat must have felt her stiffen, because he let his hands drop. She ached in their absence. He took a step back, and even those couple of inches felt like a devastating loss.

No, she thought. *No, no, no.*

"I'm sorry," he said, already half turned away. "That was stupid of me."

Tanvi was a lit sparkler, tossing scorching embers throughout the room. How in all the worlds didn't he *see* it?

She closed the gap between them. Startled, he angled his head toward her. Rising up on her tiptoes, she looked right at him, not hiding anything.

"Shut up," she ordered, fury rocketing through her. "Don't you dare say you're sorry."

When confusion flickered over his face, his sweet, beautiful face, she added, "I'm not." Then she kissed him.

He made a noise against her mouth, and she pushed herself into him. Crushing her to his chest, he kissed her back like she was his lifeline. Like if he stopped for a second, she might vanish and leave him to drown in the vast ocean of his loneliness.

Her hands tangled in his hair, caressed his cheek, found the hollow under his jaw. Nothing existed but him.

They somehow ended up with Tanvi seated on the table and Venkat leaning over her. She couldn't pull him near enough. His lips grazed her neck as he breathed her name, making her shiver, and his scent engulfed her senses.

She caught his earlobe between her teeth and felt him shudder. His skin seared her fingers as if a fire blazed just beneath.

Their mouths found each other again, lips relearning how they fit together, tongues greedily exploring. Tanvi shifted on the table, and her arm connected with the plate Venkat had set there. It hit the floor with a loud *clang*, shattering the moment. She hopped off, mortified, and glanced at the mess of food all over.

Venkat touched her arm. "Are you okay?"

She nodded but kept her head down.

He tilted her chin so that she had no choice but to look at him. Her belly flipped. "I ruined our snack," she blurted.

It wasn't what she wanted to say at all, but with her heart crying out for him, it was the only thing she could.

Venkat laughed. "Tanvi," he said, lips swollen and eyes half lidded, "I don't care about that. All I want is you."

And he pulled her back into his arms.

41

Tanvi nestled closer into the crook of Venkat's arm and sipped her caramel cider as they approached the wrought-iron garden bench in front of the house. Someone had swept it clean of the red and gold maple leaves sprinkling the lawn, as glorious as ruby and topaz dreamstones, and just as ephemeral as the dreams they'd contain. Somehow, when she'd been distracted, autumn had settled in like a relative come to visit.

"The trees are on fire, but in a good way," Venkat said. "You don't get this in Nagalok."

"It's pretty magical." Tanvi took another sip of her drink, savoring the sweet warmth. Being able to appreciate things again would never get old. So many colors, so many textures, so many sounds, so many foods to taste and smell—it was like the kaleidoscope she'd had as a kid, always shifting. Always something new to try.

The bench, which had seemed so big to her seven years ago, turned out to be just wide enough for two people. She wondered if this feeling of things not fitting right would ever go away. Did she even want it to? "Wanna sit?"

Venkat did, and Tanvi snuggled against him. "So you know," she said as blithely as she could, "Nitya said something kind of stupid."

He got that worried look that was so cute she couldn't take it. "What'd she say?"

Handing him her cup, she bent to gather a spray of leaves and spread them into a fiery bouquet.

"It's that bad?" The dread in his voice almost made her give up the game. Almost. "Do you still want to do this?"

"Well, Nitya's expecting me. I think it would be rude not to show up, don't you?"

Venkat's worry changed to confusion, and Tanvi bit back her smile. She couldn't imagine getting sick of that any more than she could imagine not loving hot drinks with shots of extra caramel or the brisk breeze on her temples.

"What's going on?" he asked. "You know you can tell me anything."

Tanvi twirled the leaves in a silly dance. "Nitya said . . ."

"Yes?"

"Could be a faerie skirt, don't you think? I'd wear it."

"Tanvi."

She'd planned to hold out a little longer, to really milk the moment, but the tenderness in his eyes made her melt. "She said I should follow my dreams unless they lead me out of Philadelphia. Then I should turn around."

Venkat's lips twitched. "And what do you think about that?"

"I think she's right."

They looked at each other, trying not to laugh, and then they were leaning in, noses brushing, lips parting. His mouth was so warm, better even than the cider. He felt like home. She could kiss him forever, and who cared if old Mr. O'Neil across the street was staring from behind his curtains, scandalized?

The front door of the house opened, and Nitya hurried out, dressed in a light gray sweater dress that made Tanvi think of winter snowstorms. She reluctantly pulled away from Venkat and rose to greet her sister. "Give us a minute?"

"Don't forget the shawl." Venkat squeezed her shoulder, then walked to the other side of the yard.

Nitya glanced after him, grinning. "Better not let Mom catch you doing that."

Tanvi rolled her eyes. "Yeah, maybe I just won't go in, and then you don't have to worry about it." When Nitya bit her lip, Tanvi immediately regretted it. "I didn't mean that. I just meant— I'm scared."

"All Mom and Dad and I ever wanted," Nitya said, her voice low and intense, "was for you to come back. They're so happy, and Dad flew back from Canada just to see you. Don't be scared."

"I have something for you," Tanvi announced. She had to break the tension, or else she wouldn't be able to do this. She took a shimmering yellow square from her pocket and unfolded it into a swath of summer sunlight. "It's a sunshine shawl. From the Night Market I told you about."

The fabric pooled like water over Nitya's open hands. "It's beautiful," she said, knotting it around her neck. "Thank you."

But her smile, the smile so much like Tanvi's and also not at all like it, stayed dim.

"Oh, no," Tanvi said. "It's not what you think. I'm not going to disappear on you. I swear."

When Nitya still didn't look reassured, Tanvi reached out and hugged her. She held her sister and let her sister hold her until they both relaxed in something close to safety. It felt weird—but also right.

Nitya finally let go. "Come on."

"Just let me say bye to Venkat first."

"Okay. I'll see you inside in a minute?" But Nitya didn't move.

Tanvi nodded. "Sixty seconds. I promise."

Once Nitya had left, and Venkat had given back her drink, Tanvi made herself say the words she'd been shoving down. "I already left my family once. I need to stay here. With them."

She dug her toes into the dirt, knowing he'd tell her they couldn't be together, then.

Venkat pressed his forehead to hers. "I figured as much," he whispered. "And it won't be easy. But I'm not going anywhere—at least, not without you. We're family, too. You're the one who told me that."

Tanvi looked up at him in astonishment. "But what about being a dreamsmith?"

"I'll still be one. Plus, I have to finish healing the other runners and get them settled here."

She ran her thumb over his knuckles. "I'll come back sometimes and help."

"I knew you would." Venkat grinned. "So we'll see each other all the time. And once you're ready, you can even introduce me to your mother."

Tanvi had never felt so shy in her life. He'd really do that for her?

Venkat held up a tiny book on a chain. "I forged this for you. It'll tell you any story you want, whenever you want. All you have to do is ask it."

He fastened the chain around her throat. As his fingers skimmed the nape of her neck, she shivered. "What if I want it to tell our story? What then?"

Venkat laughed. "I think we have to write that one ourselves." He moved aside, freeing her path to the house.

Tanvi took a deep breath, studying the red door and pondering what lay beyond.

It wasn't a dream anymore. She could rub her eyes, and the door would still be there, as solid as ever. Her life still waited for her behind it.

She didn't have to go in. But she wanted to.

Tanvi smiled at Venkat one more time. Then, touching the pendant of stories for strength, she walked toward the door, prepared to meet her family all over again.

ACKNOWLEDGMENTS

Writing a second book under contract is hard enough, but writing—and revising and revising and revising and revising—a second book in the wake of your debut *and* while in the throes of a raging global pandemic? Let's just say there were many, many points along the way where I seriously doubted this vague premise in my imagination would ever become a physical object readers could hold in their hands. And yet here we are, all thanks to the wonderful people I've been blessed to have on my team and in my life.

First, thank you, as always, to my agent, Beth Phelan, for working with me on the pitch for *The Dream Runners* until it was ready to submit and for always championing me in so many ways, some of which I'll never even know about. #TeamBeoples!

I might be a writer known for her description, but I am at a loss for words to express just how brilliant and steadfast my editor extraordinaire, Stephanie Stein, really is. While I was staring in desperation at fumbling draft after fumbling draft, wondering if I'd have to light the manuscript on fire and flee to a cave deep in the mountains, never to be heard from again, she maintained faith in my vision and guided what started out as a hodgepodge of half-cooked ideas into exactly the story I'd meant to tell in the first place, a cohesive and ambitious tale I can be proud of. I'm so deeply fortunate to work with you, World's Best Editor, and here's to us putting lots more brown girl magic out into the world!

Charlie Bowater, you knocked it out of the park yet again with your luminous illustration of Tanvi and Venkat. Every time I see my cover with its gorgeous, magical brown kids, my heart swells with joy. Thank you.

Corina Lupp, your ability to flawlessly translate the feel of my worlds into stunning cover design is its own kind of magic. Thank you so much.

And the rest of the Harper team: Sophie Schmidt, Louisa Currigan, Jessica Berg, Gwen Morton, Deanna Hoak, Mary Ann Seagren, Alison Donalty, Sean Cavanagh, Vanessa Nuttry, Mitchell Thorpe, Michael D'Angelo, Audrey Diestelkamp, and Caitlin Garing, thank you for all you do to make books happen and get them into the hands of readers.

Thanks to Jennifer Mace for the conversation a few years ago that got me thinking about how to combine my love of changeling lore and the concept of selling dreams. And then a super huge thank-you and a big squeeze-hug to Vashti Bandy and Diana DeVault for helping me figure out how to weave in Hindu mythology and actually develop a semblance of a plot. Vash, your ability to brainstorm entire universes off the cuff is a true marvel.

Jennifer Crow, I will never stop being grateful that you offered to read and cheer on each chapter of my second draft as I wrote it. Some days, that encouragement was all that got the words written and the story moving.

Diana DeVault, my darling friend, evergreen cheerleader, and intrepid social media maven, where would I even be without you? Really sad and not writing, that's where. You continue to be a tremendous blessing, and I adore you. And we *still* need to schedule our high tea!

Leanna Renee Hieber, you're always there with your heart, your ear, your spiritual sensibilities, your surprise packages, and your beautiful house. I love you.

Annaka Kalton, you are a treasure. From the very first draft so full of holes as to be Swiss cheese to the final version that went to copyedits, you believed I had something special in this novel and helped me get it to where it needed to be. Thank you, thank you, thank you.

Angie Richmond, I'm so glad we found each other again. Thank you for being so generous with your time and thoughts; the plot wouldn't have come together without you.

Renee Melton, despite many hardships, you never fail to show up, puzzle through plot snarls with me, and cheer me on. Your fingerprints are all over this book, and it's so much better for that. (We even survived losing chapter thirty-seven at the last minute!) All the hugs and rosewater brownies.

Mikey Vuoncino, the fact that you're not a reader but still always enjoy my writing and insist on filling your bookcase with my words means the world. All the love and baked goods for you.

Camille DeAngelis, thank you for your enthusiastic support and spiritual talks and your early blurb. We must cook together soon!

Nivair Gabriel, it feels like we've ridden at least fifty roller coasters since quarantine began, but the peaks and valleys have only made us stronger and more grounded, and your support and belief in what I have to offer have never quailed. Thank you always.

Jacqueline Koyanagi, heart sister and ardent fan of my work, you are the best and the sweetest, and I'm so lucky to know you. So many snuggles and kaju katli.

Lindsey Márton O'Brien, you are the enchanted heart friend I thought would only ever exist in my daydreams, but it turns out I didn't even need to be an oneironaut to find you. Your exhilaration about this book helped me realize I hadn't messed it up, after all, and your love throughout everything has been a balm to my spirit. Here's to always flooding the world with our light and magic.

Sara Cleto, thank you for all the text messages and phone calls of solidarity and loving my folktales—and for our beach retreat. All the egg breakfasts coming your way!

Sukanya Venkatraghavan and Venkatraghavan Sahasranaman, thank you for letting me borrow your name for Venkat. And Suku and Asma Kazi, thank you for your excitement and your help with the art direction.

Ciara Smyth, editor sibling and friend, I'm so glad we get to take this journey together. One day soon, we will finally meet in real life!

Lori Lee, Claire Legrand, Sarah Henning, and Anna-Marie McLemore, thank you for understanding and riding this bizarre wave of publishing during a pandemic with me.

Jialu Bao, thank you for loving the magic only I can make and demanding more. I'm on it!

Tanaz Bhathena, thank you for reading and assuring me I'd accomplished what I'd set out to do with this book.

The Make Art, Not War Collective, for plenty of encouragement and virtual writing sessions.

The Sisterhood of the Moon—Grace Nuth, Sara Cleto, Brittany Warman, Meenoo Mishra, Lindsey O'Brien, and Erin Kathleen Bahl—your friendship is like a glittering cauldron of rainbow wishes come true, and your love for me and my mythic work keeps the stardust flowing from my fingers. Thank you.

Thank you to my beloved and incredibly wise husband, who helped me keep going while we were stuck at home in lockdown, talked to me about naga lore, and didn't mind ordering a lot of takeout if it meant I met my deadlines. Work-life balance—what's that? (Kidding, kidding.)

Thanks to past me, who worked so hard on that trunked novel starring Asha and Sameer and Eklavya's Thumb. We weren't quite ready back then, but look—Asha lived to tell her tiny story in the end!

To the booksellers and librarians who loved and talked up *Star Daughter*, especially during such a strange time, thank you from the bottom of my heart for all your support. You're fabulous.

To all my readers, thank you for venturing into my fantastical universe, letting me know what it meant to you, and asking when the next book was coming. I'll do my best to keep delivering the enchanted adventures.

To the nagas, garudas, and sundry: my pranaam and gratitude for indulging my loving fan fiction of your ancient myths. What a privilege it's been to play with them and craft something new!

And finally, to Maha Durga, Sarasvati Devi, and Shri Ganapati bapa: Thank you for always showing me the way, even if it sometimes winds and slithers and coils back on itself, suddenly baring its fangs—much like a snake. This book is first and foremost for you. ॐ